Only Shot At A Good Tombstone

Robert R. Mitchell

USA

ISBN 9781453747049

Printed in the United States of America.

Ecclesiastes 1:9
The thing that hath been, it is that which shall be; and that which is done is that which shall be done: and there is no new thing under the sun.

Grace.
All the best to you!
Thanks for giving my Story a Shot!

1/26/17

Prologue

You're a goddamn fool if you expect anything new here. We're telling a story, but that doesn't mean it's a new one. Everything in this book, you should already have heard before, a million times at least. If you haven't, it ain't because it's new, it's because you're an ignorant fool. The stuff we know about, the stuff we're telling about, we know for a variety of reasons. Some of it was told to us. Other stuff, we saw with our own eyes. I made up some stuff, my partner made up some stuff, and we speculated some too. And sometimes, things were going on a thousand miles away, and we just plain knew what was going on even though we weren't there. Don't ask me to explain it 'cause I don't understand it myself.

We worked together on this story, so our words all mix together. With that said, I'm not one for fancy words, so if there are fancy words being used, they ain't mine, they're my partner's, and he ought to get the credit. One thing, though: we both tell the goddamn truth. Not because we're good men or because we never lie, but because WE HAVE TO, like that old sailor with the dead bird around his neck. Now that don't mean that every little detail in here actually happened. We had to fill in the blanks to a certain extent so the story'd make sense when you read it. Art is truth, even if it's fictional, at least that's what my partner says. So if you're one of those who pays attention to the details, take 'em with a grain of salt or even a goddamn pillar of it.

The kid we wrote about, we don't use his name and we're not gonna use it, so don't even ask. This is his story, but the last thing he needs is a bunch of goddamn strangers knocking on his door at all hours of the night asking him a bunch of questions about shit that's pretty well explained already in this book. Bob Dylan knows what I'm talking about. Crazy hippies started shimmying down his chimney, crawling through his windows, sleeping in his crawlspace. Wouldn't leave him be, because he was the voice of a generation whether he meant to be or not. Though to be honest, I don't know how the hell he could sing "Masters of War" in the sixties and not expect to be called the voice of a generation. Well this young man, this young man ain't the voice of anything except himself, and he's a good kid and doesn't need any of that shit.

Another thing: we have a straight friend who writes poems (go figure). He's pretty good. And since the general public doesn't read poetry anymore, we promised him we'd stick a poem in the story so people wouldn't have much of a choice but to read it. My partner says that poems are like vegetables: you're forced to eat them when you're young; you leave them be for a few years when you get out on your own; and then you wise up, you real- ize they're good for you, and you eat them like your life depends on 'em, 'cause at that point it does.

Speaking of my better half, I'm going to let him jaw at y'all for a bit, now.

In addition to not expecting anything new, respecting the privacy of the young man about whom this story is written, and under- standing that taken as a whole, this work is an attempt to capture and display Truth, even if particular events or people are techni- cally fictional, it's also important to know that a basic understanding of history is a prerequisite. If you don't have at least a rudimentary knowledge of American, and to a lesser ex- tent World and Ancient history, you could miss some of the more subtle nuances in the story; but don't despair: we've inter- jected, as gracefully as possible, several instructive paragraphs here and there that should help illuminate things a bit.

And with that, I'll turn things back over to my acerbic significant other.

Now I may not have a master's degree like my fancy-talking
friend here, but I've always considered myself a student of history. I read better than I talk, and I've read hundreds of thousands
of pages of history, anything that catches my eye, especially
stuff that looks at things from a slightly different angle. Because
of that, I tend to look at the world around me in terms of history.
When I see a young guy with a long beard, long hair, and long,
loose clothing, for example, I see a hippy. Now most folks today, they weren't around when there were hippies, and they
don't read the history books, so they decide how they're going to
react to this guy based on what movie star they're in love with or
what music star is popular on MTV at the moment. Me? If that
bearded dude ain't the most easygoing, love-and-peace, low
maintenance, live-and-let-live, happy-go-lucky, free-to-be-you-
and-me motherfucker the world's ever seen, then he and I are
going to have us a problem. 'Cause you can't just go deciding to
make yourself look a certain way without taking into considera-
tion the millions of people who've come before you. I mean you
can, of course; it's a free country and all, but it ain't right. You
don't put up a stop sign at an intersection and then act all surprised when people in cars begin to stop. Don't matter that you
really meant "Stop Injustice" instead of "Stop your vehicle," because millions and millions of people already know what that
red octagon means, and your intentions don't mean shit. So,
when I run into one of these vegan, hemp-wearing, dreadlock-
sporting, stinky granola kids, I feel like sitting them down with a
history book and opening it up to 1967. Take 'em on a little
stroll along Haight-Ashbury so they can see that they didn't
make up this shit, and that they're wearing a goddamn uniform
for chrissake. And the goddamn dreadlocks? Do they really
think that Rastafarianism is for their lily white selves? It's all
about Ethiopia and Hailie Salassie. Most of 'em don't even
know where the hell Ethiopia is, the ignorant little pissants. They
are using a universal symbol for something other than its mean-

3

ing, which is fine as long as they're aware of the fact and are ready to explain themselves.

Alright. So history's important. I think we've made that about as clear as clear can be. As the narrators or writers of this story, you should at least know a little about where we came from. Don't worry; I ain't gonna pull out the photo albums and goddamn baby pictures. I'll start where it makes sense to start.

In 1945 I was dumped off a naval vessel in San Francisco, nearly broke and dishonorably discharged from the United States Army in spite of my Purple Heart and Silver Star. I had lied about my age back in January of 1942 and joined the service when I was only 15 because of Pearl Harbor. I just didn't think we as a country ought to take that shit without fighting back. In the military, I realized that the thing I couldn't figure out about myself back home was the fact that I was gay. I was from Texas, and if you think Texas is backwards today, you should have seen it back in the thirties and forties. You didn't really have much of a chance of figuring out that you were gay, because as far as everyone around you was concerned, there wasn't such a thing as a gay person. Homosexuality didn't exist, at least not in Texas.

In the army, though, things were different. My commanding officer knew I was gay right off the bat. My fellow soldiers knew I was gay. And I knew which of my fellow soldiers were gay. It was all out there laid up on the table like cards, but the U.S. Army needed every able-bodied soldier it could lay its hands on, so as long as I carried my own weight, which I did; and didn't cause trouble, which I didn't; they were willing to overlook my so-called deviant nature. They overlooked it right up to VJ Day. That's when the purges began. I was blue-papered and dropped off on the pier in San Francisco with 49 other dishonorably discharged faggots. The army gave me a train ticket, but there was no way in hell I was going home.

I got a construction job and lived at the YMCA until I could afford a place of my own. After a few months, I had enough for first-and-last, and I found a cheap, walk-up, fourth-floor apartment. I was always working. Goddamn if I wasn't always working. If construction slowed down, there was always other work. I drove delivery trucks, waited tables, and worked for a painting company. On the weekends and at night, I tended bar in one of the many gay bars that sprang up after the war. That's where I met my partner.

Now don't get me wrong. It wasn't no paradise. Not everyone in San Francisco was happy that the city was getting more than its fair share of discharged deviants. And when word got out that San Fran was an OK place for gays to live, gay civilians started moving to the city too. Well, it was only a matter of time before the powers that be began to fight back. Over the years, the persecution kind of fluctuated like the tide out in the bay. Sometimes it was pretty bad, and other times it was pretty peaceful. Back and forth, back and forth, just like the goddamn tide.

In the late fifties and into the sixties, a lot of things started coming together on both sides of the fence. By that time, you had your beatniks and gays in the Bay Area making a lot of noise, saying that the uptight, cookie-cutter version of America that the government was cramming down everyone's throats wasn't necessarily right for everyone. Well that went over like a lead balloon and the backlash was on. Cops busted more homosexuals, bars got raided, and bars even got shut down by the Liquor Board. Hell, they even prosecuted the bookstore guy who sold Ginsberg's "Howl" for chrissake, the First Amendment be damned. See, when it comes to faggots, "Liberty and Justice for all" just don't apply.

You were always watching your back, watching what you said to people, watching what you did in front of people. We felt like we were in Stalingrad or Cuba instead of in the Castro district. That kind of tension and fear starts to wear you down pretty quick. It eats at your insides and weighs you down on the outside. A lot of guys began drinking too much, using drugs, even killing themselves. I'd been in the worst fighting the war had to offer and even I was on edge. This was different. In the war, you were fighting the enemy. Here, you were fighting your neighbor, the cops, and your own government.

It was a Friday night when it finally happened at our bar. The cops kicked open the door even though it was unlocked, and started swinging their billy clubs, tipping over tables, pulling down shelves, cracking skulls. You ever been hit with a lead-filled billy club? It hurts like a motherfucker and you're afraid that something's broke inside and you'll seize up and die in a matter of hours. There wasn't no AIDs back then, so they didn't hesitate to bloody us up. No skin off their backs. And that's when I met my man.

He had been passed over by the draft board because of his position on the police force and the position he'd held while the local draft board chairman, an upstanding deacon of the 1st Baptist Church, rammed his rod into his ass. He knew what he was, and the self-loathing he felt for betraying his true nature and persecuting his brothers exploded in a supercharged rage. All of his shame and guilt got shoved way down deep inside him and when it came back out again, it was sheer terror for any bugger within reach of his billy club or service revolver. He was known for pistol-whipping anyone who dared stand up after he delivered a blow with the club. Pistol-whipped them until the doctors the next day wouldn't know where to start. Made a goddamned mess out of some pretty faces, that's for damn sure. But then he met me. He had just unholstered his revolver and was getting ready to let a sweet little fairy have it, when I stood between them, my arms down at my sides. I knew better than to raise my fist. There were rumors he'd dragged one poor son-of-a-bitch out a back door one time and almost shot him point-blank in the head for openly challenging him. His partners had stopped him that time, but I didn't want to press my luck. I just stood between them and got myself ready to take whatever he had to dish out. I think I closed my eyes at some point, because when I opened 'em up again, he was still standing there and I could've sworn there was a tear in his eye. And I knew. Sure as hell knew. Right then I felt something that I'd never felt before. He holstered his gun and walked out. I knew I'd spend the rest of my life with him. The rest of my goddamned life.

His commander was a good man and let him officially resign for "psychiatric health" reasons, even though he probably knew my man was gay. Well, I suppose I should say that the commander was either a good man, or he didn't want to bring shame and scandal down on the force. One or the other, or maybe a little of both. I figured some of the officers might have known the truth, even though we never went anywhere publicly together, but it wasn't so hard to believe that a man with that kind of anger might eventually crack. I'd seen it in the army. It happens.

Staying inside and sneaking around was no way to live. We heard there were jobs in Seattle, working for Boeing. The Cold War might have made things hard for us faggots, but it was good for the aerospace industry and the American Middle Class.

Most folks in America today don't really know what a Middle Class is, at least not the way it used to be back when we moved up to the Pacific Northwest. These days, it's mostly people getting by and people living large as they say. You'd think there'd be a revolution or something, but the people just getting by idolize the rich folks and want to be like them some day. Don't matter that they never will. Marx said that religion is the opiate of the masses. Well, he was right about that as far as I can tell, but there's something else that's got people duped today. Entertainment. As long as Americans can watch the movie stars, it don't matter to them that they have to work two jobs and are still eligible for the dole. Don't matter to them that their favorite movie star spends more on a necklace or car than they'll make their whole goddamn lives.

Back then it was different. Back then, as long as you worked hard, you had a damn good chance of grabbing hold of the American Dream: a house, brand new car, a boat, a cabin on the lake, kid's college tuition, everything your everyday Joe would want, with a little set aside for retirement, even though your pension and Social Security would take care of you with enough money to spare. And that was with the woman staying home with the kids and being the homemaker like the post-war government wanted her to. You didn't see both parents working full-time much back then. Didn't need to. And there weren't no goddamn old people bagging groceries at the supermarkets or greeting shoppers at Wal-Mart, neither. Old folks back then took their grandkids fishing and played bridge with the neighbors in their goddamn golden years.

Well, we moved up to Seattle and got us an apartment in Pioneer Square and jobs at Boeing Field. We were still young, didn't want to settle down and become homeowners just yet. We had a good life down in the Square. We were saving money and enjoying Seattle's night life.

We couldn't always be ourselves, of course, but there wasn't that spotlight of attention burning down on us like we had in San Fran. I'm thinking it might have had something to do with Seattle's history. Seattle started out as a rowdy logging and mining town known more for its prostitutes than proper manners. Back then, faggots like us blended in with the con artists, whores, crooks and winos down on the mudflats. Proper folks didn't go down there. Hell, NO! It was like the Old West. Kind of a free-for-all. Folks were tough. Hell, when the city burned down in 1889, folks didn't move away, they just built a new city right on top, leaving the underground one to the rats and adventurers. You can still go down there even today.

One of the bars we drank at had a back room with a staircase leading down to the basement. There were shelves filled with boxes of booze and supplies, and a door that was usually hidden by a sheet hanging on the wall. The door opened up into Underground Seattle. The owner kept the door locked and hidden most of the time, but he'd give us a key every so often and we'd fire up a couple of kerosene lanterns and go fuck in the old bordellos. We'd made up one booth pretty nice with a mattress and blankets, and before long we'd be shaking the foundations of the city, looking up through the purple squares of colored glass embedded in the sidewalk, watching them turn dark when shoppers passed by above and blocked the light from the streetlights, shoppers probably wondering about the opposite glow coming up through the glass. It was dirty and there were rats, but we felt like we were connecting with those old-time faggots who were as good with their fists as they were with their mouths. So if you happen to go down there on a tour, look for a big blood-red heart painted above the entrance to one of the booths where drunk loggers got their rocks off with the working ladies. I painted it one drunken night and suspect that it's still there.

As Seattle grew up, the cops chose money over blood. Gay bar owners paid them off every month and were pretty much allowed to run their joints in peace. And once it had gone on for a few years, the cops were in deep enough that they couldn't really change their minds, even if they'd wanted to. Each side had plenty to lose and plenty to gain. Some queers saw this as oppression, and I suppose it was, but compared to the war zone many had left behind in the Bay Area, and the loneliness others had felt in the Midwest or the South, it seemed like a damn fine arrangement. We didn't mind spending a little more for our drinks as long as we didn't have to worry about running out the back door in the middle of a song. This went on for years and years until one owner finally got sick of it and spilled the beans in the 1960s. The shit hit the fan and the payoffs stopped. We lost our jobs at Boeing in 1971, the year that famous billboard about "turning off the lights" appeared along I-5. We migrated up the hill to Broadway the next year. Pioneer Square was changing, and Capitol Hill was the new place to be.

It could be said in retrospect that Death both sent the young man packing and brought him home again. It also seemed to guide our own lives. Death in the form of war brought my man to my city. The industries fueled by the peculiar, simmering Death of the Cold War beckoned us to Seattle. Mutually Assured Destruction cleared the way for our neat little neighborhood where we first met the young man and his family.

Death, and even more importantly, our palpable, perpetual cognizance of it, defines our lives. That's nothing new: it's the way it's always been. Life is merely the period between birth and death. We organize our lives based on our expected lifespan. Without a ballpark estimate of how long we've got on this earth, we wouldn't know whether to read 500 books or 500,000; pitch a tent or build a castle; walk across town or rocket to the far reaches of the universe. If we lived to be 200, would we marry at 25? If we lived to be 25, would we marry at all? Death rules this world of ours, more than God, governments or even greed. Death defines life and sets our schedules. Death delivers our priorities, penned on papyrus, parchment, paper and Post-Its. It greets us when we wake up in the morning, dutifully follows us about throughout the day, and joins us again in our dreams. The fact that Death can catch up with us at any time on any day changes the way most of us live. We buckle our seatbelts, eat right, get exercise, take our vitamins, avoid certain areas of the city after dark, and willingly undergo security checks at airports because of Death. We greet pregnancy with almost as much trepidation as joy, mostly because of Death. In this sense, Death defined the young man's life from the very beginning, and even before the very beginning, many years before.

Almost a hundred years ago, in the First World War, airplanes killed few enemy soldiers, the enduring myth of the Red Baron notwithstanding. World War II was a different story. In typically paradoxical form, bombers struck as much fear in the hearts of those on the ground, as flak did in the hearts of the bomber crews. Flying in a bomber in World War II was one of the most dangerous assignments you could draw. Conversely, the vast majority of bombers dropped their payloads and returned to base safely. You do the math and it comes out the same. Only in war. Only in Death.

The bombers flew higher, the guns grew bigger and the radar became more accurate. With the advent of the atomic bomb, however, it only took one plane, not hundreds, to destroy a city. By 1949, the Soviet Union had the atomic bomb, advanced jet engines, long-range bombers, and airbases within striking distance of the United States. Anti-aircraft guns couldn't shoot fast enough, high enough or accurately enough to protect the country. The specter of a communist Enola Gay, flying high and unchallenged, haunted the dreams of Americans.

Nike Ajax Missile installations were built to destroy atomic bomb-laden bombers before they came close enough to harm population centers. The missiles were thrust into the sky by booster rockets that fell to earth within about a mile of the launch site. The main engine would then kick in, bringing the missiles to their apogee and down toward the oncoming target. Nike Hercules missiles were developed to destroy an entire bomber formation in one fell swoop by detonating its payload, an atomic warhead. The development of the Inter-Continental Ballistic Missile changed everything, again. Neither the U.S., nor the Soviet Union could destroy ICBMs fast enough or accurately enough to protect their citizens, and the 1974 Salt II Treaty prohibited them from trying. An anti-missile Nike would never be deployed. Salt II closed the Nike sites that hadn't already been decommissioned due to budget cuts and the demands of the Vietnam War. Mutually Assured Destruction was our only effective remaining defense. Fortunately, neither the Soviet Union nor the United States were led by suicidal religious zealots. The commies didn't want to die and neither did we.

The land that eventually became our neighborhood used to be a military base. The federal government owned almost a thousand acres at one point, most of it undeveloped second-growth Douglas Fir stretching down an enormous hillside away from a 400-acre plateau upon which was built a Nike Missile site and its subterranean missile elevators and fallout shelters, barracks, an airstrip, a headquarters building, guard towers, rifle range and recreational facility; all of it just five miles north of Lake Washington. The woods provided a safe potential drop zone for the Nike booster rocket and good hunting for those who lived nearby: bear, deer, rabbit and squirrel. In 1974, the government sold almost all of the land, retaining only about 150 acres up on the plateau. The underground facilities were maintained, as were the headquarters building and a few barracks. An Army Reserve unit and a FEMA detachment moved in.

Before long, kids on bikes with long banana seats and triangular orange flags on fiberglass sticks cruised the neighborhood pulling wooden hydroplanes complete with broken metal files spraying sparks. Girls in tube tops and cutoffs held informal hula hoop competitions. The oil-and-gravel road wasn't conducive to skateboard use, even with the fat, soft wheels popular at the time, so the 180s and 360s were confined to the cheap, impermanent, yet smooth-as-hell asphalt driveways. The fact that the land upon which the neighborhood was built had at one point been top secret and classified territory was not lost on the new residents in a year rife with political intrigue, scandal, government corruption, and the final horrors of the Vietnam War. Today we talk about urban legends, but the stories and rumors that swirled about the neighborhood's military past were more site-specific and localized, fueled by after-dinner martinis and paranoia.

Told only half-jokingly around the dying charcoal embers of barbecues, the stories inventoried the anecdotal evidence to date: if you laid very quiet in bed at night, you could sometimes hear the clump clump of soldiers' boots in the tunnels below; bottomless holes were occasionally uncovered by AA Rentals post-hole augers; heavy-gauge iron pipes descending straight into the earth can only be cut off, not dug out; backed up toilets are found to be clogged by freshly dug earth; frequent minor earthquakes rattle the china cabinet but never make the evening news. The neighborhood's residents believed the stories in much the same jutted-chin way that acolytes believe in doctrine and political operatives believe in their chosen candidate's agenda.

In spite of the fact (amazing how often we must utter these words as we attempt to draw artificial lines of relationship between historical events) that 1974 was much like 1918 in that the world was once again left with shattered ideals and bellicose, mocking critics crying "I told you so" in a million languages simultaneously like a Hi Fi Tower of Babel broadcasting to the world; the neighborhood, it could be said, was built in simpler times, simpler times than now, at least; times before wireless communication, laptop computers, the internet, Evangelicals' Second Coming, Wal-Martization, AIDs, global warming, world-wide terrorism, cloning, night vision, NAFTA, WTO, EU, Waco, Oklahoma City, and 9/11. The fifties and sixties were over, but in their wake, the world was once again left to the children, the children too innocent to have yelled "baby killer" at soldiers disembarking Pan Am airlines; children too innocent to know what "Jesus Loves You" bumper stickers would lead to; children too innocent to have seen the napalmed little girl running naked or the Vietcong executed with a service revolver in the city street with a gut-wrenching blurp of newsprint blood; children too innocent to look beyond the bell bottoms and sunshine and jump ropes and vegetable gardens and contemplate the rudderless course of this new post-fuck-up America. Idyllic and American without the embarrassingly naked racism and escapism of the fifties. So idyllic and American that most of the kids never really moved away; and if they did, they came back and either purchased or inherited their parents' homes when it came time for their parents to downsize or die. They raised families and sent their kids two blocks down the street to the same school and the same teachers and often the same bulletin board displays to which they'd been sent some 20-odd years before.

In spite of the progressive and chaotic environment at that time, two homos living together on Americana Lane would have been a bit much, at least in the suburban Pacific Northwest. It'd be another few years before "Soap" would hit the air, and even then, it would be met with widespread condemnation from Middle America. We had enough money, and the homes were affordable, so we each bought a rambler with adjoining back-

13

yards separated only by a short fence with a gate. That little gate, of course, would wind up being the best maintained gate in the neighborhood, if not the state. We oiled its hinges, constantly adjusted its latch, kept its paint fresh, and regularly tested its return spring. The gate was as mechanically sound as a Rolex, and was used just as often. We installed some of the first motion-controlled lights to hit the market (special ordered from an electronics firm back East), and rewired them to turn off instead of on. Every night, and sometimes more than once, our backyards' night lights would briefly blink out as he or I would quietly make our way to the other's back door, so to speak. We covered our asses (at least outside the bedroom) and maintained a regular schedule filled with cocktail parties attended by beautiful women and straight couples from work, Sunday afternoon NFL barbecues, and Saturday morning fishing trips. My partner, in spite of all that I love about him, has always had this weird yen for fishing. I suspect, however, that we were the only couple of guys in the neighborhood who scored every time we hit Lake Washington.

A few months before he was born, the young man's parents moved next door to us after our neighbor died of a heart attack and his widow took the kids and moved back to the Midwest to be with family. By the time the young man graduated from high school, the neighborhood had changed dramatically. Some of the houses, for a variety of reasons, were not purchased or inherited by the owners' offspring, and were subsequently converted into rental properties or sold. The houses in the neighborhood were now the least expensive in the area by far, even though they were selling for nearly five times what we'd paid for them. Everything else was astronomically expensive. The new homes being built in newly cleared areas around our neighborhood were much larger, two- and three-storied monstrosities with three-car garages, and no yards. They were built so close together that you could almost touch the synthetic siding of each one if you spread your arms wide. Kids and adults apparently didn't play outside anymore: they played inside; in the "entertainment" room or the "bonus" room or the "guest" room or their bedroom. We had no idea who could be buying these homes or where they were finding the jobs that enabled them to afford them. The only thing we knew was that no one we knew or worked with could afford even half of what a lot of these homes were costing.

By the time the young man entered high school, the neighborhood's adult residents, in single- and multiple-income arrangements, included an electrician, a painter, a head mechanic, an HVAC guy, a nurse, a dump truck driver, a city employee, a customer service representative, a few stay-at-home moms, various retired company men (Boeing Weyerhaeuser, Paccar, etc.), a construction worker, a framer, an ironworker, an administrative assistant, a food service manager, a biologist, a guy living off a trust fund and disability payments, a real estate agent, a woman living off of two child-support payments and a monthly alimony check, a woman living off of various boyfriends, an elementary school teacher, an electrical parts salesman, an Evangelical Christian actor, a drug dealer, a school bus driver, a landscaper, a long-haul trucker, a man who slipped on a wet floor at Costco and subsequently used the settlement money as a day-trader, a window-washer, several unemployed people, members of a band who worked various odd jobs, a daycare operator, a guy scamming Social Security and an insurance company, a handful of shady-looking people whose source of income remained a mystery, and us.

Back in the day, the front yards of the neighborhood vied for supremacy in turf, foliage, color and design. As people grew older and the neighborhood grew older, unsightly blemishes appeared here and there: unkempt yards sprouted up like stubble and grime on a wino's face. The rain pissed down on empty brown-bagged 22-ounce cans abandoned on the grassy strip of city easement along the roads. The moss grew and spread on the asphalt shingle roofs, the mud rose up from beneath the drowned, trampled lawns, smearing across the yards onto the aging, cheap asphalt driveways. Carelessly abandoned toys, broken plastic and metal, succumbed to the mud and water, joining the aggregate refuse of the streets: wrappers, cigarette butts, plastic

15

grocery bags, beer cans, soda cans, newspapers, and the occasional condom or syringe.

The police began to respond to more calls from the neighborhood, mostly domestic disputes, noisy parties, vandalism, drug-dealing and burglary. One night, as I was making my way to the gate, I walked into a veritable olfactory wall of marijuana, pungent and sweet. It wasn't being smoked, it was growing. I walked back into the house and out the front door, and walked the perimeter of the property, bounded by the two streets that defined the corner lot. I could smell the weed most intensely when the wind blew from the north. Across the street to the north, the window-washer's left garage door was open, a door I hadn't seen open in months, if ever. Inside, lights shone behind what appeared to be curtains of visqueen. I found out later that the window washer and his wife had allowed the father of their teenage daughter's baby to convert the garage into an apartment. In the process, a quarter of the space was devoted to growing marijuana. Within minutes of my discovery, the boyfriend, either half-asleep, drunk, stoned, or all three, emerged from the front door, shuffled over to the open garage door and pulled it shut with a loud "kathwang." I didn't ask to sample their crop, but I didn't call the cops, either. They weren't dealing out of the house, and the window washer explained that all the pot was for personal use or the use of their friends. Within a few months, the kid left his girlfriend and baby, took all the plants and lights, and never came back.

At the end of the street was a cul-de-sac with a house inhabited by an executive administrative assistant and her teenage son. The son sold drugs out of the house for nearly a year, in spite of the complaints that the neighbors and the police delivered to the absentee homeowners. The neighbors yelled at the kid and his friends; the kid and his friends stood in their front yard and yelled at the neighbors. The neighbors gave them the bird, and they gave it back. Eventually, it got so bad that the mom moved out, leaving the house in the hands of the kid and his friends. Cars drove by at all hours of the night, pulled up in front of his

16

house, made their buy and drove away again. The cops finally caught him in the act, thanks to a lot of help from the neighbors who endured threats and retaliatory vandalism. The kid did some time in juvenile hall. When he got out, he got a legitimate job and moved out as quickly as he could. The mom stopped paying rent and the landlords found new tenants, a family of four. Unfortunately, no one bothered to tell the kid's business associates that he'd moved. Although he had turned over a new leaf, he apparently hadn't settled his tab with various suppliers, and one of them decided to make an example out of him. The young man told us that what followed was one of the main reasons he left the neighborhood.

The young man was working at a local coffee house back then, and was heading out the front door at about 4:30 one morning when he heard four or five loud, distinct pops. He knew guns: the pops were from a small caliber handgun, most likely a .22. He slipped back inside quietly and doused the porch light, reaching for the phone to call 911. Once he reported what he'd heard, he slipped outside again and made his way down the street toward the cul-de-sac, avoiding the periodic cones of weak, rusty-hued illumination provided by decrepit streetlights mounted to tarred, wooden telephone poles. He didn't see anyone or anything out of the ordinary, aside from the occasional lights furtively flicking on and off inside the houses around him. If he hung around, the cops or neighbors might mistake him for the shooter and he'd already wasted enough time to make him late for his opening shift, so he left. His parents didn't wake up and he didn't bother trying to wake them.

Down the street in the cul-de-sac, in the house recently vacated by the drug-dealing kid and his mom, six .22 caliber slugs were lodged in the recently refinished hardwood floor of what had once been the teenager's bedroom. The new residents of the house, after assembling one bed in each room, had decided on a whim to put their two kids in a single bedroom and turn the other into a play room. All but one of the six bullets struck within the rectangle defined by the four bedpost scuffs they left on the newly refinished floor when they moved their youngest's bed into the same room as his sister. Within seconds of the shots, the dad had pulled both children from their beds and covered their bodies with his own in the corner of their closet. The mother dropped to the floor in the master bedroom and called 911 with the nightstand phone. They moved out the next day and the young man was gone within two months of their departure. It wasn't the last straw, but it was damn close.

The young man, like many young men, was an idealist. He hadn't seen enough of life to understand that things and people and events don't always fit neatly into pigeonholes, and the few examples he'd encountered were dismissed as anomalies. In a sense, though, the whole country was awash in idealism, a willingness to believe that reality was black and white, that shades of grey don't exist, and that you were either with "us" or against "us," regardless of who "us" might be. Thirty years after his resignation, Nixon's Silent Majority had finally found their voices, pocketbooks and voter registration cards. They were now comfortably running the country, while the liberals, Democrats and left-wingers stood silently, impotently, arms hanging at their sides, mouths agape, angry tears trickling down their cheeks. The hokey anarchists screamed "Revolution!", the urban elite wrote "Fuck the suburbs!", the Democrats called for a "bigger tent," and the intellectuals called for a mass exodus to the blue cities leaving the red rural masses to their own self-destructive, narrow-minded, uneducated, Bible-thumping, war-mongering, right-wing, bumpkin devices. The rhetoric struck a chord in the young man. He'd always been more interested in the news and current events than his friends were, but he'd never really felt passionate about anything before. He wondered whether the yearning he felt in his gut was passion; and if it was, what he ought to do about it.

His mom and dad grew increasingly disenchanted with the neighborhood. They would have liked it twenty years ago, we'd always tell them, as we stood in our front yards drinking beer, and the father always smiled ruefully and nodded his head in agreement, taking our word for it. His other neighbors, a family of pallid, dark-haired, small-eyed Calvinists from Michigan, frowned at us drinking beer, especially outside in public, and gave me and my partner sinister, knowing looks as they drove by in their dirty white 10-seat extended Ford passenger van. When they bought the house, it boasted one of the most tastefully landscaped front yards in the neighborhood, with a generous, lush green lawn; indigenous plants, shrubs and ground cover; and boulders set here and there in a beautiful, almost natural nonchalance. The Weasel Family, as we quickly dubbed them, moved in under cover of night and within two days brought in a bulldozer and backhoe that eliminated every square inch of turf, every remnant of rhododendron, every scrap of salal, and every last limb of laurel. The backhoe than crawled into the backyard where it excavated yards and yards of soil, leaving a deep, square, vault-shaped hole smack dab in the middle of what used to be a patio. A cement mixer, two dump trucks full of gravel, and a construction crew showed up the next day. By the time they left, the front yard was a gravel parking lot and the back-yard had a new patio, poured right over a mysterious, underground, cement structure. A heavy iron hatch marked the spot, securely locked with a massive padlock and chain. The only thing that remained, thanks to the ballsy stare of the young man's father, was a 40-year old Japanese Maple inadvertently planted precisely on the property line. The bulldozer had come close, had even broken a branch, but without saying a single word, the father, sitting in a decrepit lawn chair, listening to a baseball game on a broken radio, drinking can after can of Rainier, had saved the gnarled, twisted, ancient, diminutive, Mary Jane-leafed little tree. Later, the petulant, pussy-whipped patriarch of the clan suggested they had the right to remove the tree to protect their parking strip from root damage. The father said "no," and vowed to sue if they even so much as harmed another leaf.

Three weeks later, the carnivorous Mrs. Weasel ordered her eu-nuch of a husband to cut down the tree when the young man and his parents were out of town camping. We figured they'd try something, and called the police when we saw them making their move. The cops said it was a civil matter and the Weasels laughed at us when we tried to intervene. The young man's father had advised against initiating a physical struggle in his absence, so we watched the cowardly cretin cut down the elegant miniature tree, a tree so much more beautiful and mature than its attackers; able to do little more than videotape the episode and offer a variety of off-camera epithets and curses. The Weasels muttered homophobic insults during the episode, all of which I captured on digital video, but the cops later advised me that since it wasn't OUR tree, the act didn't qualify as a hate crime.

This travesty precipitated a protracted legal battle that sapped the father's good will, patience, modest financial resources and spirit. He wasn't accustomed to fighting his battles in the courts: his fists and arms were more than adequate to settle things in a direct manner, but he knew that beating the shit out of the sneaky pissant would do more harm than good in the long run, in spite of the immediate, visceral satisfaction the option offered. The tree was worth hundreds of dollars, but it was the principle of the thing more than the money. People shouldn't be able to do bad things and just get away with it. The neighbors, unfortunately, engaged a member of their small, incestuous little church on a pro bono basis, a personal injury lawyer by trade, and successfully employed legal maneuver after legal maneuver to push the day of reckoning so far into the future that it soon grew hazy and insubstantial like a dream. As we had learned years ago in San Francisco, the law can either uphold justice or derail justice, depending on which side has the money, the time, and the willingness to turn a blind eye to ethics.

The young man was deeply loyal to his family, loyal to the point of fault, like every good son ought to be. He hated the fact that the Weasels hadn't been brought to justice and might never be, and he stared them down every time they stepped foot from their house. One time, when his nephew was visiting, the young man made a show of pointing over at Mr. Weasel and telling the kid in a voice loud enough for the whole block to hear, "See? That's what a coward looks like."

He also hated the fact that the guys in the band, across the street from the Weasels, didn't appreciate his father's patience and willingness to live and let live, leaving the street strewn with bottles, cans, abandoned cars (twice), living room furniture, and trash after their thrice-weekly keggers. Most men his father's age, especially working men who had to get up early each morning, would have called the cops every time, screamed at them from across the street, or organized the neighbors in an effort to get them evicted, but the father seemed more embarrassed for them than anything else, like it was sad to see people so disrespectful to the human beings around them; and he'd usually just walk over, have a beer with them, and try to talk some sense into them. The music would come down a few notches and they'd put out whatever was burning, but by the time he sauntered back home, the party'd be cranking it's way up to an obnoxious level once more.

One morning, his father found a pair of tighty-whities, complete with skidmarks, hanging from his pickup truck driver's side mirror. The young man watched him from the living room as he lifted the briefs with a ball-point pen, just like the crime scene investigators do on TV, deposited both items in the trash can, and calmly got into his truck and drove away. His father knew what it was like to be that age, indestructible and full of restless, furious energy and testosterone, and he knew that even though most of them were decent guys when sober (a couple of them always cleaned up their messes eventually), the alcohol- and pot-fueled haze in which they partied was a different world, a world without recollection of past apologies or promises, the ability to accurately predict or care about potential consequences, or the peripheral vision that allows human beings to care about anything outside of their own immediate desires. There wasn't much to be done about it: it was just something they'd have to outgrow.

The young man also hated the fact that the middle-aged woman who lived two houses down from our other house, the one with MS and a snippy little mutt, rolled around the neighborhood each morning on her little electric cart, walking her dog and letting it shit on everyone's front yard. It was yet another indignity that made his father clench his fists, but allowed for no recourse. "What can I do?" he'd ask his wife, "Tell her I realize she can't walk real well and will probably die before her time, but she shouldn't just go around shitting on her neighbor's lawns? She has to deal with her disease, so I suppose I can deal with her shit."

We noticed that there was something different about the young man, a level of maturity that existed side-by-side with the normal bravado and swagger of kids his age. He was young in spirit, very young, but he talked about values that old folks usually appreciated. It was a weird combination. Kind of reminded us of some of the kids I met in the military. They weren't even old enough to vote or drink but they talked about honor and duty and responsibility. It wasn't so uncommon back then, back before adolescence was hijacked by MTV. Take for example the young man's willingness to own up to his mistakes and the entirely naïve expectation that the rest of humanity ought to do the same. He hated the fact that so many people in his neighborhood seemed immune to, if not entirely unaware of, the existence and necessity of shame. Since he was young and grew up in the neighborhood, he naturally assumed the deficiency was peculiar to his own immediate surroundings. Out in the real world, he naively believed, with a few notable exceptions like the President of the United States, people felt shame when they screwed up and demonstrated this shame with appropriate actions and words. In his neighborhood, however, people did whatever the hell they wanted to do, and then stood back in bemused wonderment as their actions and the consequences of those actions wreaked havoc in the lives of others. It apparently didn't seem real to them. It was like TV without the cable bill.

Case in point: a family two houses down from the band members. A woman, her husband, and three daughters aged 15, 13 and 10 who rarely appeared together unless it was for one of four or five carefully choreographed family work days the father insisted upon throughout the year. There was Spring Clean-up Day, Summer Landscaping and Lawn-mowing Day, the Autumn Leaf Rake-up, and the Christmas Decoration Installation Day. Sometimes, he'd throw in a Detail the Family Vehicles Day, when the girls would vacuum and wash and wax and buff the family's mini-van and luxury SUV until they absolutely shone.

The father, a tall, thin, balding man with muscles, cigarette-stained teeth, tattoos and a swaggering air of theatrics about him, ordered the females around like a stereotypical construction project foreman, hands on hips except when pointing or otherwise gesticulating. Throughout the rest of the year, he was rarely around, and the mom and her girls entertained a never-ending lineup of males of all ages at the house. The two older girls took turns driving their boyfriends around the neighborhood in the mini-van or SUV, while the youngest wandered the neighborhood knocking on random doors to see if there was anyone home who could play. All of us neighbors kept an eye on the youngest and tried to steer her to houses with kids her age. She was inappropriately affectionate to strangers and talked to other kids about sexual acts she had no business knowing about, so we suspected that the father or one of the house's many male visitors was abusing her in some way. She'd be away from home all day and into the evening before her mom would get into the SUV and drive the neighborhood screaming her name.

When the father was home, unless it was time for one of the outdoor family performances, there was inevitably shouting, screaming, slamming doors, screeching tires, broken windows and cops. Two or three squad cars were the norm, because the police knew the guy and his aggressive nature: he'd once threatened the life of another guy in the neighborhood when he found out his wife was servicing him on an almost daily basis. The cops would separate the guy from the family, and he'd stew and fret and curse and gesticulate (he was quite the gesticulator) while his wife enjoyed an hour or so of jovial conversation with the other cops, laughing, joking, and shooting the breeze like it wasn't the most shameful thing in the world that they couldn't even exist without law enforcement and drama. One evening when practically the whole neighborhood was out watching the show, the young man told us he felt like asking the family if they realized that most folks aren't on a first-name basis with the entire police department.

We weren't surprised when the inevitable happened. The young man's father retired with a decent pension after 30 years with the same company and their house sold for twice what they'd paid for it. He and his wife bought an RV and headed out to discover America before it became an infinitely repeating landscape of Applebee's, Wal-Marts and SuperMalls. The young man, on the other hand, had his own ideas. He was tired of the perpetual grey, the gloom, and the brooding pissing sky. He dreamt of sunshine and heat. He was tired of bundled-up, burnt umber granola chicks; of parkas and long coats and scarves and hats. He wanted to watch girls in bikinis roller-blading past sunny beaches. He was tired of his neighborhood in particular and the suburbs in general. He wanted to leave before some kid got run over by one of the maniacal mini-van driving moms who careened through the streets in desperate attempts to get home before Oprah started. The way he talked about moving south reminded us of the Joads in Grapes of Wrath. He was a smart kid, but all he was thinking about was peaches.

Only Shot At A Good Tombstone

"Read the label."

"I know how to do it."

"Just read the label. If you want to know how to do it, just read the label. That's what they put the label on there for."

"It's not going to work. I'll do this later."

"Let me have it. I'll read the label and I'll do it."

But he had already walked away. Three sticky round metal tables reflected the glare of the late afternoon sun. Smog filtered out the yellow light. Only headache-inducing white glare beat down on the cracked, bleached sidewalk and clashed with the blaring, clanging cars stuck in rush hour traffic fifteen feet away.

A dirty, sputtering breeze rolled a cigarette butt off the curb into the fast food wrappers and crushed aluminum cans in the gutter.

"God," said the young man, pressing his temples with the heels of his hands. He stood that way for several moments until passing pedestrians began to stare. He grabbed a bleach-soaked rag and wiped down the three metal tables in ever expanding circles, squinting against the glare. Around and around, always moving outward, knocking crumbs and paper to the ground to be swept up next. He looked up too late to greet a customer entering the café, one of a 5,000-strong chain. "Christ," he said under his breath as the lead clerk watched him through the storefront window, making a mental note of the omitted greeting before moving to the cash register to take the man's order: "Welcome to-." Mercifully, the door swung shut.

The young man folded the rag and laid it gently on the third table, picked up the broom leaning against the brick wall, and started sweeping up the street-silt, crumbs and papers. A dirty little sparrow, pecking through the trash for crumbs, grabbed a dried morsel of a mass-produced blueberry muffin and flew away before the broom came too close.

A car slammed on its brakes. A little boy, his right hand held tightly by a young woman, had stepped off the curb with one foot, which hung in the air for a moment before being jerked back with the young woman's tug. "Jesus," she said.

Ten minutes to quitting. Ten minutes. Sonya appeared on the sidewalk. "Where is he?" she asked.

"In the back."

Sonya adjusted her blouse and pushed open the door, copper bob glinting in the glare.

He picked up the broom, rag and garbage-filled dustpan and pushed backwards through the door. Sonya's perfume still hung in the air. He and the customer he'd failed to greet were the only two people in sight. Out of habit, the young man scanned the café, noting the locations of crumbs, trash and latte spills before remembering he was off. "Are you being helped sir?" he asked the customer. Upon hearing that he was, the young man hollered "Corner!" and entered the back room.

"No one's in front," the lead clerk said.

"I'm off and Sonya's here."

Sonya glared at him and whispered something to another young man before sulking into the front and greeting a new customer just walking in.

The young man hung up his apron, punched out and opened his bag for the lead clerk to inspect. The lead clerk pretended to look, knowing full well the young man never stole a dime, and caring little if he did. The young man walked out into the front of the café, pushed open the door with his back out of habit, and winced at the flash of heat and glare that greeted him outside. Five steps later the sickly-sweet smell of 100-proof sweat and urine-soaked clothes reached his nostrils.

"Hey Joe," the young man said, involuntarily screwing up his face at the powerful stench and squinting to see the crazy man through the aching glare.

"A deal's a deal, Mr. Howell," said Joe. "I ain't been near-" he began, before twisting around and dry-heaving three times in the alley. The young man waited until he was done and dropped five dollar bills he'd stolen from the tip jar into Joe's four-fingered right hand.

"A deal's a deal," the young man said. Out of habit, he felt for the battered flask he kept in his left back pocket and walked into the aching din of glare, concrete and steel.

Before he'd walked half a block, the young man was sweating in the heat. Without breaking stride, he pulled a bottle of water out of his bag and drank a third of it in three gulps, spilling a few drops down the stubble of his chin onto his shirt. He replaced the bottle and wiped the sweat from his forehead up and over the shortly cropped top of his head.

The smog was bad enough that coifed news anchors in window-less air-conditioned studios advised the elderly and sick to stay indoors. The glaring gray sky looked down on the city streets in pained disapproval, muting the colors of billboards and robbing the occasional conspicuous flower bed of its brilliance. The young man passed a travel agency with faded posters advertising Caribbean cruises clumsily taped to the windows. Blue sky, white sand, turquoise water and green palm trees: "Luxurious Cruises – Pampered in Paradise." All faded.

He walked quickly, mostly out of habit, but also because it made sense to him. Smell the roses, yeah; but smell as many roses as you can!

A white metal sign bolted to a shiny metal pole marked the southern border of a newly designated "Prostitution and Drug Interdiction Zone." Not far away, a Hmong family worked their plot in a community vegetable garden, pulling weeds and arranging homemade wood-and-string trellises that would soon support Sugar Snap Pea vines. A hand lettered sign attached to the garden's sagging wooden gate announced "No Drugs, No Tricks, No Guns." The young man carefully stepped over two discarded syringes and a flaccid purple condom.

He continued walking. Moments later, three young children darted out of a ground-floor apartment, laughing and screaming, moving around him like a river around a boulder. They continued down the sidewalk towards the Pea Patch. The young man smiled at their exuberance, but then stopped, wiped the sweat up and over the top of his head and looked back at the kids: "Christ." They were headed straight for the syringes and the spent condom.

He walked a few more steps to the door out of which they'd come. It was scratched, dirty and still wide open. "Hello?" he yelled into the apartment. The doorway opened into the living room. Stained and worn shag carpeting clashed with neat green matching armchairs and sofa. A stylish glass-topped coffee table was covered with toys, sippy cups and a couple of remotes. "Hello?" he yelled, a little louder this time. No answer. Not a

28

sound. The young man muttered "shit" to himself and turned back the way he'd come.

The kids had stopped to look down a storm drain. They were pointing at something shiny down in the darkness, four feet below the iron grate. He caught up with them, slowing to a walk in order not to frighten them. "Hey. Whatcha looking at?

The two younger children, clad in t-shirts, shorts and flip-flops, stood up slowly and backed up against the older child, a girl no more than 7 or 8, with long black hair and dark brown eyes.

She looked at him for a moment before responding. "Brillante," she said. She pointed down at the glinting object through the grate. "Abajo."

The young man knew virtually no Spanish. "Si," he said weakly. He peered down into the darkness, trying to make out the object that had captured their interest. Looking back up at the girl, he asked if she spoke English. She shook her head. Looking back down, he stared for a while, shading his eyes from the glare. He could feel the coolness of the storm drain. He realized the object was an old-fashioned razor blade, all metal without the plastic cartridge – the kind you'd have a better chance finding in a hardware or hobby store than in a drugstore anymore. He remembered years ago, when his father used a razor that took those blades. Every fifth day, his father would remove the blade and slip it through a slot in the back of the metal medicine cabinet between the Alka Seltzer and Old Spice. He remembered asking his father where the blades went after he pushed them through the slot. "The center of the earth," he said, every time.

"It's a razor blade," he told the girl, motioning as if he were shaving and then pointing to the object below. She had one hand on the younger boy's right shoulder and another on the younger girl's left shoulder. "Hoja de afeitar?" she asked.

The young man looked quizzically at her for a moment and then shrugged. "Lo siento," he said.

She whispered something to the others and began to herd them back onto the sidewalk in the direction of the syringes.

"Wait," he said. She looked back at him warily. "Be careful." He pointed toward the items in question and tried unsuccessfully to demonstrate someone getting poked: "Ouch!" The girl could have easily been frightened by the way he was acting, but instead she smiled, as if amused at his awkward attempts to communicate. She shook her head back and forth and shrugged, holding her hands out, palms to the bright steel sky.

He laughed to himself in relief that she wasn't frightened. He looked around. No one else was on the hot dry street. The gardeners were gone and no one from the kids' apartment had appeared. Taking a chance, the young man decided to act out the motions of injecting something into his arm. The girl's smile disappeared immediately. To drive the point home, the young man pointed again at the junkie's trash and nodded his head with all the seriousness he could muster. The girl slowly turned her head and finally saw what he was talking about. He didn't know the word for "danger," so he opted for a more dramatic "muerte." The girl turned back around, nodded at him, and herded the younger kids back out into the street and around the danger. They rejoined the sidewalk about twenty feet later and did not turn around again as they continued on their way. The young man exhaled loudly and turned in the opposite direction, walking past the open door of the apartment, the front room still silent and empty.

The young man slipped the old flask out of his hip pocket and unscrewed the top with one hand. In one fluid motion, he emptied a few ounces of Black Velvet Reserve into his mouth, screwed the top tight, and slipped the flask back into his khaki shorts. He breathed in deeply through his nose, savoring the feel of the whiskey in his mouth, before swallowing it down and exhaling. He drank three more gulps of water from the plastic bottle in his bag and took a left at the next corner.

Two blocks out of his way brought him to a medical clinic that served low-income people in the neighborhood. Like most "pay what you can" clinics, it was understaffed and overwhelmed by the usual assortment of human scourges: AIDs, alcoholism, drug addiction, hepatitis, tuberculosis, mental illness and a shrinking budget. The line inside the clinic extended right out the front door and onto the sidewalk. Inside, babies screamed and children cried. Seven people sat on the concrete or stood leaning against the cinderblock wall, waiting for their turn, listening to the wailing, and fanning or shading themselves with whatever they had available. The young man walked quickly by those in line and stopped to speak with the man guarding the door, eliciting angry protestations: "No cuts!! Get your ass back in line!"

"Does the needle exchange program work out of this clinic?" he asked the man at the door, his back turned to the insults and protests. The man at the door was in his sixties at least, overweight and smoking a cigarette with both hands stuffed in the back pockets of an ancient pair of Levi's. He quickly looked the young man up and down and nodded slowly. "Good," the young man smiled. "There are a couple of syringes on the sidewalk a couple blocks away and I thought they might want to pick them up."

The man looked at him with a degree of incredulity suggesting that even in the midst of the city's many brands of insanity, this young man was the craziest piece of work he had ever laid eyes on. The old man began laughing, still holding the cigarette in place with his lips. "Fuck," he said out of the corner of his mouth, "there's a million needles lying all over this goddamn city. Are you new or just a dumbshit? I guaran-fucking-tee you some junkie will grab them by nightfall. The next time those needles see the light of day will be when the cops find 'em sticking out of some maggot-infested body under the fucking freeway."

31

The young man, simultaneously embarrassed by the public dressing down and impressed with the old man's ability to spew such vitriol out one side of his mouth while managing to continue smoking with the other, turned and began walking back the way he had come, smiling ruefully. The old man continued laughing until the coughs began, bending him over at the waist and threatening to finally dislodge the smoldering cigarette from his lips. His raspy hacking followed the young man as he walked back past the people in line, most of whom had heard the whole exchange and were now laughing as well.

"Hey kid!" said a burly, white-haired woman in blue scrubs looking out of one of the clinic's barred windows. "Reggie's got a bug up his ass today. Don't mind him. Put on these. Use this to pick up the syringes. And then drop them carefully in here." As she spoke, she handed the young man two thick latex gloves, forceps and a red plastic "sharps" box through the iron bars. "Bring it all back to me when you're done and I'll take care of it. Reggie was right about one thing, though: you could spend the rest of your life running around trying to protect everyone in this neighborhood." The young man smiled, nodded and shoved the items into his bag before continuing on. When he reached the apartment from which the three kids had emerged, the door was closed and he could hear a woman's angry voice and young children crying. Farther down the sidewalk, in front of the Pea Patch, the syringes were gone. He left the condom where it lay and walked slowly home.

The young man pushed open a squeaky metal gate, held onto it as a rusty spring pulled it closed again, and walked into the square courtyard of his apartment building. Weeds grew from cracks in the red painted concrete and steel-blue pigeons flapped noisily overhead, intersecting the square gray sky. He passed a small green pond with a broken fountain and started up the metal stairs to his place. Electric fans and portable air-conditioning units buzzed and hummed all around him. On the landing of the third floor, he noticed the front door of 3-H was ajar. He poked his head inside and hollered: "Hey Wilson, you asleep?" Wilson was snoring in his fully-reclined brown corduroy Lazy Boy with the television turned down low on the weather channel. He had been robbed while he slept a couple months earlier, on a hot day just like today, and most everyone in the building kept an eye on him since then. The thief stole $250 from the sugar jar that Wilson kept next to an ancient black toaster on the scratched yellow Formica counter. The thief knew where the money was hidden: nothing else was disturbed. The consensus among the building's tenants was that a young heroin addict who sometimes stayed with the young man's next-door neighbor up on the fourth floor was the thief. Things seemed to go missing whenever he came to stay.

The young man walked into Wilson's apartment and took a right into the kitchen. He pulled open the heavy olive door of Wilson's thirty-year-old refrigerator. The light was burned out and the door blocked most of the hazy daylight coming from the front window and open door, but there was no missing the half-rack of Coors Light sitting center stage on the first shelf along with a half-gallon of milk and a carton of orange juice. He pulled out three cans and walked over to where Wilson continued to snore, surrounded by half-read newspapers, Time magazines, empty Coors Light cans and a handful of remote controls. He carefully moved a stack of New York Times off a table-lamp to the floor, and replaced it with one of the cold cans of beer. Falling back onto the nearby sofa, he put his feet up and cracked open his own with a satisfied sigh.

He drank the first one quickly: it felt good in his empty stomach. He opened the second, took a swig and set it on the floor beside the couch, closing his eyes and listening to the hum of an old teal General Electric oscillating fan Wilson bought at the thrift store down the street. Slowly swiveling back and forth, with a click at either end, it cooled the front room of the apartment, rustling newspapers, stirring the dingy draperies and rustling the 500-count plastic bags of blue rubber bands lined up on the shelves beside the open front door. Rubber bands, dog biscuits, and tear-away plastic bags mounted on cardboard hangers. The shelves also held a couple outdated phonebooks, some technical manuals and a few books, mostly histories.

The young man opened his eyes for a moment and glanced at Wilson: still asleep. Wilson was a good looking man in his fifties who bore a striking resemblance to the actor Louis Gossett Jr., earning him grief from his buddies (including the young man) and a little extra attention from the ladies at work and in the apartment building. Not that it did him much good. With a work schedule like his, Wilson rarely went out and almost never stayed out late when he did. Every single morning of the year, he rose at 2:00 a.m. sharp, drank some coffee and ate some cereal, and drove down to one of the distribution warehouses for one of the city's morning newspapers. There, he joined a motley assemblage of fifty other carriers, counting out 200-some-odd newspapers, checking the reports to see if any of his customers were on vacation, and grabbing whatever ads were going out that day. Shortly after 3:00, he hit the dark deserted city streets in his rusting tan Chrysler K-Car, the back seat stacked with newspapers, plastic bags hanging from the rear-view mirror, and rubber bands erupting from a K-Mart cup caddy.

Two-hundred times a day, 365 times a year, he grabbed a newspaper, stuffed it with an ad, folded it in thirds, and bound it with a blue rubber band. He then either jumped out of the car and jogged down an apartment building hallway like a man half his age, or flung the paper on the fly, with a sharp left-handed pitch that started low outside the driver-side door and finished up near the mirror. His right hand moved from the cracked steering wheel to the gear selector and back to the steering wheel, nosing the K-Car into dark driveways and then backing up again as soon as the paper took flight toward a porch.

He worked till about 5:30 a.m., depending on the weather and his aim. Back to his apartment and showered by 6:00, he drank more coffee, made a brown-bag lunch, ate another bowl of cereal or a couple eggs and sausage, and reported to his other job at a manufacturing firm by 7:30. He spent the next 8 – 10 hours on the assembly line, testing electronic devices used by mining and excavation companies around the world. Home by 6:00 p.m.. Dinner. Beers. Bed by 9:30 and asleep shortly thereafter, if he was lucky. Each paycheck was garnished to pay his ex-wife and the IRS. He also sent a portion of the $12,000 to $15,000 per year he made from the paper route as well. The manufacturing firm gave him one or two days off each week, depending on OT, but the alarm still went off at 2:00 a.m., every single day.

Wilson awoke and sensed that he wasn't alone. "What the hell are you looking at?" he said, his eyes still closed.

"I ain't looking at nothing, Old Man, I'm resting my eyes."

Wilson laughed. "And what the hell are you doing drinking all my beer?"

"Oh, that's gratitude! I come in here to save you from being robbed again, happen to get a little thirsty...and you sit over there instigating conflict... Anyway Old Man, if you'd crank open those eyes for half a second, you'd see that there's one waiting for you, too."

"Ahh..." Wilson opened his eyes a crack and moved his left arm just enough to reach and open the beer. "It's warm."

"Not my problem. It's your lazy ass that was snoring away in the Lazy-Boy all day."

Wilson drank a third of the beer and set it back on the table-lamp. "Not bad, though."

"A real connoisseur.... How's your day going?"

Wilson grunted, drank some more beer and shook his head. "Teamsters and Management are negotiating a new contract. So, the drivers decide their union meeting this morning is going to last two hours instead of 30 minutes. Papers an hour-and-a-half late. Every goddamn customer standing there on their porch, their arms folded, looking at their watch, waiting for me to roll up an hour-and-a-half late. Sun's already up by the time I get halfway through. I ended up promising to credit back twenty-four papers this morning, and there'll be more complaints waiting for me in tomorrow's reports. Money out of my pocket. Management don't pay me back for those papers. The union don't pay me back for those papers.

"This one driver, Richie, we get along pretty well. We shoot the breeze whenever he delivers to our warehouse. Well, he told me they sat in there and played cards, read the paper, did the crossword. 'Work slow-down' is what he called it. 'Putting pressure on Management,' he says. But it don't hurt him and it don't hurt management. The only folks it hurts are the customers and the carriers. Shit runs downhill, not up. Don't know how long it's going to be before people realize that. It don't run uphill. Never has."

"Did you tell him that?"

"Hell yes! I told him that. Don't do any good, though. He understands and all, but the union bosses are calling the shots. They called for the work slow-down. It's been nine months without a contract and they're trying to up the ante. Management wants them to take a voluntary pay cut. If you ask me, the Teamsters should go after the department stores and such that are paying the big advertising bucks. Start picketing them. Don't slow down the trucks and take nickels out of my pocket. Go after the big money. If they pull their ads, management is going to feel it in the pocketbook, not us carriers."

The young man laughed. "Well shit Wilson, while you're at it, why don't you solve the Middle East crisis and end world hunger?"

"Fuck you, you little shit," Wilson laughed. "It may not do any good, but I've got a right to bitch-and-moan once in a while."

"Yeah, you sure ain't getting no other kind of moaning, lately."

"Damn, boy. You're a cruel little mo fo today. Whatcha picking on an old tired man for anyway?" Wilson drained the last of his beer. "You can make up for being such an asshole by getting me another one of MY beers."

The young man jumped up off the sofa, sending his head swimming for a moment, and then went back into the kitchen for the beer.

Wilson kept talking. "I got a right to bitch-and-moan once in a while. Everyone does. Nothing wrong with that. Long as you give thanks to balance things out. Hell, even the Good Book's got bitching and moaning in it...." The young man's groan drowned out the next few words.

"Wilson. Wilson. Here's your beer. Let's not talk about the Good Book right now, alright?"

"Well WE aren't going to talk about the Good Book. I'm going to talk and you're going to sit your ass down and listen. You're drinking my beer, another beer –what's that three, and you're sitting on my sofa. You're going to damn well listen to me sermonize a bit about the Good Book."

Wilson closed his eyes and placed his hands together, finger tips to finger tips, in an attitude of contemplation.

"Now, you may hear people talk about the 'patience of Job,' and how he was faithful and true, a regular boy scout." He drew out the last two words for emphasis, his voice melodious like a good preacher's ought to be. "But I'm here to tell you…"

The young man slumped back down onto the sofa, opened his beer, put up his feet and closed his eyes.

"I'm here to tell you that Job was a regular guy who did not appreciate God and the Devil playing games at his expense. What's that quote? Shakespeare talked about this very thing."

"Shakespeare? Damn, Wilson, you're drunk already. You were talking about the Bi-."

"Are you drinking my beer?"

"Yeah, I'm drinking your b-."

"Well then shut your hole, boy... It WAS Shakespeare...in King Lear, 'As flies to wanton boys are we to th' gods, they kill us for their sport.' You hear that? They kill us for their sport. That's what I'm talking about. Job was a good man, didn't go looking for trouble. He minded his own business, worked hard and enjoyed life. He was a straight-shooter. Well, it came about one day, that the Devil comes up to God and checks in. He was kind of on parole at that time. He could wander around all he wanted, but he had to check in with his parole officer every Wednesday afternoon. Had to pee in a cup and roll up his sleeves," Wilson said, chuckling softly.

"So he reports to his PO and God asks him what he's been up to – whether he's been staying out of trouble and such. Well jobs are scarce and the Devil don't have many legitimate skills, shall we say, so he's basically been just wandering the earth, exploring – you know, sight-seeing. Well God figures that's OK, so the Devil turns around and starts heading back out into the world, when God stops him. Now you've got to understand that the Devil was on his way out. He was through. Two more steps and he'd be out the door. Two more steps and Job would have slept just fine that night."

Wilson opened his eyes and sighed. He was lost for a moment, and then he shook his head half in disgust and half as if to clear an unwelcome thought from his mind. He reached for his beer, drank nearly half of it down, and slowly wiped his mouth with the back of his hand. "Two more steps...and Job's sons would've still been alive that night. God could have just let him go. Everything would've been alright. He didn't HAVE to stop him. The Devil was HALF WAY OUT THE GODDAMN DOOR, and you know what God DID?" Wilson's eyes were now clenched shut, his brow furrowed as if in pain. His voice was loud, but the question was purely rhetorical. He wasn't looking for any answers from anyone, least of all from the young man sprawled on his couch drinking his beer. The sun had sunk down to the horizon by this time, growing red as blood as its dying rays struggled through a world of smog. The small living room was bathed in red, but neither man was looking.

"The Devil was on his way out. Heading out the door, and do you know what God does?" Wilson was talking quietly again. His voice resonant and strong. "He starts bragging about Job. 'Let me tell you about Job,' he says to the Devil. Like Job's a racehorse or a running back. 'Let me tell you about Job.'" But at first, the Devil don't even know God's talking to him. Figures he's talking to one of the other spiritual beings assembled there. There's a good crowd, usually. But something inside tells him to stop. You see, you don't turn your back on God when He's still got business with you. No, even if he wanted to, he couldn't turn his back on God. He's halfway out the door, but he turns himself around. Takes a few steps back the way he came. And God starts in talking about how great Job is, how Job is on God's side. Starts bragging about Job. What's he doing? He's talking a little trash, if you will. Rubbing the Devil's nose in how good a man is this Job. You can read it for yourself if you don't believe me. I ain't making this shit up! It's right there. Chapter and verse. King James Version. THE RECORD. The record...will show," he said with a flourish, as if addressing a jury, "that it was God who started the trash talking. Wasn't the Devil. No, wasn't that good-for-nothing Devil. Wasn't one of the other spiritual beings standing off to the side. God the Father starts in on the Devil, and the Devil was halfway out the door."

"Well, SHIT! What did he expect the Devil to do in response? He's the mother-fucking Devil for Chrissake. Well of course, the Devil starts to talking trash right back. He tells God the only reason Job is such a good man is because he's got everything going his way. Now the Devil knows this ain't true. And the omniscient Heavenly Father knows this ain't true. Job had his good days and he had his bad days, just like anyone else. He had his ups and downs. He was a good man, but he was a man. He had a good life, but it was a life on this mortal earth. So you might have expected God, the omniscient and omnipotent God, to tell the Devil to go back to hell and shut his hole. But he didn't do that. No. He didn't do that. God didn't ignore the Devil. He didn't RE-BUKE the Devil." Eyes closed, finger stabbing the air. "He didn't say 'sticks and stones' to the Devil. No, he starts in talking trash again. He's not only instigating now, mind you. He's escalating. Es-ca-la-ting tensions. Escalating tensions. One-upmanship. Brinkmanship. A spiritual game of 'chicken.' Who's gonna blink? I just don't get it…I just don't get it…The Creator of the world and he's wasting time with this little shit of a fallen angel. Don't have no job. Out wandering the earth."

"Well we all know what happened. God challenged the Devil to do his worst. Pull a couple numbers from the old repertoire and stick it to ol' Job. Can't touch him personally – that's the caveat. You can destroy everything else, but you 'can't touch him.' Can't touch him, hunh. But what do you call it when you take away everything he owns? And then you take his sons. You kill his sons. That's not touching him? Everything's gonna be OK 'cause he don't have boils or cancer? Everything's alright 'cause he still has great skin? You kill his sons, but it's not supposed to be so bad because he's still got his health? God Almighty. God Almighty. God Almighty.' Wilson slowly shook his head, hands on his temples, eyes still closed.

"But Job took his punches, got up and walked on. He sucked it up and walked on. He pulled his broken sons from the rubble of their house and walked on. He buried his sons in his now-desolate land and walked on. 'The Lord giveth, and the Lord taketh away. Blessed be the name of the Lord.' Job says. Blessed be the name of the Lord."

"Get me another beer, boy. Get me another beer. And pull the goddamn Jim Beam down out of that cupboard and pour me a drink. Pour yourself a drink. We'll drink to Job. Blessed be the name of the Lord."

So they drank to Job. Rye whiskey and beer. And the sun sank behind distant foothills, leaving its deep red stain on the western sky. The oscillating fan hummed, left and then right, left and then right, like a soldier on guard duty after Taps. The clanging sounds of rush hour subsided, leaving the apartment building immersed in its own easy buzz of air conditioners, televisions and dinner conversations. The ancient olive green refrigerator periodically clicked and whirred with metallic hunger pains. Wilson and the young man drank quietly for half an hour before either spoke.

"Job was a good man. He was a decent man. Provided for his family. Paid his debts. Treated other people with respect. Well, he went out the next day and buried his sons. No man should ever have to bury his sons, but lots do. Job did. No man should ever lose more than one child, but lots do. And Job did. I suspect he had some help digging, but with his sons gone and his workers gone, I suspect he did most of the job himself. Probably took a couple days. It don't say how many sons he had, but sounds like a few. Probably took a couple days. When it was finished, and every morning thereafter, he stopped and spent some time with his sons and said a prayer."

"Before long, it was time for the Devil to check in with God again. Pee in the cup and roll up his sleeves. The same story. The exact same story. God stopped him halfway out the door.

He bragged about Job. Even amidst the tragedy, Job had kept the faith. God talked trash. The Devil talked trash. God cut him loose to do his worst to Job, no holds barred short of killing him. You can do anything you want, just don't kill him.'"

Wilson spoke with the quiet authority of a man who'd paid his dues. In the half century he'd walked the earth he'd listened far more than he'd talked. He'd done his time in the childhood penitentiary of 'speak only when spoken to' and still carried some of its habits and scars. He'd served his sentence. Bit his tongue. Turned away. Swallowed his words. Sometimes, he still did. When he did speak, he chose his words carefully, weighing each before delivering them, wielding them like precisely calibrated tools. At work, if a meeting lasted 2 hours, he might say four or five sentences, total. That's it. Sometimes, he wouldn't say a word. But when he did, those few words made all the difference. If you likened the meeting to the massive, iron-banded door of a fortress, Wilson's words were the unassuming hinges upon which it pivoted. Smart people listened to Wilson. They knew he had earned the right. You can't fake what he had. And even now, several beers and a few fingers of rye into the night, you didn't hear any slurred words coming out of Wilson: he held his liquor well. His words and thoughts were clear. The young man, on the other hand, was thoroughly soused. He shook his head slowly at Wilson's words, back and forth like the oscillating fan.

"So the Devil covers Job with boils from head to toe. Like chicken pox, except a hundred times worse. Running, watery, stinking, painful boils. The stench was horrible. Boils in his ears. Boils up his nose. Boils up his butt so he couldn't wipe himself properly. Boils down his throat so he couldn't eat or drink. Boils so bad that he finally broke a clay pot, grabbed one of the shards, and started scraping them all off. Scraping off the boils, head to toe. He's a madman, and a goddamn bloody mess when he's done. Then he falls down in a heap of ashes. A man who's already lost everything, covered in blood and ashes."

His best friends hear of his misfortunes and come to comfort him. They're religious friends. Pious friends. Good wholesome friends. The kind of friends your momma wanted you to hang out with. The kind of friends who never got laid. Well they sit in the ashes with him for seven days and seven nights. Good friends. Loyal friends. Friends willing to stick it out with him through thick and thin. Or so he thought. Job ain't thinking straight. He's a mass of raw flesh. Dehydrated. Half-starved. Sitting in his own shit and vomit. Sick with grief and anxiety. Cried so much that he's run out of tears. How could he know they had ulterior motives? How could he know that they secretly reveled in his downfall? He'd lost his livelihood. He'd lost his sons. He'd lost his health. And now the men he calls his friends decide it's time for a lecture. It's time for a civics lesson. It's time for a sermon (and you groan <u>at ME</u>!). It's time for a DI – A – TRIBE. His fall is their exaltation. His sorrow is their joy. His pain is their secret pleasure. And they're ready to roll. You think….", he laughed. "You think….I'm prone to preaching. You think my sermonizing is excessive. You ain't seen nothing my young friend. You've seen Jack Shit, boy. I ain't even scratched the surface this evening compared to those quote-unquote friends of Job.

"Now they weren't just self-righteous, these friends of Job, they were also long-winded motherfuckers. And they had themselves a captive audience. Job wasn't going anywhere. Even if he wanted to, he wasn't goin' anywhere. His legs were locked up from sitting so long and he's in and out of consciousness. Talk about your captive audience. He ain't going NOwhere. So his friends played tag-team preacher on his ass. When one would tire, the other would jump in the ring. They found about the only thing in the world that could have made Job feel WORSE. Sanctimonious, arrogant, back-stabbing preaching. 'Cause you know they were working on their brownie points. They weren't just preaching to Job. They were preaching to each other. They were preaching to God. 'Look at how righteous I am, dear God. And yet I'm willing to sit in the filth with this sinner Job.' Oh yeah, they're good friends. And talk about your flowery speech.

They make me look like an amateur. Make my little devotional here look like a public service announcement. Oh…And they were profound. Deep. Intellectual. PRO – FOUND. Yeah, you want to know what their message was? You want to know what they spent days preaching on? 'You reap what you sow.' Oh yeah. That was it. 'You reap what you sow.' 'This is your fault,' they told Job. 'You brought this upon yourself,' they told blood-and-ashes Job. 'We feel sorry for you, but somewhere, someplace, you screwed up, and this is what you get. Seek forgiveness for your sins and God might have mercy on you. You reap what you sow.'"

"Mercy…Mercy. If that had been me, instead of good ol' Job, I would have gathered up my last bit of strength and beat the living shit out of those guys. I would have beat the living shit out of those guys and then killed myself. Killed myself just to fuck things up. OOPS – God and the Devil look at each other. OOPS. That wasn't supposed to happen. That wasn't part of our little plan. HA!!!" Wilson opened his eyes and smiled broadly. "The Devil didn't do it. God didn't do it. It's that crazy bloody human being that did it to himself. Boy, didn't see that one coming. That's not the way it was supposed to go. Nope. Didn't see that one coming at all. Ruins everything! Ruins the end of the movie. Can't give everything back to Job if he's dead. Can't multiply his wealth and replace his dead sons if he's dead. Can't heal his wounds and restore his health if the motherfucker's dead!!!! NOW what are we gonna do? NOW, what are we gonna do?"

Wilson was laughing – cracking himself up – laughing so hard that tears were soon rolling down his cheeks. The young man listened to his friend laugh, listened to this man who'd lived a half century on this earth laughing with the abandon of a ticklish six-year old. He finally chuckled a bit himself, mostly because Wilson's mirth was contagious and funny in itself, but he couldn't quite understand the joke in it all.

"Oh me. Oh me," Wilson said to himself, taking deep breaths and wiping his eyes with his thick calloused hands. "Thank you." The young man had poured him another drink and grabbed another beer for himself. The young man was drunker than he wanted to be, but the night was warm and he enjoyed listening to Wilson, though he'd never admit it. Wilson took in a mouthful of rye, played with it a bit on his tongue and swallowed slowly. He took a deep breath of the summer night's dirty air and suddenly looked tired. And a little sad. His features slowly relaxed, his eyes focused out the front window at the darkness above the apartment building roofline.

"But Job didn't do that. He probably could of. But he didn't. I guess you could say….in some ways, he was too strong…." He said the word awkwardly, as if it didn't quite fit in his mouth right. "I guess he was too strong for that – stronger than me. Damn straight…stronger than me. Instead, he raised his head up and gave his so-called friends an earful. That he did. He summoned up enough strength and enough mental fortitude to put together a stinging rebuke to the self-righteous shit his friends had poured on his head. Even though his tongue was swollen in his mouth, even though his skin was a mass of running open sores, even though all he could taste and feel and hear and see was suffering and agony and pain, he gave his friends a verbal lashing that put their prissy little speeches to shame. His words truly had power. Are you listening? POWER! He spoke the truth, and the truth cut into his friends the same as a knife or sword. You see, it don't matter WHO speaks the truth. It don't matter where the truth comes from. Whether it's God, the Devil, or wretched old Job doing the talking, the truth cuts through all the bullshit. It tears down the towers of Babel. It rips away the facades of the wicked. It breaks the bones of the oppressors. That's how powerful the words were that came out of Job's mouth. Truth. You don't hear much truth today, boy. You hear advertisements, plenty of advertisements. You hear coercion, whining and negativity. You hear threats and insults, lies and deceit. But you don't hear much truth. You know…when it comes right down to it…truth is beauty. Yes sir.

Truth…**is**….Beauty. And Beauty is Truth. Ah yes. And Beauty is Truth. The realization of either….is Joy." The word hung over the two men. A baby in an apartment across the courtyard started crying. Wilson smiled.

"I'm tired, boy. I'm tired…and you're drunk. Should spend more time with kids your own age, anyway. I didn't even get where I was headed this evening. Only made it about halfway. But I'm tired, now. And that goddamn alarm will be going off soon. If I remember correctly, my point, way back at the three-beer mark, was that everyone's got a right to complain some-times as long as they balance it out with thanks. Well Job gave thanks every day of his life, so when everything fell apart, he had a right to complain."

"As the cloud is consumed and vanisheth away: so he that goeth down to the grave shall come up no more. Therefore, I will not refrain my mouth; I will speak in the anguish of my spirit; I will complain in the bitterness of my soul."

"And then a little farther down, just a few words later, he says 'My days are vanity.' That's right. 'My days are vanity.'"

Wilson pulled a lever on the side of his recliner, slowly bringing it upright. He stood up easily. Still steady.

"You work tomorrow boy?"

"No."

"Alright then. Good night." Wilson closed and locked the front door and disappeared into the darkness of his bedroom.

The young man awoke to the muted sounds of rush hour traffic and children playing in the square courtyard. The old G.E. fan was off, the front door locked, and the refrigerator was clicking and whirring as it always did. He closed his eyes and listened for a while, mentally picking out each set of sounds individually, and then mixing them together again. A passenger jet several miles away roared as it banked hard for its final approach. He thought about the people 25,000 feet above the city and how they were unattached to the earth.

Just a hint of a headache. Just enough to remind him of last night's drinking and to produce a modicum of relief when it eventually passed. He slowly sat up, working the stiffness out of his arms and legs. Standing, he stretched his fingertips to the ceiling and then stepped into the kitchen. Inside the refrigerator, a plate of bacon and eggs covered by Saran Wrap sat atop the remaining cans of Coors Light. "Goddamn but Wilson's a nice guy," he thought as he took the plate over to the microwave and set a can of beer on the kitchen table. Stepping back into the living room, the young man pulled a one-pound bag of ground coffee from his bag and returned to the kitchen to brew a fresh pot. The young man got a free pound of coffee each week from the coffee house. Every other week, he gave it to Wilson. The microwave beeped. He grabbed the plate, cracked open the beer and sat down to breakfast, listening to the coffee maker hiss and brew.

When he finished, he put his plate and fork in the dishwasher, the empty beer can in the recycling bin, and then poured himself a big mug of coffee. Reaching into his back pocket, he grabbed his flask, emptied its contents into the coffee mug bearing the name of Wilson's employer and for the next half hour or so, sat at the old-fashioned Formica-topped kitchen table drinking coffee and skimming through some of the newspapers stacked in front of him. About a third of the way through the stack, he opened the World News section of a week-old Morning Edition. A photograph of a small black child, sandwiched between an ad for cellular phone service and one for a day spa, caught his eye. The little boy, not more than six or seven years old, was running towards the photographer crying. The young man seemed to remember a similar photograph taken in Vietnam during the war. He had seen it in a history book on one of the shelves by Wilson's front door. The little boy in the newspaper, however, had

47

no hands or forearms. "Rebel forces" had hacked them off with a machete after slaughtering the rest of his family, the caption reported. Doctors from the U.S. and Canada were volunteering their time fitting hundreds of victims with prosthetic limbs. They spent their nights listening to the wild dogs eating the corpses that surrounded their camp. The article went on to say that over five-hundred thousand citizens of the impoverished African nation were systematically killed in the space of a month. The name of the country sounded familiar. The young man looked up at the glass light fixture over the table. One of the three dusty 40-watt "soft light" bulbs was out. Suddenly, he got up and checked the bag of coffee he had left for Wilson by the sugar jar. The coffee was from Ethiopia, not from the country where the little boy lived. Sitting back down, he wasn't sure what, if anything, he'd have done if it were.

The young man stared out the front window at the grey glare and finished his coffee. He was pleasantly abuzz with caffeine and alcohol, and figured he'd better get up to his own apartment. Despite the masking aroma of coffee that permeated his hair and clothes and every inch of his skin, the young man knew he was in dire need of a shower after a full day's work, a hot walk home, and a night spent drinking and sleeping on a couch. He gathered his things, slung his bag over his shoulder, made sure he had turned everything off in Wilson's apartment, and locked the door on his way out. Glancing in all directions, he jogged over to the metal stairway and cautiously began making his way up to the fourth floor. In the disheveled state he was in, the last thing he wanted to do was run into one of his neighbors on the way up, especially a beautiful young woman named Renee. Looking ahead up each flight of stairs, like a cop in a TV series, the young man made it to the fourth floor without encountering a soul. He didn't know what time it was, but it was already getting hot. A bead of sweat ran down the side of his face and fell on his wrinkled, mocha-spattered shirt. "Goddamn." He ran his calloused, espresso-stained hand up his forehead and over the top of his head.

First, he passed Mrs. Lavinsky's apartment. She waved at him with small wrinkled hands through her front window. She was on her sofa drinking tea and watching The Price is Right. A cat sat on the top of the couch beside her blue-haired head.

As he passed Jeffrey and Sid's apartment, he heard raised voices.

"Emotional energy."

"I'm sorry?"

"Emotional energy. It takes too much emotional energy having Ralph and Edward over. Pick someone else. It's too much for this week."

"Whatever! You best not be pulling this shit when they come over Saturday night."

"We each have a limited amount of emotional energy available to us each day or week. Some activities, some people, and some environments contribute emotional energy. They support and enhance our budgeted emotional energy. Some activities, people and environments cost us emotional energy. They debit energy from our weekly budget. When you go visit your father, for example, you lose a good third of your week's emotional energy in one fell swoop. Frankly, you're worthless for two or three days thereafter."

"He's dying."

"I'm not saying you shouldn't visit him. I'm just explaining that it costs you a lot each time you do. Similarly, when I must work with Frederick at the office, I must expend, or "spend," if you will, the majority of that day's budgeted emotional energy just to maintain an even keel and continue to perform my essential job functions. When Sally or Terrence are in the office, however, I gain emotional energy which I can then save up for Frederick's eventual arrival. Do you understand? I know you enjoy Ralph and Edward's visits. Frankly, I think you enjoy Ralph a bit more than you should, but that's an entirely different argument. I know you enjoy their visits, but I can only afford to have them visit on days when I have a surplus in my budget. They drain me. I'm shelling out emotional energy like it was a twice-yearly sale. On Saturday, I will have barely enough left from the week to make it through the day and still have a good Sunday. Therefore, if you care anything about me at all…."

"Drama."

"Master's Degree. Thank you very much. If you care anything about me at all, you'll ask them to visit next week, preferably Tuesday or Wednesday, when I still have a chance to make up lost ground before the weekend."

The young man smiled and slid past Jeffrey and Sid's window. The window was open a few inches but the blinds were drawn. Jeffrey and Sid were still talking. Their words reminded him of Lincoln Logs, the way they seemed to fit together. Jeffrey worked for the city as an urban planner. Sid was "in show business" in one way or another. They had met at church, Mt. Hebron African Methodist Episcopal Church, three blocks away, but were both forced out of the congregation when glossy 8x10 photographs of Sid in drag were circulated among the elders. Sid told the young man that the church's charismatic pastor; a former NFL running back, former cocaine addict, and convicted con artist; had banished the two "like Yul Brynner banished Charlton Heston from Egypt into the wilderness (except there were two of us, and everyone's black)." The pastor told the community newspaper that he couldn't "abide two degenerates" in his congregation. The local evening news got the juicier sound byte and some footage of Pastor Stevens preaching from his ornate pulpit: "Our Catholic brothers hate the sin, but love the sinner. We here at Mt. Hebron think that may be taking things too far. We don't especially care for either." Jeffrey still walked past the grey stone façade of the church each day on his

50

way to the bus stop. The grey stone matched the grey smoggy sky. Sid only approached the church when leading a protest of some kind or another. He once told the young man he had lost his faith the day they threw him out: "the place just gives me the creeps now."

The young man fished his keys from his pocket and opened the next door, backing his way through out of habit. He tossed the keys into a wooden velvet-bottomed offering plate Sid stole from Mt. Hebron during one of his protests. It sat atop a pine and cinder-block bookshelf below a black-and-white poster of Kurt Cobain in a torn sweater pointing a loaded revolver at the camera. He dropped his bag and lit three pungent sticks of "Instant Nirvana" incense that protruded vertically from an empty brown stubby Rainier Beer bottle, the first beer he ever drank. He hit the playback button on an old-fashioned answering machine he bought at the thrift store down the street and took a flying, back-first, high-jump style leap onto the shiny green vinyl couch pushed up against the wall beneath the apartment's two much-advertised "picture windows." The couch was warm from the morning's white sunny glare that baked his living room between 7:00 and 11:00, courtesy of the picture windows. There were two messages on the machine.

"Dude, hey I'm wondering if you can help me out. I've got this health issue staring me in the face. My wife's been working late every night on a big presentation and I haven't been sleeping well. And I think…I've started coughing a bit…and I just can't come down with a cold right now. I just don't even want a cold right now…so I'm wondering if you can help out your brother by working my shift tonight. Man, I know you just worked a shift but I don't want to catch a cold…and I think if I can just take it easy this evening and get a good night's rest I'll be OK. So anyway, that would be so cool of you to do that. Give me a call. Uh, my shift starts in a few hours."

It was Pete.

"Hey. Didn't hear back from you yet…and…well, the shift starts in about an hour…so bro', I'm really counting on you to help me out…I appreciate it…give me a call."

Pete again. Goddamn Pete. The young man liked saying "goddamn" when he was drunk. It reminded him of the stories he read that were written back in the thirties and forties when people "drank hard" and "swore with restraint." He felt he had actually invented the phrase "swore with restraint" and since he'd never heard or read anyone else using it, he felt pretty confident about it. These days, of course, everything was "motherfucking" this and "motherfucking" that. You drop a dime down the storm drain and it's cause for a mighty, gut-wrenching F-bomb. So what do you say when your buddy gets shot? Where do you go? If you start with "motherfucking," there's little room to maneuver. And although he himself used the word dozens of times a day, he realized that the stories he had read, written seventy years before, hit him harder than the new stuff he found online or in the "alternative" monthly literary magazines he found scattered about the nearby college campus.

He was about to get up off the vinyl green couch for another beer when he noticed a daddy longlegs casually walking down the pale yellow wall across the room. It was a small room; cramped, really; so it wasn't hard to pick out the grey body and long bent grey legs ten feet away. He didn't mind the yellow paint. The landlord didn't care if he painted over it, or so he'd said several times in the few conversations they'd shared, but the young man noticed his first morning in the apartment that the yellow wall turned the smoggy grey morning glare into a reasonable facsimile of real live sunshine. If he lay down on the green vinyl couch and closed his eyes, the reflected yellow light passed through his red eyelids and made a wonderfully warm shade of orange.

So Pete wanted him to cover his shift. The young man paused a moment and thought about one of the girls at the coffee house. A few weeks ago, she was acting stressed out and then one morning he overheard her talking with her mom on the telephone in the back. She lost a lot of blood, she said, enough to think it might have been a miscarriage, but it slowed enough that she was going to finish her shift. Goddamn if she didn't finish her shift. She's fucking bleeding between the legs and she finished her shift. Wasn't the smartest thing to do, obviously, pretty stupid in fact. But her determination contrasted with Pete's two messages like night and day. Night and day.

The daddy longlegs paused a moment and then continued down the wall on a different course, about 30 degrees to the east of the original. That was one thing he liked about Southern California: the daddy longlegs. The only time he remembered seeing daddy longlegs back in Washington was when he lowered his head to the ground and peered into the musty twilight beneath the pumpkin vines in his family's vegetable garden. A different world existed beneath the monstrous green leaves, a lush miniature jungle-like world in which weeds died from lack of sunlight and daddy longlegs moved about like the alien machines in H.G. Wells' War of the Worlds radio presentation his parents had on cassette tape. The young man shook his head to erase the unpleasant memories associated with listening to the recording of the infamous broadcast as if his memory was an Etch-A-Sketch. The episode was just another link in the chain of evidence that proved he was a freak.

In reality, he alternately loved and hated the memory of the blustery, rainy night back in Washington when he was home alone and the power went out. He lit an oil lamp and listened to the entire recording, old-time commercials and all, in the darkened living room, curled up in his sleeping bag. He went to sleep that night pleasantly and poignantly terrified. He was terrified by the "intrinsicality" (he made up the word especially to help describe that night) of the terror; the real, genuine, essential nature of the terror he heard in the narrator's voice. The terror of seeing the world destroyed and being alone. Utterly alone. The young man struggled to remember the person who first used the phrase "the stuff of life," but that was what it was like with the War of the

Worlds. It was the "stuff of terror." Not visually shocking, obviously; not gruesome or explicit. Just plain horrifying.

The daddy longlegs continued down the wall, paused, and for whatever reason continued on a course another thirty degrees to the east. The young man, unable or unwilling to erase the memories, began to frown as he continued down the path of thoughts that led to what he considered one of the most memorable mistakes of his young life: trying to duplicate that original night's experience in the company of a girl years later. He should have known better. To this day, he marveled at his naiveté like a little-leaguer marvels at the relative inexperience of a tee-ball team.

There were, in fact, two things in particular that he felt he should have known even at that young age. First of all, you can't relive good times. You shouldn't even try. You can remember good times. You can return to the scene of good times and remember them even more vividly, but don't try to make whatever magic happened happen again. Not only won't it happen, but you've got a damn good chance of marring the original memory, like trying to "cut" an old-fashioned album for the second time on the same "wax."

The other thing was that you don't lay all your cards out on the table with a girl. Girls (women) may say they like an "open, sensitive, sharing" man, but that held as much water as the masculine myth of subscribing to Playboy for the articles. He once read a book about the "alpha male," and had yet to find a girl or woman who contradicted its conclusions. The second you (the male) make yourself vulnerable by sharing too much too fast, or sharing the wrong thing, the woman whips out the scissors and makes like Mrs. Bobbit.

Unfortunately, that was one of Life's Lessons he had been pre-destined to learn the hard way. He was hopelessly infatuated with the girl and with the romantic notion of the "perfect evening," which in his naïve mind involved reliving the titillating terror of that rainy night years ago and making it to third base all at the same time. Everything – the rainy night, the house to themselves, the dark living room – everything was "perfect." The girl, as far as he was concerned, was also "perfect": interested in him (at least she asked conversational questions which was more than most girls would do); pretty (and with perfectly perky breasts beneath a real angora sweater); and willing, or so he thought, to sit in a darkened living room (the power had NOT actually gone out this evening – he had just flipped the breaker) and listen to an old radio program played on a vintage Radio Shack cassette recorder, all in the age of ubiquitous MP3 players.

He exercised a certain degree of caution and hid his old sleeping bag behind the sofa rather than laying it out between them, but the evening lasted mere moments nonetheless. The girl couldn't get past the fact that they were sitting there listening to a story. No pictures, no special effects. It was absurd and she didn't hesitate for a moment to say so. And she didn't give a rat's ass for the "using your imagination makes it better" argument with which he pitifully tried to prevent her departure: "This sucks!" she said over and over, building to an awful crescendo of betrayal and rejection far more horrifying than being the last man on earth after an alien invasion. She left. First she called him a freak. Then she left. He ran into the ½ bath beside the kitchen and puked. Then he jimmied his parent's liquor cabinet, forced down as much Jim Beam as he could, and then promptly puked again. He went to bed that night without bothering to clean up anything. The glass liquor cabinet doors remained ajar. The bottle of Jim Beam was left sitting on the kitchen counter. Wads of toilet paper (WTF?) lay scattered about in the general vicinity of the bathroom trash can. But his parents never said a word. When he woke up in the morning with a horrible hangover and a strikingly "perfect" recollection of the night's abject humiliation, the house was clean, the liquor cabinet repaired, and the cassette back in its plastic case. A message on the answering machine that further developed the thesis that he was a freak was erased, never to be heard again.

The young man slowly got up off the green vinyl couch, went to the refrigerator, and got another beer. "What the fuck," he thought. "What the fuck." He temporarily forgot about books written in the thirties in which characters "swore with restraint." "What...the...FUCK."

He forgot about the daddy longlegs. He forgot about the messages from Pete. He opened his beer, drank half, crashed back down onto the green vinyl couch and closed his eyes. There was no imitation sunshine now. The room was glaring, blaring, white, smoggy, crass, polluted, industrial, headache-inducing light. His eyelids glowed anatomy-class red, not Florida-fresh-squeezed orange. Suddenly he thought about his little brother swinging on the swing-set back home with his friends. He forgot about the girl. His dad built the swing-set out of 4x6 timbers since the metal swing-sets always rusted and threatened to tip if you swung too high. The young man forgot about thinking. He forgot about remembering. There was no self-consciousness at all. He was seeing clearly, without trying. Maybe he fell asleep. He had only a vague recollection when he opened his eyes an hour later. But he saw his little brother in glaring, crystal-clear imagery that looked like the trailer for THX sounds in a movie theater, every little detail crisp and independent, separated and distinct. And he saw his brother swinging and laughing with his friends. Laughing unconsciously. Laughing from within outward. He was laughing and his friends were laughing as they swung. And the young man thought to himself in whatever capacity he was thinking, that this was too "perfect" and too good. He saw his brother and he was afraid because this was too pure, too real, too joyful. He felt like crying. For every unit of joy and happiness, you inherit .9 units of fear. That's the fucking rule. Where there is no joy, there is no danger of loss. Where there is no love, there is no danger of sorrow. And here was pure, essential, unadulterated, genuine joy. Goddamn. Goddamn. He wanted to drink and drink and drink to preserve the joy, preserve it like a lab specimen in a jar of alcohol, to prevent it from deteriorating. He wanted it to stay as it was forever.

Someone knocked on the young man's door. A hesitant, almost-deciding-not-to knock. And then there was silence. The sounds of the street continued to filter into the room through open windows. The young man stirred on the green vinyl couch.

"Hey – you home?" a scratchy, tentative voice called out through the dingy-white solid wood six-paneled door. The tarnished brass doorknob turned slowly just far enough to confirm that the door was locked.

"Goddamn it Henry – I told you not to do that doorknob thing. It freaks me out, and one of these days you're going to do that and someone's going to send a load of buckshot back through the door."

"Can you open up?"

"I'm kind of indisposed at the moment. Not really presentable...."

"Just for a second?"

"Yeah, just for a second."

The young man slowly stood up, bracing for a head rush, headache or wave of nausea. He avoided all three, but instead felt that strange version of déjà vu, the kind you get after a particularly realistic dream, run down his spine leaving it tingling and aware.

"I'm sorry to be a butt, Henry. Just give me a second." He checked himself over, making sure he was fully dressed and hadn't thrown up or anything, and shuffled to the front door, unlocking the dead bolt and the doorknob. Henry was standing outside, leaning precariously far back against the waist-high metal railing, holding his head with both hands. He was unshaven, dressed in an odd assortment of pajamas and street clothes, and bleeding from his left arm. Bright red drops of blood led back down the walkway to his apartment. A small red Rorschach test was forming at his feet as the blood dripping onto the cement was smeared by Henry's fidgeting bare toes. A pair of flip-flops lay discarded halfway back to his door. His toenails were overgrown. His toes and feet were dirty and stained. Henry stank and his hair was matted. Dried blood marked his face.

"Shit Henry, what the fuck? Get in here before someone sees you and gets you locked up again. What the fuck, Henry? What the fuck?" The young man grabbed Henry by his right arm and pulled him into the apartment. Henry kept both hands on his head as he entered.

"OK. Sit down right there and don't move. Don't touch anything. Just sit your ass down and stay put. OK?"

"OK. Thanks for opening the door. Your neighbor told me to beat it or he'd call the police. He'd call the police? Shit, I thought they were Anarchists!" Henry started chuckling to himself. It was hard to tell whether he was laughing or crying. "Fucking Anarchists."

The young man ran to the bathroom and grabbed two dark-colored, ratty terry-cloth towels from a shelf, doused one with water from the bathroom faucet, and walked carefully back to the front door, avoiding the drops of blood on the floor. He peered outside and looked both ways down the walkway before stepping out and walking back to Henry's front door. The interior of the apartment was dark and it stank just like Henry did. The Price is Right was blaring on the television, the only source of light he could see. The colors were screwed up – everything was orange and green and distorted. Bob Barker looked like an evil leprechaun. He asked everyone in the audience to please have their pet spayed or neutered. The Price is Right girls leaned their breasts over a speedboat and raised their manicured hands. The young man remembered one of his first erotic dreams as a boy had been about one of the Price is Right girls. In the dream she was taking his food (he was eating dinner or something) and putting it in her mouth to "warm it." And she would keep saying sexy things like "Do you like it when I warm it?" except she supposedly still had the food in her mouth but could still talk perfectly fine.

He dropped the wet towel on the cement and dragged it along the path of the blood drops, looking in all directions as he went. Every once in a while, one of the drops had started to coagulate and he had to stop and scrub the spot with the towel with his foot. When he reached the Rorschach test in front of his door, he left the wadded-up towel on top of it and ran back to Henry's apartment with the dry towel. He then retraced the path he'd taken before, drying the cement as he went. He remembered that he still had the latex gloves from the clinic in his bag. He ran and grabbed two of them, put them on, and then cleaned up the Rorschach test with the towels. Taking a quick look around, he backed through the doorway out of habit, shut the door with his foot, and dropped the towels into the kitchen trash can. He peeled the gloves off, inside out, and dropped them in as well. Then he went to the bathroom, turned on the faucet with his arm and washed his hands with the golden, translucent anti-bacterial soap he always bought at the grocery store. He dried his hands and stepped back into the living room.

Henry was still sitting on the floor where he'd left him, both hands still holding his head, holding it gingerly with fingertips as if it were an ancient clay pot that might break at any moment. He was still doing that weird half-laughing half-crying thing, elbows resting on kneecaps. Blood dripped to the floor from his left arm, although the flow seemed to be slowing, slightly.

"OK Henry. Tell me what happened. Who did this to you?" Forgetting to put on another pair of gloves, the young man reached carefully for Henry's left arm. The blood flowed from the hairless white inside, where it was hard to see. Henry pulled away and spun about on his butt, propelling himself with his bare feet until his back faced the young man.

"Look, Henry. Goddamn it. You come and knock on my fucking door bleeding like a son-of-a-bitch, and you don't even warn me, and whoever it is could still be out there. You sure as hell better show me your goddamn arm or I'm going to fucking call the police myself. If you think for one fucking moment that I'm…" Henry slowly spun back around and showed his arms like an ex con checking in with his p.o. The young man looked carefully at the left arm and quickly realized the wounds were self-inflicted and they seemed to follow a pattern.

"What'd you do Henry?"

Henry was quietly crying now. He cried for a very long time. Quietly. Without much effort or even much feeling. Crying as if he didn't really care much. The young man settled in, leaning back on his arms, his legs outstretched toward Henry. He really needed something: beer or coffee. His mind started to wander as he mulled over his options when Henry spoke.

"This hurt a lot more than I thought it would."

"Your arm?"

"No. She broke up with me. I didn't think it would hurt this much. Or if it did, I didn't think it would last this long."

"How long has it been?"

"Five weeks. Five fucking weeks."

"And you just did this today?"

"I called her today. Again. The number's been disconnected. I called Information and there's no listing. I know I'm a fucking freak, but she didn't have to do that. It wasn't like I was fucking stalking her or anything. It was the third time I'd called. The third time in five weeks. That's pretty goddamned restrained if you ask me, especially for a basket case." The young man had long ago stopped arguing with Henry's self-diagnoses. They were usually pretty accurate.

"That's not bad, Henry. Hell, I think I called at a least a half-dozen times when my last girlfriend broke up with me."

"Did she change her number?"

"No. But I almost wish she did. She chose instead to thorough-ly humiliate me by fucking my best friend. I think I would have preferred her disappearing. At least then I would have only lost a girlfriend."

"Shit."

"Yeah. No kidding."

Henry laughed. It was definitely a laugh. "I think I'm alright now. Thanks for helping out."

"Nice try fuck-up. You can't cut yourself like that and then shrug it off like it was nothing. You're going to call your doctor right now and tell her what you did, that you're 'alright' now and that you'll see her tomorrow or today if she wants you to. I ain't letting you go until you're stabilized and under a doctor's care. Imagine the fucking liability for chrissake. I've got her number written down next to the phone over there from the last time you went bonkers. But, shit. Wait. Don't move. I'm going to get you some stuff to clean yourself up. Then you can go to the bathroom and finish. There's bandages and medical tape and shit in the medicine cabinet. You can't let anyone see that shit or they'll get you committed again. Man, you don't want to go back there, not even for 72 hours. They'll fuck you over. Sure as hell!"

"Tell me about it. I'd rather stay…can you help me clean up my apartment? I think I've let it go a bit…I don't remember much. I don't think I've cleaned much."

"You smell like shit and your apartment is thrashed. You can stay here for a few hours and get cleaned up and have something to eat and stuff. I got a whiff of your place when I went over there cleaning up your little blood trail, and I'm not in the mood to tackle that shit right now. We'll do it later. I'll go close your door so you don't piss off poseur. So he threatened to call the police on you?"

"So did you."

"Yeah, only because he did first and it was so goddamn effective. What did you write?"

"Hunh?"

"What did you write on your arm? It looks like writing."

"I started to write her name."

"Started to?"

"Yeah. And then I got about half-way through and realized I should have gone for her nickname. Elizabeth is too fucking long to carve into your arm. It would have gone up to my shoulder if I'd kept going."

"So it's not the whole thing?"

"No, I stopped after 'Eliz.' Pretty stupid, hunh?"

"Yeah, kind of. But I guess it was better that you stopped. Maybe you've got some sense left after all. So…what the hell did you use? A knife?"

"No. A coat hanger."

"Shit."

"Yeah."

"Those are fucking deep. They're gonna scar."

"Yeah. That was the idea. I didn't want to get down to the veins or arteries or shit. I just wanted it to last forever."

Henry set about cleaning himself with a couple wet washcloths that the young man dropped on the floor beside him.

"Hey, I don't mean to be rude or anything, but you haven't caught anything since the last time, have you?"

"Caught anything?"

"Yeah, you know, like any diseases, the kind that travel in blood."

"Do you mean 'do I have AIDs?'"

"Yeah."

"No. At least not that I'm aware of, and I got tested last month."

"How come?"

"I shared a needle with someone and I shouldn't have done that. It was stupid. She said she was clean, but I shouldn't have trusted her. I've heard rumors that she turned tricks a couple times when things got tight, and if she's sharing with me, she's damn well sharing with other people too, but I was drunk, I was depressed about Liz and I wasn't exactly being conscientious about my meds. So now, I've got another piece of baggage to add to the stack. 'Hi, I'm Henry. I'm psycho, my family has all but disowned me, I'm unemployed, living off handouts, newly single against my will, a relapsed alcoholic, probably going to flunk my next drug test, and I just carved half my ex-girlfriend's name into my arm with the pointy end of a severed coat hanger."

"And you reek."

"Yes. And I'm physically repellent."

"At this time."

"At this time."

"So…do you feel better, now? Getting that all out?

"No. Not especially. Getting something "off your chest" is overrated. Nothing's changed. Catharsis ain't worth shit to me right now. I don't have the energy for catharsis, and for catharsis to work, someone outside of yourself has to give a shit."

"You're sober right now, aren't you?"

"Yeah. That's another problem."

"Cause you're really coherent. You sound really squared away for someone who just…"

"Yeah. So pour me some whiskey and I'll shave, shower and get out of your hair."

"No worries. I've got food and whiskey and I'm going to help out with your apartment. Shit. You go take a shower and I'll go shut your door. I forgot."

The phone rang. The young man let it go to the recorder: "Dude. It's Pete. Hey, no big deal about last night and all. I mean it was definitely late notice and I…well anyway, I'm still thinking I might be getting sick. I kind of felt too warm last night and I'm scheduled for this afternoon at 3:00. So if you can help me out on this one that would be so cool. I wish I was like you, always healthy and shit. So anyway, give me a call."

"You know what Henry?"

Henry stopped washing himself for a moment and slowly looked up at the young man.

"I understand you're fucked up and shit. I mean I don't UNDERSTAND. I recognize, like I'm reading an article in the morning paper. I acknowledge that you may have just committed fucking suicide by sharing a needle with a smack whore. But even with all those things. Even with your girlfriend breaking up with you and you freaking out and all, you still have twice the balls and ten times the nobility that someone like Pete has. I mean it. I shit you not. You've got 'em my friend," the young man grabbed his own to demonstrate, "and that's worth something. That's sure as hell worth something. If nothing else, you give a shit. At least you're real. At least you take ownership of your fucked-up life. When it all melts down, when time ends, when the final accounting job is finished, you're going to be alright. I'm serious. You're going to be alright."

By the time he stopped talking, Henry was asleep. The bleeding had stopped. He was curled up like a dog on the floor, holding one of the washcloths like a security blanket. The sounds from the street filtered into the room. He started snoring.

The phone rang. Whoever it was hung up when the answering machine came on. Well, the day was off to an auspicious start, he thought to himself. Now what? Wake up with coffee or go back to sleep with a couple more beers? He couldn't decide. First, run out and close Henry's door.

The young man found their mutual neighbor, Jeff, his tan photogenic face screwed up in disgust, leaning forward and squinting into the shadowy stench of Henry's apartment; leaning as far as he could without touching the bloodstained doorjamb or crossing the filthy, equally bloody threshold. Entirely engrossed in his enterprise, Jeff was unaware that the young man was behind him. It was tempting as hell, the young man thought to himself, to plant a foot squarely on Jeff's Ambercrombied ass and send him sprawling into the darkness, gore and filth he so desperately wanted to glimpse and just as desperately wanted to avoid touching. But that wouldn't exactly help his chances of keeping the police and public mental health professionals off Henry's ass, and it could mean a fight. Jeff was a lazy-ass, trust-fund pretty boy who could have just as easily stepped from the pages of GQ as from his low-rent, worn-out, decidedly down-scale apartment, but he was still 6' 3" (at least), and weighed in at a chiseled 200 pounds to boot. Glass jaw? Probably. Got to look good for the cameras, after all, but you never know. Plus, one good shove and you're over the waist-high railing three floors up. So, the young man ran through the never-to-be-played scene once more in his head and dismissed it forever as the stuff of television sitcoms.

Instead, the young man peered over the railing down into the courtyard to see how many others were privy to the morning's drama. A half-dozen preschool-aged children dressed in brightly colored outfits played in the sterile grey warmth of the morning, their squeals, laughs and cries echoing upward and finally escaping into the glaring, smoggy square sky. Three women; one in a neat, pleated skirt, who crossed her legs and opened a paperback book; and two others engaged in animated conversation; had apparently just arrived with the kids. They were still getting settled and had hopefully missed the commotion. Keeping a close eye on the children, the three women didn't so much as glance up in the young man's direction.

The young man returned his attention to the task at hand. Jeff still stared stupidly into the darkness, oblivious of the world beyond the dark stinky confines of the crazy man's apartment. In one fluid motion, the young man slipped by Jeff ("excuse me"), turned off Henry's screwed-up television ("click"), and exited the apartment, closing the door behind him in Jeff's face ("sorry, man"). Sure, he wasn't looking for a fight, but there was still enough alcohol running through his veins that the young man pulled off the maneuver with confidence and prepared for the inevitable confrontation with Jeff, upon whom Henry's next 72 hours of freedom in part rested, with an unusually detached sense of amusement and calm. Ordinarily, confrontations made him stressed-out and shaky, and for this reason he tended to focus on maneuvering circumstances toward an eventual compromise that eliminated the need to designate a "winner" and a "loser," but Jim Beam and beer were still kicking about, and for the moment, at least, he was ready to lay down the law with the puzzlingly dreadlocked, blonde, one-time runway model (and industrial training video actor extraordinaire).

For what seemed like an eternity-and-a-half, Jeff continued to stare forward, mouth agape, trying to effect the look of Upper Class Disgust he had so often seen flash across his now-divorced parents' faces. He forgot entirely about Henry, the blood, and the little white-trash shit who had just slammed a door in his face, and was focusing entirely on The Look. Struggling, he imagined himself in his favorite television daytime drama, hoping this would enable him to "get into character," but it was no use. With every waitress, bartender and pool boy in Southern California reaching for that golden ring, there was no excuse for his inability to look…what did they call it… "aghast." Not willing, however, to entirely concede defeat, Jeff opted for the next best thing, the old stand-by that had greased his way out of traffic tickets and more all his life; the Top Gun Tom Cruise grin and chuckle: arrogance, sex-appeal and bravado, all wrapped up together in a multi-million dollar People Magazine cover story package. He pulled it off flawlessly, as he always did. Energized, he quickly segued to the earnest, heroically-dimpled Tom Cruise of "Born on the Fourth of July" and "A Few Good Men," preparing to confront yet another challenge that a man with his good looks certainly didn't deserve.

"The guy is fucking psycho!" he enunciated, expertly-capped teeth flashing (and almost audibly clicking with SuperBright Whiteness): "Did you see all that blood?" <Pause> <Count to 3> "Did you see what he was wearing?" <Pause> <Dimpled Smile> "What was he trying to do, kill himself?" Yeah, that was good. No denying it. The writers sucked, but his delivery was amazing.

Meanwhile, bulbous black flies buzzed about Henry's scratched, battered, bloody door. Christ, did he spin in circles? The young man's dad knew a guy who was an expert on blood spatters. He could tell the difference between someone being hit in the head with a hammer and someone being shot in the head with a nail gun, just by looking at the wallpaper. Shit, spot him the time of death and he'd write you the goddamn coroner's re-port extant. A veritable riot at cocktail parties.

The flies were loud. God. How the hell could flies be so loud? Birds weren't that loud. People walking by you on the street we-ren't that loud. Traffic was loud, sure. It was way too loud, but you're looking at tons of aluminum, steel and plastic, with spark plugs firing and gas vapor exploding left and right. Goddamn right, traffic is too loud. But these were weightless, insignificant flies, and you still couldn't ignore their filthy buzzing. Their meaningless existence intrudes upon your own like unkempt shirttail relatives showing up at Christmas. You could even smell them. Even their sound smelled. Disease-ridden hairy legs, and those fairy-tale rainbow-clear wings vibrating lasci-viously. Stinking to high heaven.

Old battle-worn, translucent plastic fly-swatters can stink up your kitchen nook before you know it. Hanging inconspicuously on that long-forgotten nail by the telephone. Some things on earth are like that. You know they're there, you know they exist, but you don't think about their aroma per se until they're up-close and personal. Elephants at the zoo. It's not until you pay your five bucks and climb up onto that harness thing, that roof-top carrier get-up (the thing you see in photographs from India), that you get the elephant smell. Jungle and dairy farm combined with a shovelful of dust. That's what it is. And what about the pages of the Bible (no sacrilege intended): sweet, tissue-paper-thin pages covered with wine-like ink. It's almost too sensual for the Good Book. Except for the Song of Solomon, of course.

No, you couldn't ignore the dirty, moist, rotting smell of the flies and the refuse they circled, just like you couldn't ignore their movements. You looked at them, initially, as a group, cloud, or swarm or whatever, and there seemed to be a pattern or connection in their movements. A choreography of some kind. But the whole is the sum of its parts, right? What individual flight patterns did they follow? Does fly #34 always zig when fly #56 zags? It's stupid, but their motions were simultaneously repetitive and random. Almost predictable, but not quite – kind of like trying to guess the next event of a déjà vu experience. You feel like you can, the déjà vu seems so goddamned familiar, so gripping, that you know you've got a chance, but it's never right. Not even once. It's so Not Right, in fact, that you're left mouth agape, staring stupidly like Jeff.

Below the orbiting universe of flies, tiny black ants, not the big ones the young man remembered from Washington State, but teeny-tiny California ants, were heading for the coagulated blood on the threshold. Drops of sweet O-Positive with just the thin surface crusted over. Lot's of good juicy liquid protein beneath. The flies and the ants. The air force and the infantry, descending upon a common target.

The young man glanced over the railing down into the courtyard. The two women had stopped talking, their hands in mid-air, and were peering upward. The third woman continued reading her book. Attempting a little acting of his own, the young man laughed as if the whole thing were a joke and waved at the women to let them know all was well. Unimpressed, the women hesitantly resumed their conversation, perfectly effecting their own versions of "aghast." The black flies, now triple their original number, buzzed aggressively, droning loudly, heavily around the two men. The young man tried to remember the guy's name that wrote that book, the one about the flies.

On the street behind the apartment building, several emergency vehicles approached, sirens blaring and engines gunning. When the noise faded into the distance, and all he and Jeff could hear were the obscenely plump flies, the kids below, televisions, air-conditioners, stereos, and morning traffic, the young man quietly told Jeff that Henry was simply very upset about getting dumped, had too much to drink, and had foolishly punched the mirror in his bathroom, cutting himself pretty severely. Jeff seemed to almost buy it

"Yeah, but it fucking reeks in there," he responded, leaning toward the young man almost like a schoolyard bully. The young man stood his ground, and received a nose full of Obsession for Men as his reward.

"Yeah, he downed a fifth of Jegermeister and puked all over the place. Then the toilet backed up. It's not pretty in there. That's guaran-fucking-teed!"

"He did all that because of some fucking bitch?" Jeff asked incredulously. The young man began to clarify that she wasn't so much a bitch as...and then realized from Jeff's tone and off-hand demeanor that this was to be the young man's "angle." This was the way he'd save Henry from a return visit to the three-day resort for the sanity-impaired.

"Yeah, what a fucking waste!" he commiserated. "A good guy like Henry getting fucked over by some little buck-fifty cunt and now he's bleeding and she's sucking some other dick."

"No doubt, bro," Jeff said, raising his hand to clasp the young man's in an awkward salute to the plight of the American white male. "Christ, that was too easy," the young man thought: "Are we all really that stupid?"

70

Jeff interrupted his thoughts: "Dude, let me tell you something," he said, licking his Val Kilmer lips. "I've had the finest pussy that Beverly Hills has to offer, and I'll tell you what: not even the sweetest young cheerleader pussy is worth putting your fist into a mirror. That's gonna fucking scar if he's not careful! Fuck! What a total dipshit!" For a few moments, Jeff shook his head in disbelief. Then a smile developed. Not a Tom Cruise smile. Not a Val Kilmer smile. An unselfconscious, distracted, goofy Jeff grin. He started laughing to himself. Still looking down as if looking straight through the cement walkway into the recent past.

Something had struck him as god-awful funny. He laughed to himself. "I told him I was gonna call the cops on him," he said, still laughing. "He was all freaked-out and crying and shit – like he was on a bad trip...and I...he was all freaked-out." Jeff was having a helluva time replaying the memory. He was knocking 'em dead – "thank you, I'll be here all week!" Involuntary laughter, the young man thought, is usually a good thing. Usual-ly. A reminder that there are aspects of human nature that aren't entirely deprived. Little glimpses of joy. Not this time, god-damn it. Not even fucking close. With every sideshow leer, with every sleezy MLM grin, Jeff defined the lowest common denominator of human experience. In place of wisdom and for-bearance, love and tolerance, there were only dirty, filthy hairy-legged flies and Jeff. Rainbow-reflecting compound eyes taking in the environment one multi-faceted snapshot at a time in a con-frontational, adversarial world.

"Yeah, he told me," the young man said dryly. "He thought it was weird that an anarchist would be calling the cops on some-one."

"Anarchist? What the fuck?" He drew the f-word out long and lazy and obscene like a two-bit actor in a triple-X flick, his pret-ty-boy face and full photogenic lips searching for the camera like a towering sunflower stretching toward the sun. He reveled in the act of pronunciation, in the activity of representation, the experience of making illusions look real. Particleboard walls, latex scars, acrid fog-machine mist…these were the ingredients of life, and he wanted to surround himself with it all. "Anarchist?" he repeated with over-the-top incredulity. "You mean those guys who live in Oregon and dress all in black and shit? I'm not a fucking anarchist – what the fuck was that guy thinking? What's his name? Harris? Why the fuck did he think that..." Jeff paused for a moment, continuing to quietly laugh open-mouthed like John Travolta in "Grease" or "Welcome Back Kotter," slowly shaking his head back and forth in mock pity. But there was something else. Something he wasn't telling. An aspect of distracted consternation in the way he carried himself. Shiftiness. Jeff slowly, gingerly rubbed his jaw as if feeling for a broken bone, continuing to stare down and through the concrete walkway, lost in thoughts and memories.

"So, why'd….HARRIS think you were an anarchist?" the young man asked, emphasizing his neighbor's new alias. "It had to have been more than the dreads…"

"Hunh?" Jeff guiltily jerked to attention as if awakened from a mid-lecture slumber by some stereotypically curmudgeonly English professor. He all but wiped an imaginary line of drool from his chin. And it would not have been surprising if he had: everything Jeff did and said and experienced was stereotypical. He was always "On." His universe was one of Hollywood-defined pigeonholes and camera angles: no matter where you rolled the Skee Ball of Life, it always ended up dropping down through one of the numbered holes. All of reality condensed to a 1 – 9 scale, with a heavy emphasis on the lowest common denominator.

"You've got dreads, but those were for that catalogue shoot, right? You didn't do 'em for political reasons. So, it has to have been more than that. And lots of white guys…well, it's not that unusual these days for white guys to wear dreads…" And anarchists certainly don't hold the trademark rights, he thought. In fact, the young man tried to think back to the last time he'd seen an anarchist up close. It was back during the WTO protests three years before. A group of self-described anarchists traveled south from Eugene to protest the international community's slavery to the almighty dollar and the resulting toll on the environment and humanity. They made the news like they always did and the young man didn't remember a single one of them with dreadlocks, let alone any tan, blonde 6-2" ones with blue eyes…

Jeff was nodding slowly. "There were," he intoned steadily like some apartment-dwelling Stone Phillips, "some anarchists here a couple weeks ago. They. They…" Jeff again gingerly probed his jawbone. "I had to throw them out. Fucking pricks." Back on track! That's the way, Jeff! "The main guy, Rodney, had come to fetch his bitch. He was all covered in tattoos and piercings and he stunk like shit, like he didn't use deodorant or something. And he was dressed like a freak. Darla and I had picked up his girlfriend over on Collegiate Avenue. Sitting there on the sidewalk, stoned out of her mind, her and her hippy chick friends, all in a row. Jesus Christ. They all needed baths. Well me and Darla, we figured we could clean her up and have a good time for next to nothing. The girls were all begging for money for bus fare back to Oregon. They had these signs that said 'Oregon or Bust' which made no sense at all…" More open-mouthed Barbarino laughs. "Sitting there with their sweet little asses on the sidewalk and none of them wearing bras...Christ, what did they expect? So I offered this bitch $50 to do a three-way with me and Darla. Darla digs that shit." Jeff crassly licked his thick lips again and rubbed his hands together like some tanning-booth porno-flick stallion. "Her sign said she needed $47 to buy the ticket, get some food and make it home. Eugene, I think it was. Some nerd name, I remember that. So I walked up to her and said, 'hey baby, you can spend the next week on the sidewalk, or you can party with my girl and me and get the whole enchilada.'" After delivering the line, Jeff mentally ran through the whole thing again, reviewing his delivery. Nodding as he mentally repeated each word. It was good stuff. "Well, she was totally stoned out of her mind, so it was pretty easy to get her into the car. Her friends didn't do much to stop her, and plus, dude, you've seen my car."

Much more of this, the young man thought, and he was going to forget Henry, forget the three-story drop to the courtyard below, and beat the living shit out of this pretty boy wannabe. Like most quiet men who exercised a high level of self-control on a daily basis, the young man often fantasized about unleashing all of his pent-up anger, bitterness, hatred and wrath in an entirely righteous attack on some filthy piece-of-shit who deserved a beating before exiting this life and going to hell. Usually, his fantasy involved the rescue of an innocent victim (most often a woman in distress), the lack of available police support (the main premise of most of Hollywood's macho revenge epics), and the drawing of first blood by the villain. Shit. The massacres undertaken by God's legions in the Bible weren't that holy. Pure, righteous, holy punishment carried out on God and Society's behalf by one quiet man who finally had had enough of the shit. Perfect. Priceless. And very, very fulfilling.

Jeff was still talking. The young man tuned back into the story.

"So I grabbed her tits as soon as she got into the car and Darla had a fucking fit. She is so goddamned jealous sometimes. And I bought this chick half for her. So we drive to my place and the girl wants to make a phone call, so I tell her that if she calls Oregon, I'm taking $10 off the price right off the bat. So, she makes her call and I get out the forty bucks and I give her twenty now, and keep twenty to make sure she does a good job sucking my dick. Doesn't wimp out and get lazy, if you know what I mean. So then she and Darla start kissing and feeling each other up and shit and I'm getting hard so I whip it out and start beating away while they get all hot and heavy and start putting their hands down their panties and shit."

The young man hated the fact that he was suddenly jealous of Jeff. Jealous of Jeff and bitter towards the two girls, who, he assumed, had at some point in their young lives passed up perfectly decent, nice guys on their way to degrading themselves by performing for slimy assholes like Jeff. Jealousy and bitterness. Envy and wrath. Two of the Seven Deadly Sins. Just like that, the young man was in hell. What had started out as a righteous mission to save a troubled young man had quickly degenerated to eternal damnation. The young man understood the jealousy and envy part. That made perfect sense. Jeff got a ménage a trois and he didn't. That's pretty straightforward. And you couldn't really blame Jeff. Shit. Guys want sex. It's not rocket science. And it's not like Jeff was the most subtle of characters, either. "About as subtle as an earthquake," the young man's dad used to say when childhood attempts at ambush inevitably failed with a crashing stumble into the kitchen's pots and pans drawer or the smacking of a shin on the cement fireplace hearth. No, Jeff was no Serpent in the Garden. (One night a couple weeks before, after a number of beers and half a fifth of Jim Beam, Wilson told him about how the serpent was "more subtle than any beast of the field which the Lord God had made." That was in Genesis in the Bible.) No, Jeff wasn't a serpent. More like a goddamned bull in a china shop. There was no mistaking what he was about. Jeff had about as much chance of deceiving a young woman as Mike Tyson had of tricking a beauty pageant contestant into his hotel room. Mike Tyson invites some pageant pussy up to his goddamned hotel room and there's some jury of twelve that will go on the record and say she didn't know what she was getting into? Christ Almighty. Tyson couldn't trick himself out of the proverbial wet paper bag for Christ's sake. He couldn't even SAY "proverbial wet paper bag" and someone somewhere believed that he pulled the wool over the eyes of some young honor student? What a fucking crock.

And that's the way the young man felt about Jeff. Jealousy. But no bitterness. The bitterness and wrath was reserved for Darla who knew exactly what was going on from the word GO. "Women are evil. Men are dumb." a wise old woman told him once, and the young man had yet to encounter a reason to doubt it. But the bitterness, wrath, and yes, even hatred toward the women bothered him more. Much, much more. The young man

75

was not accustomed to hatred. Hatred belonged in the Middle East. In Belfast. In Somalia. Hatred did not belong in his heart, but what other word could he use to describe the disgust he felt for these two young women? He couldn't help but think of these girls laughing at the geeks in P.E., turning them down for dates, ridiculing them in front of their friends. And these same girls are the ones who end up sucking some slimy asshole's dick for $50. Or helping him pick up some stoned flower child who just wants to get home. "Accessory after the fact" or whatever the hell the cop shows on TV say....

Whether the young man was truly a geek was debatable, but he still counted himself among their number like a border-line bourgeoisie counting himself among the revolutionary proleta- riat in a time of need. Half because he identified with them, and half because he had to choose a side and the nobility was totally out of the question. The nobility had no heads. So when the girls fucked with the Geeks and Freaks, they fucked with him. Plain and simple.

The young man remembered a nature program he'd watched on TV about lions. The male lion wanted to fuck the girl lion, but he wouldn't because she had cubs. So he killed the cubs and then went for it. That struck the young man as brutal, but Nature was brutal. That's the way it was. Nature was not some god- damned Disney movie with all the animals singing and dancing together. Never was, never will be. Nature is about survival and death. Plain and simple. Darwin had at least that much right. There is no mercy in Nature. Quaking Aspens give off no heat. Hug 'em as hard as you want and all you've got is an ice-cold parchment-white tree trunk in the middle of the fucking forest. There ain't no mystical warmth. Damn straight there ain't. So the male lion kills the cubs one by one. Brutal, but understanda- ble. They meant nothing to him, after all, and a guy's gotta get laid, right? No the thing that gave him chills was the reaction of the lioness. Within minutes of confirming that her children were dead, the female lion strutted herself in front of the male lion, walking provocatively by him and even rubbing her ass in his face. The young man remembered his incredulity the first time he saw it. She just rubbed her ass in his face!!! The blood of her cubs isn't even dry on his lips and fangs and she's rubbing her ass in his face as she walks by. Those were her cubs!! Is it unfair to expect more from her? Wherein does the evil lie? Wherein, the young man asked himself, does the evil lie?

Not in the Wild Kingdom, you dipshit, the young man replied to himself, briskly shaking his head back-and-forth to clear the cobwebs and heavy thoughts. Jesus H. Christ. Jeff was still talking.

He tuned back into Jeff's narrative, but desperately wanted a beer. The morning had grown warm, his buzz had worn off, he was hungry, he was thirsty, and he wanted a beer. His thoughts turned to fried eggs (over easy) and cold beer. A few strips of thick-sliced pepper-backed, hickory-smoked bacon would round out the meal. God, he was suddenly ravenously hungry and dying for a beer. Jeff was still talking and nothing of interest was being described (the topic of sex having inexplicably fallen by the wayside). And there was really very little to keep the young man there with Jeff. So, he excused himself and walked quickly back into his apartment and closed the door behind him, sliding the bolt out of habit.

He looked at a drop of Henry's blood on the floor and thought of the flies. The vulgar, bulging, hairy, big-eyed flies, buzzing about the blood. Henry's coagulating, drying, copper-smelling blood. His mind moved from image to thought to image the way a fly approaches, moves away and reapproaches an object. Were they really black or more a midnight blue? The flies. His dad taught him that the stuff that colors a gun barrel is called "bluing." And for some reason, a gun barrel came to mind when he thought about the flies' exoskeleton. Wait. Do flies have an exoskeleton, or is it just bugs like beetles?

The flies were almost lascivious in their thirst for blood. Where had he heard that word? Lascivious. It was an odd word.

People didn't say it much anymore. Where had he heard it? A scene from a movie played in his mind. A partially-clothed woman, chained and interrogated by priests...no, not just priests...special priests...Yes, Inquisitors! They tortured people and tried to make them Catholic a thousand years ago. What the hell was that? Lascivious. Wasn't that one of the Seven Deadly Sins? And where the hell had he heard about those? A friend talking about one of his college classes...yeah. It had to be. Comparative Religions or Medieval History or something. Maybe someone at the coffee shop. The national coffee house chain was lousy with English and History degrees. "Unmarketable," a recently graduated coworker told him. But does anyone think about all that shit anymore? The only reason he knew there were still priests in the world was because they were in the news for molesting little boys.

Did anyone think about that old stuff anymore? Anyone, of course, besides the old white-haired professors his friends told him about, holed up in their musty, cramped history department offices. Hidden away between classes up rickety flights of sagging, cock-eyed wooden stairs, down dark hallways smelling of dust, yellowing books and peeling paint. He accompanied a friend of his to a professor's office one time to drop off a paper. The professor was the only one in the department who still required a paper copy. An emailed copy was fine for everyone else. Books. Old, thick-papered, dust-covered books. He thought about that old professor he'd met. That old professor who still loved his books. When they dropped off the paper, he was looking for a book about the Middle Ages. He found it and gently pulled it from the shelf like it was the goddamn holy grail or something. He blew the dust from the top and carefully opened it, turning the pages so gently you'd think they were spun from spider webs.

Lascivious. The young man liked saying it. He didn't, however, like his thoughts bouncing about like one of those old-fashioned multi-colored "superballs" his parents used to play with when they were kids. It seemed to him that everything from thirty or forty years ago was called "super" something. He thought about making a t-shirt with the word "Lascivious" in black block letters on a white background like the old-fashioned "generic products" that grocery stores used to sell at a discount in the old days because they didn't have pretty packaging. Paper Towels. Facial Tissues. Beer. That wouldn't fly these days. People buy things because they're told to and because they feel like they're buying a piece of life. Pickles. Paper clips. Dishwashing liquid.

Lascivious was one of those words that almost felt like its definition when you said it. What were those kinds of words called? He couldn't remember. Onomatopoeia? No. He remembered from his senior-year English course that Onomatopoeia is a word that sounds like itself. But this was different. This was a word that FELT like itself. Maybe there wasn't a word for that. His mind shot back and forth. Christ. He needed a beer to settle down. It was like his face was strapped to a computer with a million different screensavers alternating without rhyme or reason. The only thing he could really focus on was blood and flies. When he concentrated, he could still smell the copper in the air around Henry's apartment door. It smelled like a big pile of wet pennies.

Henry was still asleep on the floor, snoring softly, curled in the fetal position. The young man fetched a pillow and blanket from his bed, slipped the pillow under Henry's soiled head, and spread the blanket over his filthy, blood-stained body. He reeked of sweat, vomit, urine and blood, but he was alive and probably happier now, asleep, than he'd been in days. The young man hoped the nightmares in Henry's life didn't invade his dreams. Sleep should be a refuge, not a battlefield or a chamber of horrors. There always ought to be someplace you can go to escape your problems, he thought. Sleep was good because it didn't produce the side-effects that drugs and alcohol did. But he knew that sleep was not always an escape.

He thought about the boys without forearms he'd seen in the newspaper. He wondered whether their dreams were filled with images of sunny days spent playing soccer, or of machetes hacking their little limbs in two. He wondered whether the machetes were those cheap plastic-handled ones you can buy in the army surplus stores here in the states or if they were heavier, with wooden handles, that were maybe passed down from father to son like a hunting rifle or pocketknife. A family heirloom employed in an atrocity. Did Grandpa know his machete would end up cutting through the bones, muscles, tendons and nerves of a young child's arm when he gave it to your father? Did your father know that the son he and his wife gave birth to would one day destroy the life of another child? How do you reconcile something like that?

The young man remembered the last history class he'd taken. It was his senior year of high school and the teacher was a Vietnam vet who later resigned after a scandal involving pot and an 18-year old female student. The teacher always spent one class period each trimester covering the Mai Lai Massacre. The young man remembered silently watching the video with the class, reading the text, and listening to his teacher who had done his year "in country" and lived to tell about it. As soon as class was over, the young man went to the restroom and puked.

Henry looked like he was resting peacefully. When he woke up he could take a shower, borrow some clean clothes, and get some decent food and some beer in his stomach. That's where he was at right now. Bare bones living. Eating when you're hungry, drinking when you're thirsty. Sleeping when you're tired. Cleaning yourself when you're filthy. Nothing fancy. Basic. Meeting the needs. It's a satisfying way to live, at least for a while. Fulfilling. Nothing tastes better than food eaten when you're truly hungry. Nothing feels better than a hot shower and a clean bed when you've been without both for awhile.

That's one of the things wrong with America, the young man thought. No Frontier, no Depression, no World War. No Sacrifice. No Need. No words in capital letters. No Vision. No Passion. But it all comes back to no Need. Compared to so-called Third World nations in which thousands of children die from malnutrition and adults are lucky to reach the age of 40, America is a fucking Disneyland where most dangers are imaginary or easily avoided. Sure, there's poverty. Yeah, there's crime. Yes, the Middle Class doesn't exist like it used to in the 1950s and the country is made up mostly of those getting by and those getting rich, but "getting by" means a whole different set of circumstances today. Even "The Poor" in America turn up their noses at certain items in the food bank's free grocery bags. "Wish Lists" emailed to eager donors by major charities list expensive electronics and designer fashions rather than the basic necessities of fifty years ago. Most Americans are no longer concerned with meeting basic needs. Food and shelter are givens. That's where you start. Penniless immigrants are given at least that much by charitable organizations and the government. Yeah, we're way the hell beyond that. The Basic Need Market is Saturated. Totally. Public housing today is more luxurious than the Depression-era hovels the young man's great-grandparents proudly owned. He'd seen pictures of their freshly swept, tidy tarpaper shack.

Midway through the twentieth century, about the time the young man's parents were born, American marketing geniuses realized they were no longer able to sell enough products based solely on Need. So they turned to the twin gods of Convenience and Luxury. Americans, they quickly proved, were willing to pay more than a product was worth if it carried the promise of Convenience or Luxury.

The lower and middle classes bought Convenience. The upper-middle class and everyone above them bought Luxury. It even became a category of car for chrissake. Luxury. You've got a lot of growing room with Luxury. Damn straight. You can never have too much Luxury. Luxury is a relentless ruler who never sleeps. And Americans buy that. We buy and buy and buy. And that, at least according to the economists and political scientists, fuels Freedom. Give me Liberty, or take my shopping malls! Ask not what your country can do for you, ask what you can buy for your country! At Valley Forge (does anyone know about Valley Forge anymore?) they starved and marched barefoot in the snow. Feet frost-bitten and bleeding. And they did that for Freedom. The Continental Army's payroll department was a tad behind to say the least. A lot of them weren't going to make it home even if they never saw the muzzle of a musket. Have you ever stood barefoot in the snow? The young man, freak that he was, stood barefoot in the snow for as long as he could once when he was a kid after reading a book about Valley Forge just to see what it was like. It gave the neighborhood kids yet another reason to call him a freak, and he was, he supposed. But even then, it wasn't even close to what the poorly trained farm boys went through back in 1778. Obviously. There were blankets and hot dogs and root beer and a color television only fifteen feet away from the spot on which he stood. Had he ever marched for miles in the snow with only soiled rags covering his bleeding feet? Knowing full well he was going to die? Knowing that he'd never see his family again? No. Goddamn it no. But they marched on. Yeah. They marched on. It made him cry then and it still did today when he thought about it enough. Goddamn. Goddamn. Those young little shits walking barefoot through the snow. And they fucking won. They didn't just survive. A bunch of sick, starving, freezing, bleeding, frostbit, half-trained hick soldiers. And they fucking won. Why? So we can buy luxury cars? The young man knew his thoughts were those of an old man. And he didn't give a good goddamn.

The young man was in the middle of the room, his left hand absentmindedly scratching the back of his closely-cropped head. Staring at something that didn't exist. Finally, he realized that Henry was awake and watching him.

"What the hell were you thinking about? Shit. You were gone, man....", sounding a little like Dennis Hopper. "Totally detached. It's been like 10 minutes and you just stood there rubbing your head and looking off into nothing." Henry started laughing. "We may have more in common than I thought."

The young man, thoroughly embarrassed, smiled sarcastically at Henry and told him to fuck off.

Seemingly energized, Henry sat up, but the smile quickly disappeared from his face. His eyes closed involuntarily and he winced, putting one hand on his head and shakily holding himself up off the floor with the other.

"Head rush?" the young man asked, initially enjoying the opportunity for payback, but then quickly feeling guilty and concerned when he remembered the amount of blood he'd mopped up off the floor. He went and grabbed an extra pillow, one with coffee stains, from the closet next to the bathroom door and walked over to Henry. "You alright?" he asked, kneeling on one knee beside him.

"Damn…"

The young man noticed that Henry had broken out in a sweat. The color had drained from his face and he held his eyes tightly shut. The young man figured he was waiting for the spinning to stop.

"I've got another pillow here. You lost a lot of blood, Henry. More than I realized until just now. Do you feel like you're gonna pass out?" Henry slowly nodded. "OK, let's lie back down," the young man said, supporting Henry's weight as he eased his torso slowly back down to the floor. The young man passed out once after giving blood and knew what it was like to have the liquid blackness envelop your eyesight just before slipping into nothingness. "I'm sorry, man. I didn't realize how much blood you lost. When was the last time you ate?" Henry, still screwing up his face in the effort to stave off unconsciousness, slowly shook his head and half-shrugged. "OK, then," the young man said. Henry was laying back on the two pillows now, and seemed to be relaxing a bit.

"Fuck," he groaned.

The young man got up; and went into the kitchen for some water. He returned to see Henry tentatively opening his eyes and holding his head with his hands like he had when the young man first opened the front door.

"You OK now?"

"Yeah, I'm sorry. What a fucking pain in the butt."

"No worries. Don't sweat it." Although outwardly he was the picture of empathy and reassurance, the young man didn't argue with Henry's main point because it WAS a royal pain-in-the-butt to have a loony neighbor monopolize his time on his day off. Working retail sucked in so many ways, that he valued days off like holy days. He would never do something like this to Henry, the young man thought. Hell, if he was going to pull a stunt like this, he'd go up in the mountains so if he bled to death, he wouldn't bug anyone. If you want attention, fine. Just tell someone that you need attention. Don't pull a stunt like this. And if you're going to do something like this, go up in the mountains and let your life bleed away. What would that be like? Just going to sleep?

And then your body decomposes and is carried away piecemeal and consumed by coyotes and ants and maggots. And the digestive systems of the creatures turn your flesh into shit. The shit enriches the soil and allows new sprouts of lichen and wildflowers to prosper. Then, some hiker, poking around in the brush finds your femur or skull or something and tells the forest rangers who alert the sheriff's department who call in search & rescue volunteers and police cadets and cadaver dogs to search the alpine meadows and salal-covered clearings for the rest of what remains of your body. They find some clothing shredded by mice and marmots. A few bones. Identification is made through dental records. The missing person bulletin is canceled, and the family mourns and at the same time rejoices that they finally have "closure."

Don't inconvenience everyone around you because you don't have your shit together. That could pretty much be the Rule for Life. Don't inconvenience others. The Golden Rule, "Do unto others what you would have them do to you" was OK, but patently unrealistic. Just don't inconvenience others, and everything will be OK. And when you DO have to inconvenience others, which you will because all rules are broken almost immediately after formulation, do it as quickly and painlessly as possible and then apologize. But these were arrogant thoughts. These were not humble thoughts. The young man shook his head back-and-forth again.

These were egotistical, cold-hearted, juvenile thoughts that he really didn't want floating around in his brain, but they were there and they were real. And he had to deal with them. We've all got our faults, the young man reminded himself, and we all inconvenience others when these faults get the best of us. Whether it was true or not, that was the position the young man felt he should take. Just like that old cliché', "There, but the grace of God, go I." Or something like that: really religious-sounding and ironically self-righteous in its humility. Back and forth. Everything is yes and no. Ying and yang. Everything is black and white simultaneously. Is THAT wisdom? Realizing that you have to believe in the yes and the no at the same time? The young man thought back through the histories and biographies he'd read and remembered that all the "great men" and "great women" were forced to work with more than one reality at a time. Each reality equally real and yet diametrically opposed to the other. JFK, supporter of freedom and proponent of clandestine operations in Vietnam. What kind of men do you suppose were assigned those missions in the early 1960s? Liberal, left-wing, progressive civil rights protestors? Hell no! You had your right-wing, homicidal, gun-freak spooks out there.

85

How do you think they treated the locals? All in the name of national security. The more power you get, the less lily-white you're allowed to be. You've got to assume responsibility for both the evil as well as the good. Creator and Destroyer. You carry the weight of both. That's what real power is all about. You can be holy as long as you're not important. The more important you become, the more compromised you become. And then, when the final tally is taken, the only thing that matters is the 51%. 51% good and 49% evil equals a winning season. That's all that matters. Think about it. There's no celebration after victories because you're thinking about all the evil it took to accomplish the good.

Henry was quietly puking on the scratched, scarred, stained hardwood floor. It was a thin, gruel-like, unsubstantial spittle, the kind they show on the movies. This guy hadn't eaten in a while. Puking up bile. That sucked. Impulse and Reaction without Solid Results: over the past several weeks, the young man's thoughts had begun forming themselves into philosophical pronouncements, and he didn't exactly know why. Lots of capital letters and colons in his brain. Henry transitioned to dry-heaving, and finally stopped, exhausted. A thin line of vomit still clung to his chin. He didn't wipe it off. He didn't seem to know it was there. The young man looked at it, and felt like taking the towel and cleaning Henry's face. Henry either didn't know it was there, or he just didn't care.

The young man remembered the flies on the faces of African children on Saturday afternoon charity infomercials on TV: "For the price of your daily cup of coffee, you can feed..." Flies on the faces of armless children in the newspaper. When there were enough flies, they'd wave their butchered arms to shoo them away. But they couldn't do it constantly. That would be stupid. They waited until it got bad enough, and then they did the best they could with what they had. That's the only thing they could do. The flies would always be there. They'd always return to their faces as soon as the stump of an arm stopped impotently flinging itself back and forth. Unless they were inadvertently swallowed, it seemed that they never died. 24-hour life expectancy? The young man heard that once. Didn't know if it was supposed to actually be true, but he'd stayed in a studio apartment with four or five flies buzzing around for an entire weekend and had seen them maintain their population with apparent ease. The flies didn't drop dead. They just kept on living. Creatures like flies are defined by their overall population. People don't pick out particularly troublesome flies. It's just "the flies." Dirty, hairy, six-legged, bug-eyed flies, irresistibly attracted to the weeping, seeping, leaking, oozing, bleeding orifices of the human body. Beat them away and they just keep on coming.

The young man looked down at the small pool of vomit, the bloodstains and the sweat that now covered a small area of hardwood floor. The floor and Henry reeked. The line of vomit was drying on his chin and his right hand lay inert on the floor in a coagulating smear of blood. He would let Henry sleep and worry about cleaning up when he awoke. He was concerned about the loss of blood. Re-hydrating him would be easy. He didn't know what to do about the blood. He could call 911, but then Henry would be committed again. He didn't know what to do.

He walked over to a window overlooking the street and opened it. The lead weight inside the wall bumped clumsily downward as the heavy wooden window frame slid slowly upward in its track. Across the street, where a historic music hall had once stood, expensive new condominiums with balconies and electric awnings glared back at the young man in the late morning heat. Exclusive street-level shops with expensive security systems and designer names meant a constant flow of luxury SUVs, limos, Mercedes and BMWs. It was only a matter of time, the young man thought, before his old apartment met the same fate as the music hall. There were seven months left on his lease, and he figured he'd have to move after that. Rumor had it the owner was going to either double the rent or level the entire building and sell.

The window glass was old and thick, occasionally pockmarked, and subtly rippled by the force of gravity pulling its molecules downward over the decades. Acting as a prism, the distorted glass projected hundreds of rainbow polygons into the apartment's interior. His apartment was a good place to live, overall, and he was going to miss it. Henry stirred, breathed deeply, and settled back into the two pillows on the floor. One night, months ago, after many beers, Henry told the young man his story. Everyone has stories, and most people have one or two that they only tell after drinking lots of beer.

Henry once lived in a high-rise condo worth four times as much as the luxury condos across the street. High up on the 34th floor of a blue-hued glass tower downtown, the extravagantly furnished, 2,000 square-foot loft saw innumerable parties and dinners in the short six months Henry called it his own. He didn't really live there. He partied and sometimes slept, but he spent most of his time seven blocks away on the 10th, 11th and 12th floors of the Denton-Howard building, home to one of the many dot-com companies to rocket skyward and just as quickly plummet back down to earth in the nineties. Henry was a millionaire on paper after 14 months. The first thing he did upon passing $999,9999.00 was buy the condo and throw a party.

The parties he threw. Music: Big Names doing hush-hush private shows, up-and-coming acts, friends, everyone played Henry's Loft, as it came to be known, if they played anywhere at all. The 30,000 cubic feet of the loft, $50,000 in sound-proofing, and 9-to-5 office space above and below, meant the jam sessions could be as loud as anyone could stand. And of course, there were drugs, alcohol, schmoozing with the city's young society standouts and celebrities, and sex. Lots and lots of sex. He wasn't sure how Bill Gates got down-and-dirty (hadn't read the book), but when money was no object and pressure at work was the name of the game, there was gonna be T&A on the weekends. And despite the fact that Henry and his compatriots were in many ways full-bore nerds, there were always women around. College girls, models, local television personalities, actresses, artists, musicians, you name it. And if a night looked a little sparse, then the local escort agencies were more than happy to supply window-dressing for an elegant dinner party or a night of rock-and-roll.

It was on just such a night, a Wednesday night, that he called the two agencies he usually dealt with and asked them to send over a total of ten girls, the regulars who knew how he wanted things to be. $15,000 (at least) for the night and it was no more to Henry than $5.00 for a six-pack of beer was to the doorman 33 floors down. They were celebrating the latest release, and it was hard drawing a crowd on a Wednesday night, even with the free booze, music and food. Henry never supplied the drugs. He just turned a blind eye to the byoc crowd and instructed his security detail to do the same. This particular night was noteworthy, however, because it promised to be the first time a bonafide punk act played his loft.

As a geek, albeit now a millionaire geek, Henry grew up listening to the music of the disenfranchised, freakish, ugly, outcast and pissed. And he knew, better than anyone else, that no true punk would play his loft. In fact, that would pretty much define a true punk: someone who wouldn't play his loft if it was the last venue on earth and a cool million waited in the dressing room. So, Henry, sharp thinker and aggressive strategizer at work, did what he did best. He made it happen. He hired an experienced documentary director and crew, and paid them to do a 30-minute documentary on the local punk scene, complete with on-location shots, vintage footage, talking-head interviews and a show in his loft. It was genius. Even though it required close to $95 grand, it was genius. There would be punk in the loft, the band wouldn't be any wiser, and the agency girls were asked to dress appropriately.

There was one girl in particular, a girl named Lucy of all things, whom Henry hoped to see that night. He didn't know she was 38 and had two teenage kids (she looked no older than 27). He didn't know she fled a life of heroin addiction and domestic abuse when she was 19. He didn't know she was working her way through a nursing program. He did know that she was bright, intelligent, charming and utterly devastating. Long, curly red hair; enormous, hazel, crystalline eyes; and an ass that he could watch all night. He let out an audible oath of relief when an anonymous message flashed across his laptop's screen: "short skirt, tall boots, 15 minutes away." He knew Lucy would be there. He hated the fact that he cared so much and reveled in it all the same.

One of his colleagues, a heavily bearded man with black plastic 1968 GI glasses, a sleek black ponytail, and a prominent set of teeth that constantly challenged his lips to fully cover them, was standing in the room, watching him with dark ganglionic eyes. Henry didn't hear him enter. He quickly double-deleted Lucy's email and said hello to the man everyone called Rasputin when he wasn't around (his real name was Reginald Covey). He reported directly to the CEO as "Assistant Vice-President, Strategic Planning," but answered to no one else, not even the President, Strategic Planning. He was universally feared and hated, arbitrarily exercising great power with apparent impunity. When challenged to slash hundreds of thousands of dollars from the budget, he hired two HR temps and a private investigator. He directed them to read through each of the company's 600 employees' applications, resumes and subsequent quarterly reviews. Within three weeks, they were able to identify 63 previously missed errors, inaccuracies and/or offenses significant enough to allow immediate termination. Occurring just two weeks before Christmas, three weeks before a hefty yearly bonus was to be paid out, and ninety days before the board of directors was to have begun offering obscenely generous severance packages to encourage attrition, Rasputin saved the company somewhere in the neighborhood of 13 million dollars. Three subsequent attempts at retribution by terminated employees and their families failed miserably, derailed by personal tragedies, disasters and/or heavily-publicized scandals that seemed to materialize out of thin air.

It was not outside the realm of possibility that at least a few of his victims, of which there were soon hundreds, were desperate and vengeful enough to consider violence up to and including homicide. They were forced, however, to reckon with the fact that Rasputin could apparently not be killed. Two years before the Christmas terminations, he inexplicably stopped in the middle of a crosswalk when the light turned green, and was thrown thirty feet through the air against a fire hydrant by a 1-ton diesel king cab pickup truck doing 45 miles per hour while the driver fiddled with his cell phone. Rasputin suffered a fractured skull, dislocated shoulder, collapsed lung, five broken ribs, a lacerated spleen, and a detached retina. He walked ten blocks to the hospital and politely asked the ER nurse for assistance. After recovering fully from his injuries, he collected $800,000 from the pickup truck driver's insurance company.

Eight months later, scaffolding outside his office collapsed as he spoke with the construction workers who were repairing a brick façade damaged in a recent earthquake. A heavy-gauge steel pipe swung downward like a pendulum and struck him square between the eyes. He was in a coma for 17 days before awakening. When he opened his eyes, he asked for a Neapolitan ice-cream cake from Baskin-Robbins. Four months later, he was shot in the chest by a sixteen-year old holding up a 7-11 at 3:00 a.m. It was an accident. The kid backed into a Cheetos display comprised of life-size cardboard cut-outs of Barry Bonds and Christopher Walken and unintentionally pulled the trigger. The .45 caliber bullet tore through a pyramid of Hostess Twinkies and lodged itself an inch from Reginald's heart, a smidgen of cream filling still clinging to its copper-coated, mushroomed, lead mass. Thirteen weeks later, he contracted E Coli from a discount breakfast cereal. And finally, only ten days previously, he was struck from behind in the company parking garage with a cinder block, either by one of his enemies or a random assailant. Aside from some cement fragments permanently lodged in the base of his skull, he escaped unharmed.

"Duhkha!" said Rasputin, his prominent upper and lower teeth cutting through the air. "To quote Thanissaro Bhikkhu's translation of a passage from the Samyutta Nikaya, 'With desire the world is tied down. With the subduing of desire it's freed. With the abandoning of desire all bonds are cut through.'"

"Furthermore," he continued professorially, "'Birth is duhkha, decay is duhkha, sickness is duhkha, death is duhkha, so also are sorrow and grief... To be bound with things which we dislike, and to be parted from the things we like, these also are duhkha. Not to get what one desires, this is also duhkha.' The venerable Alan Watts pondered that famous passage in his popular 'The Way of Zen.' Jack Kerouac read Alan Watts. Even a dumbfuck like you could too.

Mr. Watts suggests that duhkha is frustration. I think he's right. Another scholar defines duhkha as 'unsatisfactoriness.' I think they are right as well. And Who made it so? Who bestowed impossible desires upon human beings? Who created duhkha? Who programmed people to desire what cannot be fully obtained? Who put a gun to your head and then magnanimously offered his Son as a substitute hostage? It's a stacked deck. Those who know, don't say, and those who say, don't know. Which one are you, Henry? Whatcha gonna do, Henry? You going to search for nirvana?" he laughed, baring his teeth. "Ah, nirvana." He slowly closed his eyes and tilted his chin upward, speaking, slowly speaking, enunciating each word, gingerly holding each word like a dove before releasing it towards the high vaulted ceiling: "No more karma...no more karma...no more impotent striving...but is all striving impotent? Mr. President," he said, snapping to attention, "is all striving impotent? Mr. Astronaut, is all striving impotent? Mr. Athlete, is all striving impotent?" Rasputin smiled, his lips barely covering his teeth. He opened his eyes, met Henry's, closed them again, and tilted his chin up once more. "Without Desire, is there duhkha? Without lust, is there duhkha? Without effort, is there Life? The Hindus embrace desire and lust, knowing that once you've shot your load, you'll be looking for something more. Once you're spent, you're more likely to seek a higher truth. It's not until your dick is limp, you could say, that you begin to see the spiritual realities of life. Oh, eunuch... You there, Eunuch. Are you the holiest and most enlightened? NO. You are not spent. You are merely forgotten."

"Hey now," Henry carefully protested, looking about the room at everything he stood to lose if Reginald had him fired. "What's with the eunuch shit? Are you...stoned, or something?" Reginald laughed quietly to himself and returned his gaze to Henry. "I am stoned without having become stoned. I was stoned and will be stoned. You? You and the others? You must change yourself. You must reach out for an 'other' state. Are you, like those Mr. Morrison sang about, 'stoned immaculate,' Henry? If you ARE, then you're stoned. If you ARE, then you ARE. But I don't think you ARE. Are you?" Reginald giggled through his teeth and ran his hand down his black ponytail, giving it a flip when he reached the end. "Now the Heavenly Father," he slipped into an obnoxious, dirty, trailer-trash southern accent, "told Moses 'I Am that I Am.' THAT was the straight shit, and THAT was enough for Moses and the Israelites. Didn't need any more than that, and they understood that. For once, God had made himself perfectly clear. But 1500 years later, things weren't so clear. God Incarnate has to spell it out for his disciples. Jesus had to explain Himself. The Son of God, for chrissake, and he has to define his terms like some multi-level marketing guru working a crowd of lazy-ass moochers in a smoky Red Lion Inn conference room. Jesus Christ. Jee-sus Chrrrist. Jesus had to amplify and clarify and DEIFY. 'I AM the Way, the Truth, and the Life,' he said. 'I AM the Way.' Two distinct statements in one: 'I AM & The Way.' Keep in mind, little Henry, that dharma, the Way, had already been defined by Buddha 500 years before Christ. Buddha's words were half a millennium old when Joseph and Mary held hands in the dirty straw of a dirty stable and watched the King of the Jews drop ignobly into the filth of this world. No, Jesus was not injected into a vacuum, so-to-speak. A womb, perhaps, but not a vacuum." Coarse horse laughs. "Buddha was here first,

Christ….no….no…no, Christianity…yes…Christianity in many ways only feebly reiterated what the world had already figured out, that the Way must be found, that the dharma must be followed."

"You look at the email message on the screen, Henry, and you feel desire. It invigorates and infuses you with Life. It makes you more you. If you believe King James, and if you believe experience, Desire is different than Lust. Related in some 2nd cousin-twice-removed kind of way, perhaps, but really completely different. Lust will stiffen your dick, and it will spark the surface of your imagination, but Desire is something entirely more consuming. It is indeed like a fire. Cliché or not, that's what it's like. Sure, it stiffens your dick. Of course it does that, but it also burns your soul. It grasps, roars, consumes, destroys, creates, spreads, focuses, illuminates, darkens, breathes. When denied, and REALLY," Rasputin paused, eyes closed, anger flashing across his face for the first time, "when is it NOT denied, it will pull your innards out like a hunter pulls the offal from the carcass of his prey. But you keep right on feeling it. You're dead. The object of your desire is gone, forever. But you keep right on feeling it. Like a soldier feeling pain in his amputated leg, you keep right on feeling it. It's already ripped your guts out and you still can think of nothing else. You poor…sick…fuck." Reginald was sweating. His chin dropped to his chest. He stood, muscles tensed. He'd lost track of where he was. He thought nothing of what had brought him into the room. All of that was gone. All of his power meant nothing, because he wouldn't have been able to pull the trigger on this one if his life depended on it. None of that seemed real anymore. Only God, Desire, Henry and Lucy's words remained. He didn't know their content, only their nature. He knew as much by Henry's reaction as by any otherworldly ability he might have possessed.

"Lucy is it?" Rasputin smiled lasciviously. He licked his lips, the tip of his tongue searching the strands of his mustache and beard. "St. Lucy. Did you know she was a saint, Henry? Will-

94

ing to die rather than spread her legs. I'm not making it up, Henry. It's right there in the little Catholic schoolgirls' history texts. Read their books, Henry. Lucy wouldn't open her legs. They tried to burn her, but she wouldn't die. So they pushed a sword through her gut and then her heart and then her lungs. The air rushed through the wounds when she tried to breathe. Ever get the wind knocked out of you, Henry? Try to breath with three-inch holes in your lungs. With blood bubbling up your throat. She spent several minutes dying, Henry. It takes a while for a woman to die. Your Lucy. St. Lucy."

"John Donne," Rasputin continued, his chin tucked against his chest, perspiration dripping down from his forehead and face to the marble floor. "He sacrificed everything for his Lucy. Career. Family. Freedom. And then she died. Have you read Mr. Donne's words, Henry?" He didn't wait long enough for a response. "Mr. Donne, three-hundred years before Hemingway wrote "our nada," wrote 'I, by love's limbeck, am the grave of all that's nothing.' He wrote that for St. Lucy. He wrote that for HIS Lucy." He slowly began nodding. He lifted his head slightly and let it fall again. Over and over again, like a worshiper at the Wailing Wall. Nodding, nodding. Over and over. Then his shoulders and chest began to move as well. Up and down, up and down. Forward and back he was rocking, arms limp at his sides. Sweat dripping onto the floor. Eyes clenched shut.

Was he stoned? Was he drunk? What the fuck? Was this a performance? Some bizarre scheme to drive someone else out of the company? Someone like him? It didn't seem like it. Henry didn't know what the hell was going on, but it didn't seem real. Where's the fucking camera? There's gotta be a camera!! Then again, maybe everything the prick had done had finally cracked his gourd. Full mental and emotional breakdown. And how did the asshole know what he was thinking? Rasputin was still rocking back and forth, sweating and......chanting? Eyes clenched shut so tightly that his eyelashes had disappeared. Out of control. Simultaneously enraged and in agony. The situation was

95

way out of hand and whatever the hell was going on, Henry didn't want to be around when Reginald came out of it, or all hell broke loose. Shaking, he ran from the room.

Christ. Thoughts chaotically jerking about like he'd had way too much to drink. Focus. Damn. Vertigo. Just like the bed spins he used to get years ago in college when he drank too much…but this time he wasn't drunk. Not even close. Not yet.

Henry reached up and put his hand on the wall. He was still shaking. The wall needed painting. Too many drunk bastards sliding down the hallway to the elevator leading to the side entrance to waiting cabs, limos, girls. Hand shaking on the wall, waiting for everything to stop spinning. His wall. His wall in his hallway. Fucking Rasputin had just chased him out of his own den in his own house. Jesus H. Christ!! Henry was almost pissed off enough to go back in and rip him a new one, but he cared about his job too much, and that would have been suicide. No doubt. And then…and then there was just enough of the whole crazy scene that didn't seem right. Reginald's words, the almost supernatural detachment with which he surveyed the world, the way he looked into and through Henry's eyes as if they were lenses focused on his mind. Penetrating. It was wrong. The whole fucking thing was wrong.

He slowly leaned up against the wall and then slid to the ground, legs buckling a bit on the way down. He was still shaking, so he tried to breathe deeply to regain control of his nerve-wracked body. God, if someone came along right now…

He heard a woman's laugh and singing outside. A door down the hallway opened and he could now hear Lucy singing her favorite song. Henry jerked and tried to scramble up off the floor, legs still rubbery, head still reeling... Christ. What was wrong with him? Maybe Rasputin slipped a Mickey into his drink or something. He struggled once more to stand up. Off-balance and spinning, he fell forward and smacked his forehead against the opposite wall. "SHIT!!!!"

Lucy, still singing and laughing, an open bottle of Grey Goose in her right hand and a shiny black leather pocketbook in her left, turned the corner and saw Henry holding his forehead, face screwed up in pain, $600 Italian shoes stomping the marble floor in fury and frustration. Lucy stopped, pretty red mouth wide open, and then recognizing Henry, laughed loudly, splashing vodka on herself and the wall, her bright hazel eyes, albeit both a bit bloodshot, wide and shining. Scoldingly, she wagged the index finger of the hand clutching her purse in Henry's direction. "Why you little fucking prick!!!"

Henry stopped rubbing his forehead and looked up through the red glaring blur of pain to see Lucy effecting anger. She was quite an actress when she wanted to be, sculpting her face into whatever mask the occasion demanded. Rough times had toughened her looks a bit, but they hadn't aged her and they hadn't detracted from the powerful sensuality she exuded without even trying. Some women carry their beauty like a burden: a cross they bear throughout life, painfully displayed to the grasping, ugly, dirty masses who unworthily steal furtive glances, glances that soil all they fall upon like filthy fumbling fingers on pure white silk. The women avert their eyes and avoid the glances, walking steadfastly forward, carrying their beauty like a banner into battle, seeking others of their Kind with whom to fight the good fight. But Lucy was not like this. She stood, a bit unsteady from the vodka, now smiling coyly at Henry still rubbing his head.

"You fucking little prick. You weren't supposed to get drunk until I got here. Didn't you get my message? Couldn't you wait 15 fucking minutes?"

She hadn't lied. Tall, black leather boots. Black tights. Short plaid skirt. White blouse. Short black leather jacket. Her full head of beautiful curly red hair tossed this way and that. Henry straightened up. Smiling, he walked deliberately toward her, immediately forgetting his vertigo, throbbing forehead, fucked-up crazy V.P. in the den and his wobbly legs. He took the bottle from her hand, tilted it back into his mouth, and then kissed her while the vodka still tingled his tongue. Her red lips always felt small beneath his, and they were so soft and supple that he sometimes couldn't tell whether or not she was slipping him the tip of her tongue.

Henry breathed in deeply and immersed himself in her. Body and soul, as the saying goes. Body and soul. He touched her lightly, below the curve of her breasts, and pulled on her lower lip with his teeth.

"I missed you."

"What?"

"I missed you."

She stretched upward and kissed him back. "Let's fuck."

They turned and walked back toward the end of the hall.

Henry had never fucked Lucy. He tried on a number of occasions, but something always seemed to get in the way: usually one of the other girls. It got to the point that he started to suspect she didn't like him. That she detested him, in fact. Then, one night, a girl from the same agency, a stunning blonde with enormous silicone breasts, got really, really drunk and admitted, just before passing out in Henry's bathtub, that Lucy was playing with him. That when she was good and drunk, she gushed about him like an infatuated 7th grader.

When Henry and Lucy stepped out into the warm, smoggy night, the agency driver and the stretch limo were gone.

"Shit!"

"Don't worry. I'll call Fred."

Fred answered the cell phone, slowly and deliberately.

"Hey Fred. We're at the loft. Can you bring the car around right away?"

"Boss, I'm sorry. I wasn't expecting you to need me until...later. I'm uh...kinda fucked up at the moment. Can you give me an hour or two?"

"Shit!"

The vodka was gone. The bottle was nowhere to be seen. Lucy's right hand slipped into the right pocket of his slacks and reached around the front.

"Uh...Fred. Do the best you can, bud. OK? Just take it slow. You can do it."

Henry and Lucy made out until Fred arrived, scraping the hubcaps on the curb. Henry and Lucy didn't notice. They piled into the back seat, never breaking contact.

Fred was in bad shape. He was drunk to begin with, before he cinched his belt around his left arm. They didn't really stand a chance.

After four blocks they were going fifty miles an hour, scraping the underbody as they passed through intersections, orange sparks flying into the night. For Lucy and Henry, the vodka and some pills she pulled from her shiny black handbag were enough to keep their attention on each other and not the ride. Fred, struggling mightily to keep it together, was on his own.

There were no skid marks. An iron cleat, set a bit low on a telephone pole, ended Fred's life when it contacted his forehead and continued through his skull into his brain. Henry was thrown over the front seat, through the windshield, over the hood and into a dense thicket of trash-infested blackberry bushes that broke his fall and shredded his skin from head to foot. Lucy stepped from the wreckage with a broken arm and random lacerations. She pulled a foil emergency blanket from the car's first-aid kit, followed the path Henry's body cleared through the vines, and spread it over him to stave off shock. She checked his breathing and pulse, nursing her right arm. Then, she felt inside his slacks pocket once more, this time for his cell phone, and called 911, calmly giving the operator the exact location of the wreck and the condition of the one surviving victim. Then she put the cell phone back into Henry's pocket, kissed him on the lips and walked away.

Henry was in a coma for 49 days. He was in the newspapers. Lucy received one call from the police. Lucy didn't know anything and the cops never called again. Fred's autopsy revealed an enormous amount of heroin, cocaine and alcohol in his bloodstream. Henry was over the legal limit, but hadn't been driving. They were sure of that because Fred died behind the wheel. The steering wheel embedded itself into the flesh of his chest and the telephone pole cleat traveled four inches into his head. The car was a restored classic: no airbags.

Lucy, despite a broken arm, had collected her belongings and left little if anything for the cops to trace. She made her way to the emergency room, blamed the injury on a bad date, and walked through her apartment's front door at 9:30 the next morning with a fiberglass cast on her arm. The kids were at grandma's. She drank herself to sleep, missed a mid-term, and didn't begin calling hospitals until she woke up at 7:30 the next evening.

Within hours of the accident, Rasputin received a phone call from "a friend" in the accounting department warning that Henry had submitted at least two T&E reports listing Fred's chauffer service among the many restaurants, stores, hotels and other service providers he patronized while "on the clock" and "entertaining clients." Rasputin ordered the reports to be altered, the expenditures "reallocated," and the receipts placed front and center in the middle of Henry's kitchen table where they were found a few days later by the police. Fred's girlfriend came forward a few days after his death and told police and his family that Fred called her that night from his cell phone, complaining that Henry was "making" him drive when he was "shit-faced" and "high." Within a week of the accident, a private investigator (recommended by the company) and a high-priced lawyer were on the job, and a lawsuit was quickly filed in superior court alleging that Henry was personally responsible for Fred's death. The company was in the clear. Fred never kept any records and there was no way to prove Henry was reimbursed when the T&E reports listed no such expense.

Henry's father assumed power of attorney, hired his own lawyer (who was later disbarred after selling illegally modified semi-automatic weapons to undercover ATF agents), and settled out of court for 2.8 million dollars. The company ended its relationship with Henry. The bank foreclosed on his loft, and the settlement eliminated what remained of his liquid assets. Henry was still in a coma. Doctors were forced to drill a hole through his skull to relieve intracranial pressure caused by the swelling of his once vibrant brain. Blood and fluid shot out like a geyser when the drill bit pierced the membrane between his brain and skull, inundating the surgeon's plastic face-shield and drenching the neckline of his scrubs. The hospital refused to speculate on how much, if any, mental function would remain if and when Henry ever came out of the coma. The longer he failed to respond, they said, the darker the prognosis.

On the 50th day, Henry briefly opened his eyes.
On the 53rd day, his eyes followed his father as he walked around the room.
On the 57th day, he smiled at his mother. She broke down, for the first time since the accident, and cried for nearly an hour, sobbing like she had never sobbed before. It was another week before he spoke. His first word was "Mom." Within two weeks, he was sitting up in bed, but still only beginning to interact with

his family and other visitors. He was only awake for a few minutes at a time, his speech was slow and stilted, and he couldn't remember new information. Nothing.

Anything that occurred before the accident was easily accessible in his memory. Any information he received after coming out of the coma was forgotten in minutes. He knew who he was. He remembered the events leading up to the accident (the lawsuit settlement included a clause prohibiting claims for additional damage based on new information captured post-coma). He remembered his childhood, high-school graduation, the first time he got laid, his stereotypically meteoric rise to success, and Lucy's beauty and charm. As he lay in bed, in pain, a morphine drip barely taking the edge off, with metal plates and screws securing broken bone, with internal sutures and external staples, with a shaved head and the hole in his skull, and the absence of all short-term memory, Henry's thoughts inevitably and stubbornly turned to Lucy and then to the enormous burden of guilt he felt for making Fred drive.

His last memories; confused, drunken, hazy memories, were of speed, a racing engine, laughing, and Lucy in the back seat with him. They had found a half-full bottle of Jack Daniel's under the driver's seat along with a newspaper and some trash. They drank the JD down, kissing as they drank, spilling and laughing. He remembered her soft red lips and enormous hazel eyes, and the way she wiped a drop of whiskey from her chin, all the while eagerly looking into his own eyes as if searching for something. He remembered hearing something up front, he wasn't sure what, and turning away from Lucy to look at Fred. Fred was asleep. The car was going way too fast and Fred was asleep, slumped sideways against the driver's side window. Lucy, seeing the blood drain from Henry's face, looked over as well and let out a scream; a childlike, terrified, anguished scream that woke up Fred just before they hit the telephone pole. And then there was darkness. He remembered darkness and muffled sounds, sounds like you hear when you're under water. He remembered the sensation of having things broken inside him. A

102

grating sensation of bone on bone. Something wrong in his gut. A searing, immobilizing pain behind his eyes. And then silence.

In a hellish cycle that repeated itself literally dozens of times before his family and doctors finally agreed to sedate him and to henceforth lie about Fred's death, Henry would wake up, ask for food or water, and then ask about Fred and Lucy. No one wanted to tell him. They'd try to change the subject, but he would quickly grow angry and abusive. Angry like he'd never been before the accident. There was an intimation of violence and recklessness in his voice and eyes that was foreign to those who knew him from before. He'd begin yelling, shouting obscenities, and cursing everyone in the room until he was told what had happened. And then it was like he'd been kicked in the gut. A split-second of jubilation immediately followed by utter devastation and horror. Lucy was alive. Fred was dead.

His memory would quickly flash back to the telephone call he'd made that night. Lucy's hand, slipped into the pocket of his slacks, slowly stroking him, and Fred's voice on the phone, asking for a little time to sober up. Henry remembered telling him no. God. He told him no: "Uh…Fred. Do the best you can, bud. OK? Just take it slow. You can do it." The words, his words, now reverberated throughout his memories like the echoes of a gunshot, twisting his stomach into a sickening knot. What a weak, sorry fuck he was. He wanted to fuck Lucy so badly that he ordered an impaired employee to drive. Other people could have been killed. Not just Fred. Pedestrians, other motorists, Lucy. And Fred was dead. Henry shut his eyes tightly, and tried to hide his face in his hands. Unable to lift his arms that high, he turned his head to the side and wept bitterly. What weakness he displayed. What selfishness. He listened to his dick instead of his brain and now Fred was dead.

Each time someone reluctantly gave Henry the bad news, he asked to speak to Fred's family, not believing that he had already done so once, twice, three times. He would call almost unable to speak through the sobs, experiencing the horror all over again as if he had heard for the very first time, his mother or father or a nurse holding the phone to his ear and he'd try to apologize: "I'm sorry. I'm sorry." Over and over again, tears and snot running unheeded down his face, eyes red and swollen. The first time he called, Fred's sister answered. She told Henry she was glad he had been hurt. That she hoped he would never walk again. She told him that she hoped he'd be a "fucking retard" for the rest of his life and rot in hell after that. And then she hung up. Henry sat for five minutes without moving. The nurse asked if there was still someone on the line. Henry nodded, mouth open, snot dripping down onto the hospital sheets. The nurse couldn't hear anyone talking and Henry wasn't saying anything. Finally, she leaned down and heard the busy signal indicating that the phone had been off the hook too long.

She gently removed the phone from Henry's ear and replaced it in its cradle. Henry slowly looked upward, turning his head to look up at the people standing around his bed, his face twisted up in despair, his mouth agape. The first few times, most of them were crying too. He looked each person in the eyes, but he wasn't really making eye contact, because there wasn't anything there for him anymore, inside. Death. He awakened to Death. Why had he awakened? Why hadn't he called a cab that night? There was no excuse. He replayed the scene in his head over and over again. There was no way out of it. He was guilty. He killed a man. He didn't pull a trigger and he didn't grasp the handle of a knife, but it almost would have been better if he had. He killed a man through carelessness, arrogance and selfishness. Somehow it seemed it would have been better if he'd done it on purpose. Action rather than inaction. Strength instead of weakness. But Fred would still be dead either way. Fred's life was over. Fred's family would never see him again. They never had a chance to say goodbye. Henry's life was over as well. No matter what he did in life now, it could never make up for the life he'd destroyed.

And although he experienced the horror and shame anew each time, unaware he'd played out the same scene minutes or hours or days before, an underlying sense of sadness, guilt and loss began to overtake him, accumulating subconsciously each time he learned of Fred's death, each time he ran through the events leading up to the crash in his tortured mind. He stopped smiling. Didn't talk much. He stopped eating. He stopped drinking water. When the nurse put in an I.V., he pulled it out as soon as she left the room. He couldn't have told you why he felt the way he did, but he was dead inside nonetheless. His outbursts grew more violent and disruptive. He wouldn't leave the I.V.s alone. Kept pulling them out. When he used the I.V. needle to dig into his arm, soaking the bed sheet with blood, the decision was made to sedate him. Everyone agreed that until his short-term memory was restored, they would lie and tell him that Fred was alive but had moved away, leaving behind no contact information. Hopefully, he'd believe them and see no reason to call Fred's family. Just in case, they removed the phone from his room. A certain degree of isolation would be necessary if their plan was to work. They looked for Lucy and found out that she had left the agency shortly after the crash and changed her telephone number. Even if Henry tried, he wouldn't be able to find her.

A voice from outside, out on the cement walkway, interrupted what was left of the morning. Loud, embarrassingly hyper, raucous, staccato and awkwardly juvenile, the voice pierced the walls and door, the glaring grey sky, the neighborhood and the street, invading the quiet morning like an oblivious drunk getting thrown out of a skid row bar. But Mandy was sober. Loud, but sober, and trying to carry on conversations with people two floors up and all the way across the airy expanse of the courtyard. Distance was not a factor for her. If she could see you, you were fair game, and her voice was like a sniper's bullet when it came to killing power. The people two floors up finally reached their door, and nodding and smiling slipped into their apartment.

105

Mandy was 45 years old if she were a day, but she "hung" with kids half her age (and younger) and dressed like a late-blooming high school senior intent upon getting laid before graduation. Today, it was a tight-fitting grey nylon sweat suit worn over short shorts and a low-cut, midriff-baring tee. Her dark brown hair, streaked with grey, was teased and hair-sprayed in the same manner as it had been back in high school.

"Hey baby! You awake hon? C'mon sweetie, open the door for Mandy. I need your strong muscles to carry my laundry downstairs. Hey honey, you awake?

"Jesus H. Christ, why doesn't she just knock on the door like a goddamn human being?" The young man looked at the mess on the floor and at Henry, walked slowly to the door and checked the peephole out of habit. "Hang on a second..."

She was laughing and sliding something along the walkway with her feet. He could hear it scraping along whenever she paused to take a breath. Probably her laundry basket full of satin thongs, sweat-suits and push-up bras. She was chattering on to herself and anyone else within earshot. A second person was not a requirement for conversation.

Wilson often commented that having that much nervous energy wasn't normal for a woman her age, not even a white woman. He and most everyone in the building suspected she was addicted to cocaine or meth or speed or something. She was jittery as hell and her make-up never stayed in the lines. She always seemed "impaired" in some way, but no one had ever seen her with the shit. And no one knew where she'd get the money, either. Crack? Yeah, she could afford it, but with these neighbors and that mouth, she wouldn't have been able to keep it under wraps for so long.

It was public knowledge that she got money from at least two sources. First, every month she cashed a check from the insurance company of the drunk driver who hit her head-on two years

106

ago and changed her life forever. The drunk crossed the center line as smoothly and as easily as if changing lanes. Cruising along at three times the legal limit and 65 miles an hour, he hit her passenger side headlight with his own. She was deemed "lucky to be alive" by the doctors, paramedics, witnesses, judge, the attorneys, newspaper reporters, her family, her friends, and the boyfriend who left town shortly thereafter; but the jagged naked white scars that crisscrossed her neck and back and chest and skull and abdomen suggested that "luck" was relative and not necessarily an end in and of itself.

Ordinarily, the young man dismissed people who constantly complained about their health, especially those who insisted that accommodations be made on their behalf (Mandy forced the landlord to replace the aging railings on all the apartment building staircases at a cost of $37,000). Basically, anyone who met life with anything less than defiant stoicism was suspect in his young, inexperienced eyes, but the glaring albino lines intersecting her body bore testament to the pain and physical devastation she'd endured. Her case was legit. Her body was fucked up enough that no one could claim otherwise, in spite of her flaky demeanor and airhead mentality. What bones had not been crushed in the accident had been cut and shaved to provide the materials with which surgeon after surgeon attempted to reconstruct her shattered self. She'd been dealt a bad hand. No fucking doubt about it.

As if this had not been enough, shortly after she was discharged from the hospital, just when she was beginning to see the proverbial light at the end of the tunnel, she was brutally raped by one of her home-care physical therapists, a man who, police later determined, was a registered sex offender in another state who'd gotten the job caring for Mandy by applying with forged documents and a stolen identity. After the AIDs tests, the DNA evidence, the trial, the sentencing, the surgery to repair the damage the man did to her, the counseling, the publicity, the lawsuit that finally secured her a second source of income, and the return to the scene of the crime (her own apartment), Mandy fell completely apart, about as broken as a person can be.

Three days after the rapist was sentenced to 23 years in prison, his replacement, a young woman who'd just completed training, arrived two hours early due to a scheduling snafu and found the front door slightly ajar and Mandy unconscious with an empty bottle of pain killers beside her cold, purple hand. She'd taken the entire bottle. It wasn't a cry for help. The physical therapist was two hours early. Mandy did everything short of putting the barrel of a gun in her mouth and pulling the trigger to make damn sure she'd never wake up.

She was rushed to the emergency room four blocks away where they pumped her stomach, administered the appropriate anti-dotes, and watched her slowly come back to life. Brain damage was a definite possibility, but once again, she was officially deemed "lucky." Not lucky enough to go home, however. Committed to the psych ward of one of the many hospitals that tried to put her body back together previously, she spent three months in a vacuous stupor. The doctors weren't entirely sure whether the overdose or the horror did the most damage. CT scans were inconclusive. No drugs were necessary during those three long months because she was as close to comatose as you can be while still knowing enough to get out of bed before taking a shit. Soon, even that wasn't an issue because she stopped eating, lost a total of 50 pounds, and only survived because they finally strapped her into bed with an i.v. pumping nutrients into her body and a pee-tube siphoning urine out of it.

Her family paid her bills but never visited her in the psych ward. Not even once. Maybe it would have been too much for them to "see her that way." Maybe they weren't comfortable with someone being so royally ass-fucked by Fate as she'd been. Then again, they were a cowardly lot, and at least a few of them feared having anything to do with Mandy just in case lightning struck a fourth time. Better to clean up the apartment (or rather have it professionally cleaned so they didn't have to personally see the blood and cum on the living room's dark brown shag carpet), and pay the rent and utilities than to visit psycho Mandy in the nuthouse. When she finally got out, they sent the occasional check, but otherwise kept their distance. She was very much alone.

And now she was outside his door. Chattering away, a mile-a-minute, loudmouthed and embarrassing, calling him out onto the walkway, for all to see and hear. And he felt so guilty (even though he wasn't the one who'd decided her fate), that he could do little but plan on how he was going to disengage himself once he got her laundry basket down to the 'mat.' The mystery that no one in the building could authoritatively address, was whether her age-confusion, hyper behavior and perpetual ditziness, were the result of all the trauma she'd been through or if her personality disorder predated the accident and the rape. No one could remember what she'd been like before. And in the end, it didn't really matter.

The young man looked back at Henry. How could he sleep so soundly for so long? Maybe he'd lied that morning about being clean and was sleeping something off. The young man, cursing to himself, flipped the lock and opened the door the usual four inches allowed by the chain. Big-toothed, big-haired, sloppy-makeup Mandy, awkwardly upright, as if in a full-body brace, was right there in his face, attempting to peer into the apartment, leaning over a laundry basket full of satin thongs, push-up bras and midriff-baring tees.

"Hey Mandy. Laundry Day again? I'll go ahead and carry that down for you." He spoke to her as he would an eighty-year-old woman, with exaggerated concern and loud enunciation, but she never seemed offended and actually seemed to understand better than when he communicated in a normal manner. The information SHE communicated was always conveyed in rapid-fire, scattered triplicate, and never seemed to pertain to more than that day's immediate concerns: i.e. who was hosting the party and which DJ was "Da Bomb" at that given moment. He closed the door briefly to unhook the chain, and then opened it only wide enough for him to squeeze out, locking the door behind him. She didn't see a thing.

"What's the matter, baby? Hot date last night? She still there? You two get it on, sweetie? Oh, you're blushing, aren't you? How cute! How cute! You're blushing. She's a lucky girl, babe. Any girl in her right mind would love to hook up with you. Oh, did you take her someplace nice? That new place over on 4th, the one that just opened, is just da bomb! They've got stuffed mushrooms that are just to die for. You've got to take her there! You'll love it! You've got to! I love stuffed mushrooms, but I can't make them. I always screw up and they come out looking lame. The place on 4th, they just opened up last month, is just da bomb! The mushrooms come out on this huge platter with pretty garnishes. Presentation is everything, sweetheart, but you probably know that cause you're always looking so phat when you go out. Don't think a girl doesn't notice, hon. You've got it together alright. You got it happening. I hope she appreciates what she's got baby. You make sure she treats you right, or someone's liable to step in and take her place." Mandy moved sideways up against the young man's hip when she said this and giggled impulsively.

If she were attractive and he were less principled, it would have been tempting to take advantage of her. If there were ever an opportunity for an "on-call fuck," this was definitely it, but Mandy projected such pain, dysfunction and mental instability that any inkling of arousal was quashed before it had half a chance. Other guys in the apartment building, of course, felt no such compunction whatsoever, and unflinchingly used her and abused her until finally becoming bored with the "freak fuck" and casting her aside with insults and disdain. She would disappear for days, blinds drawn, never once opening the door or answering the phone. Her papers would pile up and the mailman would notify the manager when her mail slot was full, and she'd open the door with a pass key and Mandy would at last come out, looking like someone who'd been trapped in a caved-in mine without food, water or light, and had just been brought back to the surface, barely alive. Within a day or so, she'd be back to "normal," hitting on the young man and almost every other guy she ran into. The young man felt like someone ought to protect her, but no one did, and although he occasionally tried to steer her away from the vilest opportunists, it always came back to "if not him, then how about you?" And while he wondered what it would be like to do an older woman, he sure as hell wasn't going to find out with her. Fortunately, he was able to simply ignore the frequent sexual references knowing that literally within seconds, her manic, unending monologue would focus on an entirely different subject.

He hurried as much as he could, but Mandy couldn't walk fast. She was too broken up inside and limped along painfully, metal bolts and screws holding her body together. She had no problem talking, though, and seemed to accelerate when feeling uncomfortable or stressed. Kind of like the folks who say the most when there's really nothing to say, except a lot faster.

"I just love it down here. It's just da bomb. There's sunshine, phat cars, movie stars, rich guys in limos, clubs, restaurants, beaches. It's just so awesome, hon. Don't you think so? Why would anyone live anywhere else? It's just so wonderful and glamorous like on Entertainment Tonight. There was this red carpet thing last night downtown and there were all these stretch limos lined up and they had these little bars inside and everyone was drinking gin-and-juice and playing music videos with these built-in DVD players with those flat-screen TVs and bumpin' stereo systems that make your whole body vibrate, honey, especially me with all this metal inside. And we were all the way on the sidewalk! Imagine if you were actually inside one of those rides. And then we went into this club, it was like a jungle with all these plants, I think they were plastic, but they looked awesome with all the lights and the black lights made this little white t-shirt I was wearing all glowing and all the guys couldn't take their eyes off it, and I was watching everyone dance and we were drinking and it was just da bomb, honey. Why don't you ever go out with us? Don't like to have fun, sweetheart?"

They had managed to make it as far as the building's only elevator and the young man scrambled quickly to remember the last thing she'd said so he could answer in a polite manner. The elevator opened and she stepped inside, turning awkwardly and repeating the question: "Why don't you ever go out with us, honey?"

"I, uh…I'm just a lightweight. Two drinks and I'm ready to go home. I wouldn't last with partiers like you guys."

"Mmmmhmmm. That's not what I heard," she said, throwing her hip out to the side and her nose into the air, in an attempt to effect a miffed pose. The young man was content to let her stay that way, the laundry basket under his arm and safely between them as the elevator slowly made its way to the ground floor as if conspiring with Fate to keep them together as long as possible. Apparently Mandy's mind wandered, because they made it down and the doors opened before she started up again.

"Did you hear that?" she asked, big-haired head cocked to one side. The young man put his left hand out to hold the elevator doors for her, but she wasn't moving.

"Uh, I've got the door here, if you want to…"

Mandy wasn't moving. The elevator doors tried to close, bounced back upon meeting the young man's hand, slowly moved back into the "wide-open" position, paused, and then tried closing again.

"Hey Mandy? We were going to go to the Laundromat, right?"

"That sound."

The young man couldn't tell where she was staring. It wasn't at the backlit plastic numbers above the door. It wasn't outside. He thought he could hear people upstairs starting to complain about them holding the elevator, but it could have been his imagination.

"When the elevator started moving…That sound behind the walls of the ropes and shit moving up and down…It sounded like the beginning of the old Scooby Doo cartoons when the spooky words are appearing and the bats fly out of the castle. Did you hear that? It was exactly the same sound. I always wondered how they did that. That's my favorite cartoon."

"Hey!! What the hell are you doing down there? You making out with Mandy?"

"Jesus Christ. OK, Mandy, I'd love to talk to you about that sound, but we need to let Phillipe and his wife use the elevator right now, OK? Mrs. Carillo has the bad leg, remember? She needs to use the elevator. Now."

Mandy stepped out of the elevator and the young man gratefully followed her, yelling his apology up to Mr. Carillo and his wife, and picking up a hot pink underwire push-up bra that had fallen on the crack between the elevator floor and the cement walkway outside.

"OK, so the sound, like right when the elevator started moving? Or when the doors closed?"

"Thanks honey. Ooooh, I hope that cute Latin boy is down here," she said as she took the laundry basket from the young man and walked awkwardly into the Laundromat.

The young man, hearing the elevator containing Mr. and Mrs. Carillo approaching, ran quickly down the walkway to the stairs and started upward, taking two steps at a time. The last thing he wanted was to be around when those doors opened. Within 60 seconds, he was back to his door and checking his pockets for his keys. He checked front, back, right, left, and lower, and no goddamned keys.

"Goddamn it!" he muttered, a little louder than he meant to. Looking around to see if anyone had heard, he absentmindedly put his hand on the doorknob, turned and opened the door. Jesus Christ. Unlocked. Henry was gone. The floor was clean. The young man found his keys sitting in the offering plate on the bookcase where he'd left them. The incense had burnt out long before. A note on the floor, exactly where Henry had been curled up asleep, read simply "Thanks. I'll arrange to have my sty cleaned. I owe you two towels." The young man turned, double-checked that the door was unlocked, and walked down to Henry's apartment. There was a note taped on the door: "ServiceMaster people. This is the place. Get key at office."

The young man walked back to his apartment and started some coffee brewing. He grabbed the cardboard container of eggs and some thick-sliced pepper-backed bacon out of his dingy white refrigerator with duct tape covering the bare metal of the worn handle, shut the door with his hip, snagged a nonstick pan from one of the lower cupboards, and started three strips on medium heat. The coffeemaker steamed and spat and slowly poured hot water through the darkly-roasted, freshly-ground coffee. Within a minute, the bacon began to sputter and complain in the pan. The young man took in a deep breath and closed his eyes, enjoying some of his favorite smells in the whole world and trying to get a grip on everything he had done and thought and heard over the past 24 hours. Jesus Christ. It was almost noon.

Grabbing each strip of bacon with his fingertips, he flopped them over one-by-one, enduring the spatters of stinging hot bacon grease without even wincing. His hands were calloused and toughened by the last few years of work as a janitor, delivery man and barista. Weekend do-it-yourself projects and his affinity for the outdoors had done the rest. And he liked it that way. A certain tolerance for pain is valuable in life, if for no other reason than because life is full of it. As a young boy, he'd cried much too often, but his 1970's-pop-psychology-influenced parents did little to stop him. Rosy Grier and Marlo Thomas won that battle. Only when he was picked on in school did he realize the importance of gritting your teeth in the face of pain. He looked at the people who did and the people who didn't, and he knew which ones he wanted to be like. Wilson always said, "You can judge a tree by its fruit." He said that was in the Bible. You can't always judge a person by what they say or how they look. Watch what they do over a period of time. That's their fruit. A walnut tree won't bear lemons. A maple tree won't give you acorns. "It's a fact of life," Wilson said. And the young man saw that those who met hardships with stoicism were generally the folks you could rely upon.

Sometimes when he drank a lot, he'd test his own tolerance for pain, giving himself small burns from a borrowed cigarette or a set of barbecue tongs left over the coals too long. His hands were tough enough that he usually chose an inconspicuous place on the inside of an arm or on his lower leg where he wouldn't have to apply the heat for very long and the resulting burn wouldn't prompt people to ask questions the next day. It might have just been a macho thing, but the only time he ever did it in front of a girl at a party, she called him a freak and walked away. His attempt to explain the ancient belief that mortifying the flesh was the path to enlightenment fell on deaf, quickly retreating ears.

One night, a year or so before his humiliating attempt to impress the girl, the young man was drinking with a buddy of his who was married, smart as hell, decent, and torn between his responsibilities as a husband, homeowner and dad-to-be; and his longing to do something quote-unquote significant in life. The two of them were hanging out on the guy's back patio, sitting on rusting lawn chairs, the kind with the woven nylon straps, drinking beer and toasting marshmallows over the last few glowing red briquettes in the barbecue. His friend was saying something about how he felt like he was "on the verge" of something,

something big. Something significant was going to happen real soon, something that would impact his family and even his community. His words, at that time, sounded like prophecy, they carried a lot of cosmic weight after that much beer, but nothing ever materialized. Turns out he had developed a business plan for a used bookstore/café, but a week after the barbecue, the bank denied his loan application after three months of paperwork and meetings. His savings account was depleted. His wife's salary and the money he made doing carpentry on the side were no longer enough to pay the bills, let alone set aside a bit for the baby on the way. He took an anonymous office job earning just enough to get by and wondered what he'd been thinking that night on the patio when he'd drunkenly defied Fate and predicted his luck would change. The young man's friend laughed bitterly to himself the third day on the job when he reached down to scratch at a fresh scar on his calf, just now beginning to scab over. It was all he had to show from the night he spent drinking beer with the young man. The young man had pressed red-hot barbecue tongs against his calf as a joke, but had drunkenly left them pressed against his flesh a few seconds longer than he should have. When the young man saw the pain in his friend's eyes, he promptly reheated the tongs and applied them to his own bare calf not once, but three times, leaving a criss-cross of burns that prompted questions and rumors at the coffee house for weeks thereafter.

His leg healed, he avoided an infection, but the pinkish white scars remained, more prominent in the summer when his legs tanned, but always a visible reminder of that night. The young man flipped the bacon strips once more, glanced down at his calf and laughed to himself. He pulled the bacon out of the pan and laid the strips out on a paper-towel-covered plate, poured most of the grease into an old soup can on the counter and cracked three eggs into what remained. In two minutes they were done "over easy" and he put the three strips and eggs on a plate, poured a big mug of coffee and sat down at the kitchen table. The kitchen table was actually a beige, wooden, six-paneled, solid-core front door (without a knob) covered with a large heavy

116

sheet of clear Plexiglass and supported by four cast iron pipes. He ate his eggs and bacon, drank his coffee, and read the obituaries.

They were formulaic by necessity. So-and-so: died doing what he loved. That was the best. Like that matters. Cut-and-paste. After a long battle with cancer. Peacefully in her sleep. Surrounded by family and friends. After a long and prosperous life. In lieu of remembrances. In her name. Medic One of Valley General Hospital. To Evergreen Hospice Association.

You can add a neat logo for a nominal fee. More options on our website. Flowers. Flowers. Flowers. But yeah, they're dead too. In lieu of flowers. We've got it down to a routine, and why shouldn't we? It's the most reliable event in Life. Death. It's gonna happen. Guaran-fucking-teed. A million times a day. It's a business. It's a relief. It's "closure." Death and Taxes. Benjamin Fucking Franklin.

He always scanned for the young ones. The ones like him. Mostly, they didn't say how they died. Statistics tell us it's pretty predictable: car accident, suicide, homicide, accidental overdose, leukemia, accidental shooting, freak accident, drowning, etc. If they did mention it, it seemed like it was often leukemia. But mostly, they didn't. They talked about their smile, their friends, their love of life. The joy they brought others.

He read through the rest of the obituaries, paid his respect to the veterans, the men and women who ended up paying their dues to America face-to-face, often in their own blood. Survivor guilt? Fuck yeah! He felt guilty that men born 10, 20, 30, 40 years before him were assigned a different fate based on the day on which the employees at Farrell's would bang the big drum and bring them a big free chocolate sundae. So here's your birthday, here's your fate. You get to live, and you get to die. During the Vietnam War those who didn't impregnate their wives, who weren't born Caucasian, who weren't signed up for college courses, who didn't have senators for fathers; they were sent to the rice paddies to stand up and die for their country. Like the ragtag soldiers in The Beginning. In 1776. They stood up and died. Jesus Christ. A lot of them back then didn't stand a chance because they had to follow the rules. Stand up, march forward and receive a big ol' slug of Redcoat lead in the chest without an ER, without antibiotics, without IVs, without Trauma Units, without defibrillators. Big ol' plug of lead in the chest and then you hemorrhage. You look at the hole in your chest and feel the pain and see the blood and slowly, surely, anonymously, singly, die. And yet, in The Beginning, they were fighting for something. And in the Big One, they were fighting for something. How was it standing in the rice paddies while everyone around you was saying "this war don't mean nothing." The first war in which we came to that conclusion WHILE it was happening. And you're slopping around in the jungle and mud and water and rice paddies and you look down and your intestines are getting wet. They're getting all muddy, and you have to fucking pick them up and try to stuff them back where they belong, and some motherfucker is still shooting at you, and you're standing upright now like a greenhorn or a soldier in 1776, and even though there are now helicopters to airlift you to the mobile hospitals, you're standing upright and the choppers aren't going to make it in time and it's not even your fault anymore because your brain ain't working right. And you're still standing.

Even if you're a senator, or a professional baseball player, or a rock star or an astronaut, you might only get a third of a page when you die. Once in the morning edition and once in the evening edition if you're lucky. Movie stars get a nod in People Magazine and on Entertainment Tonight, but that's mostly because there's advertising money to be made with a touching retrospective. But a third of a page? That ain't much for a lifetime. Fifty, sixty, seventy years of living and your entire life is summed up in less than ten paragraphs. And that's for "famous personalities," not brilliant or decent or brave or creative people. Hell no. Those folks can pass away without so much as a ripple on the surface of the national consciousness. And what about us? We slip below the dark waters without a sound. Us ordinary folks, the "extras" in this Made-for-TV Sunday Movie. We walk back and forth on the "street scene" set, consciously being unselfconscious, counting our steps after the 27th take because there's nothing else to do. And then the scene's cut out of the movie. Never even makes the "little screen." And the star gets a third of a page, if they're lucky. Is that all there is?

You're a fucking waste of plasma if you go 70 years and never once ask "Is that all there is?" You make your daily trip to the mall to exchange time, money, ambition, creativity and soul for unnecessary material possessions, and never once ask yourself who built the mall and why. And why must I buy in order to be happy? You never ask that. Jesus. That's one thing about the folks in the military. They get down to brass tacks in a goddamn hurry when folks start shooting at them. You can be goddamn sure that they'll be asking the big questions after they slam themselves to the ground behind the burning wreckage of their Humvee, cramming every inch of their body into every nook and cranny of the vehicle, trying to become one with it as hundreds of skull-crushing rounds rattle and ricochet inches above their head. They'll be asking the big questions. But is that what it takes? Do you have to come within inches of dying before you ask yourself what the hell it's all about? And even then…And even then…how long does that last? By the time you're discharged, home, punching a civilian time clock, eating your TV dinner on your painted aluminum TV tray, do you really care anymore? Do you ever ask that question again?

The young man sat back down and picked up where he'd left off in the obituaries. Wilson laughed at him when he brought up philosophical questions. "What does a young little shit like you know about anything?" he'd ask. Whenever he came to the young man's apartment, which wasn't very often, he commented on a particular picture on the wall. Not the poster of Kurt Cobain, but an old print in a black-lacquered wooden frame carved to look like bamboo. "Now that's a guy who took time out to think things through," he'd say. "He sat and stared at a goddamn wall longer than you've been allowed to drive," he'd scoff, laughing to himself. But Wilson refused to tell the young man who the guy in the painting was. He'd just say "look it up in the dictionary," which didn't make much sense to begin with, let alone when you considered that the young man didn't own a dictionary. The picture portrayed a stout man of short stature, sitting on the ground. He had large bulging eyes, kind of like Kermit the Frog, a prominent nose, big bushy eyebrows, and a furrowed brow. A G.I. Joe beard and mustache. A cowl with many folds partially covering a heavy-set chest and draw-string pants. Who the hell was he? And why did he stare at a wall?

The young man knew where to find the answers, but he'd have to swallow pride, arrogance and some unpleasant history to go there. A girlfriend whom he'd sophomorically and defensively nicknamed "Brainiac" because she was smarter than him and was constantly trying to get him to "broaden his horizons" and "live up to his potential" gave him the picture for his birthday almost a year ago at one of the few points in his life in which two girls were interested in him simultaneously. He ended up dumping her in favor of the "hotter" girl who promptly dumped him when her old boyfriend got out of jail. The quiet, nerdy and yet seductively funky used bookstore clerk missed an entire day of work crying at home when he awkwardly and brutishly told her of his decision. She thereafter quietly and permanently re-moved herself from their circle of mutual friends in utter humiliation. The damage he did was not easily repaired. The young man never apologized, in fact never spoke to her again, and never once ventured into the used bookstore again. There were only a few acts in his life for which he still truly felt shame and this was one of them. Regrets. He knew people who claimed they had no regrets in life. People a lot older than him. It didn't make sense. The fact that a person claims no regrets in life says more about their lack of self-consciousness than it does about their accumulated actions. If you are a human being, if you are self-actualized to any degree and even half-honestly eva-luate your own actions, you will have regrets. If you say you don't, you're either ignorant or a goddamn liar.

One of his other regrets, one that still bothered him every time he picked up a basketball, dated back to his sophomore year in high school. Often, during lunch period, he'd go down to the gym and join pick-up basketball games. He identified and empathized with the geeks and freaks, so he often ended up shooting hoops with them. In that particular circle of kids, he excelled as one of the best shots and ball handlers. One day, one of the guys from a much more athletic clique asked him if he wanted to join their game. They were short a guy and were impressed with his play. The young man, flattered by this vote of confidence, ditched the geeks and joined the pseudo-jock game after only a moment of hesitation. He left the geeks hanging with only five guys, and their lunch period pick-up game folded before it began. The young man held his own in the more competitive game, but had to face the ditched geeks when he hit the showers on his way to American History. There were no illusions among the geeks and freaks. These were the kids who saw things most clearly because their illusions were systematically deconstructed by their parents, siblings, teachers and everyone else in the school. They ate lunch with brutal reality and sat side-by-side with unseemly truth during Study Hall. Their quiet protestations cut deeper than any chair-flipping tirade. The next day, the young man returned to his usual place on the court. A week later, all was forgiven, but he never forgot how quickly he'd ditched his friends when given the opportunity. Sure, he hadn't killed anyone or ripped off a liquor store, but he'd sunk to the lowest common denominator, something he never expected himself to do.

The young man sighed and shook his head to dispel the memories. He finished the coffee, dropped the newspaper into the recycling bin, walked into his bathroom and flipped on the light. The bathroom was white: tiles and paint. A mirror-faced medicine cabinet was recessed into the wall over the Formica-covered vanity and sink. The sink's enamel was scratched and stained and the Formica bore the scars of cigarettes, razor blades and unattended curling irons. He opened the medicine cabinet and grabbed a plastic disposable razor and the can of shaving cream (with soothing aloe). He turned on the hot tap and cupped his hands beneath the opaque stream, splashed his face three times and then filled the sink up halfway. He lathered up, using too much shaving cream like he always did, and started to pull the blade of the razor up his neck and over the line of his jaw in neat parallel lines, rinsing the blade in the warm water every few seconds. He always thought of J.D. Salinger's book "Franny and Zooey" when he shaved. The shaving scene, in the Zooey section of the book, was one of his absolute favorites. Zooey was so cool. Cool and edgy. He shaved with one of those old-fashioned razors with the loose blades like the one the little kids had seen shining down in the storm drain the day before. In the book, Zooey stood in the bathroom, shaving and talking to his chain-smoking mother about his crazy sister and the "Four Great Vows" and he called her a "fat Irish Rose" and they told each other to shut up and said "goddamn" a lot of times. The shaving scene lasted about fifteen pages, the bathroom scene in its entirety was about fifty. Fifty pages of conversation in the bathroom and it flew by. You didn't even notice it.

The young man looked up at himself in the mirror and went over a few spots the razor had missed. Four small circles of blood appeared on his face, two on his neck and one on each cheek. The red blood stood out starkly against the white shaving cream. That's why he always shaved before taking a shower. He always got nicks. Even when he didn't have zits, his face had these little bumps that always got nicked. Didn't matter how careful he was. There was always blood. A fly buzzed between his face and the mirror and then headed off toward the shower stall. He wondered whether this particular fly was one of the dozens that feasted on Henry's blood. For a moment, he contemplated catching the fly and cutting it open to see. Instead, he finished shaving, rinsed the sink, and started the shower. The fly was gone. Just like that. He didn't even see it leave. The tile in the shower stall was kind of dirty and he needed a new rubber bathtub mat and plastic shower curtain liner. With no steady girlfriend, the only people who used his shower on a regular basis were his buddies when they drank too much and had to spend the night, and they didn't give a shit what the shower looked like.

The hot water felt good. Full stomach, caffeine and alcohol coursing through his veins, a full night's sleep, and a day off. The young man smiled and washed himself with the last few little mangled pieces of a "family size" bar of Ivory. Maybe he'd walk down to the drugstore and buy a shower curtain liner, more soap, a bathtub mat and whatever else caught his eye. He had some cash and it wouldn't hurt to clean up the bathroom a bit. The young man washed, shampooed, and then just stood face-first in the shower for several minutes, letting the water, warmth and noise envelop him. If nothing else, the apartment building had amazing water pressure. Even cheap no-frills shower heads like the one in the young man's shower felt like fancy shower-massage units that cost fifty bucks at the hardware store. Fifty bucks for a shower head.

He turned off the water, grabbed a towel, dried off, flossed, brushed his teeth, stuffed his dirty clothes into the white plastic hamper, and padded contentedly to his bedroom, towel around his waist as he passed by the large picture windows. He pulled a on a well-worn pair of jeans, a hole-free forest green t-shirt, clean socks and Vans. Grabbing his wallet, keys, Chapstick, two Kleenexes folded in half together and his pocketknife, he was off; double-checking that the door was locked behind him. He shuffled quickly down the metal stairs, through the courtyard and out onto the street.

He was happily mellow and acceptably melancholy like an old "10,000 Maniacs" song. The sidewalk felt good beneath his feet. The city sounds melted together into a pleasurable level of white noise. He forgot about the smog, the glare, and the monotonous, market-driven, show-biz-conscious, homogeneity of Southern California. Instead, he looked at the people walking on the sidewalk, driving the cars in the street, and riding the bicycles that weaved annoyingly and dangerously through traffic and pedestrians, with a bemused detachment.

This, perhaps, was a taste of bliss. The young man couldn't be sure how he arrived at this state, nor could he sufficiently explain it. He wasn't drunk, but he couldn't rule out the effects of alcohol entirely. He wasn't high. Wasn't sleep deprived. Hadn't just got laid. It was a zone, of sorts. A level of consciousness that took everything in and held it suspended in his mind with a 360 degree view. As close to omniscience as a person can get, perhaps; unless of course you're psychic or really good at meditation or something. He'd always been interested in the paranormal, even as a young boy, and always read all the Scholastic Books about unexplained phenomenon that he could order off the tissue-paper-thin order sheets he brought home from elementary school. But he'd never really experienced anything of the sort himself. For the young man, the paranormal was a tantalizing realm that suggested truths about ultimate reality. If there were experiences or abilities or beings outside the realm of conventional understanding, he reasoned, it would not be so terribly hard to believe in God.

This was one reason the young man developed a peculiar habit of asking new acquaintances whether they'd ever experienced anything out of the ordinary. Often, he'd act as if the conversation had petered out to an uncomfortable silence requiring a new subject, ANY new subject to fill the void: "SO, ever see a ghost?" he'd ask, all self-mocking and over-the-top. But then he'd listen intently to whatever story the person had to tell. Almost without exception, however, his acquaintance would only be able to offer second-hand accounts of objects mysteriously appearing to have moved overnight, of strange sounds or scents, or dramatic temperature differences within the same room. It was quite rare to speak with someone who actually had a credible-sounding account of their own, unless they themselves were not credible to begin with. And if a person didn't effectively evaluate the everyday realities around them, how could you believe their stories of the paranormal? If they couldn't hold down a job or pay their rent on time or remember to meet you at the bar for drinks, how could they accurately communicate something beyond the realm of human reason? Then again, wasn't there something in the Bible, something Wilson must have mentioned, about God choosing the unlikeliest of people to convey his truths? Basically just to fuck with us?

One girl he'd known, who worked at the coffee house for a year or so before moving Back East someplace to take a job with an aunt at a major pharmaceutical company, was the only person who'd really offered a convincing first-hand account. She was very intuitive when it came to reading people. Whereas the young man often found himself getting screwed by people because he automatically zeroed in on whatever good existed in a person however insignificant it was, the young woman inevitably picked up on whatever evil existed in a person's heart or mind or soul. As a result, she kept her distance from the folks out to do wrong and was often perceived as stand-offish, snooty, arrogant or just plain weird. Her ability to pick out potential problem-makers, however, eventually made her an integral part of the coffee house's interview process. It only took three predictions regarding three "stellar" applicants to establish her value in the mind of the previously skeptical store manager. An internal transfer from another downtown store turned out to be a mental case who tended to flush her medication and flip out while on shift: she once asked a customer to please disguise the antenna protruding from his head because it was upsetting other patrons. Another applicant, a small unassuming woman, a senior citizen no less, turned out to be a back-stabbing, conniving instigator: within two weeks, the coffee house's delicate balance of personalities and egos collapsed into a maelstrom of drama. And the clincher: a clean-cut, red-haired kid from the local seminary who carried a Bible to work and read scripture on break. He was caught failing to ring up every third or fourth sale and pocketing the surplus when he counted out his till at the end of each shift. All three had impressive résumés, terrific references and nearly perfect interviews, but in each case, the young woman offered the manager a one-sentence warning. For the seminarian, it was "watch the money." That was it. The manager laughed it off ("Yeah, right!") until sales began to slip whenever the pious, freckled young minister-in-training worked the register: even on the busy nights, Fridays and Saturdays, when the movie theater next door dumped literally hundreds of customers on their doorstep. The manager's first step upon discovering something wrong? Dragging the young woman into his office with two sneering misanthropes from business security for an hour-long interrogation seeking to prove that she was connected in some way to the thefts. When they failed to get anywhere with the young woman, they pulled the carrot-topped Bible-thumper into the office and confronted him with two months' worth of suspect receipts. He promptly broke down, sobbing, and offered a full confession regarding the money as well as his use of the office computer to surf porn sites after closing. Two weeks later, the manager promoted the young woman to Lead, a position that allowed her to sit in on interviews and give the manager a high sign whenever she picked up bad vibes. And that's all it was, really; just bad vibes coupled with a single image: money, drugs, violence, laziness, whatever. Kind of like the Seven Deadly Sins in a retail context. It was an unspoken arrangement for the most part, and it worked out fine until he came in drunk one evening and made a pass at her. Her only surprise was that it had taken him so long, and she had no other recourse but to quit and take her aunt up on a long-standing offer of a place to stay and a cushy job with her employer Back East.

The young man was the only other person to realize she could "see" things when others couldn't. He even asked her about it one time, but she quickly changed the subject, blushing deeply. She did entrust him, however, with her first-hand account of a paranormal encounter. One evening, a warm, quiet evening that lent itself to conversation as they made their way through the nightly "clean-up list," the young woman asked the young man if he believed in ghosts. He immediately perked up, of course, and realized that he had known his coworker much longer than it usually took him to broach the subject himself. "I don't know," he said, hoping she'd explain why she asked. She appeared a bit shaken, which surprised him because he assumed that one paranormal experience was basically akin to any other. But she didn't see things that way. Something outside of herself had invaded her world, leaving her quite unsettled.

So as she swept muffin crumbs and scone morsels into a pile on the hip tile floor, she told the young man about a night at home a couple weeks before. Her daughter was alone in their bright, funky yellow-walled bedroom. They lived in a cramped one-bedroom apartment in a less-than-upscale neighborhood 10 blocks from the coffee house. The little girl liked to lie on their bed and watch cartoons after dinner while her mom washed the dishes. The apartment didn't have a dishwasher and had poor water pressure to boot, so after-dinner clean-up always took a little longer than it should. When she finished rinsing the dishes, leaving them to dry in a rack on the counter, she heard someone talking in her daughter's room. The hair on her arms stood up and a chill ran up her spine because it sounded like an adult, most definitely not someone on the television. The young woman grabbed a knife from the dish rack and slowly made her way to the bedroom, pushing the door open with her bare foot.

The little girl was looking at something in the corner of the room. Entirely ignoring the cartoon on the TV, she was sitting cross-legged on the bed, cocking her head this way and that, and speaking in an animated but quiet voice to someone the young woman could not see. The little girl was not afraid, and didn't hear her mother open the door. The young woman checked to make sure the window leading out to the fire escape was still closed and latched and then ditched the steak knife on the buffet table just outside the room.

"Hi, Pumpkin Pie."

The little girl didn't hear her mom. She squinched up her nose and laughed at whatever she saw in the corner. "You're funny," she said, softly clapping her pudgy hands.

"Hi, Pumpkin Pie."

The little girl slowly turned around and smiled at her mom. "Say hi to gerbil!" she said.

"Hi, gerbil. You're awfully tall for a gerbil, aren't you?" she asked, noticing the focal point of the little girl's gaze. The young girl looked confused for a moment.

"She's not too big, she's just right!"

"Oh, OK. So how long have you been talking to the gerbil, Pumpkin Pie?"

"Ever since the Rugrats went off." The young woman glanced at the current cartoon and then up at the kitty-cat clock with the swinging tail and quickly calculated twenty minutes.

"That's an awfully long time. Your gerbil must be fun to talk with."

"She is. She's funny."

The young woman smiled and quietly half-closed the door on her way out, snagging the knife from the buffet and dropping it in the kitchen sink. She promptly forgot about the "gerbil" until they visited her parents in Nevada a week-and-a-half later. She drove the two hundred monotonous miles to her parents' small house every few months so they could see their granddaughter, but her relationship with them was strained and it always felt good to head home the next day. There was an air of artificiality in their greetings and expressions of affection, perhaps no more than in most families, but she had never been close to either parent and they struck her as people who had been born to become elderly. Even as young adults, in her first memories, their mannerisms and values resembled those of people thirty years their senior.

The beige hollow core aluminum door opened slowly after the peephole grew dark and then light again. Her parents had obviously been sitting on the couch and chair closest to the front door waiting for their arrival. They offered fragile hugs for her and her daughter who immediately ran towards the kitchen and the "candy drawer" as soon as her grandparents finished kissing her freshly scrubbed chubby cheeks. Halfway to the kitchen, however, she stopped dead in her tracks and began jumping up and down, clapping her hands and pointing to the "picture wall" of the living room. Above a buffet table that matched the one they had in their apartment, the wall was covered with framed family pictures; some recent, most dated, several quite yellowed and old.

The little girl, still jumping, said "Hi gerbil! Hi gerbil," her pointing finger quickly replaced with a pudgy, squeezing wave. This continued for a few moments until she realized that something was different. "Gerbil's not talking," she turned and said to her mom, her smile quickly transformed into a pout of disappointment and concern.

"What is she saying?" asked her grandparents, looking up at the young woman and bending down towards their grandchild. The young woman was caught off guard. Ordinarily, whenever she was around her parents, she felt entirely self-conscious and awkward, examining every statement before speaking; careful not to sound negative; touch on politics, music, art or movies; mention the names of any boyfriends; or God Forbid, swear; but her daughter's exclamations threw her for a loop. After hearing the word "gerbil" she stared openmouthed at her child and the picture wall as if watching a movie without a soundtrack. She didn't hear her parents' questions, struggling simply to focus on her daughter and keep back the sick feeling that crept up from her stomach. Finally, she broke through the shock as if surfacing from a deep dive. She could hear everything now, the sounds were loud and brash and she struggled to pick her child's small voice out from beneath those of her parents.

"Where's the gerbil?" she asked quietly, ignoring her parents and speaking a notch below the volume of her child's quizzical words. The little girl stopped jumping and put her hands on her hips in a picture-perfect imitation of her mom mid-scold, and said simply, "Gerbil's not talking to me." Then she pointed to a point on the wall two thirds up from the bottom and two thirds over from the left. The young woman, still quite oblivious to everything and anything her parents were saying, dropped her overnight bag with an audible thump on the thick-pile, freshly vacuumed carpet, walked slowly over to the buffet, put her shaking left hand upon its antique surface for support, and slowly raised her right hand to point at the pictures while her daughter vigorously shook her head up-and-down for "yes" and back-and-forth for "no," abundant brown curls bouncing about with three-year old abandon.

One by one, she pointed at the people in the snapshots, family pictures and formal portraits. She paused at each one until her daughter shook her head, and then moved carefully to the next. Halfway through, her daughter triumphantly nodded her head up-and-down. The young woman's finger pointed to an elderly woman in a plain grey dress. The picture had been taken years before, and the young woman didn't recognize her. Keeping her finger on the image of the woman, the oils from her fingertip smudging the glass to her mother's immediate consternation, the young woman slowly turned her head around and asked her parents what the woman's name was. "Mary," they said in unison.

"That's your great-aunt Mary Goerbald, for goodness sake," her mother said. "She passed away a week-and-a-half ago. Don't you read any of the letters I write…" she began, but then reached up and toyed with the top button of her blouse with her index finger and thumb. "You know, I may have forgotten to mail that one, come to think about it. Let me go see if I can find it," she said, quickly exiting the room.

The young woman began to chide her retreating mother for steadfastly refusing to use email, but it didn't really matter, and she stopped before a word left her open mouth. Instead, she turned and looked down at her daughter again, and watched her little face peer searchingly up at the picture on the wall. There was something in her daughter's eye, something that actually frightened her. Recognition. Her daughter knew the woman in the photo.

"Dad, did you and Mom ever talk to Pumpkin Pie about great-aunt Mary Goerbald?" she asked.

Her father was looking out the front window at a car that had stopped momentarily in front of their home before moving on down the street. He didn't hear her.

"Dad."

"Did you or Mom ever talk about great-aunt Mary in front of Pumpkin Pie?" she asked, summoning up all the nonchalance she could. Her father looked sheepish.

"Your mother doesn't like talking about her. Still doesn't, even now that she's dead. Great-aunt Mary was a bit of a wild one in her day, and frankly, right up until she died. Your mother never really got along with her the few times they were in the same room together. I don't remember her speaking a single word about her for years until a couple weeks ago."

At this point in the story, however, the woman had to stop and concentrate on the register and a quickly growing line of customers. The young man, standing behind the espresso machine, one hand on a steaming knob and the other on a black plastic portafilter handle, was working his way down the line, calling out the drinks of the people he recognized, and asking with raised eyebrows the preferences of those he didn't. His coworker, suddenly confused by an abbreviation on the touch-screen register, totally forgot about her story and the queasiness in her stomach. They were slammed until closing and had to blink the lights three times before the last of the movie theater crowd reluctantly exited into the comparatively brisk night air.

They were now behind schedule, at least behind THEIR schedule, and had to work their asses off in order to quickly bring the coffee house to a point of temporary cleanliness and repose sufficient to placate the Type A personalities who populated the opening shifts mere hours away. The young woman and the young man parted company after mutually confirming that the alarm was armed and the front door was closed and locked, and they never spoke of the matter again. Shortly thereafter, the manager made his pass and the young woman picked up her life and moved east.

The young man suddenly realized that he had walked three blocks and crossed two main streets in an almost entirely detached daze as he remembered the young woman's story. He couldn't recollect who he had passed or whether he'd had to wait for the crosswalk lights to change or had jay-walked with the rest of the people in a hurry. Anything could have happened in the preceding minutes, he reasoned, and he was utterly oblivious. So much for eyewitness testimony. The greatest bank heist in history could have occurred and he would have unconsciously muttered "excuse me" as the robbers passed him by on the way to their getaway car idling at the curb.

It's even scarier, he thought, when this happens driving. He took a road trip one time with two of his friends and had the sensation of "coming to" in South Dakota after three hundred miles of largely uninhabited, barren landscape. He couldn't recall a single detail about the preceding four hours. Nor could he remember any landmarks, signs or exits. One moment he was accelerating up the onramp after a convenience store pit stop, and the next he was decelerating down an exit ramp beneath the enormous lit sign of a fast-food chain. How could that be? How could he have successfully navigated almost a ton of steel, glass and rubber down a narrow asphalt ribbon without so much as an anecdotal memory? No wonder there were so many people out there claiming to have been abducted by aliens. When the most advanced brain on the surface of the earth can hiccup and miss three hundred miles of travel, who's to say the abductees are full of shit? It was exactly this type of sensory failure that made the young man question whether the world we perceive every day is really "real." If our senses and cognitive faculties could be so easily fooled, who's to say that this didn't happen all the time? The Deconstructionists, Wilson told him, took this apparent "gap" to heart. If our senses are fallible and incomplete (have you ever seen the back of your head without the use of two mirrors?), how could we base our world view, our cosmology, our philosophy and religions upon them? For our religions may claim to be independent from our sensory experiences, but where would fundamentalist religions be without the chill that runs up a convert's spine during a fiery sermon? And ironically enough, if it were not for "sinful sensuality," fundamentalism would have little to vilify. Cold rationalism eats fundamentalism for dinner (and vice versa).

A pretty-faced, slightly plump young twenty-something in sandals, floral skirt and white, button-down, close-fitting top, stepped halfway into his path with a smile and asked him how his day was going.

"So far, so good," the young man said, making a conscious effort to look into the woman's green eyes rather than the bit of cleavage she was displaying above the clipboard she hugged with both arms. He kept walking. "How's it going for you?" he asked, looking back over his right shoulder.

"Well. Well." The words sounded strange coming from a woman this young. "Would you be willing to spare a couple minutes and answer a few questions from my survey?" she asked, smiling a provocatively sweet smile and leaning in his direction. The young man stopped, retraced his steps, and gently steered her out of the middle of the sidewalk with his left hand on her right elbow. "Excuse us," he said as they weaved their way through the pedestrians to an empty patch of sidewalk up against the rough stone wall of a building.

The girl said "thank you," and flipped her medium length hair back over each shoulder before bringing the clipboard down away from her breasts so that she could read the questions and jot down the young man's answers.

"OK," she said, before quietly clearing her throat. "Do you ever ask yourself what your purpose is in life?"

"Oh Jesus," he responded before realizing that the young woman might work for one of the storefront churches established to minister to the street kids, runaways, drug addicts, squatters, punks and petty criminals inevitably drawn to the college district's used bookstores, arcades, noodle shops and all-night coffee houses. The young woman saw him wince and smiled reassuringly. "Uh, I've always, I mean it's not like I'm old or anything, but for as long as I can remember, I've wondered what it's all about. Doesn't everyone?"

The girl wrote hurriedly and apologized when her note-taking extended several seconds beyond the end of his answer. There was something printed along the length of the ball-point pen. It was one of those pens that companies order to give out free and advertise their business. "Do you think there might be something in life that would make you happy and fulfilled?" She bit her lower lip for a moment and seemed to silently read through the question again as if making sure she'd gotten it right before looking up and earnestly reestablishing eye contact.

"I hope so." The stupid survey had hit a nerve and he blushed upon hearing the longing in his own voice. "Jesus Christ," he thought to himself, "next thing you know I'll be bawling at Hallmark cards." He looked quickly up and around at the constant stream of people passing them by. A grimy green taxi pulled over into the far right lane marked as a loading zone, pumping oil-rich exhaust directly at them. The cab's chrome hubcaps were dirty and scratched. A thin man in his thirties with dark skin and high cheekbones leaned forward and fiddled with something on the dash and then looked around as if confirming that he and his cab were safely out of traffic. The young man turned his gaze back to the girl, hoping she had not sensed his knee-jerk earnestness. She was looking at him rather blankly, and she waited a couple more moments before saying "OK" and moving on to the next question. Already, the young man thought, there was a hint of boredom in her voice, a subtle relaxation in her features. He knew the look. "She's just doing her job," he thought, once again feeling rather stupid and juvenile, much as he had his first time in a strip club when one of the dancers asked him if he wanted to rub her shoulders for a while, only to have her bail when an overweight man in a business suit pulled out a wad of hundreds. "Jesus, there's nothing worse than knowing a woman's bored with you. Much better that she be pissed off or bitter or hateful. At least then, she cares. He decided to bail after the next question whether the survey was finished or not.

"If you had a chance to learn how to be happy and fulfilled in life, would you take it?" The girl shifted positions, transferring her weight to her left leg and raising her promotional ballpoint pen in preparation for his answer.

"Yeah, why not?" he said, his resolve crumbling as his eyes focused on the soft upper curves of her breasts.

"Follow me," she said, turning abruptly around and passing through a dingy doorway into a dimly lit, aging foyer with long-abandoned mailboxes built into the wall on her left. She no longer stood upright, but slouched a bit, and her left hand holding the clipboard fell carelessly to her side, the ballpoint pen clipped to the survey upon which she'd jotted his answers. When he looked down, however, he noticed that her "notes" were merely random loops and scratches and doodles, much like the "pretend writing" a five-year-old girl would pen before learning to write.

"God I'm a dumbfuck," he thought to himself. "What the hell have I gotten myself into?" Ignoring the ancient beige elevator to the right, the girl started up a carpeted staircase towards a landing lit by a large stained-glass window. The colored glass was arranged abstractly, with no discernable pattern or theme. Ah, if only he were drunk, then this would be an adventure and he'd tell whomever he was about to meet to shove it up their ass. But he was entirely sober now, and this was an uncomfortable waste of time on his day off. The girl continued up the stairs, climbing them as if she'd climbed them a hundred times before. "She doesn't even have a nice ass," he thought, having unsuccessfully tried to salvage something of value from the quiet, awkward march upstairs. She didn't look back once or even acknowledge his presence. No small talk. No "So what's your name." Nothing.

Turning the corner at the landing, they continued upward, the young man alternately eyeing the girl's boring flat ass and looking up over her shoulder. He noticed the smell of brand new carpet and paint as they approached the top of the stairs, and a hum like that of a hundred people talking simultaneously behind closed doors, an almost ominous murmuring. The second floor was decorated in typical modern office fashion with generic framed abstract prints, potted plants, wainscoting and neutral colors. A drinking fountain hummed and shuddered like Wilson's refrigerator. The young man felt for his flask but it wasn't there. There was an unattended reception desk in the center of the large room surrounded by six sets of beige, double, six-paneled doors complete with keycard sensors. The murmuring, now reminding the young man of a Pentecostal church service he'd once attended with a friend, in which hand-raising worshippers throughout the sanctuary spoke up in an unknown language when moved by the Holy Spirit, seemed to be coming from one of the sets of doors on the right. The girl led him to the second set of doors on the left, swiped a keycard she surreptitiously retrieved from between the pad of questionnaires and the clipboard, and opened the door after the locking mechanism was released with an awkward-sounding, metallic clunk.

She waited for him to clear the doorway and then closed the solid wooden door behind them, pausing for a moment until she heard the locking mechanism click. Returning her keycard to its hiding place beneath the survey sheets, she stepped around the young man and walked forward toward a wall with a single six-paneled door and a sliding window to its right like you'd see at a doctor's office. A frumpy, overweight woman sat behind a desk at the window. She looked up over a computer monitor at the girl, nodded, and manipulated a mouse, clicking several times. The girl waited for her to finish and make eye contact once again, and then spun about and told the young man that "Henrietta" would be assisting him further. She walked to the double six-paneled doors, swiped her keycard, opened the one on the left, and disappeared.

As if on cue, Henrietta piped up: "Someone will be here to see you, shortly. Feel free to have a seat." She never looked up from the computer monitor, moving her head only centimeters in an apparent attempt at a directional nod. The young man, as if waiting for a yearly physical, retreated to one of the waiting-room chairs up against the wall to the left and picked up a magazine called "Bountiful Living." He began absentmindedly flipping through the slick pages, paying little attention to the articles about physical and mental health, time management, financial success, family dynamics and spirituality. There were lots of pictures of upper middle-class families of every ethnic origin gathered around enormous dinner tables and stone-faced fireplaces, eating multi-course meals and playing board games. Advertisements offered video courses; training seminars; books-on-tape (i.e. CD); financial planning services; "exciting" once-in-a-lifetime business opportunities; family summer retreats at one of three sunny, family-oriented "Bountiful Living" resorts; "positive" CD ROM games for the kids; books; day-planners complete with daily inspirational messages; elaborately matted and framed, "hand-detailed" reproductions of Bountiful Living's resident artist's most cherished works; and so on, and so on.

The overhead music, upbeat instrumental tunes that reminded one of old Beattle songs, but weren't, faded away and was immediately replaced with the voice of a middle-aged Caucasian man of Midwest origins. He was evidently speaking to a large, enthusiastic crowd, perhaps a couple thousand people, who clapped and cheered after particularly stirring statements. If nothing else, his voice was easy on the ears. Down-home and folksy, but strikingly intelligent and eloquent. He enunciated well without seeming to try too hard, the exact opposite of evening news anchors. His apparent age notwithstanding, his words were infused with a youthful energy and spirit. He was talking about Life and Happiness, talking almost conversationally one moment and like an old-time orator the next. His cadence was not exactly that of a preacher; Southern Baptist, Methodist, Assembly of God or otherwise; and yet the emotional effect of its rhythm was similar. It was almost as if the young man had heard him before or had seen him in a movie or on TV.

"I met a man in a small town who had just lost his job. My associates and I were sitting at the counter of a coffee shop on Main Street, a block away from the motel where we were staying. It was a warm summer night, and the coffeehouse had a single squeaky ceiling fan in the middle of the room. No air-conditioning. The windows were open, just the screens keeping out the June bugs and crickets, and this squeaky ceiling fan moved the warm night air about the coffee shop, mixing the aromas of freshly-baked pie, coffee, buttermilk biscuits and gravy. I do enjoy a big old plate of biscuits and gravy." The young man heard many in the audience murmur their assent. A few clapped and whooped. The speaker paused. You could almost hear his smile. Then it grew quiet. You could hear the scrapes of shoes on the auditorium floor and occasional coughs.

"A man was sitting a couple stools away from me on my left. He looked crestfallen. Staring down at a cup of coffee that the waitress topped off every once in a while. He looked like he didn't have a friend in the world. You ever see someone like that? Someone who looks like they don't have a single soul with whom to share the thing that's troubling them? Well I got the waitress' attention and I motioned toward the gentleman without him noticing. She looked over at the man, pulled a ballpoint pen from her apron, the one she used to take our orders, and wrote 'Lost job today' on a napkin which she scooped up and threw away immediately after I had read it. Then she went down and warmed up his coffee again. The man had lost his job. That very day. And here we were, three fellas with Bountiful Living, sitting at the same counter, drinking the same strong coffee as this man who'd just lost his job. What a coincidence!" The audience laughed quietly, clapped, murmured expectantly, realizing that something powerful was going to follow. A few, having heard this presentation before, smiled the knowing smile of those "in the know."

"What a coincidence that was. Out in the middle of nowhere in this small town of no more than a few thousand citizens. What a coincidence. Now for some folks, calling an event or circumstance a 'coincidence' is a kind of dismissal. 'Oh that's just a coincidence' they say. 'No need to pay attention to that.' Well, our Bountiful Living Family feels differently. We feel that a person should pay very close attention to coincidences, that COINCIDENCES COUNT. In fact, for those of you following along in your workbook, that is our first bullet point on page 27: 'Coincidences Count." That's the first of the 'Three Cs' we'll be looking at tonight. 'Coincidences Count.'

"So I decided to make this coincidence count for something in this gentleman's life. We're in the business of bountiful living, and he's just been removed from the job he counted on to get by. To make a living. Not even a bountiful living. Just a living. And now even that's gone. What a coincidence that we'd find ourselves seated next to this gentleman. No one else in the diner. Just us. So I think to myself, 'Let's make it count.' 'Let's make this count.' So I asked the man to pass a packet of artificial sweetener, the blue kind, because the small porcelain container in front of us only had real sugar and the pink kind. Now I don't usually use the blue kind," the man said chuckling into the microphone, "but it gave me a chance to start up a conversation with the gentleman."

"I told him my associates and I were in town on business. That we were looking for some positive-thinking, self-motivated, dynamic individuals to join our organization and start building their future. Well, the gentleman was stunned. He sat silently for a moment, eyes wide and the beginnings of a smile creeping up on his face. And do you know what the first thing out of his mouth was? The first thing he said? That is, once he could put some words together?" The speaker paused and people throughout the crowed began saying and murmuring and even shouting "it's a coincidence," "what a coincidence," and just the word itself, "coincidence." The sound of applause and people's happy voices grew. The speaker chuckled confidently into the microphone and warmly affirmed, "That's right…that's right…what a coincidence. Well in no time the man was telling us his story. Everyone's got a story, don't they? Well, he was telling us his story. A sad one, as you might expect. Five years working for the same man in the town's hardware store and without so much as a day's notice, he was told to hand over the store key and his name tag, pick up his things and leave. Not a lot of dignity in that. No, not much dignity in that. Now there may have been a good reason. I don't know. I didn't ask the man. My intention wasn't to pry…would you have? The crowd quietly murmured "no."

"No I didn't ask him why he'd been fired. Didn't really matter at the point, did it? My knowing why he had been fired wouldn't have changed his condition. My knowing why he had been fired wasn't going to get him his job back. That was done. In the past. And I wasn't concerned about his past. No, I was concerned about his present." A pause. "About his current condition. If you're following along in your workbooks this evening, that's your second bullet point. The second 'C' is a person's 'Current Condition.' Where he was AT, at THAT exact moment: that's what I focused on. That's what I zeroed in on. And it was pretty obvious that emotionally, financially, and in such a small town, socially; he was hurting. The man was in pain. It hurts when a man or a woman loses their job. THAT was his current condition. And THAT'S what I cared about. And I would suggest that his current condition was what concerned him the most as well.

"The man was recently divorced, paying child-support, living in his cousin's basement, just getting by, and now he was unemployed. That was his current condition, and that's what he talked about. He didn't talk about Plato and Aristotle." Titters from the crowd. "He didn't want to debate the importance of Fate versus Free Will. He didn't have anything to say about international politics, free-market economics, eastern philosophy or feminist sociology. Great works of literature were not on his mind. Neither was religion. He just wanted to tell us about the position he'd found himself in, and he wanted to hear how he could pull himself out of it. He wanted to hear the good news that we had to share. People always want to hear good news, don't we? Many years ago, it wasn't unusual to hear people call out 'What's the good news today?' to their friends as a kind of greeting. Kind of like how we say 'How's it going?' these days. In the early 1970's, more than one television network chose to close each evening newscast with a segment of unabashedly 'good news' to balance the steady stream of stories about war, famine, oppression and social unrest they were delivering to America's living rooms each night. Everyone wants to hear good news.

"So we listened to him pour out his sorrow in the little diner. The waitress kept the coffee coming, and she seemed relieved that the man she'd seen a thousand times before was getting the attention he needed. Working class folks understand how close they are to the end of their rope every single day. Working class folks don't harbor illusions about their financial outlook. Living paycheck to paycheck is no longer the exception…it's the rule."

141

A long pause. Quiet. Nervous clearing of throats. A couple coughs. The rustling of workbooks.

"But it doesn't have to be that way." You could almost hear the collective sigh of relief. An awkward smattering of applause grabbed hold, faltered, and then expanded and moved through-out the assembled people, growing until it almost sounded like people were standing up. Then, a perfect 45 degree decline in the applause left the speaker with his attentive audience ready to hear the good news.

"IT DOESN'T HAVE TO BE THAT WAY." The young man waited for another, even stronger round of applause, like the President receives throughout his State of the Union Address, but there was quiet instead.

"And that's what we told the gentleman in the diner. We told him he could be his own boss. That he could have peace of mind, stability, happiness, fulfillment. He could live bountifully, not paycheck-to-paycheck. He could meet unexpected chal-lenges with confidence. He could move forward in life, rather than simply treading water. He could be a leader. Make his kids proud. Be his own boss. All of this could be his. Right then. Right where he was. All he had to do was say the word." Ap-plause. Strong, confident, ardent applause. "And he did, ladies and gentlemen." The speaker almost shouted over the ovation. "He said 'yes' and he pulled his checkbook from his jacket and wrote a check for $475." Thunderous applause. The micro-phone was overwhelmed for a moment. Distorted applause and cheering flowed from the waiting room's hastily mounted sur-round-sound speakers. "Yes, he wrote that check. He signed that check. Lost his job, lost his family. And he signed that CHECK and forged a new future! Ladies and gentlemen, Mr. Richard…"

The young man stood up, walked over to the reception window and looked down at Henrietta who stared intently at her comput-er screen, the bright blue background reflected in her bifocals. A sliver medallion hung from a silver chain around the folds of her neck. Impressed in the metal was an image of a teenage girl and the words "Saint Agnes Blannbekin." On the computer screen reflected in her lenses was a similar picture of a young woman.

The young man, not wanting to startle the older woman who sat oblivious to her immediate surroundings, occasionally fingering the medallion with her left hand and clicking the mouse with her right, quietly said "excuse me." No response. A little louder. "Excuse me." Still nothing. The young man smiled to himself and walked back to the polyester-cushioned waiting room chair and sat down. He couldn't see Henrietta and Henrietta couldn't see him. His mind tuned back into the sounds of applause and enthusiasm piped into the room. A different man was speaking. Probably the guy at the diner who lost his job and now was a fantastic success and a prominent member of the Bountiful Living Family. The nasal, almost whiny tone of his voice was harder on the ears than the first speaker's had been. He sounded less intelligent and more heavily scripted, more white trash than folksy. Nevertheless, the audience was with him, echoing his points and participating like they had with the first man. His segment of the program was apparently much shorter, for he was already building up to a finale. With what sounded like another standing ovation, the guy from the diner shouted into the microphone: "Bountiful Living is the Foundation of Enlightenment!" and then the sounds of applause faded away and were quickly replaced with more Beattlesque music.

The young man heard two people coming up the stairs beyond the door through which he'd entered. They weren't speaking, but there were definitely two sets of feet making their way upward and he figured the young woman with the distracting décolletage was one of them. Already embarrassed about the ease with which she'd maneuvered him to this point, he was not in the mood to share the moment with another gullible mark or give her the satisfaction of seeing both of them sitting quietly in side-by-side chairs like two guys dubiously waiting for barium enemas.

On top of that, he had a good half-pot of coffee in his bladder and no idea what time it was or how much of his day he'd wasted on this detour. He quickly stood and walked over to the reception window as loudly as he could without actually stomping his feet. This time, Henrietta was looking up at him when he looked through the window, a look of irritation on her elderly face. With her head turned toward him, he couldn't see her computer screen reflected in her bifocals any longer, but her left hand still toyed with the medallion and her right hand still grasped the rather dingy-looking mouse.

"I'm sure someone will be out to see you in just a moment. If you'd like to just take your seat and…"

"I need to use the restroom, please."

"Like I said, I'm sorry you've had to wait this long," she looked back over her shoulder at the closed door behind her and then turned back to the young man. "Just take a seat, it will be just a moment."

"Look, I don't mean to be a jerk or anything, but I either need to use a restroom here, or I'm going to leave and use one someplace else." If the two people weren't already on their way, he would have done just that without a second thought, but he wasn't even sure the door would open, remembering the girl's use of the keycard. Henrietta's face told him she'd lose a point or a bonus or a trip to Miami if she lost a potential member of the Bountiful Living Family, and she quickly told him the bathroom was through the double doors across the room to her left, and then two doors down on the left.

The young man heard the beep of the woman's keycard as the door swung closed behind him and he found himself in a bare hallway of unfinished sheetrock walls and a concrete floor. The second door on the left was labeled "Men," as Henrietta had promised. The first door was unidentified, and the only other

144

door in sight was a heavy-duty steel door with a push bar down at the end of the hall beneath another "Exit" sign.

"Perfect," the young man thought to himself as he turned the smooth, brushed-steel doorknob and found himself in a small austere bathroom with a tile floor, one sink, one urinal, and a toilet stall with a broken white door. The urinal was the kind that stretched upward from a rectangular porcelain receptacle built into the floor to a point just about chest-high, topped with the chrome flushing mechanism and rod-like handle. There was a brand new pink circular cake of toilet deodorant in a triangular white plastic screen bearing the words "Just Say No To Drugs" and "Johnson Janitorial Supply." The young man quickly unbuttoned the fly of his Levi's and began relieving himself with a satisfied sigh. This kind of urinal is cool, he thought, you don't have to hit it in just the right place to avoid the back-spray. No need to adjust aim or velocity: just don't hit the deodorant cake or miss entirely and you're fine. He thought if he ever built his own house, he'd have a urinal in each bathroom, or at least in the guest bathroom. The guys would think it was pretty cool. The young man looked downward and noticed three wads of chewing gum on the plastic screen: one white, one pink and one green. "Jesus Christ," he thought to himself, don't guys think about the poor son-of-a-bitch who has to clean that shit out of there? It's not like he's got a great job anyway, but you throw shit into a urinal and it's adding insult to injury. Basic disrespect, selfishness, and an inability to put yourself in another man's shoes. The young man had worked for two years as a janitor in a rest home, and often subconsciously sized up a bathroom in terms of how many minutes it would take to clean. He wondered whether normal guys threw shit into urinals because they just didn't think it through, or if it was just the sociopaths, the guys who got off on others' misery, beat their girlfriends and picked barroom fights for no reason.

The young man looked up at the white-painted wall above the urinal's chrome flushing mechanism. The graffiti, obviously written and drawn by many different hands, was almost entirely produced by the same black ball-point pen ink. Directly in front of him, at eye-level, was the old standby: "What are you looking up here for? The joke is in your hand." There were several variations of "fuck you," a couple of poorly drawn depictions of gay fellatio, a misspelled admonition to "eat slimy green pusy," and way up high, at least seven feet up and to the right of the urinal, near one of those metal, electric air-freshener units, was a large black and white sticker. It was a depiction of Christ with the subtitle "Suicide Christ II." Instead of being nailed to a cross, this Christ had hung himself by the neck with a heavy-duty extension cord secured to an overhead water pipe like you'd see in an old unfinished basement. He was handcuffed, and below his wound-free feet was a toppled folding chair. His eyes were closed. Thin streams of blood flowed from a crown of twisted barbwire. Boxer shorts replaced the loincloth. A crucifix tattoo marked his left shoulder. The young man, entirely distracted by the suburban Twelfth Station, stared stupidly upward, his "lizard" long having "drained," until he abruptly came to his senses and flushed. He washed his hands thoroughly with the pink liquid soup, used his forearm to ratchet down two sheets of brown paper towel from the dispenser, and stepped out into the unfinished hallway.

Walking further down the hall, he came to the heavy steel door with a push-bar and an illuminated "Exit" sign. Opening the door, he was offered the choice of an immediate left or an immediate right. No arrows or indicators of any kind adorned the plain sheetrock before him. Turning right, he heard the faint sounds of Henrietta back in the waiting room calling out "Sir? Sir?" as she stood and leaned forward through the reception window. The second "mark," a bird-like man with John Lennon glasses and a maroon bow tie sat stiffly in one of the metal-framed, polyester-upholstered waiting-room chairs and cocked his head to the side like a cockatiel in order to better observe Henrietta's distress. Henrietta muttered "fuck" under her breath and exhaled in disgust, buzzing the door beside her open and stepping out into the subdued corporate colors of the waiting room. She rarely ventured beyond her receptionist station: you never knew what kind of crackpots followed the girls up the stairs. They averaged one psycho requiring police attention every week. The cockatiel man cocked his head back and forth, flipping pages of a Bountiful Living magazine without looking downward. "Freak," thought Henrietta. She hesitantly walked over to the door through which the young man had left, fingering her silver medallion with her left hand. She opened the door and called out "sir?" once again, out into the empty unfinished hallway, before erasing a tick mark from her mental bonus tally sheet and allowing the door to close. No luggage or BBQ this month, she mused discontentedly as she turned and slowly returned to the receptionist station. The bow tie guy was now immersed in the magazine. She slid her keycard into the sensor, waited for the beep and click, opened the door, and returned to her computer, waiting for the door to swing shut and latch before sitting back down and immediately logging into her personal email account and checking for responses to an online personal ad she'd submitted the day before.

The young man stood quietly, listening to Henrietta open the door and call for him. He heard the door close and then it was quiet. He smiled and once again reached for the flask that wasn't there. The hallway in which he now found himself had several doors on either side, all white, un-marked, steel "fire doors" with brushed-steel doorknobs and heavy duty hinges with hydraulic returns. At the very end of the hallway was another green "Exit" sign. "Jesus," he thought. "Good thing there's not a fire or something. I'd be toast." He walked quickly but quietly down the hall toward the second exit. Halfway down the hall, he noticed that a door on his left was ajar, held open by a wooden doorstop fashioned from a piece of two-by-four. The heavy-duty return had pulled the door nearly shut. The doorstop was wedged between the door and the doorframe. It was dark inside. Curiosity getting the better of him, he reached inside and felt along the wall to his right for a light switch. Several large fluorescent light fixtures, hung from the ceiling with small-gauge chain, hesitantly flickered to life.

He stepped halfway into a large room filled with metal shelving units holding hundreds of brown boxes of all sizes, each marked with the Bountiful Living name and logo, a brief description, item number and a barcode. Allowing the door to quietly return to its position three inches ajar, the young man walked through the room surveying the merchandise: cassettes, CDs, DVDs, calendars, day-planners, books, framed paintings, desk lamps, desk-top waterfalls, sets of luggage, wind chimes, aromatherapy candles, mouse pads, financial planning software, Hibachi barbecues, household cleaning products, laundry soap, closet organizers, everything he had seen in the waiting room magazine and more. "Look at all this shit," he thought. For all the apparent security this operation had on the front-end, there wasn't much on the back-end to prevent someone from walking off with a shitload of this crap. No security cameras and wide open access. Then again, the folks out there spending a week at the Bountiful Living family resort and forking out hundreds and even thousands of dollars for "masterful reproductions" of Bountiful Living's resident painter's works, weren't the types to be buying stuff out of the back of a van. He laughed at the thought of a Bountiful Living black market, and then realized it probably wasn't as far-fetched as he had first thought. You'd just have to present the transaction in the right way. Make it look more like a "sample sale" or a garage sale or sell it on freakin' eBay. No need for the back-of-the-van type scenario these days. Anyway, people interested in getting rich quick love a good bargain and often aren't too picky about the logistics of the situation, even if they're ostensibly concerned with "spiritual well-being" and enlightenment. Case-in-point: movie stars aligned with major religions who have no qualms about pursuing the Hollywood high life while simultaneously touting religious leaders who practice and preach asceticism.

Either way, the mental exercise was an almost entirely hypothetical one for the young man, for aside from the $5 he stole weekly (without fail) from the tip jar at the coffeehouse, he rarely, if ever, stole anything.

A heavy-duty, battered blue hand truck and a cheaply-made, brand-new red hand truck stood side-by-side against one of the few stretches of wall not covered by shelving. A fire-extinguisher, a clipboard and some workplace safety documents hung on the wall above them. The room was long, and the young man quickly realized that at least two more of the doors he had passed on the left opened into this same room. Not wanting to get caught and growing bored with the whole episode, he left the storeroom and began walking down the hallway toward the exit sign again, pausing only a moment to reach in through the propped-open door to flip the storeroom lights back off.

As he approached the last door on the right, he heard the same low, persistent murmur of voices he had heard upon reaching the top of the stairs with the young woman. He didn't know exactly how long it had been, but the voices sounded exactly the same. Different conversations, possibly even different people, and yet the murmur was indistinguishable from the first. Kind of like the coffee blends at work. When the coffeehouse chain was in its infancy, when he was a loyal customer rather than an employee, varietals were its claim to fame. Distinctive, unique flavors that varied from season to season, often eliciting comparisons to fine red wines from the passionate, bohemian coffee-lovers who initially represented the majority of the chain's employees. As the company grew, however, and the number of stores multiplied exponentially, varietal beans were stretched thin. If each store were to continue offering the same coffees, and the company was to maintain the same level of quality, blends were the only way to go. With a blend, you never tell the customer exactly what varietals it contains. You tell them only that the "Sunshine Blend" is a combination of Central American Arabicas, and then you've got a hell of a lot of room to maneuver if one coffee plantation fails to produce one year or one country's beans are ruined by drought. "Sunshine Blend" tastes the same day after day, month after month, year after year. If Costa Rican beans are in short supply, you can make up the difference with Mexican and Guatemalans. That's the way it was with the noise from behind the door: Joe might get up to take a leak; Joan might press "the button," temporarily removing herself from the automated flow of calls to finish up her notes on an account; Sally might finish out her shift and straighten up the small cube she shares with Frank, scheduled to begin 15 minutes after her quitting time. The parts might vary, but the sum remains the same. Homogeneity.

His pride still smarting at the ease with which the young woman in the close-fitting top had maneuvered him up the stairs, and his curiosity piqued by the speech he listened to in the waiting room, the young man ran back to the storeroom, flicked on the light, grabbed the clipboard he'd seen hanging on the wall, and returned to the last door on the right. Even with the increased security you saw everywhere in America after September 11, 2001, you could still make your way almost anywhere in an office building with a clipboard and a determined demeanor. The young man had once piggy-backed his way through a secure entrance, walked past two fully-staffed security desks, rode an elevator up 23 floors, and even asked a receptionist for directions to visit his friend's office (he was a tax lawyer), all with just a clipboard in his hand and an earnest, perturbed look on his face.

The young man opened the door effecting a confident, distracted air, alternately peering down at the clipboard (holding what appeared to be inventory sheets) and glancing up at the diverse group of people he saw before him. It was a large room served by multiple doors like the storeroom, filled with at least a hundred men and women, both young and old; fitted with various styles of headsets; sitting side-by-side before dummy terminals in beige, upholstered "mini-cubes;" tapping away at ancient, filthy keyboards; speaking in scripted phrases and modernized versions of decades-old sales pitches. Snapshots, inspirational mementos, quality awards, comics, contest tracking sheets, and pin-up girls/boys covered the few precious square inches of each cube. Only a few of the customer service reps/Bountiful Living "Ambassadors" looked up. The rest continued to work their way through their day: rattling off as much of the "outbound" script as the unsuspecting consumer allowed before interrupting or simply hanging up, and expressing as much empathy during the inbound "Family Member" calls as they could stomach before offering the almost inevitable "courtesy credit" or "complimentary upgrade" to make up for the inconvenience of delayed orders, the shortcomings of highly-touted financial seminars and the frustration of lost reservations to Bountiful Living Resorts.

The young man remembered that Wilson once described modern-day customer service reps as "cannon fodder," placed in harm's way at minimal expense, in a calculated move to mitigate the negative impact of brazen assaults on the interests of consumers. "The CEO can either spend $15 million on a promotion that genuinely benefits the company's customers, or he can spend $10 million on a promotion that fools most everyone and $1 million on customer service reps (and the courtesy credits they administer), to placate the consumers willing to take the time to call in and voice their displeasure. Overpromise and underdeliver and let Customer Service take it in the groin for pennies on the dollar.

And here they were. Lined up, ready to take their bullet over and over again for 25% less than the "living wage." This was the "better than many" job, the "not bad for entry level" job, the "stick it out for a year and post out" position. The job attracted many hard-working "intelligent" folks who reasoned that a pay cut up front was worth the promise of advancement down the road and a decent benefits package.

The young man, of course, didn't see all the anti-depressant and anti-anxiety medications in the purses and satchels and backpacks, but as he walked along the periphery of the large room, he heard the candid asides when a rep pressed the "mute" button on a particularly abusive customer, and voiced the words that could never be said "live." He saw hollow looks, stoned stares, clenched jaws, cynical sneers, disinterestedness, determination, flippancy, depression, despair and one or two almost euphoric, jubilant smiles. Maybe one in a hundred were truly suited for

151

the job: thick-skinned, persuasive and naturally predisposed to appreciate every aspect of human interaction, even the most negative. Cops were the only other group of people the young man could think of who spent most of their time taking people's shit just so they could occasionally help a genuinely needy person. Day in and day out, all without retaliating or becoming hateful or bitter. Some pulled it off, but a lot didn't.

Two thirds of the Bountiful Living customer service representatives were women, most in their early to mid twenties, many with snapshots of young children pinned to the interiors of their cubes. If the snapshots were an accurate measure, more than half of the young moms were single. The young man honestly wondered what he'd do if he got lucky one night only to get a call a couple months later. He figured he'd do "the responsible thing," but would that necessarily mean marriage? He reached for the flask that wasn't there and peered unconvincingly down at the inventory sheets secured to the clipboard.

Banners and posters covered the walls. Colorful pictures of Bountiful Living Resorts and products, and bold slogans in Times-Roman like "Upsell! Upsell! Upsell!"; "Financial Success = Foundation for Enlightenment!"; "Remember Add-on Sales!"; "Move Product and Win Big!"; "Quality Month = Hawaiian Adventure!" Lot's of exclamation points. The young man noticed for the first time that multi-colored, plastic fake leis were haphazardly draped over random cubicle walls, miniature cardboard and crepe paper palm trees stood atop computer monitors, and Waikiki screen-savers of Diamondhead graced the room's few idle computer monitors. And about half the people in the room were wearing gaudy Hawaiian shirts, flip-flops, Bermuda shorts, MuuMuus, sunglasses or combinations thereof.

Monochrome monitors suspended from the ceiling indicated the number of active outbound calls, active inbound calls, the longest period of time a Bountiful Living Family Member had been waiting on hold, the names of all Ambassadors taking themselves out of queue to finish work or simply slack, the number of inbound "abandoned" calls (when the customer got tired of waiting and hung up), and the total number of Ambassadors working at that moment. Even at first glance, it was obvious that everything in the room, including the current Hawaiian "incentive" program, was constantly evaluated, quantified and measured. Even the coffeehouse, with its corporately programmed, cookie-cutter chic atmosphere; nationally consistent signage and display hardware; and often draconian security measures, seemed almost libertarian in comparison. He remembered the old Police song "Every Breath You Take" and thought of being chained to a cube for eight hours each day with a "Quality Assurance" team and your supervisor monitoring every word you speak into the headset microphone. You can't even take a leak whenever you want without impacting your stats. Case in point: the young man saw a girl with multiple piercings and short orange hair done up in two little "handlebar" pigtails stand, tap a button on her telephone console, and begin walking in his direction. The name "Traci" immediately appeared on the overhead monitor. She glared at him as she passed, toying with a silver stud protruding from her tongue, glancing at his clipboard and coming to her own conclusions. Her perfume caught him off guard. He expected 120-proof rebellion and anarchy, but was left with a delicate impression of Chanel. Her hips swayed provocatively as she strode just slowly enough across the thin grey carpet in tall black, heavy-heeled leather boots and a black polyester skirt, for him to take it all in. She didn't look back. "They never do, when you want them to," the young man thought. Traci pulled open one of the heavy-duty steel doors and disappeared into the nondescript, unfinished, echoing hallway. He heard her boots clunking down the hall toward the women's restroom. The door initially began to swing closed rather quickly, was slowed by the hydraulic return, and finally clicked shut.

Traci's name was racking up the time on the monitors. A few Ambassadors looked over at her vacant seat before returning their attention to the screen in front of them. They appeared to be organized into teams. The young man continued on his way,

153

brazenly examining the contents of each cube like an anthropologist. He'd never had a job that required him to sit in a cubicle.

The girls with pictures of their children, the girls he assumed were single mothers (no pictures of Dad anywhere), weren't much older than him, and they reminded him of a girl he'd worked with at the retirement home. Not particularly attractive, more than a little overweight, the girl was a "housekeeper," the female equivalent of a janitor. When speaking with her during breaks, it was hard not to come away with the impression that if it weren't for her child, she'd have nothing to talk about. No interests, hobbies, or ambitions outside of those intrinsically tied to her daughter. She graduated rather anonymously in the middle of her class, didn't consider college, and after graduation drifted from entry-level job to entry-level job without any evidence of a game plan or strategy. By all accounts she was a good mother, but maybe Wilson was right. He sometimes called children "SPs," which stood for Suicide Preventors, Species Preservers, or Shitty Pucks, depending on his mood and the number of beers under his belt. He had kids, but he didn't talk about them and grew angry if you asked.

People without a strong "life force," he said, begin burning out about the time they turn twenty. College can add a few years of purpose, focus and momentum, but the denouement can be even more devastating than the one following high school graduation especially for idealistic English Major types who find that not only is the "real world" entirely unlike MTV's version, it's nothing if not antagonistic toward wide-eyed, jittery poet-types who scoff at the business world but expect to be paid nonetheless. Love can add a year or two. Marriage a few more. But kids. Kids are our salvation. A tautology, of course, but propagation of the species is but one short clause of this expansive metaphysical insurance policy.

Traci was back. He didn't hear her return, but there she was, slowly settling back into her ergonomically-correct plastic and polyester swivel chair, shifting the taut curves of her ass back

and forth, tugging at her funky tight t-shirt top, and finally crossing her legs, lifting one heavy black leather boot up and over the
other, and petulantly tapping the "Automatic In" button on her
telephone console. The call rang in, she immediately muted it,
breathed a deep condescending sigh, relished the customer's
confused reaction to the silence, hit the toggle mute button once
again and exhaling the standard Bountiful Living greeting, began
the 47th call of her day. The polyester skirt was short and as
tight across her ass and upper thighs as the form-fitting top was
across her ample round breasts; and the cumulative effect, when
combined with her short, orange hair and strangely prim posture,
was enough to move the young man to a state of distraction.
There's definitely a difference, he thought, between girls who
simply give you a "woody," and those who move you on a more
visceral level. Those who both excite your dick and hit you in
the gut are almost irresistible. Throw charm, intelligence, wit,
sensuality and a healthy dose of spirituality into the equation and
it's scary as hell.

He'd never spoken to the girl, of course, and most likely never
would, and yet he felt the impulse to kneel and declare his undy-
ing devotion to her like the acolyte of some ancient goddess.
The fact that today, at least, he wasn't going to humiliate himself
as he would have only a few years earlier made him think this is
what the beginning of wisdom and experience must feel like. He
thought about old folks he knew like Wilson, who had seen
enough of the world and knew enough about themselves, that
they could evaluate most impulses, drives, emotions and external
circumstances before taking action. The fact that he did not immediately embarrass himself with this girl, he thought, was a
good sign. A quantum leap behind Wilson, but reassuring nonetheless.

But God Almighty, she was captivating. She was a distraction,
an unexpected value in the equation of the day. He hadn't asked
to be derailed, hadn't looked for an opportunity to relinquish his
autonomy and free will, and yet here she was impacting him
without effort, planning or even awareness, aside from the time

spent becoming who she was at that moment and putting together her look for the day. She looked familiar, too, and not just because his mind was racing through excuses he could potentially use to speak with her. He looked around the room again, and no one struck him with the same sensation of familiarity. Perhaps sensing his presence, she began to swing her desk chair around. The young man quickly turned away and looked down at the inventory sheets on the clipboard.

"Shit." He could feel himself blushing as she looked him up and down before swinging back to view her monitor. He felt the boredom in her gaze. Beads of perspiration appeared on his forehead. He tried to casually wipe them up and over the top of his closely-cropped head. Jesus, these office buildings are always so goddamned stuffy, like an MD80 towards the end of a five-hour flight. Wrapped in plastic, sealed air-tight, every molecule of oxygen long ago replaced with carbon dioxide. And yet, even with the climate-control set to what felt like a blistering temperature, the young man noticed that many of the young women still wore large, down-filled jackets as they took calls. Some had maroon or hunter green fleece blankets with the Bountiful Living name and logo stitched along the border in white thread, spread across their laps. He decided it was time to get the hell out of Dodge. He was sweating, and the orange-haired punker chick was too much for him, anyway. He knew it, and she sure as hell knew it. She could have any guy she wanted when it came right down to it, as long as he was looking for a little "alternative" entertainment. Doctors going through a mid-life crisis, lawyers looking for a little punk-rock pussy. She could call the shots. No young coffeehouse geeks need apply.

"Goddamn!" he thought, and then gasped and froze like a second grader playing "statue tag," thinking he might have said it out loud. He had finally put his finger on the sense of familiarity he felt towards Traci. He slowly looked up from the clipboard. The babble of voices had not subsided. No one other than an overweight, middle-aged African American woman with a Mary Tyler Moore hairdo and a four-legged aluminum cane with rub-

156

ber stoppers was looking in his direction. He smiled at her, she returned his smile, and turned her attention once again to the screen before her.

The girl, Traci, seemed familiar because she was a dead ringer for a girl he saw one strange night when he and his buddies went downtown for a typical evening of mindless carousing. They began the night in the central business district, dropping seven dollars for each imperial pint in a polished hardwood pub, saying "excuse me" to suits talking on $400 cell phones, and admiring the young Ally McBeals in short business skirt ensembles. After a couple stops, they progressed outward, away from the gentrified mixed-use blocks of street-level, high-end retail and over-priced, upper-story residential; to the land of three-dollar well drinks; mass-produced, vinyl promotional banners; garish neon signs and four-dollar pitchers of Bud. They wandered throughout the hind quarters of the city, stopping at each and every dive they encountered, without discrimination or direction, drinking cheap beer and playing pool, electronic darts and pinball; making fools of themselves, flirting with the occasional pretty girls, but mostly concentrating their efforts on the average-looking girls and the homely ones who trashed themselves up to the point of being sexually provocative, because they at least gave a shit or were so needy that they were willing to relinquish the age-old advantage of the female.

In this mixed-use area of the city, businesses, community centers, factories and residential areas seemed to randomly intermingle and share space as if in an ad hoc declaration of the necessity of flexibility. There were no perfect lines drawn here. People lived, worked and played in facilities stacked atop each other or scattered randomly throughout the low-rise urban environment. There was no rhyme or reason. No master plan. Lax or non-existent zoning enforcement. Almost like the city planner had smoked a bowl or two and didn't really give a shit.

The young men drank their beer, for the most part oblivious to the people sitting beside them, people working on their 20th or

157

30th year of service to the same company, often the very company their fathers and even grandfathers had worked for in eras past. It was different for these folks, though. Times had changed, and they were not rewarded as their forefathers had been. Companies no longer offered perks or benefits or advantages to compensate them for their reliability and impressive track records. They were basically treated the same as the rookies: heavily scrutinized and expendable. The years they dedicated to the company were tallied with regret, condescension and fear, rather than pride and appreciation. The most qualified and experienced employees were often ridiculed as know-nothing, lazy hacks who did not possess the ability to better themselves. All too often, they tirelessly worked toward retirement, weathering the storms of layoffs and reorganizations, only to find themselves suddenly unemployed a month before becoming eligible for a pension.

In this world, you maneuver the dark mile or two home from the bar, and you don't even notice the holes in the carpeting, the chipped and dingy porcelain in the bathroom, the various extension cords stretching from the only three-pronged outlets in the house, the duct-taped refrigerator handle, or the crack in the front window. After all, your neighbor's house is in the same condition or worse. It's only when an outsider is due to arrive that the veil of familiarity and denial is lifted and you see the sorry state of your surroundings in painfully crisp resolution.

It was in this world that the young men found themselves, and they drank beer and flung their heads about in time to thrashing, rocking garage bands playing on dilapidated beer-drenched plywood stages. It was getting late and they had just been thrown out of a bar after a down-and-out power lifter picked a fight with them in the haze of an anabolic steroid rage. He was a regular, so he got a cab and the boys got the door. Reeling and raucous, they stumbled and swaggered along, baggy jeans sagging, sneakers shuffling, strong lungs breathing in the testosterone cloud in which they traveled. Jaywalking and shouting, they finally came upon a faux-black-marble storefront sandwiched between an adult bookstore and a decrepit pawn shop. They stopped for a moment and looked around. Like any group of drunk young men, they were variously exuberant, sullen, staggering, euphoric, sleepy, horny, theatrical, earnest, nostalgic, grandiose, antagonistic, conciliatory, wide-eyed and squinty. Fifty feet down the sidewalk, a dark alleyway neglected by a broken mercury-vapor street light filled the late night air with the pungent aromas of rotting cabbage; stale chicken wings; sour milk, soggy Jo Jo potatoes and grease-trap offal. Saxophones, electric guitars, cameras, DVD players, TVs, cell phones, computers and guns sat quietly beneath the sporadically blinking, ticking, dingy fluorescent tube in the pawn shop window. Iron bars separated the lowlife humans occupying the filthy sidewalk from the riches within. The adult bookstore was open. A laminated cardboard sign said so. Taxi cabs and beater cars with ragged tinted windows schlepped by loudly, stereos thumping and buzzing with bass and feedback.

A light, smoggy rain began to fall and the guys were looking for another establishment within which they could escape the grimy wet night and have yet another cheap, mass-produced beer. One of them joked that standing in the luke-warm rain was like getting pissed on by God. They were drunk. The young man put his hand on the rough brick exterior of the adult bookstore and closed his eyes momentarily in response to the spinning in his head. The others stared down at the stained, dirty, chewing gum-spotted sidewalk, checked their watches and cell phones, and tried desperately to calculate the remaining minutes until "last call" with the few still-functioning synapses at their disposal. Soggy cigarette butts and fast-food wrappers were laminated to the sidewalk by moisture and foot traffic. It was getting late. They either needed more booze or a distraction.

As if on cue, a guy not much older than themselves, wearing an olive trench coat with a turned-up collar, stepped out of the adult bookstore, lit a cigarette, and walked out into the wet night, licking his thumb and rather brazenly counting the folded bills he had removed from a brass money clip. Satisfied with the total, he replaced the money clip and thrust the bills back into the right front pocket of his neatly creased gray slacks. He took a long drag on the unfiltered King and then pointed to the storefront entrance with two fingers and the glowing cigarette as he exhaled.

"We're open," he said with a nod. "The next service is due to begin in about ten minutes. Are you gentlemen interested in joining our congregation tonight? Twenty-five bucks in the offering plate gets you a seat in a pew. Here's tonight's bulletin," he said, pulling a number of small pamphlets from an inside breast pocket of the trench coat and attempting to distribute them to the drunken young men standing dubiously in the dirty drizzle.

"Fuck," they drawled, suddenly afraid they were being roped into a skid row mission revival of some kind. The young men began uneasily backing away from the doorman as if he had open running sores or a communicable disease. They backed away, that is, until one of them saw the nude woman on the front of the "church bulletin." She was thin and fair; with short, mussed, punk-rock, red hair; green eyes and large natural-looking breasts. Kneeling before what appeared to be an altar of some kind, her eyes were uplifted in obvious ecstasy.

"Church of Diana Universal," it said across the top in gold lettering. "Come worship with us!" it said below the picture. That was followed by the "church" address, phone number and internet address. More than one of the young men mentally tucked away the "www" address for safekeeping, knowing there'd be at least a few "free pics."

Inside the glossy brochure were more pictures of the girl from the cover: green eyes darkened with heavy eye-liner that continued outward Cleopatra-style; full, Molly Ringwold lips; expansive areolas; taut, pink nipples; and that striking shock of spiky, blood-red hair. She, as well as other girls, had been photographed engaging in various sexual acts with each other and a few anonymous men with long, substantial penises. What little clothing there was suggested antiquity, although it was difficult to discern from the costumes whether the wardrobe folks were shooting for ancient Greece, Rome, Egypt, Africa or pre-Christianity England. The guys, of course, didn't give a shit. They were now, however, confronted with a conundrum older than the civilizations supposedly represented by the women's gold lame' thongs, fur-trimmed bodices and extravagant head-dresses: booze or sex. They were in no danger of sobering up before the night was through, but there's that ambitiousness young men feel when they're drinking together, a drive to consume until passing out or vomiting, and then to consume more. Booze or sex. In a perfect world, of course, they could choose both, but this is not a perfect world, and the bulletin stated plainly that there'd be no alcohol inside. They looked at each other, the glossy pictures and the establishments around them. A couple of them muttered something and rather unsteadily jogged down the street to the corner and looked down the cross-street in both directions. Craning their necks, they peered through the night, searching with the heartfelt urgency of young men on a mission, before turning around slowly, shaking their heads and jogging back to the group.

"What's the verdict gentlemen?" the doorman asked, a half-grin holding what was left of his cigarette.

The young men looked at each other and in unison began pulling their wallets from their pants with sheepish grins. Two of them were short.

"Is there a fucking ATM anywhere?" Hey Dan, when you guys went down the street, did you see an ATM?"

"We were looking for a bar."

"Yeah, but did you see an ATM?"

"We were looking for a fucking bar."

"OK. Shit. So can I bum ten bucks?"

"Yeah, is that all you need?"

"Fuck, I dunno….we might have to tip, and buy drinks. Drinks are what, five dollars? Dude. Hey Dude!'"

The trench coat guy took a long drag before looking up. He looked down at the sidewalk, and then slowly looked up at the dark, starless sky, squinting a bit at the falling rain. You could tell he watched a lot of old movies when no one else did. He had the timing down. He moved slowly. Black-and-white movies, like black-and-white photos, are intrinsically dramatic. Dramatic like black next to white. Tension. Demarcation. A number of his friends, most of them in fact, had not seen a single black-and-white movie from start to finish. Temple of Diana on Skid Row. This was black-and-white. Stark. Glaring. He wanted to be an actor, and this was his first professional role. Beggars can't be choosers. He exhaled slowly. Absentmindedly, he felt the breast pocket of his dress shirt and found it empty. He looked up at the young man who had asked the question and advised with a near-perfect combination of aloofness and grit, "Look man, it's twenty-five bucks up front with no tipping and no drinks. It's a church, not a strip club."

Flicking the cigarette onto the sidewalk with theatric flair, like Bret Boone flipping his bat after a game-winning home run, he looked up at the soggy young men assembled on the sidewalk, took a deep breath and pointed to the text of the brochure he held in his steady young hand.

"Church of Diana, Universal. Dedicated to the worship of She who illuminates the night, wields the silver bow, and infuses the earth with Life and Regeneration. Huntress, Silver Goddess, Universal Mother. She about whom Existence turns. Life-giver, guardian of the Harvest." He looked up expectantly.

"Come worship She who unites all sentient beings. She who spares us the suffering of old age by cleaving our breastbone with arrows flung from her silver bow." He knew he was quickly losing his audience and his "cut," so exasperated, he shoved the brochure back into his trenchcoat and moved quickly to close the sale, reciting the last line from memory: "Come worship the Goddess of the hunt, the patron of the working class, the many-breasted protector of the beasts, honored with human sacrifice and ritual sex."

"Fuckin-A!" muttered more than one in drunken affirmation. "She's got a million tits!" a pimply-faced, curly-haired kid named Randy announced upon reaching the last page of the brochure with its image of the goddess' multi-breasted statue from the temple in Ephesus. "Shit, count me in motherfucker!" With drunken bravado, Randy pushed his way through the group, deposited $25 in Trenchcoat's soft-skinned, callous-free, outstretched hand, and stumbled up the cement steps into the dark, black-light illuminated interior of the "Church of Diana, Universal."

Randy turned his head at the sweet scent of incense, and peered down at his white t-shirt and tennis shoe laces glowing purple like they did in the county fair's low-budget haunted house in which he and "Stoner Sally" were quickly rounding the bases when a disembodied nasally voice broke in via a cheap speaker advising them that inappropriate displays of affection were not allowed. Randy stepped unsteadily, drunkenly, through the darkness, the thumping beat of loud techno music vibrating the air in his lungs. Bolted to the sloppily painted wall, upon which he placed a sweaty right hand to steady himself, were dimly back-lit plexiglass panels emblazoned with the same text that Trenchcoat had read from the brochure. And there was the photograph of the statue with innumerable stone breasts, standing amidst a colorful illustration depicting what the temple might have looked like with its shining brass censers, altar, priests and priestesses.

He closed his eyes, waiting for his beer-drenched brain to stop rotating within his skull. Drank way too much. Sure as hell don't want to puke or pass out. Shit. Fuck. Don't lose control. His brain was slipping. C'mon motherfucker. Maintain mother-fucker. He steadied himself, steeled himself against the spin, and wondered where the restroom was, eyes still closed, beads of sweat appearing on his acne-scarred forehead. A familiar dark warmth began to envelop him, and his thoughts turned to something that had happened to him back in the seventh grade, something about which he never spoke, even when he was really drunk, like now. He was in his school's state-mandated sex ed class when that warm feeling crept up on him as stealthily as a lioness stalking a springbok antelope on one of those nature shows on TV. He remembered looking down at his photocopied handout, looking up at the generic round black-and-white clock to his left, looking outside through the portable classroom's window on his right at the soggy, dirty, rainy afternoon. Closing his eyes helped at first, but he couldn't sit there in the middle of sex ed with his eyes closed and a giant three-foot-wide, black-and-white, line-drawing cross-section of a breast up on the over-head projector screen. The moment Mr. McKlusky uncovered the overhead transparency, it was all over. Randy wasn't a prude, his parents didn't shelter him from the world any more than any other parents did; and as much as the jocks in the lun-chroom begged to differ, he was pretty sure he wasn't gay. But the fact remained that a black curtain was falling on his world and in mere seconds he would forever be known as the kid who passed out in sex ed.

He had no fucking clue what was wrong with him, and the anger almost brought him out of it, but not quite. For Chrissake, he was more than fine when he saw Paula Gwinn's left breast be-hind the gym one glaring summer day. He gawked for several seconds, in fact, before she matter-of-factly pushed it back into her training bra beneath the surface of her bright green top. She said something which he didn't quite catch, turned abruptly and left, swinging her immature hips to-and-fro until she turned the corner and disappeared from sight. No problem, whatsoever, and a resounding woody to boot.

And in the portable classroom, it was only a drawing, but the anonymous illustrated breast neatly sliced in half and beamed onto the speckled-silver, pull-down screen by the ancient overhead projector, was enough to push him over the edge. Maybe it was the clinical environment that was responsible for his swoon. He sure as hell didn't faint when Paula flashed him the goods. Not even close. And he was fine when he rode his silver-blue fifteen-speed mountain bike down to the mini-mart and rummaged through the rusty green dumpster out back with the red-and-white warning sticker that said "Don't Play Upon," retrieving expired issues of Playboy, Hustler and Penthouse. Shit, they showed pussies and everything in Hustler. Sex, he decided as he tried to effect a swagger on the way up to the front of the room to retrieve the laminated bathroom pass hanging on a hook on the wall, should be tan, air-brushed and sexy, not stark, lily-white and scientific. If someone talked about a tit like it was a fucking medical procedure, he was basically fucked, just like the time he snapped his eye with a rubber hose (the kind you filled up with water and used as a squirt gun) and puked in the eye doctor's office as the doc explained the intricacies of his injury to his worried mom. There was a big cross-section of the human eye on the wall in the exam room. Fucking cross-sections. A lot of things in life are fine until you start talking about them.

He managed to walk shakily up past three rows of desks to the front of the room, mutter an apology to Mr. McKlusky who was now intently tracing the outlines of the Cooper's ligaments with his laser pointer, and request permission to leave; exiting out the portable's aluminum doorway, briefly obscuring the enormous tit with daylight, a royal blue laminated construction-paper Bathroom Pass clutched in his trembling left hand, only to black out seconds later, the heavy black curtain finally dropping once and for all before his eyes, forcing him slowly to the rain-soaked cement in the open-air courtyard between Mr. McKlusky's, Mr. Friedman's and Ms. White's portable classrooms. His baggy jeans immediately began soaking up the dirty rainwater. He came to moments later, and struggled to pull his head between his legs like he learned in First Aid.

There he sat, muddled and soaked in sweat and rain. The fact that no one walked through the ordinarily busy courtyard or even bothered to look outside convinced Randy that there was indeed a God, re-energizing a once-fervent faith and leading him to delete all the porn and rap songs from his computer's hard drive at home and answer a "rededication" altar call at his family's conservative Baptist church the next Sunday. Instead of a shocked witness, Randy was examined only by a crow sitting on a power line, and then only disinterestedly, surrounded by the sounds of school and suburbia; a plane flying overhead invisible above the clouds; cars whizzing by the "Slow Children" signs out front; band class performing scales inside the main building.

As soon as his mental fog cleared enough to stand, he hurried inside the main building and dove into the first available boy's bathroom. For fifteen minutes he squatted on a white porcelain sink bolted to the aquamarine, tile-covered bathroom wall; sticking his wet ass as close to the spout of the hot-air hand-dryer as he could without falling, and trying to listen for anyone coming through the door; before splashing cold water on his face and returning for the last five minutes of the class. All of which, fortunately, were conducted with the lights on and the overhead projector off. After the bell and an uncomfortable two minutes explaining the duration of his absence to Mr. McKlusky as the result of a "major, huge dump," Randy ditched his next class in a futile attempt to locate Paula Gwinn.

Trenchcoat guy smiled as Randy disappeared into the darkness. "Gina is the priestess for this service. She's the redhead on the cover. Twenty-five dollars reserves a seat in a pew. The service is about to begin." Peering inside, the young men formed a single file line, handed over $25 each, and entered the dark streetfront "church" with drunken, horny, expectant curiosity.

166

Half of them at least had been in strip clubs before, but the air of overt sensuality commanded their undivided attention nonetheless. They didn't understand the goddess shit, but if the redhead in the brochure was going to strut her stuff, they didn't really give a flying fuck about the context in which she was performing. Every guy who walked through that door was simultaneously very much the same and very much different from the others. Even in their drunken haze, they were focused and attentive. Three of the guys already had die-hard woodies; at least one guy was gay and secretly hoped Gina would be joined by a handsome, oil-slicked stud during the "service;" and one other was feeling rather guilty about stepping foot inside what most certainly was the modern day equivalent of the biblical "den of iniquity" with a healthy dose of idolatry thrown in for good measure.

Gina, meanwhile, tilted back a bottle of Jim Beam yellow label, draining two fingers of its copper contents, her expertly shaved pussy, covered only in a g-string, resting distractedly on a cold blue metal folding chair set up in the closet-sized dressing room lit with a single, overhead fluorescent tube. The only good thing about the sterile white light was that it highlighted imperfections requiring a bit of make-up. Out on the stage (the owner required that everyone refer to it as "the temple" when in her presence), the dramatic lighting was far more forgiving. Some of the girls were downright ugly, but when the lights were lowered and the men's imaginations combined with the previously consumed alcohol in their bloodstream, the music, and the costumes, it didn't really matter. Lowering the bottle, she licked the whiskey from her lips, the same lips that kissed her 3-year old daughter good-bye that morning and brushed her boyfriend's ear that afternoon; the same lips which would soon drain the contents of Rick's dick in front of a crowd of strangers.

She placed the open bottle of rye on the scarred surface of a beat-up vanity, the only other piece of furniture besides the chair, and applied a thick layer of moisturizing lipstick, stopping every once in a while to pucker up and look in the cracked, dingy mirror. She was pretty, and like most pretty girls, she knew it; but she had been used and discarded enough times in her life that she didn't rest on the laurels of her beauty. She almost never failed to use it to her advantage, either.

Rick was a loser blessed with decent looks, a very long dick and the ability to come almost at will. Rick never worried about the "money shot." That was as much a certainty in his life as Benjamin Franklin's Death and Taxes. What he worried about was longevity in the business, not longevity in bed. There's only one Ron Jeremy, and there will always be only one Ron Jeremy. And he was NOT Ron Jeremy. Not even fucking close.

Gina methodically lubricated her vagina and anus, pushing the water-soluble clear gel deeply into each with a hefty, purple, silicone vibrator. Rick was hung and occasionally too rough, and she wanted no chance of him ripping her or causing abrasions. Depending on her mood and the guy with whom she'd be performing, she sometimes got a head start on things with the vibrator and allowed herself to become involved in the sex enough to orgasm on stage. But usually she just drank a lot and only used the vibrator (turned off) as a lube dispersal device. There was a time limit on the "service," so Gina didn't care either way when it came to the guy's response (if he didn't come, he'd just fake it with his dick still inside her), and although she had forsworn heroin, cocaine and sedatives, she still worshipped the 750 ml bottle as surely as the "priests" worshipped the multi-breasted Diana. She was able to distance "herself," whatever it was that made her "her," from the body that went through the motions of sex in front of a room full of strangers. She separated herself from the lipsticked lips that rode his erect penis, rhythmically moving up and down the shaft with a voraciousness that sometimes even surprised herself; her trusty, muscular right hand keeping the flagpole upright and the testicles part of the show.

As she sat in the room, shifting her compact naked ass on the cold blue chair and fiddling with the poorly sewn gold lame' headdress and push-up bra, she thought about the fact that her greatest triumphs and greatest failures had occurred when she was drunk. Her most mundane musings and tragic conclusions were entertained and drawn, respectively, when she was drunk. She had been arrested for a number of offenses, had lost her license to a DUI, and had most recently been charged with misdemeanor assault when a long night of drinking was interrupted by a particularly bitchy teetotaling aunt who told her one too many times that she "wouldn't find the answer to her problems at the bottom of a bottle." The charges, however, were eventually dropped when the aunt found herself needing help making the mortgage payment on the decaying, asbestos-filled, 800-square-foot rambler she shared with her unemployed, two-timing, paranoid, meth-addicted boyfriend.

Gina sucked dicks for a living, but she was easily the most responsible member of her immediate (and most of her extended) family. Her mother was an alcoholic who lived off alimony payments and L&I. Her father was in prison for aggravated assault, burglary, mayhem, and felon in possession of a firearm. He wasn't getting out soon, if ever. The judge was only reluctantly considering his attorney's appeal of her "three strikes" ruling. Gina's sister was diagnosed as bipolar when she was eighteen after three suicide attempts and was finally committed as a "threat to herself and others" when she abducted a young cousin and drove their car into a 6-foot deep irrigation ditch filled with muddy water. The child was pulled unconscious from the water by a passerby ten minutes after Hannah climbed out the driver-side window, stumbled 100 yards down the road and lept from a steel girder bridge into the Mansfield River. A state patrol chopper picked her up on its infrared scope a half mile downstream where she was apprehended by a couple of pissed-off, soaked-to-the-skin county sheriff deputies. She was ruled incompetent to stand trial (not even close), and eventually was committed indefinitely to the state hospital for the criminally insane. There, she was doped up and restrained for so long she developed bed sores. A lawsuit was filed, but Gina's family had a hard time showing up for court, let alone putting on a good face, even when hundreds of thousands of dollars were at stake; and they eventually settled for a much smaller, undisclosed sum that paid off a few debts, the lawyer, Uncle Sam (who was about to foreclose on two of the extended family's homes in an effort to recoup unpaid back taxes), and nothing more.

Ruby was the boss ("head priestess") of the "temple," and she appreciated the fact that Gina was always on time, even when she was drunk; and that she never missed a day of work (even when she was drunk). Away from work, Gina always paid the rent on time, was almost never late picking up her daughter, and deposited money into a savings account from each paycheck she received. She only partied when one of her trusted friends agreed to baby-sit. She sucked dicks for a living, but she was bettering herself, protecting her daughter and planning for the future. Jim Beam helped gloss over the rest. God bless Jim Beam.

Her cell phone vibrated on the vanity. She picked up the petite, color-screen phone with a Disney Tinkerbell faceplate and read the text message: "You're on!" She turned off the phone and stashed it in her purse; locked the purse, vibrator, lubricant, Jim Beam and the book about Jungian psychology Ruby gave her to read in a combination safe bolted to the floor beneath the vanity; adjusted her headdress and bra, checked the straps on her 4-inch high heels, and walked out into the dimly-lit, bare hallway. It was cold and her nipples reacted accordingly. Her heels clacked loudly on the cement floor. The customers, she thought, would have found the sound provocative. Fucking perverts, sex offenders, lonely old guys, sheltered young guys, macho dudes thinking they'd score a free ride after the "service," the curious, the horny, the moved. She was glad it cost $25 to get in: that weeded out most of the street-crazies.

Her heart beat a little faster and she hated that. Stage fright. She slipped into the swaying "sexy walk" she used during the two short weeks she danced at a "traditional" strip club, but began to laugh and had to stop for a moment to collect herself before

170

opening the brown door and stepping into the "temple." An unknown number of guys sat in "pews" behind the one-way glass.

Rick reclined in a chaise lounge beneath a papier-mâché statue of the goddess Diana. At least three of the goddess' breasts were cracked and ready to fall from her chest. Flecks of newspaper, paint, and flour-water paste clung to Rick's ample chest hair and feathered coiffe like dandruff. He absentmindedly worked his circumcised, limp penis like a cow's udder in reverse beneath the surface of his polyester toga, ignoring the one-way windows and thinking about the new big screen TV he planned to buy if he landed a role in the next Natasha Spy flick. Natasha was a royal cunt, but the pay was good and the director moved the production along at a decent pace.

He picked at his nose a bit with the index finger of his free hand and watched "the priestess" slowly approach him with dramatic, measured steps; her head reverently bowed; her hands outstretched, palms up, before her. The strains of a techno-symphony swelled as Gina raised her manicured hands to heaven and threw her head back to look up at the statue of Diana beseechingly. Her nipples were hard and erect. The hair flip was actually one of the moves she used at the strip club when her hair was still long and blonde. Guys used to cheer when she flipped her hair like that. Then she'd give them a sly, knowing look and do the "sexy walk" to the nearest brass pole where she'd swing about once and then magically remove her top the second time around.

A white spotlight burst into life, shining down on Gina with beatific candle-power and enough heat to bring beads of perspiration to her heavily made-up forehead. Trenchcoat guy doubled as the lights and sound man. After a few dramatic moments, the music thundered with bass as the spotlight was cut, and green floor lights positioned out of sight beneath the one-way windows shone upon Gina and Rick as he pulled his toga up and she slipped out of her gold g-string and heels. Really, most of the "acting" was done at this point. Now all she had to do was move through a series of positions, making sure to keep Rick hard and to present the action in such a way that the "congregation" could clearly see where "the rubber met the road," as Ruby always said, quoting an old-time radio preacher to whom her parents listened religiously.

Gina had the routine down, moving through half a dozen typical positions like clockwork. Giving head, receiving cunnilingus, riding him forward, riding him backwards, taking it doggy style, doing it missionary with her legs up and over his shoulders, and then back to giving head until the "money shot" upon her beautiful breasts (if the guy made it that far). Fortunately, the female owner of the "church" forbade facials, so it was either on her ass or her breasts, neither of which bothered her much. All the "priests" and "priestesses" were tested for STDs monthly, and were tested randomly for intravenous drug use. Ruby didn't care about drugs as long as there weren't disease-spreading needles involved and as long as you showed up to work every day and did a good job. For the sake of general hygiene and to help put her mind at ease when the whiskey wore off, Gina washed herself with anti-bacterial soap from head to toe after each service, douched, and usually stood in the shower for 20 – 30 minutes. The "temple" used to be the first floor of a hotel and the ancient boilers were still in place down in the basement. They provided a shower that seemed as hot and forceful as a jet engine blast. She knew her routine wouldn't protect her from AIDs, and she considered making the guys use a condom, but tips always tailed off when she did, and in the end she chose a dose of denial instead.

By all accounts, she was the best actress when it came to giving blowjobs. The audiences preferred her, the actors preferred her, and the owner preferred her. Her "services" brought in the most "parishioners" by far, and the offering plate set up near the exit was almost always overflowing with "love offerings" in the form of tens and twenties, often paper-clipped to personal notes written on Post-Its, old receipts, paper napkins, etc. In part it was her style: she didn't twist her head in 45-degree arcs like some girls did. This looked goofy and tended to make the audience slightly dizzy as they tried to follow the action. Neither did she stupidly, unemotionally run up and down the guy's erection like an anonymous engine piston. She had great lips, both top and bottom, and if she had learned nothing else in life, she learned to exploit her assets. She truly sucked dick. She moved up and down like she needed to, but the lips moved about the shaft and head, at perigee and apogee, in an almost supernatural sensuousness, like a fucking incubus, insanely-green eyes looking up from above the sweet, red, full-lipped mouth full of cock. Her eyes, God, her eyes, they looked up with impossibly simultaneous aggression and submission, and she made sure to look through the one-way windows several times during the "service," as if making eye contact with the congregation sitting in the dark. The way she lingered over the head, not just to flicker-lick it like the porn stars do, but to truly worship it, never seemed trite or rehearsed partly because she never worshipped just Rick's dick or Frank's or Saul's. No, she worshipped the archetypical dick, the phallus, the mana. At least that was what Ruby said, and although Ruby seemed to believe in that shit more than she did, the books she loaned her described a world that closely resembled her own in terms of sexuality, love, power and truth. The latest, a book by Charles Jung, described a source of truth called the collective unconscious: Jung wrote that the "collective unconscious" contains the spiritual life and history of mankind. Gina didn't believe in God. God was for people with three-car garages and timeshares in Aspen, not for girls like her. So, being able to tap into the comprehensive psychic reality of all humankind from the dawn of time to the present, seemed as close to godhood as she could imagine someone attaining. The idea that every one of the billions upon billions of human beings who had ever walked the earth or who walked the earth today, shared a consciousness of some kind was extremely comforting to her. It made humankind sound more like a family and less like the disconnected, chaotic assortment of isolated, lonely creatures she sometimes felt it to be. She hadn't read enough to know whether Jung himself thought about it this way, but one thing she believed was that truth was truth no matter who brought it to the table. Great Minds could get you started and save you a lot of time, but the fact that you believed something that the Great Mind did not, didn't necessarily mean you were wrong. Ruby said that "mana" was the word Jung used to describe the power derived from, and intrinsic in, the collective unconscious. People from the beginning of time worshipped entities representing power beyond the realm of the conscious human experience. Often, these entities were represented by idols emphasizing virility and fertility. Male figures with enormous phalluses and female figures with enormous vaginas or multiple breasts like the goddess Diana. Even Christianity was not exempt from the influence of this paradigm. The officially sanctioned Adoration of Mary actually began shortly after the arrival of Christian teachings in Ephesus. In order to effectively install Christianity as the predominant religion, early Church leaders sought to co-opt the Cult of Diana's fervor and focus by replacing Diana with the Virgin Mary. Mary was even given several of Diana's titles. The first time Gina was in Ruby's office; a crowded chaotic collection of computer equipment, stacks of paper, books, pictures (including several of the Virgin), and knick-knacks more closely resembling the working space of a stereotypical absentminded professor than the owner of a live sex show; she picked up a figurine made from clay. It was a male figure clad only in a loincloth. A giant penis, easily the size of the gentleman's leg, extended upwards from beneath the loincloth. She laughed as she picked it up: "Sure hope he doesn't work for you, Ruby. I wouldn't be able to walk for weeks after servicing that guy." Ruby laughed.

"So tell me this. If the collective unconscious is in the brain, why the hell does he have a huge cock? I think they got the wrong head."

Ruby smiled and said simply, "THAT, Gina, is exactly what I'm trying to find out." Gina remembered Ruby seeming genuinely pleased with the question, almost giddy in fact, as if by uttering it, Gina had identified herself as a kindred spirit, a woman who questioned life (embracing Jung's "animus"), rather than accepting the worldview of her family or the men who inevitably tried to control them. She knew that most people figured she was a crackpot or a cynical businesswoman using the "temple's" categorization as a church to avoid paying taxes and complying with city codes regulating adult entertainment, but here at least, was a woman who might just stand beside her. And Gina was indeed willing to give her the benefit of a doubt, even though she sometimes got the impression that Ruby was turned on by more than her kindred spirit.

Sure enough, it wasn't long before the cops, the city council, and several downtown churches heard about the activities going on in the "temple," and ridiculed Ruby's faith as "fantasy" and "sacrilege" on the 5:00 Evening News. Gina, however, stood by Ruby as the Armani-clad investigative reporters grilled her with unabashed condescension, arguing that she was selling out to male sexist fantasies and was no better than a two-bit madame exploiting down-on-their-luck young women. Ruby, however, performed well on camera and Gina's eloquent support played well with the viewers. Alternative newspapers fashioned them into folk heroes, standing up for "the new sexuality" against an anal-retentive, prudish city government.

In feet and inches, the young man's hard dick was closer to Gina's taut, tan, compact ass than any of his drunk compatriots'. He stared forward, mouth slightly agape, nose mere inches from the smudged one-way glass, like the stereotypical kid peering through the window of a Main Street toy store in some twisted Norman Rockwell painting. "God," his breath fogged the glass, and he drunkenly wiped it off with the sleeve of his t-shirt. He felt more euphoric than the alcohol justified: "What the fuck is this?" he wondered to himself. He was abso-fucking-lutely bewitched. No other way to describe it. If Gina's head had spun about three times and she had spewed out a hefty stream of slimy green effluent, it would have made no difference. He would have done her bidding: sacrilege, assault, armed robbery, whatever. He was bought and paid for. He was committed: he saw no discrepancy, he saw no conflict, no contradiction, no complication, no caveats. He was hers and he submitted his soul for her appraisal like a British widow offering up an heirloom wall-clock LIVE on the Antique Roadshow. The low lights and his intoxication combined to airbrush away Gina's stretch marks, moles and the three pimples on her back. She was more than a young, underemployed mom about to suck some lucky bastard's dick. She was an Ideal. An Archetype. She was Sensuality and Beauty and Lust personified. The young man forgot about the companions around him. He did not hear the music, did not recognize the existence of Rick's face, nor did he notice his buddy Joe not-so-subtly masturbating through his jeans.

Derek, seated two pews back and snorting a line of cocaine off the back of his hand, told him years ago that the secret to enjoying a strip club is the suspension of disbelief. Like any novel, movie or play, you've got to allow a little artistic license, a little liberty, if you're going to get the full benefit. And the young man allowed the artistic license. He didn't speculate about how many infants may have suckled at her less-than-pristine breasts. He didn't wonder whether the calmness with which she approached the reclined man indicated a state of intoxication and possibly a drinking problem. Nor did he think about the kind of relationships she may have had to endure, the abuse she may have suffered at the hands of men who considered her a whore deserving only to be kept in line. No, it was all about her near-perfect body, her explicit sexuality and the voracious look in her haunting, green eyes. Without those eyes, without the million strands of communication streaming outward from her starburst irises like pulsing, light-filed fiber optics; without the dark mystery of her wide black pupils, she'd just be a body. A fucking hot body, to be sure, but merely a body, nonetheless.

She looked down at Rick's erect dick and took it slowly, aggressively, fully in her mouth, taking it in until it hit the back of her throat and her lips brushed his testicles, before moving up and down, backing off a bit and then turning her head just enough to look out through the one-way glass towards the pew in which the young man sat. She looked at him as if the glass did not exist, as if she could see into the darkness, and the corners of her mouth turned up as she smiled with Rick's dick still held firmly between her Molly Ringwold lips and naturally straight, white teeth. If she had reached out and grabbed the young man by the balls, he would have been no more attentive, no more rapt than he was at that moment. She effortlessly, unconsciously consumed him with her eyes like a force of nature, a black hole devouring a solar system millions of light years away from earth. And that's where he felt himself to be: in a different world, thanks to the alcohol, the hour of the night and the darkness. Suspension of disbelief. Fucking A.

He looked at her hair, the curvature of her back, her ass and her shapely legs, and finally her small, perfectly feminine feet. She was curling her toes, slowly in and then slowly out, while she earnestly, sublimely worked Rick's penis with her mouth. Her toenails were painted gold like the bra she'd removed and the headdress still adorning her short red spiked hair. Those feet belonged on a beach somewhere, a sandy beach baked and bleached by an unforgiving, tropical sun, and washed by gentle aquamarine waves. There was white sand covering the floor of the "temple," and her toes caressed its grains with the same care that her elegant, manicured hands caressed Rick's abdomen and groin. Yeah, those feet belonged on a beach someplace very far away, and the young man thought of her footsteps in the sand at sunset. The aquiline curve, the gentle toe prints. There was something sublime about her footprints: he wanted to touch them, signs of her supernatural beauty made manifest in an earthly medium.

He stared at her footprints in the sand on the "temple" floor for a moment wondering why they struck a chord of recognition within him. As much as he'd moved to Southern California for the sun and beaches, he couldn't handle the crowds and rarely went. He was just about to dismiss the sense of familiarity as yet another facet of the fervent wishful thinking in which he was engaged at the moment, when he realized that they reminded him of a time many years before when he was a young boy stay-

ing with his great aunt and uncle in a mobile home park surrounded on all sides by the Oregon Dunes. Every morning he'd
wake up early, just as the sun was beginning to rise. The deer
were returning to their beds, etching their hoof prints in the dew-
dampened sands. One year he brought plaster of Paris, mixed it
with water and poured it into the indentations of the prints.
When he came back a few hours later, the plaster was hard and
he pulled it from the sand like a trophy.

Sometimes, he'd catch a glimpse of one, its white tail disappearing into the firs, tall grass and salal. The prints would dry in the
sun and gradually disintegrate as the wind swept up and down
the dunes. He'd wander back to the mobile home park, smelling
the bacon frying and coffee brewing, and his uncle would be sitting on the Astroturf porch smoking a dark wooden pipe, the
pungent sweet smoke curling up around his head and disappearing into the morning. Later, they'd go fishing in a nearby creek,
so shallow that only a few cool, dark holes were deep enough to
hold the 10-inch trout his aunt would fry up for dinner. Three
times a day, his uncle hung from a chin-up bar mounted between
two posts, to ease the pain in his back. He was tall and thin, and
could almost touch the bar if he stood on his tiptoes and
stretched his long, thin arms upward; calloused hands reaching
for the cold steel. Because of his back, he couldn't lift the boy
up, so he'd have to shimmy up one of the posts himself if he
hoped to hang down like his uncle.

One morning out on the dunes, he noticed small human footprints following those of a large buck. He figured it was a girl
about his age. The prints were almost the same size as his, and it
looked like she wore a ring around her right big toe. He pulled
off his own shoes and socks, stashed a sock in each shoe, and set
them neatly beside a small patch of dune grass, before making
his own prints next to those of the girl. And so the three traveled
across the sand, none of them seeing the other, but all following
the exact same path, separated only by time. Neither the deer
nor the girl had been in a hurry. Each set of prints were produced by almost perfectly vertical actions. No scraping or

sliding or scattered sand. He walked for fifteen minutes, losing the trail once when it intersected a rocky patch of ground where crystalline, mineral-rich rock lay crushed and scattered about. He picked it up again on the other side, and before long he saw a girl sitting on a log at the edge of a stand of firs, a hundred yards ahead. She did not look up as he approached but sat quietly with her hands in her lap and her head bowed a bit, as if she were looking at something on the ground.

The sun was slowly burning through the morning fog, appearing occasionally as a mysterious two-dimensional white disk, still low in the sky, before disappearing once again, obliterated by the grey mist. A few songbirds rehearsed the day's trills and a crow battled a fast food wrapper caught in a thorn bush. No breeze. Quiet. The occasional sound of a squirrel dropping a fir cone to the ground sounded muffled, dead. When he drew near to the girl, he noticed she was crying. Not bawling or sobbing, but just sitting there quietly with tears slowly rolling down her cheeks. She had long dark hair and wore cut-offs and a tank top. She shivered occasionally, but gave no indication that she was aware of his presence. He sat for a while at the far end of the log, thinking she'd look up eventually, but when she didn't, he resorted to making coughing noises, clearing his throat, and finally speaking.

"You OK?" he asked, expecting the girl to leap up startled. But she didn't move. Not a muscle. She was still crying. He tried again. Finally, she nodded her head, ever so slightly and wiped her nose with her hand, still looking down.

"I have to leave today," she said quietly, "and I didn't see a deer. Not a single one."

"They're awfully hard to see, really. You got to be pretty lucky."

"I followed this one all the way out here and now I can't find any more tracks. And when I go back, I'll have to leave." She played in the sand with her toes. A sliver and jade ring adorned her right foot's big toe.

"They're all sleeping now. They'll be deep in the brush. They're hard to find in there. It would take a long time."

"I know. I tried that last year. That's why I'm sitting here."

The boy had an idea and offered to walk her back. He told her he had a surprise that might make her feel better.

"You're staying with the Staffords, aren't you?" she asked quietly, peering up a bit with her head still bowed. She asked what his name was. "I was right," she said, smiling for the first time. Your aunt and uncle are friends of my grandparents. We're four trailers down, by the cabana.

"I thought you were going to jump out of your seat back there, but you didn't."

"I knew you were following my tracks. I looked back from the top of that last big dune and saw you far away, coming closer."

As they walked back, following the three sets of tracks in reverse, the young man looked off to the west and saw that someone had drawn something on the side of a dune with a stick. It appeared to be a heart, some twenty feet wide, with something written inside, now partially obliterated.

"What's that?"

"I made it."

"What's it for? What's it say inside?"

"It used to say a name."

The boy looked at the girl. She smiled at him, peering up with big green eyes, her head still halfway bowed.

"Can't tell," she said and then raced back to the mobile home park.

The young man "came to" as Rick was saying something to Gina. She reached back under herself with her right hand and fondled his balls as he thrust himself into her over and over again. His face tightened and he turned up toward the statue of Diana. He wasn't acting. He always looked up right before he came. Which he did, immediately after withdrawing from Gina's pussy and stroking his long cock once, twice, three times. His semen shot out upon her ass, still moving slightly, slowly unwinding from the preceding five minutes of grinding. Rick continued working his dick before finally dropping his head and hands as the lights fell. When the lights came back on, a curtain had been drawn across the window and Trenchcoat guy was standing on the opposite side of the room, motioning towards the exit and an offering plate sitting upon a four-foot tall wooden Roman column. The offering plate reminded the young man of the one he had at home.

"Thank you gentlemen. Thank you for joining our worship service. As you exit, please leave any "love offerings" you may wish to give Priestess Gina in the offering plate. The next service begins in half an hour and will be led by Priestess Amber. I'll join you at the entrance momentarily."

Although he didn't say so, the "offerings" would be divided three ways between Rick, Gina and himself: 35%, 55% and 10%, respectively. It hadn't taken long for everyone to realize that they received five times more tip money when they said it was all for Gina, than they did when they mentioned the guys were getting a cut. Trenchcoat guy also got 5% of all the door fees plus minimum wage, so the more people he packed in, the more money he left with each morning.

181

As the men filed out of the "sanctuary," vulgarly praising the virtues of Priestess Gina and marveling that the establishment had not been shut down by the authorities, Trenchcoat guy kept an eye on the offering plate, mentally tallying the take; and visually checked out the "sanctuary," making sure no one had spooged on a pew or left any syringes or trash. He looked up at the plexiglass panels depicting the ancient worship of Diana. They needed a good dusting. He'd attend to that tomorrow, before the first service. Ruby purchased the panels for a hundred dollars on eBay from a conspiracy theorist being charged with tax evasion. He had planned on building a Center for Truth in his hometown of Flint, Michigan, dedicated to unveiling the secrets of the coming New World Order and the unholy alliance between the Illuminati, the U.S. Federal Government and sinister forces of the occult. The panels Ruby bought were part of a planned display illustrating how rogue CIA and British Intelligence operatives murdered Princess Diana in order to prevent her boyfriend, an Arab, from joining the royal family and someday becoming stepfather to the king.

Diana, like the rest of the royal family, the Flint native claimed, was deeply involved in the occult. So deeply involved, in fact, that the forces of evil had all but achieved a resurrection of the ancient Cult of Diana, with further funding to be obtained upon her marriage to the multi-millionaire. Somewhere along the line the Masons and brainwashing were involved, but Trenchcoat Guy had become confused at that point in Ruby's narrative. If he was ever curious enough, she advised, the whole story was on the conspiracy theorist's website.

"Goddamned bitch," Traci muttered, pulling off her headset and tilting backwards in her chair until she was looking at the speckled off-white ceiling tiles. "Goddamned, motherfucking bitch." A few of her teammates cupped their hands over their headset microphones and glared at Traci. The young man also heard, and as he looked up at the object of his current infatuation, he noticed a middle-aged woman in a conservative blouse and skirt enter through one of the far doors. She was looking at several papers in her hands and nodding and smiling at various customer care "ambassadors," silently mouthing their names as she walked by.

"Shit." When the young man's gaze returned to Traci, she was looking right at him. They made eye contact and the young man thought "What the hell?" and walked directly over to her, leaving the clipboard in a vacant cube.

"I don't really work here."

"Duh."

"This girl stopped me on the street and started asking me questions and she was kinda cute so I followed her up these stairs and then realized I had been kinda tricked, and bailed on the receptionist. Can you tell me how the hell I get out of here?" Traci looked across the sea of cubes at the approaching woman. It was her supervisor.

"So you're an escapee, hunh? Yeah, I can tell you how to get out of here. YOU get out by helping ME get out," she smiled deviously. "Follow my lead. Your name is Ted. Don't fuck this up and we'll go for a cab ride."

"Fuckin A," the young man thought. "Cool, I'm Ted."

Traci's name was up on the monitors again. Apparently she had hit the same button she hit when she went out the heavy metal door earlier. The glares around her intensified. The middle-aged woman, sensing something was amiss, pushed her eyeglasses up into place and looked up at the nearest monitor and then over at Traci and the young man. Her face tightened a bit and she began walking towards them, still trying to quietly greet reps along the way. A few more names appeared on the overhead monitors as other "ambassadors" chose to watch the scene unfold before them without the distraction of another call ringing through.

"Cheryl, this is my cousin Ted. He came to the front desk looking for me because his mother, my aunt, was just in a car wreck. She's going to be alright, but the whole family is heading down to the hospital to see her. They're keeping her overnight."

"Traci, we just had a discussion regarding your attendance. I haven't even had time to type up the "Note to File," and now you're leaving an hour-and-a-half before your shift ends? This will put you at the limit. You could lose your job tomorrow."

"Cheryl," she responded in a patronizingly patient and overly familiar tone, "what would YOU do in this situation? I understand you have a job to do, but I've got responsibilities to my family. My aunt could have died today. Thank God she didn't. I need to be there for her."

Cheryl's face grew redder as she struggled to maintain her composure in front of her employees and keep the volume of her voice as low as possible. Sensing the attention their interaction was garnering, she shoved her glasses up with her index finger once more and quickly peered up at the overhead monitors. Six names suddenly disappeared, and with a cynical grin, she turned to Traci.

"Traci, why is it that the only time I hear about your family," she nearly whispered, "is when you're missing work? Other people who have families talk about spending the weekend with them, going on vacation with them, going to their houses for dinner after work. Your teammates tell me the stories with which you regale them on breaks and lunch, and I don't recall a single reference to your aunt or your mom, your step-brother or your great-grandma. Why is it that you're the only Fleisser in this city until tragedy strikes?" The young man made a mental note of her surname while Cheryl mulled over the realization that her anger and frustration were eating away at the decorum and tact that usually kept her in "the clear" with the Human Resources folks when it came to personnel issues. She had crossed the line. She knew it, and so did Traci.

Traci was calm. She knew she had won, and yet her face still showed the concern she felt for her fictional aunt's well-being, and even a bit of empathy for Cheryl's frustration and burden of responsibility. She looked away abruptly for a moment, and lifted a ring-festooned right hand to her mouth, blinking quickly. Her delicately proportioned hands were worn and weathered, calloused and scarred, with prominent knuckles, quite unlike what you'd expect to see with someone who talked on the phone and typed on a computer all day. Cheryl rolled her eyes and sighed in disgust. She didn't notice Traci's hands. She was looking out at the sea of direct reports and mentally tallying those whom she felt contributed to the company's success and those whom detracted from it. Then, she returned her focus directly into Traci's dusky emerald eyes. Traci accepted the challenge and maintained eye contact. The young man looked at her darkly-lined lips.

"Cheryl, you do what you have to do, and I'll do what I have to do. I'm not asking for special treatment, just to be treated fairly. But I have to go." She blinked quickly several times and turned away. The young man marveled at her acting abilities. He wondered whether she was in theater. He pictured her in a period piece with a corset and hoopskirt like Helena Bonham Carter. He wondered how grateful she'd be when they got outside, and realized almost instantaneously that he was dreaming if he thought he'd get anything from this chick. She was holding the cards. He couldn't even think of something clever to say to facilitate their escape. Instead, he just stood there, comfortingly patting Traci's delectable shoulder and wishing he wasn't quite so befuddled with lust and amazement. He caught himself checking out her ass and quickly looked down at his shoes, hoping Cheryl hadn't caught him sizing up his "cousin." Fortunately, Cheryl's gaze hadn't budged. She looked into Traci's eyes as if to decipher a code or see something through a dirty window. Traci finally had to look away. Cheryl shook her conservatively clipped head, turned, and walked away: "I can't promise you you'll have a job tomorrow," she said over her shoulder desultorily. Traci, however, had already turned around, grabbed the young man's arm, hit five buttons on the phone console (erasing her name from the overhead monitor), hooked her purse (a pink, hard-sided retro number with a vinyl shoulder strap) and headed for the heavy metal doors with an ass-twitching stride that accentuated the escalated nature of her retreat.

No one applauded or smiled. She was an interesting diversion, but a dangerous friend, and she invariably weighed down whatever team was unlucky enough to count her as one of their own. And yet, the vast majority of the people in that vast cubicle-cluttered room knew something was up and couldn't resist gawking. And Traci knew they knew. She reveled in the attention, the notoriety and the infamy. She was tempted to turn around and fire a heroic f-bomb salvo at Cheryl's retreating figure for dramatic effect, but she knew this would simply be erasing a hard-fought victory and eliminating a job that paid an average wage with above-average benefits at a time when she could really use a few visits to the doctor. Her back hurt like hell, there was something wrong "down south," and she saw stars when she stood up too quickly. It was all probably nothing that a good multi-vitamin, a gallon of cranberry juice and some Darjeeling couldn't clear up, but she might as well wait until the doc checked her out before she burned this bridge. So instead, she smiled smugly and soaked in the attention, negative though it was.

When the heavy steel doors closed behind them with a satisfying double-click, she released the young man's arm (to his dismay) and let out a relieved sigh as she fell back against the beige-painted stairwell wall. He watched her breasts heave upward and fall several times before she shook her shocking orange head to-and-fro, handlebar pigtails flipping about with the motion, and opened her eyes, catching the young man scoping out her

186

tits. She smirked as he quickly averted his head, and noting the hard-on he'd developed, she sighed.

"Did you see the people in there, Ted?" she asked, as if conducting a television interview or another version of the very survey responsible for his current predicament. In response, he told her his real name. She didn't seem to hear. "As we were walking out back there, Ted, did you see them sneaking looks, all guilty-like, twisting around as we left the room, like people gawking at a rollover accident on the fucking freeway?" Her laugh was a barroom laugh full of sex, cigarettes, warm beer and punk rock. He imagined her laughing at the men she'd left behind, mocking them and their pitiful need for her ass, tits, lips, pussy and attention.

The young man told her his real name again. "I heard you the FIRST time, Ted. Look, fuckchop, I don't really give a flying fuck what your name is. Those people back there? You're just like them." She paused, a smile slowly growing on her face: "You are, aren't you? HA! Oh honey, don't feel bad. It's not your fault. Sweetie, that's the way life is: millions and millions of people who have absolutely no connection to anything REAL." He stood there looking at her, his smile gone, his face growing warm with embarrassment. "Do you know why they were watching ME?" she continued, pointing her finger back in the direction of the other "ambassadors."

"Do you know why they put themselves into 'aftercall,' jeopardizing their own pitiful quarterly bonus and undermining their team's pitiful productivity? Because they were watching something closer to REALITY than anything else in their fucking pitiful lives." She spat the words venomously, contemptuously, tossing her head about in a way the young man would have found provocative if not for the emasculating tone of her tirade. The door through which they exited began to open and Traci bolted down the stairs, much more quickly in her tall boots than the young man would have thought possible, swinging on the steel pipe handrails at each landing and careening down the next flight with childish abandon. Disgusted with himself for having been duped by cute girls twice in as many hours, the young man slowly, dejectedly followed her down the stairs, listening to her heels echo off the cement below, resigned to going his own way, alone, as soon as he hit the street.

Upon reaching the bottom of the stairwell, Traci threw her slight frame against the steel push-bar of the door on the left and burst out into the stale, hot, smoggy daylight. The door swung out-ward with enough force to knock over anyone foolish enough to have been standing in front of it, and bounced backward with surprising elasticity toward the young man who was just reach-ing the ground floor, forcing him to throw up a forearm in self-defense, only to see the hydraulic door return catch the rebound and slow the door to a crawl before it made contact. The young man, untouched and humiliated, slowly lowered his left forearm and let if fall to his side, as he watched Traci hurrying down the dumpster-filled alleyway toward the street.

Out of stubbornness, if nothing else, he caught up with her and stood determinedly beside her as she hailed a cab. He furtively, absentmindedly glanced down her shirt, relishing the brief glimpse of her smooth, round breasts pushed upward with a deli-cate black lace bra. There was a brown birthmark on the left one. He felt for his wallet, figuring he'd end up paying, and marveled at the volume of the fingerless whistle with which she pierced the air and his left ear. A green taxi, identical to the one that pulled to the curb when he foolishly stopped to answer the first girl's questions, cut off a battered red compact pickup and careened to within two feet of his shoes, brakes screeching. Out of habit, he reached for the door handle to let her in, but she was too fast and he was left having to dive into the backseat beside her as she rattled off directions to the cabbie. He reached back behind him and grabbed the door closed a split-second before it would have slammed into a weathered two-door Toyota parked at the curb with a parking ticket tucked under the driver-side windshield wiper.

As he pulled himself upright he looked down at his left hand tightly gripping the worn vinyl upholstery mere inches from Traci's right hip. Her black polyester skirt was riding high, and he sensed that a glimpse of her panties (if she was wearing any) was mere centimeters away, but instead of fabricating an excuse to bend down and look back up, he righted himself and leaned back confidently into the seat, slouching and pushing his knees upward in front of himself.

Traci pulled a black flask from her purse, swallowed three times and handed it over to the young man who watched the girl in unadulterated adoration as he tipped the flask back and swallowed three times as well. He wanted to look into her eyes as the vodka vapors dissipated in his mouth, but she stared forward over the cabbie's right shoulder, watching the street signs and toying with the stud in her delectably pink tongue. He looked at her ears, her miniature pigtails, her breasts, arms, thighs and tall black boots. Traci brought her chin down to her chest, turned her head and peered sidelong at the young man with her heavily made-up eyes.

"Whatcha doing, Ted?" she asked softly, smiling slyly.

The young man looked directly into her eyes. She met his gaze and held it, still smiling, still looking sideways at him as the taxi moved through traffic. God, he loved it when girls looked right back at him, unflinchingly. Her eyes and the taste of vodka in his mouth made him brave: "I'm looking at you," he said. She smiled, turned her head away, and looked down at her boots for a moment. She rubbed a smudge from her left boot with her thumb. Although the boots were old, she wore them more often than anything else. Traci slowly brought herself upright, arching her back in a feline stretch, and then looked outside at the people on the sidewalk. The cab stopped for a red light and the young man noticed a couple of young men, about his age, walking along with their arms around each other. His first thought was that they were drunk, but he quickly realized, upon seeing two middle-aged women with stereotypically short haircuts and dangly, metal earrings holding hands at a crosswalk, that their taxi had entered one of the city's gay enclaves. Aside from a McDonald's and a Starbucks, he didn't recognize any of the businesses. Nor did he recognize the names of the streets.

The light turned green and the cab accelerated. The young man looked to his right and saw a red stoop and a heavy, red metal door with a rectangular peep hole like the old speakeasies had back in the 1920s. There were no signs, just a five-digit number painted in black on a red canvas awning over the door. It seemed strangely familiar, but in a few moments it was behind them and out of sight.

He sat quietly, straining to figure out why that anonymous establishment struck him with such familiarity. Had he seen it on the news or online? The young man's face was screwed up in concentration. Traci, meanwhile, was preparing to exit the cab. She looked up ahead, about a block down on the right side of the street; and a few moments later, suddenly perked up and offered a feminine half-wave to someone waiting on the sidewalk. The cab slowed and pulled to the curb.

"Excuse me honey," she said, as she unselfconsciously moved past the young man, her right pigtail, breast, hip and black leather boot electrifying the four points of contact on his body. But then she was gone. He looked up and saw her embracing a woman about their age, maybe a little older; with long, elegant brown hair, a knee-length black skirt, white blouse with wide cuffs, black high heels, and a black leather attaché. Traci's perfume still hung in the air. The young man inhaled deeply as he forgot himself and stared stupidly at the two women kissing. When they finished, Traci turned around, stepped back to the curb, and bent over to address the young man.

"Hey Ted, thanks for the ride," she said quietly. "By the way, in case you didn't realize it, you're cute. And if I weren't a dyke, I'd be taking you upstairs right now and fucking your brains out." She smiled broadly, carefully closed the door making sure the young man's hands, feet and head were safely inside like she would with a small child, spun around, cocked her head to one side and slowly walked up to her girlfriend, ass twitching from side to side, to kiss her again, laughing.

"Where to?" the cabbie asked, accelerating away from the curb and entering traffic in front of a U-Haul truck with Arizona plates. Still confused and distracted, the young man muttered the name of the drugstore he'd been heading to before stopping to talk to the girl with the clipboard. He settled back into the seat, lifted his pelvis up and pulled his wallet from the back pocket of his jeans. It was a good thing he'd double-checked his cash before getting into the cab. As it was, half of the money he had set aside for the drugstore would be used on the cab ride.

He closed the wallet and put it between his legs on the seat so it'd be handy. The scent of Traci's perfume was quickly re-placed by the worn-out smell of the cab and the city around him. He replayed the scene of Traci kissing her girlfriend over and over in his head. God. If they had been naked, it would have been as good or better than any girl-on-girl porn flick he'd ever seen. It was real. He could have watched them kiss all after-noon. And then he suddenly remembered where he'd seen that red door before. Almost a year ago, after a night of drinking with his friends, he'd split cab fare with one of his gay friends, Jerry. Halfway home, Jerry decided he wasn't ready to call it a night, and instead asked the young man if he'd like to see what it's like inside one of the city's most notorious and exclusive gay sex clubs. Jerry knew two of the doormen and had dated one of the bouncers: sometimes he got in and sometimes he didn't. While the bathhouses in the neighborhood had for the most part been shut down by aggressive, persistent police raids and equal-ly aggressive AIDS prevention efforts, there were still a few clubs around in which you could make your way past a buffet of sexual dishes, all available, for a price of course, with no ques-tions asked. The cover charge, usually a hefty sum, guaranteed your right to be a spectator and the opportunity to "pay and play." He never made it inside. Both he and Jerry were very drunk, but he was faring the worse out of the two. As they pulled up to the curb a couple hundred feet from the entrance, the young man opened the door and puked in the gutter, almost falling out of the taxi. Jerry grabbed his shirt and hauled him back into the cab when he stopped heaving and then told the cabbie to take them home. "So that's where I was that night," thought the young man.

The cab passed a decrepit x-rated theater with faded posters of buff, shirtless men; passed through a major intersection and three blocks later entered an African-American community. It was as if he had crossed an international border. The young man marveled at the degree of segregation that still existed in his supposedly "modern" city. From 3rd to 15th, same-sex couples walked hand-in-hand. From 18th to Capitol Street, the majority of the people walking by were heterosexual African-Americans, and there wasn't a single openly gay couple walking hand-in-hand to be found. Both demographic groups were living freely and for the most part happily, but they were separated by a no man's land like that separating the two Koreas. On 15th, the First Community Unitarian Church was led by an openly gay female pastor who joyfully presided over same-sex unions. On 18th, fire and brimstone rained down from the pulpit upon Sodom and Gomorrah. Could Francisco's Martini Bar exist side-by-side with Momma Ruth's Soul Food Kitchen? The young man didn't know.

Lost in thought, the young man rode for another five minutes, not paying attention to where he was going, until the cab swung over to the curb and the cabbie turned around and told him the fare. Embarrassed to have been caught zoning, the young man blushed and gave the cabbie too big of a tip, climbed out and awkwardly walked away from the cab which quickly merged back into traffic and was gone. It was getting hot out, and the white sun shone down on the noisy street like a halogen bulb. He ran his fingers up and over the top of his closely-cropped head and down the back, spraying a mist of sweat behind him, and felt for his flask which wasn't there. A beer. He wanted a beer. Five doors down was an Italian restaurant that had just opened up for the day. The front was a folding wooden façade they opened on nice days allowing tables to spill out onto the sidewalk within an area bounded by a low, green steel fence. White-and-red checkered vinyl tablecloths covered each small round table. A glass container holding Sweet N Lo, Equal, and Sugar in the Raw; a bud vase with a real flower from the shop around the corner; and two round glass shakers of Parmesan cheese and crushed, dried red peppers sat on every table. The aromas of spicy sausage, tomatoes, garlic and freshly-made pasta had filled his nose before he even saw the place. The darkly stained wooden front door with two glass panes and a little red curtain was propped open with a cement-filled coffee can. Three faded peeling stickers on the door indicated the years in which the restaurant had been rated among the top ten Italian restaurants in the city. From the dates on the stickers, you had to assume that either the restaurant rating company or the restaurant itself had gone downhill the past few years. But all he wanted was a beer after all.

It was dark inside and the palpable, all-consuming presence of garlic nearly pushed him right back out the door through which he'd entered. A girl in a tight t-shirt bearing the restaurant's name and a monochrome depiction of its storefront as seen from the street, greeted him and showed him to one of the tables outside, one he had pointed at, off to the side in the corner, beside a potted Japanese Maple. She handed him a dog-eared lunch menu, rattled off a couple specials, and said somebody'd be out in just a second with some ice water. He had almost gone into the tavern next door, but it was dark and dirty inside and he wanted what passed for fresh air in the city. On a cold, rainy night, he had no problem secreting himself in a dark hole of a tavern like a hibernating bear in a cave, but during the day, he usually preferred to be outside in the sun, watching people go about their business.

Another girl, older than the first and wearing her oversized t-shirt untucked, brought out a large, burnt-sienna colored plastic tumbler full of ice-water and asked if he'd decided on something. He ordered a beer, and in deference to the delicious smells surrounding him, a small plate of spaghetti and meatballs with a side of garlic bread. What the hell: the bathtub mat could wait. The girl left and for the first time, the young man looked around to get his bearings. He saw the drugstore directly across the street and laughed to himself. It was the right chain, but definitely not the one near his apartment. He really didn't know where he was.

This part of town looked vaguely familiar, but he wished he had paid more attention to where he'd been taken. What the hell, he thought, it was his day off, the morning was already blown, and he had just sat down for a beer, so it could definitely be worse. The girl brought the beer. He drank down a third of it right away and then slouched in his chair and reveled in its flavor, watching the people go by. All these people and he didn't know a single one of them. All these people and no one's talking to each other. This is kind of what that movie was like, he thought, remembering an art-house flick he'd seen once with Brainiac. The movie was called "Wings of Desire." It was long, mostly black-and-white, and in German, but he remembered chills running up his spine as he watched these two angels, just your "average Joes" really, wander the earth watching the living human beings and listening to their thoughts, but never being able to actively engage them or make a human connection. He remembered thinking that if heaven was like that, he'd rather not go. As they left the theater, Braniac turned to him and said, "That's the way we all are, really. We're dropped into this world only to spend the rest of our lives trying to connect with something real. Those angels? That seemed more like hell than heaven to me." The young man remembered smiling broadly because he had thought the very same thing and he proceeded to tell her so. He looked around and thought for a fleeting moment that her bookstore might actually be nearby.

He finished the first beer just as the waitress brought the spaghetti and bread. She left to grab another beer and he began eating. The spaghetti sauce was a rich, dark, brick-red color, full of meat and onions and garlic. This, he thought, was the way spaghetti sauce should look and taste. The family-size can of Franco-American spaghetti he had at home was fine if you wanted a quick dinner that didn't taste anything like real spaghetti, but for chrissake, the sauce was orange and had carrots in the ingredients! What the fuck is that? Orange spaghetti sauce? He ate it on a regular basis nonetheless, always smothered with a quarter-inch layer of Parmesan cheese. The girl brought another beer and the young man enjoyed the food, the people walking by, the breeze and the glaring white sunshine. The smoggy sunshine made everything look black-and-white, just like that movie he'd seen with Braniac.

Some people took their time walking by, some people moved by quickly, weaving their way through the crowd: stop and smell the roses, and smell as many roses as possible, respectively. He was partial to the second crowd, when push came to shove. Life is damn short. Don't fucking waste time on worthless shit. If you're getting into something simple, like walking along the sidewalk; digging the texture, tuning into the way it feels beneath your feet, that's one thing. But to just walk slowly cause you're lazy or dense? That's fucked, he thought. "When I'm on my deathbed," he thought, "I don't want to think that I could have seen more of life if I'd only walked a little faster."

People walked by. Goofy, deformed, retarded, beautiful, average, brilliant, arrogant, afraid, oblivious people walked by. The young man drank his beer and watched the people pass by in the glaring white sun. The supply never ended. The stream was never stanched. People were popping out babies as quickly as people were dying, and they all ended up on the sidewalk in front of the Italian restaurant eventually.

The young man lifted the beer to his lips and drank thirstily. The lager satisfied his thirst and pleasantly buzzed his senses. Closing his eyes, he carefully set the pint glass back down on the red-and-white checkered vinyl tablecloth and tilted his face upwards toward the sun, soaking up its warmth like his dogs used to out on the back patio on the occasional Spring afternoon that turned warm back when he was growing up. The long, dark, wet winters of the Pacific Northwest, winters that flowed almost imperceptibly into long, wet, grey Springs, imbued dogs and humans alike with an almost demonic lust for sunshine that often erupted in orgies of sunglasses, swimming, yard work, biking, rollerblading, running, hiking, barbecues and trips to the beach as soon as summer approached and temperatures exceeded 65 degrees for more than two consecutive days.

Their two black labs Joey and Joani, brother and sister, were no exception: when the perpetual drizzle slowed and then stopped, and the sun rose in earnest for the first time of the year, they'd turn a circle or two, lazily lie down on the white, sun baked concrete, sometimes rolling completely on their backs in slow motion, bent legs held luxuriously upward at all angles, soaking up the warmth radiating upward from the patio and beating down from above. That was always a good day. After a day of sunbathing, they curled up together inside the oversized plywood doghouse his father built for them and slept some more.

The young man smiled at the memory for several moments, unaware of the busy street in front of him, the waitress who came out to see how he was doing, and the old man who was shown a table in the opposite corner. The smile on the young man's face, warm with sunshine and nostalgia, slowly faded, however, and his brow furrowed as he remembered the end of it all. On a frosty Autumn morning, the same day as the second game of the World Series, he found Joey dead, stiff and cold beside the doghouse, Joani curled up against him, shivering horribly.

Every morning, before he left for school, after cold cereal and cartoons, he stepped outside and checked their water, got them some breakfast and said hello. Usually, the sliding glass door would make enough noise to get them stirring inside their doghouse, intentionally placed beside the house and directly in front of the clothes dryer vent. Filled with cedar chips, it smelled good in the morning as the two dogs stretched and slowly poked their heads out of the rectangular door. An elaborate routine of yawns and stretching would follow, regardless of the weather, varying from day to day, and yet almost always the same. That morning, though, both dogs were outside, millions of slivers of frost mixed in with their fur, a small icicle of bloody drool hanging from the fur beneath Joey's left canine. He was on his side, but he didn't look right. It wasn't the same as when he rolled over. It looked more like he had been laying on the ground Sphinx-like, and had been unceremoniously tipped over like a trash can or a sawhorse, cemented to the ground by the frost, stiffened and hardened by rigor mortis.

Until that morning, the boy had always thought of death as he had been taught to think of death, as a peaceful "passing away;" unless of course you were fighting in a war or had cancer or were being tortured to death or something like that. Joey didn't look peaceful. Joey looked like he'd been through a little bit of hell on earth. His lips were curled back in the snarl he reserved for truly evil people, eyes open, nose dry, saliva-matted fur along his jaw. Joani looked up at the boy but stayed curled up beside Joey.

The young man could still remember the way in which she looked up at him that cold morning so many years ago: calmly, almost concerned, as if she were afraid he might take it hard and wanted to be strong for him. She seemed to know more than him. Animals weren't supposed to know more than humans. They were just stupid animals. But maybe, just maybe, Joey's last moments were etched in her memory, her dull-witted, loyal, loving Labrador memory: the way he had faced death, teeth bared, a low, gravelly growl rumbling out from his strong, thick throat, eyes searching the fence line for the invisible intruder. The boy wondered if he'd felt fear during those last few moments, if he'd realized that this particular intruder wouldn't run away at the sound of his bark. You shouldn't have to be afraid when you die. There shouldn't be panic in your blood. You should face your death bravely, calmly, like Joan of Arc, or Nathan Hale standing on the gallows, the rough hemp about his neck, with the composure and balls to say what he said. That was death. Heroic. Peaceful. Even joyous. That's what he learned at school and at Vacation Bible School. But this didn't seem peaceful or heroic.

Joani raised her head up slightly again, just enough to quietly whimper for a moment as if trying to speak, before placing her chin carefully down upon her folded paws once more. His Dad, already late for work, noticed something was wrong and came out and stood beside him for a few moments before exhaling loudly and telling him to get a shovel.

The boy slowly walked across the pockmarked, weed-ravaged lawn to the dilapidated, rusting metal shed from Sears, filled with decomposing chemicals and fertilizers, lined up on rotting, pressed-wood shelves; and an assortment of busted-up lawn tools. He jerked and pulled the dented, rusting shed door, sliding it, screeching along its cheap, bent tracks. An abused gas-powered mower sat dejectedly on the shed's dirt floor, rotting cut grass caked around its cracked black plastic wheels and bag attachment port. Even in the cold, the chemicals made his eyes water and burned his nose. Rat droppings dotted the mildewed shelves. He grabbed a shovel with a cracked handle and bent blade, and slowly returned to his Dad's side, leaving frost footprints as he went. His Dad turned without saying a word and walked slowly away from him to the corner of the yard where their compost pile sat, smoldering in the cold Autumn morning, literally steaming with organic heat, and dragged his heel along the ground twice, marking an "X" in the wasted sod beside the pile. "Dig a hole there," he said. His Dad stepped back out of the way and folded his arms as the boy thrust the shovel blade into the earth, cutting through the thin, summer-burned sod, and then pressing the bottom of his shoe down on the flat steel edge and driving the blade home. Shovelful after shovelful piled up beside the hole. The silt-like soil snaked back down into the hole until he stopped and moved the whole pile farther away. "Deeper," said his Dad. "Shave off that side, over there."

The young boy dug for nearly twenty minutes, an eternity when you're young on a school morning, or old and late for work. Sweat trickled down his forehead and into his eyes. He smelled his sweat mixing with the "Tearless" children's shampoo his mom bought at the local drugstore. His good school shoes were dirty and he tasted the salt of the sweat on his lips. He sniffed hard and ran his dirty hand up through his short hair and down the back. Good thing his mom was still asleep: she'd freak if she saw the "state" he was in only minutes before the first bell was to ring.

Blisters began to form on his unprotected palms. His hands were pink and aching. He shoveled as hard as he could, grunting with each thrust of the shovel. He wanted to do a good job. "Good enough," said his Dad finally, taking the shovel from him and tossing it carelessly aside. The two of them walked slowly back to Joey and Joani.

Joani, still shivering, seemed to know something was up. Her lips slowly pulled back into a snarl as the young man and his father approached Joey's body. The frost was already melting in the morning sun and the boy noticed a smell he'd never smelled before: the sickly sweet smell of mammalian death, of flesh beginning to deteriorate, of congealed urine and blood-tinged drool. His father raised his hand at Joani and she ducked down immediately, her snarl replaced by submissive whimpering. She tried to get up, but couldn't. Her legs were almost as stiff as Joey's. His father gently picked her up and held the cold shivering dog to his chest, dirtying his coat. He took her inside and placed her on one of the cedar-filled, oversized burlap pillows in the unfinished rec room. The other one remained conspicuously unoccupied. He stopped half-stride and looked back at Joani laying there by herself, barely able to keep her eyes open. He turned the light off and closed the door behind him.

Leaving his soiled jacked on, his Dad stepped back out into the crisp Autumn morning and walked directly over to Joey, picking him up all in one motion and carrying him over to the hole the young man had dug. The man held the stiff body as far away from his chest as his strength allowed. His right hand, of course, slid directly into urine-matted fur and he swore. Upon reaching the hole, he squatted as low as he could until the tops of his Levi-clad legs were parallel to the ground, and then a little bit further, before stretching forward to set Joey down as carefully as possible. The boy didn't even try to help. He hadn't been prepared for this this morning, and he was having a hard time taking it all in. How did his father seem to know what needed to be done? It seemed like he had done this before. The boy felt dazed, kind of like the time in junior varsity football when his amazing catch down the opponent's sideline was rewarded with a defensive back's helmet in the earhole on the next play.

He was glad his Dad came outside to say goodbye that morning. Sometimes he left long before the boy even woke up, although he always walked in and checked on him no matter how early in the morning. The boy stared at Joey in the hole. His Dad had to maneuver one of the stiff legs so it would fit right. The boy wasn't sure what his Mom would have done if she had been the one left to deal with it all. He had neither seen nor heard her since his father came out and stood behind him almost forty-five minutes ago. He was glad that the hole was deep enough. He'd worked hard on that hole.

Slowly, he emerged from his reverie, shaking his head a bit to clear the cobwebs and turning around to retrieve the shovel his father'd tossed aside. Shovelful after shovelful began to fill the hole. He wondered whether he was supposed to bury the head first or leave it for last. He decided to evenly cover the whole body, and was relieved in spite of himself when the dirt finally rose up and covered Joey's eyes. He remembered the day in school when his friend Marvin tried wearing his big brother's contact lenses and the school nurse had to take them out because his eyes clamped shut like clams. He had really, really sensitive eyes. All you had to do was start talking about having an itch on your eye or something like that and he'd start fidgeting and rubbing his eyes and blinking real fast. Sometimes, he'd have to get a bathroom pass from the teacher and go splash cold water on his face before he could function again. That's what death is, the boy thought: it's not caring when dirt gets in your eyes.

"Mound it up," his father said, showing him what he meant with his hands. He still hadn't wiped the blood, urine and drool from his rough, calloused hands. The young man carefully mounded the dirt so it looked like a freshly dug grave on a scary movie. His Dad looked down at it and said "Good job. He was a good dog and you did right by him." With that, he turned and walked back across the cratered lawn, over to the utility sink he had installed a few years ago by his wife's potting table. He flipped the long flat levers for both hot and cold water with his elbows and began washing the gore from his hands. When he removed most of it, he reached over and pumped liquid soap into both hands and rubbed them together over and over again. "Come wash your hands," he said, pulling a couple paper towels from the roll over the sink. The boy did what he was told. The water felt hot on his blisters and he winced when he rubbed his hands together. His Dad watched him wash, sighed, and opened the squat, old-fashioned white refrigerator with the long, vertical chrome latch that he kept out on the patio beside the utility sink. He looked down into the fridge and then up at the house, checking the sliding glass door and the windows, before ducking down and pulling out a can of Olympia beer. The refrigerator light had burned out months ago. He closed the door with his hip. It still latched with a satisfying, air-tight "ka-thunk." The man looked down into his son's sad eyes for the first time that morning and marveled at the fact that he was a father. He could still remember the day when he was a young boy and his first dog died. He remembered the day, the sounds, the smells, what was on television that night, and the special dinner his mom had made to cheer him up: Hamburger Helper Chili with store-bought garlic butter bread, and salad with oil-and-vinegar dressing. He didn't understand how that day could still be so real. Not when his own son stood quietly, devotedly, looking up at him. He turned away from his son's gaze for a moment, focusing on the decay-

ing cedar fence, before walking slowly back towards the freshly
dug grave. The boy quietly followed, wiping his wet hands on
his jeans, soap bubbles still clinging to his fingers.

The man reached the grave and opened the can of beer with one
hand. He carefully poured out a swallow or two, just behind the
grave so as not to mess up the mound, and then drained two
thirds of what remained. He licked his lips and briefly considered calling in sick before handing the can to his son and
nodding at him to do the same. His son carefully poured a bit of
beer in front of the grave and then nervously put the can to his
lips and drained the remainder, squinting a bit at the taste. He
handed the empty can to his dad and they walked back to the
house.

"Would you like another beer?" asked the girl.

"What? Yeah. Sure. That'd be great. Thanks."

The girl left, taking his plate and balled-up paper napkin with
her. The spaghetti was good. Good as any he'd ever had. They
must simmer that sauce for hours, he thought, just like they used
to in the old days. People didn't simmer anything for hours anymore. Most of his friends didn't even have stoves in their
apartments. Coffee-maker, microwave, InstaHot and toaster
oven. That was all they ever used. The girl brought his beer.
He thanked her, shielding his eyes from the sun's glare with his
left hand, and then looked around at the other tables. He and an
old man were the only ones out on the patio. The restaurant was
filling up inside with the lunch rush. There were TVs inside.

The old man in the opposite corner of the patio was drinking red
wine from a large, snifter-shaped wine glass. The cork and bottle stood on opposite sides of the bud vase on the vinyl red-and-
white checkered tablecloth. The man looked absentmindedly
down at the wine in the glass, twisting it and tilting it in the glare
of the hot white sun. When he drank, he drank heartily, rather
than sipping. His hair was as closely cropped as the young

man's, but it receded far from his forehead and was dominated by hundreds of coarse, erect grey hairs. His face was lean and experienced. His hands, one coddling the wine glass and the other grasping the bottle, were calloused, scarred and muscular. He looked like he was ready for whatever life had in store, and yet there was a sense of melancholy and resignation that hung about him like a funereal shroud. The old man looked into the glass of wine as if reading tea leaves or panning for gold, swirling and watching and tilting and turning. The wine shone blood red in the white glare. The old man had vibrant hazel eyes, eyes that glinted blue one moment and dulled to muddy green the next. There was something familiar about him. The young man couldn't put his finger on it, but he'd seen this guy before. Or at least it felt that way. He racked his brain to make the association. Goddamn it. Where did he know him from? After several moments of random, chaotic mental searching, the young man decided to approach the question like an investigator, a coroner, a crime scene investigator. He imposed a grid on his life and began to move from one square to another. School. Work. Family. Social outings. Travel. Sector by sector, he searched for the old man. Several minutes passed and he could not place the face. Fuck. Maybe it's one of those déjà vu things. Maybe, the familiarity he felt was because the guy resembled a movie star or because he epitomized the archetypical "virile old guy" like Paul Newman. And then again, you really can't trust your feelings, anyway. Jesus Christ. The young man was a firm believer in that. Braniac once told him that you've got to separate yourself from your tangible feelings because the chemical reactions responsible for them are detached from the reality you're trying to define. Feelings are "simpering mistresses," ruled by agenda and whim, she said. And he couldn't argue with that. One of his friends from high school who was diagnosed with paranoid schizophrenia his junior year in college, felt all kinds of emotions that had nothing whatsoever to do with the reality his friends and professors could perceive. He felt genuine fear. Genuine panic. Broke out into sweats and got all wide-eyed and shit. Those were real feelings, real emotions and real physical reactions, but the people around him weren't really after him, and the government wasn't really listening to his calls or reading his mind, and CIA "remote viewer" operatives weren't psychically torturing his clairvoyant little sister. We define our reality with imperfect tools. No way around that. Our senses, our thoughts, memories and feelings are all terrifically flawed. Witnesses can't remember whether the bank robber had a mustache or was wearing a red or blue shirt. Jeans or khakis? Glasses? Can't remember for sure. Do you smell that? No. Jesus Christ, that stinks like ass. I don't smell anything. Jesus H. Christ how can you not smell that? Merlot. Cabernet. Merlot. Cabernet. Smooth finish. Crisp finish. Berry. Oak. And THESE are the building blocks of our lives, our history, our future. So do you say "fuck it all' because you can't trust a goddamn thing, or do you work with what you have and try to finger that "fine tuning" knob to just the right location where you reduce the interference and pump up the signal? Do you sift through the gravel for the one small nugget of gold, or chuck the whole damn mess and go plant a field full of corn? And if you do, is the corn real? Can you taste it? If it's rotten, will you know?

The old man ordered another bottle of wine and some food. The young man wondered what he was going to eat, whether he'd order the same thing he'd had or something fancier, more "mature," something with a long, hard-to-pronounce Italian name. The man's eyes looked like they could see through anything. The young man remembered Wilson telling him that human beings are all born with blackened glasses. You can't trust your senses in the first place, and to top it all off, you're born with these thick, old-fashioned, dark glasses, like the kind Helen Keller wore, that you can't see shit out of, even if you're not blind. You don't know shit beyond the sound of your parents' voices, colors, temperature, patterns of light and darkness. You don't know if you got a clitoris or a penis, whether you're black or white, got hair or not. As you grow older, life cleans a little bit of that blackness off your glasses and you begin to look around and recognize shit. You recognize the people who take care of you, your favorite blanket, a bottle of milk, whatever. By the time you're in high school, everything seems bright and clear.

You think you see everything there is to see and because of that you figure you know everything there is to know. "Well, shit!" this is easy, you think, pronouncing your version of truth to whomever will listen and a lot of people who won't. "That's why you got so many Young Republicans," Wilson said. "Republicans see everything in terms of right and wrong, America and America's enemies, good people and lazy lowlifes, black and white. But that's wrong. That's not the way it is, 'cause you see, this whole time you've been looking out of only one lens. The other one's still dark. You think everything's clear, but everything's 2-dimensional, and you only got half your peripheral vision. Your depth perception is fucked up, so you end up running into things, running over people, pulling up way short sometimes. It ain't just the Young Republicans, either. It's the young revolutionaries, the Anarchists, the Communists. The fuckers who asked me how many babies I killed, how many little Vietnamese girls I raped. Same fucking thing. Different side of the spectrum." The people who sent him to Hell to pad their pockets, and the people who treated him like shit when he came back. Same fucking difference. The young man didn't understand why people would spit at soldiers returning home. There was a draft, for chrissake. And he was pretty apolitical when it came right down to it. He knew what he thought was right about the country and what he figured was wrong, but all the folks in charge seemed the same to him, regardless of what side of the aisle they were on. It was all about the money and the power, two things the young man knew nothing about.

A college student with a red backpack, a goatee, and curly blonde hair rode by on a long skateboard, the small, hard wheels rhythmically kathunking over the expansion joints in the sidewalk as he slowly wove his way through the pedestrians as if they were cones on a slalom course. That guy. He couldn't be any older than 19. That was the kind of kid they drafted and sent to Vietnam. Wilson told him that's one reason why guys get so fucked up when they're sent to war. "It's cause their glasses get wiped clean all at once. Like Adam and Eve eating the apple and all of a sudden seeing their nakedness. You go from two-dimensional idealism to three-dimensional horror. Nothing gets filtered out. You're staring at the sun, or the pit of hell, and it burns your eyes and your mind and your soul. You're seeing all the horror and evil the world has to offer and you're not fucking ready for that." A lot of men and women who served in Vietnam talked about aging twenty or thirty years in thirteen months, about not recognizing themselves in a mirror. About coming home and finding themselves with nothing left to learn about life. Nothing would ever compare to the highs and lows they experienced in Nam: saving their buddy's life, watching another buddy die. In the space of two years, they went from high school graduation to boot camp to some anonymous ville in which the guy next to them nonchalantly caps some old Vietnamese guy cause he looked at him funny, to a helicopter, and 37 hours later they'd be back in the World, sitting on their old bed upstairs with pennants pinned to the walls and Playboy magazines stashed behind boxes of baseball cards.

The girl brought out another beer and the young man was feeling pretty damn good by this time. He said something to her that made her smile and touch his shoulder as she left. He resisted the temptation to swing around and watch her ass retreat back into the darkness of the restaurant. People walked by, cars and trucks drove by, jets overhead roared loudly as they banked for final approach. A dirty little sparrow stabbed at French bread crumbs in the shade beneath his table. The white sun filled all of existence with a constant, unwavering, white light that made the young man squint and raise a horizontal hand to his brow when he looked at something on the opposite side of the street.

He looked over at the old man. The wrinkles on his face betrayed a lifetime of squinting against the sun. And the young man wondered what kind of man he was. After all, by this time, he had already become who he was going to be, right? You can't teach old dogs new tricks, and even if you do, you don't turn a German Shepherd into a Schnauzer. What was this guy? Was he a good guy? A bad guy? A tormented soul or a tormenter of other souls? Only one thing was certain. He was a son. Just like the young man, the President of the United States, Jesus Christ, and the serial killer on death row. All sons. And that was kind of fucking weird if you thought about it, especially if you were drunk or stoned. At one point in time a woman had given birth to them. A woman set their life into motion, squeezing them out from between her legs, out of the fluid, warm darkness into glaring, brilliant, intrusive, cold light.

The old man took his hand off the bottle of wine and slowly, gently rubbed his lined forehead with his forefinger and middle finger held together as if taped in a makeshift splint. He slowly traced circles on his forehead with his eyes closed, unaware or not caring that the young man or anyone else might be watching him, like there was something in his brain, something that he couldn't forget. Maybe something he hoped to massage away with his two fingertips like Jesus touching a blind man's eyes, one-by-one eliminating the glaring white cataracts. The young man turned away and squinted at the cars in the street and the people on the sidewalk. How do you get to be an old man like that? Do you wake up one morning not sure where you're at, disoriented and confused, not feeling quite yourself, kind of like you might feel the morning after a long hard night of heavy drinking, and look up at a face in the mirror that only vaguely resembles your own? Like those kids in Vietnam who get air-lifted out of the rice paddies halfway through their tour with half their leg somewhere down in the jungle below and the first time they see themselves in a mirror they nearly jump out of their rack, stub and all? Or are you pursued, relentlessly, day after day, like a convict on the lam? At first, you've got yourself a good head start. Sure, you're always looking over your shoulder, but it's almost fun. Exciting. You know the cops are closing in on you, tightening the noose, little by little, but you've got wiggle room, you take risks, enjoy the thrill of tempting fate until they get close enough that you're afraid to show your face in the daytime. Each escape becomes more desperate. You no longer take chances because of the thrill. You take them because you've got no choice. And really, honestly, it's not so much of a thrill any more, anyway. It's just a big fucking pain in the ass and you're getting tired of it all. Tired of running. Tired of hiding. Realizing that it's just a matter of time, and not really caring much. And then one day, there's the proverbial knock on the door and you look around and all the windows are barred. There's no back door, no basement, no attic. Just you and the knock on the door and the revolver sitting on the kitchen table among empty beer bottles, stale room-temperature pizza and ashtrays.

"God. I'm doing it again. Fuck." The young man "came-to" and sat up quickly in his chair, bumping the table and almost spilling his beer. He looked around: the patio was filling up, but fortunately no one, except perhaps the old man, had noticed. "God, I'm such a freak," he thought, trying desperately and un-successfully to settle back into a state of nonchalance. He felt like everyone around him had been monitoring his thoughts, shaking their heads in disgust, in pity. Conversations, however, continued around him. People were enjoying their lunches and drinks seemingly oblivious to his mental embarrassment and shame. Perhaps it was all in his head. He looked quickly, ob-viously, back at the old man. He was eating spaghetti. After a few furtive gulps of beer, the young man began to relax again, taking deep breaths and half-smiling like someone having just avoided a major injury through sheer dumb luck, gulping up the relief, relishing the sensation of relief like a runner at the end of a race in 100-degree heat relishing the act of gulping down a pa-per cup full of pure, crystal-clear, ice-cold water.

He was painfully aware of the fact that one of the many reasons his acquaintances and friends considered him something of a freak was because he thought quite a bit about death and what it's like to grow old (if you're lucky enough to do so). And not death in the Goth kinda way: all bloody, black, vampirish and suicidal; but death in the obituary way, the tallying of people who were no longer "with us." People who were permanently "excused" from the assignment of life. People who'd never an-swer the telephone during dinner and hang up on a telemarketer or mow a lawn or think dirty thoughts about some pony-tailed hotty driving a pick-up truck in the next lane. Death in the "erased from the ledger" kind of way. The "life goes on" kinda way. It wouldn't have been so bad if it hadn't started to influence the way he lived his life.

A lot of times, people he knew decided they just wanted to "hang out at the mall," or "hang out at home and watch TV." The young man would usually excuse himself at that point and head out to do something else. "Watching TV" especially bothered him, because he figured if there was something you really wanted to see, that would be one thing, but if you're just wanting to veg in front of the TV regardless of what may or may not be on, that was a big fucking waste of time. Sure, maybe every once in a while, if he was both physically and mentally spent, he'd spend a couple hours surfing channels before going to sleep, but usually he read or DID something. Watching a show was one thing, watching TV was another. "Life is short," he'd say when pressed, but they usually didn't understand what he was trying to get at, and would call him a "freak" and move on.

A number of factors contributed to his unusual stance: working as a part-time custodian in a rest home for a year, hanging out with old people like Wilson, and reading biographies and autobiographies rather than watching MTV. Reading books about people's lives was a no-brainer, he thought. It takes an entire lifetime to figure out how things work, so why not check out the conclusions other people have drawn shortly before their death, rather than waiting on your own? If there was a God, he or she had a twisted sense of humor, putting human beings in a world that takes at least 90 years to figure out and then putting most folks' life expectancy 20 years shy of that. "Here are the rules to the game. They will take 90 years to read and if you live long enough to read them through, you won't completely understand them. Have fun!"

That's why reincarnation is so attractive. You just keep coming back until you get it right, learning more and more each time un-

til you reach eternal bliss. And you've got to be a complete asshole to come back as a beetle or snake or jack ass, and even
then, it's just like going back to the beginning and starting over.
If you are an amazingly decent beetle, you can move up to a bird
the next life, and then maybe a dog or chimpanzee. He wasn't
sure if the phases of reincarnation mirrored Darwinian evolution,
but it would make sense if they did. That's something Braniac
would know.

Custodians in rest homes do a hell of a lot more than mop up
shit, pureed beef and Ensure. They are confidants and counse-
lors, friends and advocates, witnesses and historians. Nurse aids
are too busy to talk with the patients much, and the nurses are
running the show: they have even less time. And the residents?
These are people warehoused in long single-hall wings with
heavy oversized doors and room numbers to the right of the
brushed steel knobs. People, not minks or chickens or veal.
And most people require one thing in life aside from food, water
and shelter. From the time they're born to the time they die,
they require meaningful human contact. Hermits are the exception, not the rule. And even hermits require meaningful human
contact in order to confirm their status as hermits. Otherwise,
they're just people living by themselves in the woods.

As he mopped and vacuumed, unplugged toilets (rectal muscles
relax with age), mopped up overflows, dust-mopped and wet-
mopped, he wondered what it'd be like when he was the one in
the generic hospital bed. Is this the way it ought to be? An
Idealist would say "NO!", but he'd met some of the families and
the rest-home was the only logical thing they could do in their
particular situation. In a perfect world, we'd all be the Waltons,
but the Waltons didn't face Alzheimers, incontinence, dementia,
psychosis, bed sores, cancer, heart disease or Parkingson's. The
old folks in the rest home were being cared for, if nothing else.
They had a window, a TV, human contact. And if he could
make them smile five times a week, then that was something real
that he was accomplishing and something real that they were
experiencing.

Sometimes he asked them questions and sometimes they initiated conversations. Either way, he soon realized that some people who grow old feel the same as they did when they were young, but they're forced to live with a degenerating, visibly aging, physical body and brain. They are still themselves way deep inside, the same young person they'd always been, but are trapped within a decrepit, deteriorating sack of skin, shit and bones. They're 8, 12, 16, 21 and 30. They're not 60, 70 or 80. Others, however, were born to be old. They lived their young lives as anachronisms, never fitting in, never connecting to anything that seemed real, until they grew old and became grandparents or sages or geezers or fogies. It was only at that point that they hit their stride. The girl at the coffee shop's parents, in fact, had been like that. They didn't make sense until they hit 55. Only then did they begin to seem comfortable in their roles.

There were a few occasions on which he spoke to a resident one day, and watched the morticians wheel them out in a body bag the next, but that was unusual. Usually, he'd come in after a couple of days off and find the room empty, personal belongings gone, floor freshly mopped and buffed by another custodian, ready for another resident. That was death. Someone else sleeping (themselves slowly dying) in your bed. That was death. Someone else's underwear in your drawer. Someone else's knickknacks on your shelf. It's a circle, a wheel, a cycle. Name your religion, cliché, philosophy. Over and over and over again. He couldn't remember which one, but some religion he had read about used prayer wheels. Kind of like an old-fashioned mill's water wheel, but with prayers written on it, so that every time it completed a turn, God or the gods would accept the fact that a prayer had been said. That was like life, in a way. One turn around and you get God's attention. And then you're done. On to the next prayer, on to the next life, on to the next soul.

The old man was gone. The day had changed. The way people walked the sidewalk in front of him was different. The white

211

sun had dropped a bit in the grey sky. People around him were wiping their mouths with paper napkins, checking for their belongings, and taking their checks to the cashier. He no longer had to raise his hand to shield his eyes from the glare when he looked at the sidewalk across the street. The constant stop-start flow of vehicles before his eyes reminded him of the movies he'd seen in high school health class about blood cells moving through arteries and veins. He couldn't remember which one went to the heart and which one came from the heart, but he remembered the blood vessels hastily, impatiently, bumping their way forward, like they were running a tad behind schedule.

The sweet-assed waitress came back to his table at the same time that he noticed a man across the street sitting atop the back of a bus-stop bench, combat-boot-clad feet on the seat, ragged beard and long brown hair. She looked down at the young man and smiled, remembering his earlier comment, and asked if he'd like another beer, her right hand holding the check in the hip pocket of her tight, faded jeans, mere millimeters from the very ass the young man relished and lusted after. Thankfully, responsibly, the young man said "No, thank you," and she smiled and handed him the check, glad she wasn't going to have to eventually cut him off. He seemed like a nice guy.

She noticed the attention he was paying to the homeless guy across the street. "That's Harold," she said, her voice as sweet as the rest of her.

The young man didn't think he'd had enough beer to slur his words, but he paused before responding and then carefully, self-consciously, enunciated his question, just in case. "Who's Harold?" The girl smiled and slowly took a seat, looking around to make sure no one needed anything and that her boss wasn't looking. "He's homeless. No one knows where he stays. Doesn't use shelters but you never see him sleeping out on the street, either. He can paint and play the guitar. Sometimes does that for money and he preaches, but not like the preacher guys over on 18th. He's pretty famous. Been on TV a couple times and in the newspaper. Some people say he can tell you what your life will be like and how you can be happy and what Life means. Some people say he's psychic or some such shit. Sometimes you'll see him in protests, but usually he's hanging out talking to people." Her leg touched his beneath the table. His dick responded accordingly, and his right hand began moving slowly in the general direction of her leg, when her boss hollered something from the dark confines of the restaurant. "Go listen to him," she said. "He's a kick. He earns enough money playing the guitar and selling his paintings to buy a glass of decent wine from me almost every night, and a fifth of the hard stuff from the grocer down the street every other day or so." He watched her leave, noticing an additional, delicious twitch in her stride, and then looked down at the check which tallied one small spaghetti, one beer and a phone number.

The young man left a tip equivalent to half the total on the check, paid up out front, and carefully made his way out the door back into the white glare of the afternoon, tucking the phone number into the back pocket of his jeans. He was drunk enough to have a little party going on in his head, but collected enough to be ultra-conscious of his appearance to the outside, non-partying world; making a conscious effort to take it slow and easy, one step at a time. Easy does it, don't smile too big, don't close your eyes for too long while you're walking. And then he was across the street and standing behind a small group of people gathered around the guy the waitress identified as Harold. Harold reminded him of a hippy from the sixties or seventies who was photographed eating a peach or apricot in a park someplace and wound up as part of a segment on a Sesame Street anniversary show. He thought it was for the letter "P," but it could also have been for the letter "A" or the letter "E." Regardless of which one it was, the man epitomized an era in the young man's mind, like an icon on a computer desktop, as powerful an image as any gleaned from one of Wilson's stories. The mustache and long brown beard; the full, prominent red lips; thick, black plastic eyeglass frames; the long hair, long fingers, and the juicy pinkish-orange peach; all captured the hedonism, environmentalism, freedom and joy of the hippies, at least in the young man's mind. To anyone else, it may very well have just been some fucker eating fruit.

Harold was chatting quietly with a young, thin woman with long straight blonde hair, standing to his right. She was fidgeting with a vintage beaded purse, and she stopped every few seconds to pull the hair away from her face. The other six or seven people listened intently, huddled in a semi-circle around them. One guy, an older man with a big grey mustache, collar-length grey-black hair, and a plaid wool driver's cap, steadied himself with a gnarled wooden cane clutched in his large right hand. In his left, he cradled a copy of the day's Christian Science Monitor. It looked like he wanted to cup a hand to an ear, but couldn't. A freckled-face girl with bright green eyes and strawberry blonde dreadlocks stood quietly on Harold's left, offering blue 8 ½ by 11 inch flyers to passersby. They advertised an upcoming symposium, sponsored by the local Unitarian Church and the nearby Buddhist temple, being held at the Eagles Hall down the street: "Universalism: individual enlightenment through association with others." Harold, first name only, was listed as a "special guest." The young man took one, smiled at the girl and returned his attention to the thin man sitting comfortably, almost jauntily, atop the forest green bus-stop bench.

The street behind the young man was now packed with cars, barely moving, bumper-to-bumper. He had lost track of time and wondered whether he'd pissed away the entire day and was now witnessing rush hour. Exhaust pipes pumped carbon monoxide into the air of a city known first and foremost for its air pollution. Some jerkoff decided he needed to move from the far left lane to the far right lane, bringing everyone behind him to a complete stop in the process. When the young man drove, which was rarely since he didn't own a car, he always tried to avoid inconveniencing others. If someone behind him was trying to squeeze themselves out of an intersection when the light turned red, he'd move up as far as he could in order to give them the room. He always flipped on his turn signal with plenty of time to spare so the folks in oncoming traffic could take advantage of the opportunity and turn left in front of him if they so wished. And if he was in danger of missing a turnoff, he did NOT hold up three fucking lanes of traffic to inch his way over. He instead cursed himself for not being better prepared, took the next exit, and doubled back, inconveniencing no one other than himself. That's the way it ought to be, he thought again. In this fucked-up crowded world, the best thing you can do is make a concerted effort to avoid inconveniencing other people. But he was thinking arrogantly again.

The young man's attention turned back to Harold. He was listening, fingers casually interlaced, forearms resting atop his jeans-clad legs, combat boots laced and stationary on the seat of the green bench. The day raced around the stationary man like those time-lapse movies of a bean sprouting and growing serpentine toward the sky while the world whirls crazily around it at supersonic speeds. An African-American man in his late forties or early fifties in a rumpled grey three-piece suit was telling Harold about a dream he'd had. He spoke quietly, gesturing here and there with thick, sturdy hands that belied his corporate appearance. Harold listened carefully, happily, without the slightest indication of boredom, impatience or distraction. He listened like the man's story was the most fascinating story he'd ever heard. He was more interested in listening than in talking himself. "Damn, that's weird," thought the young man. Most people listen to others out of courtesy and expediency. It's polite and you can't talk until the other person finishes what they're saying anyway. In fact, you can often use other people's stories like you would a Rorschach test. Their random ramblings often provide useful segues to the topics you wish to cover. Harold, on the other hand, appeared content to listen to the people around him share their thoughts, dreams and experiences for the rest of the day and into the night. And this guy wasn't some regular person. This guy's whole existence depended upon his prophetic and insightful statements; at least that's what the young man had gathered thus far. Harold maintained eye contact with whomever was speaking, but didn't play the "who will look away first" game. Instead, he occasionally looked down at his boots, sometimes closing his eyes for a few moments, other times looking at the others in his group, all the while obviously still focused on the man's voice. "And then everything slowly grows dark and all I can see is blackness. But not one-dimensional blackness like a wall. It's three-dimensional blackness like a moonless night or outer space. What do you think that means?"

"Is it warm or cold?"

"Excuse me?'

"The three-dimensional darkness. Is it warm, or is it cold?"

"It's warm."

"Do you stand and observe it, enter it, or travel through it?"

"I travel through it."

"For how long?"

A grimy reticulated city bus lumbered by in a cloud of diesel exhaust and noise. Harold smiled and waited for it to pass before repeating himself.

"How long do you travel through it?"

"For the rest of the dream. For the majority of the dream."

"And are you happy, sad, afraid, angry or indifferent?"

"It's hard to explain. It's like I've got a fighting chance. It's like I'm setting out to do something. I guess I'd describe it as hopeful determination."

Harold smiled at the man, smiled at the words he'd chosen. The man, suddenly embarrassed, looked down at a scrap of paper on the sidewalk to the right of his polished leather dress shoes, and then back up at Harold. He fiddled with his briefcase a bit and straightened his suit jacket. The old man in the wool driving cap standing next to him looked down at the head of his cane and thoughtfully stroked its polished surface with his forefinger. A cabbie in the traffic jam behind them leaned on his horn and swore in Punjabi.

"It's tempting to drift into cliché, into pop psychology, into convenience, and to think of the warm darkness in the ubiquitous symbolism of the womb, but one would think that being 'hopefully determined' would only apply if you were exiting the womb, not entering it, or more accurately, re-entering it. In the dream, you are not hiding, not seeking shelter, not looking to escape responsibility. You aren't looking for nurturing. You are entering an environment with a job to do, but you can't see anything around you. You can't 'see' as we ordinarily think of 'seeing,' and yet, you're not afraid. You're suddenly blind, but you do not panic." Harold licked his lips and smoothed his mustache with his left thumb and forefinger. "How often do you have this dream?"

"At least once or twice a week. It's the only dream I ever remember."

"What do you think it means?"

Harold looked up at the man, the receding hairline of his fade highlighted by grey. The man met his gaze with a determined jaw.

"I wish I knew."

"I know what I think it means to me, but that's not really important, is it?" Harold wasn't fishing for compliments. He wasn't looking for the strokes that followed, a series of murmured

217

praise-filled remonstrations from the small crowd of impromptu urban commuter disciples gathered about him. The man looked down at him, met his gaze and genuinely believed in the selflessness he saw in Harold's eyes. For a fleeting moment, amid the grinding, droning, crashing din of the city, he was in that multi-dimensional, limitless darkness, and he could see clearly. He was enveloped by it and yet there was no "him" to envelop. He was one with the darkness and yet there was no "him" or "darkness." To "become one" suggested pre-existent dualism, and that's what struck him at this moment. There never was a "him" or "it." That was the whole fucking point. He looked down at Harold and Harold looked up at him with a smile of recognition.

"Thank you," the man said and quickly walked away, confused, enlightened, calmed, exhilarated, embarrassed, emboldened, and entirely disconnected from the cars, signs, traffic lights, billboards, crosswalks, storefronts, pedestrians and trash-strewn curbs around him. He hopped on a bus and rode it home to his wife.

The strawberry-blonde girl leaned over to whisper in Harold's ear: "What happened?" Harold didn't answer the girl, but instead watched the man walk away. He climbed up into the city bus and found a seat on the opposite side. Harold couldn't see him when the bus pulled away from the curb with a dirty diesel roar. Harold watched it move away, half-smiling, but then a cloud seemed to pass over him and he rubbed his eyes with his right forefinger and thumb. The people around him were asking questions. "What happened?"

"Harold, why did he say 'thank you'?"

"Did you see what he was thinking? Were you two speaking to each other with your minds?"

A grimy, skinny, tall man with a patchy two-day growth of beard, a faux leather jacket and bad teeth muttered "fucking bullshit" and stalked away, his long-fingered hands stuffed into the front pockets of his worn holey high-water jeans. Harold nodded quietly, slowly, as he watched the man lurch his way down the sidewalk in his old, paint-spattered leather work boots. Harold watched the man's strange gait and wondered whether one leg was shorter than the other, or whether he'd been in some kind of accident.

"Harold? Harold?"

The small group of people looked in the direction of the small voice. The sidewalk was crowded with two-way pedestrian traffic. Tall thin super-model types strutted here and there with their designer leather attaché cases and short skirts. Business people walked and talked on their cell phones; hands-free headsets and earpieces transforming them into Star Trek characters and pop stars. Humanity flowed like two rivers colliding and flowing through each other in opposite directions, swirling around anyone who stopped to dig into a pocket or purse, or to reassess their location. A small, frail-looking Asian lady in her seventies or eighties stood shakily for a moment, ignoring the imminent danger of being overrun, and cupped her hand to her mouth to yell Harold's name in her loudest voice. She wore a neat plaid dress with big buttons, and walked shakily with the aid of a wooden cane with a red rubber stopper on the end. She carried a slim cream-colored leather purse under her left arm and used the cane with her right. Her voice was small but strong. Harold looked down for a moment when he heard his name amid the city's noise, and then returned his gaze to the retreating malcontent. He wanted to get inside this guy and see for himself what he was all about, but he couldn't connect, as much as he tried, and he wondered whether he could really connect with anyone at all, already experiencing doubts about his experience with the man in the rumpled three-piece suit.

"Harold! Harold!"

"Jesus Christ, now what?" he wondered, as he heard the tiny sing-song voice somehow emerging unscathed from the pale, glaring city's monotonous, raucous clamor. The corrugated cardboard world's harmony grew discordant, the easy spinning of the spheres began to scrape and wobble, and a screeching, worn-brake-pad dissonance rose from the anonymous urban bedlam. It pierced Harold's ear drums like screaming jet engines, but everyone else barely heard it."

"Harold! Harold!"

He heard his mom, calling out through the screen door, ready to give him another chore, another task, another time-consuming wild-goose chase. She was insane and had to take her medicine every day so she didn't flip out and drag the whole family down into the cellar to hide from the government spies and the deadly x-rays. She got them up in the morning, got them dressed, fed them breakfast, and got them off to school. As long as you didn't pay much attention to what she was saying as she did these things, everything was pretty much OK. But even his mom warned against sharing their "talks" with classmates and teachers. "They don't understand us," she said. Her alternate reality was almost entirely parallel to their own, so although the labels and names were different, the activities and actions were almost always the same. There was no reason for drama. No more reason than if your mom spoke English as a second language. Reality was their mother's second language and she spoke it rather well, except when she got off her meds.

It did not take long for her to realize that he was different than his brothers and sisters. He almost never got in trouble, but not because he was a saint. He knew when she was coming in to check on him, and he knew what she wished for him in her heart. That's why her occasional "episodes" didn't frighten him. He saw that there was love and kindness in her heart, even when she didn't recognize the neighbors.

Harold had the unique ability to turn others transparent, like the fish in his brother's aquarium, the ones you could look right through, their hearts pumping away, their digestive systems changing food into shit. He warned his mom when the social worker was coming to visit, he reminded her about her medication, and tucked her in when she "self-medicated" herself with too much Wild Turkey. In so many ways, he was her savior, so it should not have been a surprise when he discovered, however reluctantly, that he could be a savior of others.

"Harold! Oh, Harold!" She finally saw him clearly, and her rapidly beating heart finally began to relax. As long as she could tell him face-to-face, it would be OK, but she HAD to tell him to his face.

"The tumor is nearly gone!" The doctors don't even understand! But they said it is almost entirely gone!"

"Mrs. Yokohama," Harold smiled somewhat awkwardly, feeling the stares of the people around him, all of whom leaned in to better hear: "that is great news, but haven't you been taking medicine for the tumor?" He looked down at her expectantly, as if coaching a child to say the right thing, all the while trying to suppress the condescension in his voice, the condescension he felt was almost necessary to prevent the scene he feared from unfolding.

"Yes, but it wasn't working. I didn't tell you that," she said hesitantly, looking up at him; a lifetime of joy, pain, sorrow and determination readily apparent in the lines of her face and the single tear slowly making its way down her cheek, apparent even to those without Harold's abilities. The young man looked at her small slight frame. She was five foot nothing and probably tipped the scales at 90 pounds soaking wet, and yet the earnestness with which she spoke to Harold was powerful. She secured the undivided attention of every person standing around him. Only the young man noticed the tremor in Harold's hands and the beads of sweat that appeared on his brow.

"I was talking to you and there was a collision two blocks down and the police cars and medics came racing through. It was late in the morning and the traffic was light. Do you remember?"

Harold had lost control of the conversation if he'd ever had it in the first place. Once again, he found himself a character playing a part, his consciousness detached and standing nearby, watching as if at the theater. His next actions and words were scripted, so there was little use pretending that anything other than the inevitable would occur. He knew what Mrs. Yokohama was going to say, and he was both thrilled and horrified by the fact that people, not just Mrs. Yokohama, but others as well, experienced what many of them described as miracles after coming into contact with him.

"Doctor Reynolds and Doctor Lee both said the tumor is nearly gone and they're not sure why. That day, that day that the police and aid cars went racing by, you turned around to watch them, and when you did, I touched the fringe of the poncho you were wearing. I didn't really think it would help, but I didn't have any choice. I couldn't discount any possibility, and after you made that girl Gwen get better, I figured it couldn't hurt."

Everyone in the neighborhood and many people in the city at large either knew Gwen or knew of her. As the lead singer of the all-girl punk band "Fender Bend Her," she experienced a modicum of fame, if not fortune. The group toured most of California's I-5 corridor, from San Diego to Redding, and had a couple CDs out, but none of the girls abandoned their day jobs, and no one was counting on making it big. Their faces regularly graced the staple-ridden telephone poles of the neighborhood and the entertainment pages of the local weeklies. And Gwen's antics weren't limited to the cramped plywood stages they played. She was loud, garish, lewd, raucous and was even worse when drunk, which was often. It was said that she'd been thrown out of every single bar and tavern within a five mile radius at least once, had been arrested for disorderly conduct and public mayhem in three counties, and had made love with more local celebs and notables than the Fantasy Girls of Fantasy Escort Limited, a local establishment catering to the well-heeled traveler and businessman (and on four occasions, Gwen). Everyone who knew her told her to slow down, but one night she was found alone, beaten nearly to death in one of her friends' apartment. The door was kicked in, but the cops suspected it was done for show (the door sprayed blood droplets when it swung open), and the assailant failed to take anything of value. The hospital rape kit ruled out sexual assault, and the DNA retrieved from beneath her broken black fingernails never found a match. The cops also found meth and heroin in the apartment, but the only thing coursing through Gwen's blood that night was a fifth of Jack Daniel's and a pack's worth of nicotine.

Gwen lost a lot of blood before she was found, and her heart stopped once in the aid car and once on the operating table, but the defibrillator brought her back each time. Her friends, fans, a couple newspaper reporters, and the few family members who lived in the area gathered in the hospital waiting room and maintained a vigil throughout the wee hours of the morning and into the glaring hot day. She remained unconscious in the ICU for another 24 hours, various bodily functions shutting down as if in protest, only to be nudged and sometimes violently forced back into operation by the hospital staff. The second day, her vitals once again headed south. One of the doctors cagily suggested that Gwen's mother prepare herself for the possibility that her daughter wasn't going to make it. It was one step short of the "let's just make her comfortable' speech she'd delivered innumerable times before. And then Harold showed up.

The first miracle attributed to him that day was that he made it into the ICU. The second was that as soon as he left, Gwen's battered body came back to life. A few family members saw Harold leave the hospital wing in a hurry and shortly thereafter the head nurse came out into the waiting room with a big smile on her face.

"Do you remember?" asked Mrs. Yokohama, pleading as if this acknowledgment meant as much as the cancer's apparent remission. She was crying now, and Harold took her into his arms as much to conceal the tears and prevent a "scene" as to comfort her or take part in her joy. Quietly, so quietly that no one around them could hear above the grinding gears, squeaking timing belts, and thumping car stereos, Harold leaned his head down to Mrs. Yokohama's ear and simply whispered "yes." Her sigh of relief overtook her body with a shudder and her legs gave way beneath the weight of the miracle she knew was occurring within her body. She survived racism in the forties, the death of her first husband in 1962, abuse at the hands of her second, and she was going to survive this as well. Harold held onto her, struggling to support her without crushing her, until he felt her gain her feet and she whispered back "thank you."

Mrs. Yokohama sat down on the green bench, pulled a handkerchief from her purse, and dabbed at the tears coursing down her wrinkled face. Sighing once more and replacing the handkerchief carefully back into her purse, she pulled herself up with her cane, smiled at Harold, and entered the pedestrian flow. The young man instinctively reached out toward her with his left hand, inwardly cringing, like a driver when the car in front of him attempts to merge onto a busy freeway going only forty miles per hour, but she was fine. And Harold was gone.

The small group of people turned around bewildered, checking each other out like audience members at a Vegas magic show, all trying to figure out who was in cahoots with the magician. The only clue was a grimy city bus pulling away from the curb some thirty feet away. One by one, the people looked at their watches, their cell phones, the sky, and walked sheepishly away in a cloud of confusion. The joy of the moment was lost upon them, at least for the time being; but one by one, in their own time, they replayed the scene they'd witnessed over and over, squinting at it like a crime scene investigator holding up a revolver with the tip of a pen, realizing that something entirely unpedestrian had occurred on that entirely unremarkable stretch of sidewalk that day. The young man was the only one who remained by the green bench. Even the strawberry-blonde dreadlocked girl abandoned her stack of flyers and stomped away in a huff, the pink satin of her thong panties conspicuous above the equator of her low-rider camouflage cargo pants. The young man smiled in spite of himself, felt for the flyer in his pocket, and sat down on the green bench. He instinctively reached back for the flask that wasn't there, ran his hand back over his closely-cropped head, and watched the people rushing to get home.

The young man felt like he had just witnessed something, like seeing a car accident or something; something that cuts through the glazed-over routine of the day, the anonymous monotony, everyone just doing what they're doing, moving along in their little bubbles like blood cells in a vein. And then something REAL interrupts everything: SNAP, and all of a sudden you're outside the flow, looking at it like some scientist, entirely separated now, examining what just happened like an independent third-party. It was kind of like this story Wilson once told him about how he'd fallen asleep during a movie at school, some biology movie about cell division or something, boring as hell. It was back when movies were on reels, and if you could stay awake long enough, the teacher would sometimes let you see it run backwards super fast when he rewound it. If the class was "bad" or not paying attention or something, he'd just rewind it with the classroom lights on and the little bulb in the projector turned off.

In addition to an after-school job at the supermarket, Wilson had a paper route every morning before school. He'd ride his bike around the neighborhood as the sun was coming up, tossing papers onto porches for about an hour. So if there was a movie in school, he often took advantage of the darkness to catch a few extra Zs. This time, though, the film snapped and everyone except Wilson jerked upright in their seats as the projector went right on spinning the reel and the film just flapped like crazy: flap/flap, flap/flap, flap/flap, flap/flap. Loud as hell. And the

225

teacher flicked on the classroom lights and shut off the projector and everyone started laughing because Wilson was still asleep.

Well that's kind of how he felt, just then. Like the day was a movie and it had just broken and was flapping like crazy, and he was wide awake and needed to make sense of what he'd just seen; mending the film as it were, before he could resume the division of cells or growth of bean sprouts or migration of the salmon. If there was even the slightest chance anything he heard was true... He thought about the young mother he'd worked with at the coffee shop, about her ability to see certain things about people immediately, without even knowing them.

"Excuse me," someone said from behind him, tapping his shoulder. "Excuse me young man, were you here with Harold?"

The young man rose slowly from the bench, hands on the worn knees of his jeans, and took a step forward before turning to look at the shoulder-tapper. On the storefront side of the green bench, bending over to pick up the abandoned fliers just as a breeze began to stir them, was a pasty, thin, balding, wiry, almost translucent middle-aged man with John Lennon glasses; soft, uncalloused hands covered with spidery blue veins; and a big bristle-brush mustache that hid his top lip, leaving the thin, bright red lower lip to fend for itself. The mustache, the hair above each ear, and the few thin wisps that clung to his white, freckled scalp were light red. The young man caught himself staring at the man's oval head. The skin reminded him of the skin you see when you removed a two-day old band-aid. It was like the skin of creatures that live deep in caves. He almost felt that if given the right angle and light, he'd be able to see the man's skull. He wore loafers, brown corduroy pants, a black "X-Files" t-shirt, and a brown blazer. He was clutching the blue fliers to his chest with his left hand and counting them with his right. Upon finishing, he turned and retreated towards a heavy steel door painted green with a brushed-steel doorknob, a peephole, and the number 27. He quickly punched a series of numbers into a worn keypad affixed to the stucco beside the door, shielding them from passersby with the fliers in his left hand, and pulled open the door with almost comical effort, like some half-starved serf struggling with the enormous iron-girded door of his lord's manor. Having almost opened it wide enough to slip through, he attempted to turn, twisting his neck to look back over his left shoulder, John Lennon glasses slid down upon his nose. He appeared to be motioning for the young man to follow him with lateral jerks of his head. His wispy red comb-over caught the breeze that had threatened to scatter the fliers and flew upward like the crest of a cockatiel. It reminded the young man of a TV commercial he'd seen once. The comic relief notwithstanding, there was no way in hell he was going to follow the dude. The young man could easily take the X-Files guy, but there was no telling who might be waiting inside or what kind of place existed beyond the heavy green door.

"Uh, no. That's alright. You go ahead. Thanks though." The young man waved at the guy and gave him a polite nod and smile.

The brown blazer-clad man was losing his battle with the fliers, his glasses and the door. He looked incredulously at the young man's wave as if it were some foreign salute he didn't recognize, and made a strange impatient noise in his throat, as loud as he could, like someone trying to get someone's attention in a crowded room without actually articulating any words. The young man began laughing in spite of himself when a scene from one of the old British "Mr. Bean" episodes played out in his brain.

One flier slipped from his grasp and somersaulted to the sidewalk where it skated a few feet, pivoted, caught some wind and flipped up into an evergreen shrub in a redwood planter beside the front door of a hair salon. At that point, the John Lennon eyeglasses perched precariously on the man's sweaty, narrow, sun-starved nose; slipped and fell towards the pavement. In one surprisingly fluid motion, the man thrust his right foot into the doorway, locking his heel in place against the door, released the

polished steel handle, and swung his now free hand in an under-
hand arc cutting off the glasses' descent with only a split-second
to spare. Surprised himself, the corduroy-clad man looked down
at the unharmed glasses nestled in his quivering, clammy, white,
blue-veined hand, and looked up at the young man and smiled.

"Nice catch Phillip," said a Latino girl with sleek black hair
pulled back in a ponytail as she stepped out into the evening,
easily pushing open the heavy door, gym bag slung over a
shoulder. Phillip replaced his glasses, repositioned the fliers in
his hand and turned to see who had spoken. By the time he focused on her slim, nylon sweatsuit-clad body, she was several
yards down the sidewalk. Phillip called out "thank you" and she
raised her slender left hand high above her head and waved
without turning or slowing down. The young man and Phillip
watched her until she was enveloped by the rush-hour crowd. In
moments, she was gone.

"Do you have a few moments? I'd like to ask you about Harold." He had taken advantage of the girl's strength to reposition
himself completely inside the doorway, his left hip holding the
door open. The young man, reassured by the girl's friendly interaction with Phillip, still buzzed from the beer, and wanting to
"mend the film" of the day, decided to follow the pallid man into
the building, like Frodo following Gollum up the cliff at the Mi-
nas Morgul in that Lord of the Ring movie.

The foyer was small, dingy and dimly lit like every old foyer in
the city. Phillip and the young man climbed two flights of stairs
and left the stairwell for a white hallway lit by several rectangular fluorescent office-style light fixtures. The young man looked
at Phillip, half expecting the stark, sterile white hallway to ab-
sorb his waxen body like the flow of pedestrians on the sidewalk
had enveloped the pony-tailed girl. The clinical lighting and
white walls reminded him more of a hospital or clinic than an
office building. Along the left side of the hallway were white
painted wooden doors, and plexiglass plaques identifying the
company and suite number. The young man, warily peering

228

over his shoulder every few steps, read the names on the wall: "Ahmad's Money Transfer," "Bio-Genetics, Inc.," "Svelte Publishing," and finally, "Friedrichson Institute." Phillip fished a silver ring of keys from his blazer pocket and unlocked the door. The light wooden door swung open easily and silently. The sounds of the street met the young man's ears as he and Phillip stepped into a decent-sized office with an enormous ancient wooden desk atop which sat a laptop and a desktop computer; a printer/scanner/fax; several stacks of papers; an anachronistic aluminum desk lamp like you'd see in a really old P.I. movie; several coffee mugs; and a white Styrofoam take-out container with some kind of stewed meat and sauce over rice. Phillip walked in and sat down behind the desk in the creaky steel and vinyl desk chair facing the doorway, motioning for the young man to have a seat on a wooden chair to his right. To his left, prostrate on a prayer rug, was a young African-American man with a white crocheted kufi covering his head. He wore a black t-shirt and blue jeans. A pair of Nike tennis shoes sat behind him on the worn, scratched hardwood floor.

The young man stopped and waited until the man finished praying. Despite an open window and a fan, beads of sweat ran down the black man's neck. When he finished, he sat slowly upright and then stood, turning slowly to greet the visitor he heard accompany Phillip into the room. He extended his hand and introduced himself as "Reggie." He motioned along with Phillip for the young man to take a seat and then turned and carefully rolled up the prayer rug and stowed it in a wooden cabinet. Reggie sat down on a wooden chair identical to the young man's and replaced his tennis shoes. City noise flowed in through the open wood-frame window. The young man guessed that a second wooden door between Reggie and the filing cabinet led to a small bathroom.

"How long have you known Harold?" Reggie asked, while Phillip tapped away at the laptop computer. "We don't remember seeing you around here." The young man looked out the open window and realized from the storefronts on the far side of the street that the green bench was almost directly below. It creeped him out a bit, thinking that Reggie and Phillip had been watching the whole thing from the office window.

Reggie removed his kufi and wiped the sweat off his brow. He replaced it, taking care to position it correctly. He was slim but muscular, over six-foot, and at ease, as if talking to strangers about street prophets was part of his normal daily routine, or that he had seen enough in life that he now took everything in stride, no matter how bizarre. The young man glanced back at the open door and took in as many details of the room as he could, a bit more wary now that he was outnumbered and had a formidable foe in Reggie if things got weird. One of his friends had a cousin who'd been questioned by some low-level mafia types because they thought he might have seen something he wasn't supposed to. These guys didn't look like mafia types, at least not like the ones on TV.

"I don't know him at all, really." The young man mentally reviewed the day he'd had thus far and decided to lie about how he'd ended up in this part of town. Phillip lit up a cigarette and adjusted his glasses. He was listening, but couldn't bear to take his eyes off the two computer screens for more than a few moments. His fingers tapped the keyboards in sporadic bursts. The young man guessed he was instant messaging a lot of people simultaneously. "I met a friend out here for lunch and when she had to go home, I noticed this small crowd of people around this guy with a beard and decided to see what was going on." Reggie looked over at Phillip's cigarette smoldering in a thick clear glass ashtray and frowned.

Phillip looked up, although his eyes darted obsessively downward every few seconds. His translucent scalp was dotted with perspiration. He saw Reggie frowning, sighed, and turned his attention to the young man. "The elderly Asian woman who embraced Harold. What did they talk about?" The young man thought about the few words he'd managed to hear. He felt uneasy about repeating them, but decided that the woman made no effort to conceal her purpose in talking to Harold, and had actually drawn quite a bit of attention to herself by calling out his name. Plus, if these two guys knew something about Harold, it might give him what he needed to splice his day back together.

"The lady said that guy Harold healed her cancer." Reggie and Phillip looked meaningfully at each other and turned back to the young man.

"You heard this?"

"Yeah. Crazy shit, hunh?"

Reggie laughed quietly: "Yeah, crazy."

"So, Mrs. Yokohama is the third," Phillip said.

"Possibly the fourth," Reggie said.

"OK dudes, I'm sorry, but this is getting king of weird. I told you what you wanted to know. How about filling me in? I mean, I got friends to meet back home." He stirred as if to stand, half to force their hand and half because his curiosity and sense of adventure were slowly waning as his blood alcohol level slowly fell and thoughts of getting back to his own neighborhood crept into his mind.

Phillip smiled and closed his laptop. "Of course. I apologize. Our desire to know the truth sometimes distracts us from the equally important obligation to share the truth." He stood and walked over to the window, looked outside, and turned back to the young man. He stood stiffly, almost formally, his right forefinger and thumb stroking his mustache outward in opposite directions, his right elbow supported by his left hand, left arm held stiffly across his stomach. "Where to start, where to start."

The young man quickly realized that Phillip was the kind of person who enjoyed hearing himself talk and unconsciously assumed that everyone else did as well. The young man once had a teacher who felt that every occasion in life deserved a speech, and that HE was the one person talented enough and intelligent enough to deliver it. He was the perennial M.C., the quintessential keynote speaker, the supreme Turner of Phrases. Mr. Tocsin had a speech for the first day of school, the second day of school, and the third day of school. He had a speech for the school year's first Friday, the first time he passed out homework, and the year's last test. He gave a speech when he joined students in the lunchroom for stewed turkey and rice, and when he joined an impromptu game of HORSE after school in the gym. Phillip, the young man guessed, was probably of the same ilk. Harold, on the other hand, in the short time he had been with him, seemed to speak unselfconsciously, sparingly, focused on the people around him rather than on himself or on his own words; and when he did express something of gravity, he did so with the unique humility of someone delivering an important message that was not their own.

Phillip licked his small red lower lip excitedly. The young man thought that he looked most like a rabbit. The whiskers, small lower lip, small oval darting tongue.

"In the 16th episode of the very first season of the X-Files, enigmatically titled 'E.B.E.,' Dana turns to Mulder and says, 'Mulder, the truth is out there, but so are the lies.'" Phillip stood with his unblinking eyes wide open for a moment, as if to emphasize the import of what he just said. "And that profound statement, spoken by such a lovely individual, summarizes where I was at six months ago. After seven-and-a-half years of searching for the truth, I realized that while my searching in and of itself was legitimate, the assumptions under which I was operating were faulty. When my beloved mother and founder of the Friedrichson Institute was only moments away from herself entering the great unknown after a horrible bout of pneumonia, she motioned me to the side of her bed and whispered a single word." Phillip paused, eyes again wide open, fixed, unblinking as if watching the event on a screen suspended somewhere over the young man's head. He paused, not saying a word, not even making a sound. Finally, after several awkward moments, the young man looked quizzically over at Reggie as if to silently ask "What the fuck?" Reggie nodded understandingly, and with the look of a slightly irritated yet indulgent parent, muttered quietly, "Phil. Hey. Phil….PHIL!!"

Phillip stood there silently for a few more moments, as if not wanting to admit that Reggie's voice had successfully spurred any action on his part, and then slowly relaxed his eyes, returning his gaze to the young man and Reggie. He carefully pulled a neatly folded handkerchief from one of his blazer's inside pockets, removed the John Lennon glasses for a moment, dabbed at his eyes and commenced cleaning the round lenses. Carefully folding and returning the handkerchief to his pocket and replacing the glasses carefully on the bridge of his nose, Phillip turned to the young man and Reggie, and dramatically said the word 'Other.'"

He allowed the word's significance to reverberate throughout the small room as if it were a gunshot in an acoustically superior concert hall. "My mother looked up at me and said 'Other.' And for seven-and-a-half years I ignored that simple, yet profound admonishment. I did not seek 'The Other,' as she asked. I believed, in the arrogance of my knowledge and extensive schooling, that there was no 'Other,' that the truth I sought was a truth that could be quantified, dissected, measured and displayed for all the world to see. And I was going to be the man who did it. The man who would finally prove for all the world to see, that the human being is simply one of a million different organisms, all slowly fashioned through the methodical processes of evolution, and that there was no Almighty God looking down on creatures which He fashioned in His own image. And how was I going to prove that once and for all? Rather easily, I had thought back in the day…" Phillip chuckled, looked downward, and shook his head slowly back and forth, theatrically indicating just how ashamed he was of his past hubris, and unintentionally demonstrating that he remained oblivious of his ego's still-robust health.

"I was so entirely convinced that I knew the truth, so utterly engrossed in the seemingly pedestrian task of documenting the truth, that I ignored Scully's admonition to watch out for the lies. I ignored my mother's admonition to look beyond the staid halls of science and the self-congratulatory promises of Gnosticism, solipsism, and New Age mysticism and see that there is truth entirely independent from Homo Sapiens and our near-vertical forehead and 1200 cc brains. Saint Augustine argued that there is a 'God-shaped vacuum in every man,' and that is the psychological and philosophical reality that demands our attention every minute of every day. There is an intrinsic…one could almost say physiological…need for something outside of ourselves. From the moment we are born, to the moment we die, we are reaching outward. Why then….why would human beings of every country, of every ethnic origin, every language, tradition, era and race, be constantly reaching outward unless there really were something out there for which to reach? This drive, a component of a universal human consciousness, like that which Jung spoke of, has been with us since the beginning and continues to shape our behavior, thoughts and desires to this day. Wherever we find evidence of ancient humans, we find evidence of this quest for connection with some Other, some being or force or presence or energy which DOES NOT LIE WITHIN." Phillip's eyes grew wide again and he stabbed the air with his right forefinger to punctuate his words.

"Years ago, I argued that there was no 'Other' and that the desire to search for one was an intrinsically illogical impulse encouraged by fear-mongering religious leaders intent upon lining their pockets and increasing the power of their particular organizations. I longed to humiliate them in the public's eyes. No, more than that: in History's eyes. I wanted to be the ultimate iconoclast. Bringing down the hateful, cowardly hypocrites like Jim Bakker and Jimmy Swaggert is one thing. Bringing down the entire religion out of whose dying, diseased loins their televan-

234

gelistic empires sprung was another. I was going to be the Samson who finally pushed over the pillars supporting Catholicisim, Protestantism, Judaism and Islam. I envisioned myself as a liberator of minds, as a Moses leading millions out of Egypt into a Promised Land of rationalism, science, logic and Reason. Darwin explained how we humans came to be and why we no longer had to fear an angry God, but I was going to be the one who proved it! I was going to be the one to rub the Truth in the collective face of those who would take advantage of sincere, well-meaning millions, all wanting to believe, wanting to be safe, wanting to live free from fear. And I figured all it would take was a single body. A single corporeal offering to the gods of science and public opinion and the matter would be settled, the gavel would fall, the pronouncement 'Case Closed' made, forever sealing the fate of organized religion.

So I searched for extraterrestrials. Physical, organic beings from other planets. I also spent a short period of time up in the Pacific Northwest working with an expert on the Sasquatch. I just wanted a body. Even a part of a body. Something no one else has ever been able to produce. So many people, literally millions over the millennia, have encountered these physical, organic, carbon-based beings. Millions of encounters, and not a peep from the main three monotheistic faiths. All I needed was just enough flesh for DNA samples. With that, I'd be able to pull the great curtain back and reveal the bumbling nondescript "wizard" working the controls of modern monotheism. The snake oil salesman whose name means false hope, weakness, fear and stupidity. I could single-handedly bring modern religion to its knees, not to beg for its life, but to suck my atheistic dick; and in the process, free untold millions of poor misguided believers. I imagined taking the corpse with me on the lecture circuit, the talk-show circuit, take it to the U.N., the Vatican, cryogenically preserved in a Plexiglas cylinder like Michael Jackson; and meet with the rabbis, the preachers, the imams, the pastors, and all those priests; and ask them to show me the passage in the Koran, the Torah, the Catechism or the New Testament that discusses the extraterrestrial flesh laying there

235

before us, let alone counsel us on how we should interact with alien life forms. How could an omnipotent, omniscient God not have the faintest idea that entire worlds existed next door to this small blue globe? How could a Deity fail to address part of His Creation that constantly visits this world? How could an omnipotent, omniscient God inspire holy men to write scriptures without recognizing at least ONCE the fact that his followers were encountering travelers from other parts of the galaxy on a regular basis?"

Phillip's small, pale, clammy head shone with perspiration, droplets interspersed with freckles and random, isolated strands of red hair. He breathed heavily, his shoulders rising and falling, looking distractedly forward but seeing the infinite cold Cosmos before him, not the faded, nicotine-stained walls of his office. His small, red rabbit tongue licked his walrus mustache and he rubbed his translucent hands together slowly as if washing. Reggie was eating the food that the young man had noticed on the desk, looking on in bemused forbearance. If it were not for his sometimes overpowering curiosity, and Reggie's apparent normalcy and calm demeanor, the young man would have fled the X-File guy's office long before.

It was nearly dark outside. The young man could see the storefronts' lights through the window. Phillip put both hands on his head. The young man remembered a line from a Doors song Wilson liked to play. Phillip held his head like an egg, as if his nearly translucent flesh and skull were as fragile as a paper-thin wasp's nest. So this was the sum, the apex of the human evolution he had once heralded as the true religion, a slight, frail, weak, hairless, thin-skinned, brittle-boned, humanoid; cradling his oversized, vulnerable brain in his own cold, clammy, blue-veined hands. Aside from the enormous bristle-brush mustache, he looked a lot like the very aliens he had obsessively hunted for almost eight years.

Reggie was finished with his meal. He placed the Styrofoam container and plastic fork carefully into a plastic bag-lined trash

236

can and walked over to Phillip who still stood there, his head in his hands. Phillip was a bit over the top thought the young man, but there was something compelling about his quest, if you disregarded his obvious megalomania. At least he gave a shit. The young man remembered a cartoon he used to watch when he was a kid, called "Pinky and the Brain," in which a mouse and his cohort spent each episode unsuccessfully attempting to take over the world. He struggled not to laugh to himself as Reggie guided Phillip back to his chair, where he slumped and pulled the neatly folded handkerchief from his blazer's breast pocket once more, this time to mop up the perspiration on his head.

Reggie wiped his mouth carefully with a brown paper napkin, walked over to place it in the trash can, and returned to the wooden chair upon which he'd been sitting. He slowly turned the chair around in order to straddle it. The metal cap on the bottom of each chair leg scraped along the worn wood floor with a sound that reminded the young man of sandpaper. A military helicopter flew low overhead. He could feel the thump-thump throb of its rotors. He still didn't know exactly how to get home, and he began mentally counting up how much money he'd spent, wondering if he had enough for a bus. Another taxi ride wasn't going to happen.

As if reading his thoughts, Reggie looked at the young man and asked him how he was getting home. "I'd give you a ride, but I don't have a car right now. Where do you live?"

The young man told him the cross-streets about three blocks from his apartment. He didn't trust either one of them.

"Alright. Well this is what you do. Two blocks from here, at 4th and Alder, there's an Express Bus stop. Straight out that way," he said, pointing out through the wall towards the Italian Restaurant at which the young man had eaten. The young man felt for the slip of paper with the waitress' phone number, making sure it was still there.

"The Express Buses come by every fifteen minutes and they take you almost non-stop to your neck of the woods. You're going to want to get off at the second or third stop after the stadium. You know where I'm talking about?"

The young man looked slightly upward as he mentally tracked the route of the bus which would be taking him home. He smiled as he remembered the way the main drag snuck behind the new stadium and went another half mile before coming to a "T." Halfway to the "T," he'd get off and catch the 88 bus down to his apartment. He felt better knowing where the hell he was.

"And then you take the 88 and go about 12 blocks and you're home free." Reggie knew the bus routes like he knew the back-roads and forest trails back home. If nothing else, this was a city in which you didn't need a car. A bus pass, patience, and a good book, in this case an English translation of the Koran, were all you needed. No car payments, no insurance, no gas money, no oil changes, no mechanic bills. The only drawback? Trying to date without a car. But then you just planned as best you could, went out with friends who had rides, or coughed up the dough for a taxi.

"So we cool?" asked Reggie. "You've heard Phillip's story. I've got mine to tell, and then you'll understand what we'd like to know about your encounter with Harold. Cool?" The young man nodded: "Cool."

"Everyone's got a story to tell, and most folks have several. A wise man once said that the best place to start is at the beginning. So I will. My name is Reginald Masters Jefferson." Reggie enunciated his name with relish. His name was one of the few things his father had given him, and he treasured it. It was one of the few things Life couldn't take away. His father was taken away from him, long before he had a chance to get to know him, but the only way Life was going to get his name was to kill him like it had his Pa. And even then, one of the first things he'd done when he made some money, was buy a burial plot for his family back home. Land is cheap in the South, whether it's for people who are alive or people who are dead. Everyone in his family was going to have a place to rest their bones and a stone with their name permanently engraved, and he had the papers in a safety-deposit box to prove it.

"I was born and raised in the South. I didn't move out here to start my own life until I had fulfilled my duties at home. I was the oldest of six kids, and took the place of my father when he died in a car wreck. I raised my brothers and sisters as if I were their daddy. My mother worked two jobs and took us to church all day Sunday, her only day off, so they saw more of me and their school teachers than any other authority figure. When the youngest ones hit high school and could help my mother enough, I came out here. I wanted to see what life was like away from the South. And I wanted to see the ocean. Not the Gulf of Mexico, but the ocean. The Pacific or the Atlantic. I chose the Pacific." Reggie spoke as if he enjoyed telling his story, as if relating his past somehow helped him shape his future. "I moved from job to job, apartment to apartment, girl to girl, drug to drug, and could not find satisfaction, just like that old song. Before long, I began to feel old, because the inner drive, the inner purpose I had felt when I was helping support and care for my family back home, was gone. The enjoyment of basic pleasures, sex, booze, drugs, whatever, became fleeting and more and more expensive. A sense of emptiness I had never felt before weighed on me like the weight of the world on Atlas' shoulders, but unlike Atlas, the only thing I was holding up was a heavy, hedonistic lifestyle. I wasn't doing anyone any good, and yet I felt more pressure and anxiety than I had when I was holding together an entire family.

"When I was younger, I helped my mother shape my brothers and sisters into good little Christians. It meant so much to my mother that each of her children be "saved,' that every last one of them had knelt at the front of the church on a Sunday night and confessed their sins and accepted the saving grace of the blood of Jesus. I did all of it, knowing that deep inside my heart

I didn't really believe. It wasn't so much a decision as it was a realization. At least that's the way it felt. It was like looking outside and seeing that it was raining. You don't decide that it's raining. You don't intend for it to rain. You just look outside and say 'It's raining.' It was just recognizing a reality. It's not that you hated the sun and loved the rain, it's just that it was raining and that's what you saw."

"Communion Sundays were the hardest. The preacher'd be up there, big hands on either side of the pulpit, sweat pouring down his big round face, and he'd warn us, he'd warn all us brothers and sisters against the damnation awaiting anyone who partook of the blood or flesh of Christ with an unbelieving heart. I condemned myself a million times before I left home, simply by swallowing the grape juice and crumbled crackers. Paper fans on wooden tongue depressors, advertising the local funeral home, waving back and forth like the leaves on a quaking aspen in Colorado, fluttering all over the sanctuary, and brothers and sisters praying and testifying and saying "amen," saying "yes sir," saying "Sweet Jesus," and there I am, committing sacrilege more times than I can remember, like some ancient Roman desecrating a temple, and even though I didn't believe it, I didn't like the fact that I had to live a lie in order to save my brothers and sisters and make my mother proud and happy. But sometimes you don't get an easy choice. You just have to suck it up and do what you have to do. Just like in football. Twice-a-day summer practices, sweating every last drop of moisture out of your body until your stomach is twisted into a cramping, dry knot, and the salt is in your mouth, but you suck it up. Balls to the wall. White coach yelling at you. Balls to the wall. And I wondered every Sunday, what this crowd of black men and women were doing worshipping a white savior. White coach, white teachers, white mayors, white governors, white presidents. Our pastor's grandfather had been lynched for looking at a white woman. One of my mother's uncles was sentenced to die for a murder he didn't commit by an all-white jury. Why were we worshipping our oppressor? Why was our God white? We didn't learn about Jesus until we came to America, and we came to America as slaves. We adopted the God of the slave owners and sang hymns to the white savior whom our taskmasters worshipped. It's hard for me to swallow."

"So these days, these days, I'm trying something new." Reggie smiled, a genuine, relived smile, like someone waking from a nightmare and realizing that things are OK. "I was walking one day, not far from here, and all these men; black men, white men, and Asian men; all these men were walking toward a mosque. Here in America, on the West Coast for Pete's sake, there's all these men walking together in unity and brotherhood, getting out of SUVs, stepping off of buses, parking their taxi cabs, hopping off bicycles; all moving in unison toward a building that represented to me, inclusion. It reminded me a lot of Malcom X's experience in Mecca."

"My church back home was a traditional southern Baptist church. White-washed clapboard exterior and a single steeple, rising toward heaven. But this mosque, this mosque had a dome, like the earth, like the atmosphere, like the solar system, and it wasn't so narrow and focused and limited. It was like here is an artificial horizon beneath which you can worship the one God who created everything, and everyone in the mosque, regardless of where they're kneeling, has the same view, the same position, the same advantage, the same place beneath the great dome of existence."

"It was really cool, but I didn't feel comfortable going inside. I didn't know the prayers, I didn't know the traditions, the Dos and the Don'ts. I didn't know what to do or what to say, and I'm a perfectionist. I don't like to do something unless I can do it well, and I don't like to look stupid. So I started studying. Very quickly, I realized that in order to learn as much as I wanted to learn as quickly as I wanted to learn it, I'd have to go high tech. Card catalogues at the city library weren't going to cut it. I needed translations, email, newsletters, chat rooms and instant messaging. So I've been borrowing Phillip's computers and re-searching. Researching Islam to see if this is the way I should

241

go. Researching to see if this third member of the Big Three is the Truth I've been searching for all my life. I figure in another three months, I'll have learned enough to blend in at the mosque. That's not saying much, but I hate attracting attention to myself. You may have already figured this out, but I work three doors down at the money transfer company. The employees are all Muslims, and they are helping me understand the way, but I don't like to do research in front of them, and I don't want to use work time for my own personal development, so I ran into Phillip one day, and he offered the use of his computers in exchange for information about the Jinn."

"Jinni," Phillip began, rising from his seat and stretching his clammy white hands toward the ceiling, before letting them fall to his side and shaking out the kinks in his shoulders, "are entities described in Arabic as originating from 'smokeless flames of fire.' Think about that for a moment, and you'll realize its significance. 'Smokeless flames of fire.' It's a cliché: 'Where there's smoke, there's fire.' Similarly, the obverse is almost always true: 'Where's there's fire, there's smoke,' but the Jinn are like fire without smoke. Entities that can be seen and even felt; entities that can act upon our physical world, effecting physical change, even occasionally destroying physical objects (much like a UFO leaves burn marks in the grass at a 'landing site'), but leaving no physical trace of themselves. No physical trace, because they are not truly physical. THAT explained my reality. And the imagery is aligned with other elemental motifs of the Big Three. The Koran associates mortal humans with 'clay,' much as the Old Testament portrays the First Man being created from the dust of the earth."

Reggie closed his eyes and recited: "And the Lord God formed man of the dust of the ground, and breathed into his nostrils the breath of life; and man became a living soul. Genesis chapter two, verse seven. There are similar passages in the Koran, but I haven't memorized them, yet."

"Angels are Light, Men are Clay, and Jinni are Smokeless Flames," Phillip continued, smiling and stroking his enormous mustache with his right forefinger and thumb. "Jinni are entities which often mislead, manipulate and impede human beings. They can take different forms, sometimes appearing as animals or even people. They sometimes commit 'shirk' by leading humans to recognize deities other than Allah or to attribute Allah's characteristics to entities other than Allah. Particularly evil Jinni are called Shayateen, the singular of which, Shaitan, sounds remarkably similar to Christianity's 'Satan.' The word Jinni, plural for Jinn, is the basis for our word 'genie.' If you cross-reference Islam, Judaism and Christianity, you come up with an amazingly coherent multi-monotheism. Throw out the wild cards and you've got what I think of as the marrow, the central truths, agreed upon by the majority of the world's religious adherents. I'm sure it's already been done, but if it hasn't, or if it's been done before but only poorly, I'd love to embark upon a journey to discover and analyze the commonalities of Judaism, Christianity and Islam, to cross-reference them as it were, and produce a tome containing the shared stories, doctrines and values of all three."

Reggie stood, said "excuse me," and turned and opened the wooden door between himself and the filing cabinet. Inside, the young man saw a stark white bathroom with an old white porcelain toilet, a urinal and a sink with a cracked mirror mounted to the wall above. A bare 60-watt light bulb hung from the ceiling beside a small metal chain used to switch it on and off. Reggie paused before entering the bathroom and quietly recited "Allahomma Inny A'ootho Bika Mina 'I 'khobothi Wa 'l 'khaba'ith" before entering the bathroom, left foot first, and closing the door behind him with his left hand.

"Roughly translated," Phillip explained, "that means 'O'Allah: I seek refuge in you from male and female noxious beings,' referring, of course to Jinni. Inside the bathroom, he'll use his left hand whenever possible to take care of business, since the right hand is the one with which you greet others and eat. There are a number of other rules, many of which dictate how one relieves oneself out in the desert or woods. This is all in the Koran and in officially accepted scholarly commentaries. Islam is much like Judaism in that way: in addition to a single most holy book, like the Koran or the Torah, there are innumerable documents recording holy men's comments and thoughts which are esteemed almost as much."

The young man nodded and walked over to the window to take a look outside. What a fucking weird day. Below him and to the left was the green bench he had sat on earlier. Across the street, a waiter was lighting the black torches surrounding the patio area of the Italian restaurant. The young man looked up at the evening sun, smoldering blood-orange through the smog of the Western horizon. A passenger jet, miles away, banked and flashed silver and disappeared. The traffic was lighter now, and there were fewer people on the sidewalk. Rush hour was over and the street's nightlife was still hours away. To his right, a young woman in high heels and a short skirt stood impatiently talking on a little silver cell phone and craning her neck to see down the street. The young man leaned against the chipped, dirty window sill, his head half-way in and half-way out. He listened to the woman's loud rancorous, whiny voice, and watched her tight ass twitch this way and that as she alternatively shifted her weight from one fuck-me-pump to the other.

"Goddamn it! Where the fuck is the driver? He better show up in the next five minutes or I'll have Freddy rip his balls off. Fucking idiot probably can't find me. Jesus, I stand out like a sore thumb on this shitty street. Tell him to look for the pink Dolce & Gabbana skirt and my black Gucci motorcycle jacket. Ugh, I am so fucking pissed.

"NO. Jesus, you're a dumb bitch. Of course I didn't wear my Michael Kors. Did you not listen to a single goddamned word I just said? Dolce and Gabbana skirt, pink. Gucci leather jacket, black. Prada pumps, pink. It's the same fucking thing Rachel

Leigh Cook had on at that awards show the other night. Get a fucking clue, Shel.

"Right. So I asked her, is that a REAL Debbie Brooks bag? It sure as hell better be for $800. So I bought that, made the bitch clean a spot off it first, and then got the ring, too. If I'm gonna suck Freddy's ugly cock, he's gonna fucking set me up. I sure as hell ain't doing it for his looks."

The young man saw a black town car pull into traffic a couple blocks down. It accelerated recklessly and lurched to the curb in front of the girl. A guy in his fifties or sixties stepped out and quietly began talking to the woman. He spoke so quietly that the young man could barely make out his voice, but it sounded like a heavy Eastern-European or Russian accent. He gestured down the street from where he had come. He used his hands a lot. It looked like he was pleading his case. The girl was in his face and wasn't having any of it.

"Two minutes my sweet ass, motherfucker. You're fucking ten minutes late and I'm going to have you fired. Now open the fucking door and get me out of this asswipe neighborhood. Fucking shithole."

The young man heard a toilet flush and he turned from the window and saw Reggie step out of the bathroom, right foot first, with the words "Ghufraanak. Alhamdu Lillah, Allathy Afany Wa Akhrajha Al Atha Minny." Phillip stopped typing and looked up: "Upon exiting, he asks Allah's pardon and gives thanks for protecting him from harm or impurity. Reggie is teaching me some of the more common phrases as he learns them himself." Reggie smiled and once again straddled the backwards-turned wooden chair. The young man remained standing and leaned back against the wall by the open window, with Phillip on his right, Reggie on his left, and the open door in front of him.

"After seven and a half years, I finally accepted the fact that I was never going to find the physical proof I had so arrogantly sought. The visitors are real, and they often appear to have physical characteristics; leaving crop circles, areas of high radioactivity, burn marks, etc., but no one in the history of mankind has ever held the proof in their hands. So what does that tell you? They're real, but amorphous. Like clouds, you can see them, they can cast a shadow, you can even feel their effects in terms of temperature changes and precipitation, but you can't hold them in your hand. You can't find pieces of clouds lying about on the ground ready to be picked up. Clouds don't get hung up on fir trees as they move through mountain passes leaving behind tufts of fluffy whiteness.

"It was in the midst of this epiphany that I came across a website maintained by a proponent of Gordon Creighton's hypothesis that UFOs and aliens are evidence of Jinni. I had read Creighton's 1988 essay before, of course, but had dismissed it outright, since after all, I was a de facto atheist and felt even less compelled to believe in spirits or angels than I felt compelled to believe in God. And he wasn't the only expert to posit an alternate theory. Carl Jung believed UFOs were a sociological phenomenon, that 'extraterrestrials' were actually 'ultraterrestrials,' entities existing on different planes of existence. But Islam's position, championed by Creighton, made the most sense. Jinni can shapeshift. They can take on physical characteristics, can even appear human, and we've had the answer in our hands for nearly 2,000 years. And longer, really, since spiritual or supernatural explanations for the paranormal have been around since the dawn of recorded history. We in the west, however, dismissed tales of spirits as superstition, and only recently began paying attention to Islam, and then only in the context of terrorism or religious conflict. Muslim nations gave the world advanced mathematics and saw no contradiction between their science and their faith. When Chechen rebels watched a UFO buzz Russian troops, they immediately recognized the assistance of a good Jinn, while the Russians scrambled several fighters in an unsuccessful effort to engage the brightly lit craft.

"The other piece of the puzzle fell into place when I began to look at history in terms of a struggle between monotheism and its enemies both temporal and spiritual. I'm a sucker for a pattern that fits, and if anything has ever fit, it is this. Think about it. When a person sees the Loch Ness Monster, or Sasquatch, or a UFO, or an alien, does that experience draw them closer or push them farther from a monotheistic faith? The paranormal has always tempted humans with the promise of hidden knowledge without the need for direct intercession from a supreme, judgmental deity or a hierarchical, equally judgmental religious institution. In fact, the woman who maintains the website names names, indicting various 19th and 20th century leaders of what we now call 'New Age' movements, movements which intersected and eventually culminated in cults like the one that constructed an underground city in Montana, stockpiling guns and supplies for the day Soviet nuclear missiles would slam into American soil. The missiles never hit, and the Feds didn't appreciate the heavy artillery the cult assembled, channeled 'knowledge' notwithstanding. You can follow the thread from the mystery religions of ancient Egypt to Zoroastrianism and Gnosticism, Rosicrucianism, the Theosophical Society, to the 'I AM' Movement. Shit, right now there are hundreds of people living on and around Mt. Shasta who claim to channel the 'Ascended Masters' like Saint Germain and even Christ. They look to the mountain's subterranean cadre of ancient Lemurians for direction and wisdom. The carry on conversations with worms and stop eating food on the advice of channeled entities. And there's never any real doctrine you can say Yea or Nea to, it's all a stream of circular reasoning, vague niceties and claims to speak for dead wise ancients. Which is EXACTLY why Reggie and I are so interested in Harold. Real shit happens around Harold. All these other so-called mystics, they don't ever do anything real or say anything real. The prophecies they receive from dead religious figures don't come true; their promises of health, wealth and enlightenment fizzle amid excuses, obfuscation and condemnation. But people are healed when Harold is around. And the things he says are true."

The young man looked at Reggie and Phillip. He turned and looked out into the night. He felt for the waitress' phone number and the damn flask that wasn't there.

"I can't tell you much about Harold. I feel bad, cause you guys have spilled your guts and I don't have much to give you. But what I CAN tell you is that little old lady wasn't faking it. Whatever happened to her…whether she was cured or whatever…she believed it. I was close enough to see that. She was crying and shaking and shit and the way she looked up at him was weird. It was like those Jesus movies where he heals some guy and the guy is like 'Oh my God,' you know?" He looked at Reggie and then looked at Phillip. They were listening intently. Phillip was typing like crazy on the computer like he was taking notes. Reggie was smiling and nodding. The young man continued, "And you know the weird thing is that Harold acted like he was trying to hide what had happened. I mean, you'd think he'd be announcing what he'd done so he could get on TV and make some money so he wouldn't be homeless anymore, but he acted almost a little afraid that we'd hear what was going on, or embarrassed. Almost like he was afraid of getting in trouble for healing people without being a doctor or something. And before that, before that there was this guy who had a recurring dream he didn't understand. And it was bugging the hell out of him. Not like a nightmare, but you could tell it was troubling him, the fact that he kept dreaming about this 'darkness' or something and didn't know why. Well I figured Harold would interpret his dream and tell him what it meant like a fortune-teller down on 3rd Street, you know, and then ask for twenty bucks or something. And I suppose that's what happened, but I never actually heard Harold TELL the guy anything, and he didn't ask the guy for money. It was like he helped the guy see whatever it was on his own. And then the guy just left. It was fucking weird. There was something going on alright, but I don't know what it was. But you could feel it in your gut. I can tell you that. It freaked me out a bit."

Phillip typed for almost a full minute after the young man stopped talking. Reggie and the young man patiently waited.

"Does that help?" the young man asked. He didn't know these guys and still didn't trust them, but nothing they'd done that night suggested that they were anything other than what they seemed, and in that way, they were apparently very much like the Harold guy.

"Yes. Thank you," Phillip said. "Here's my card. If you happen to stop by our part of town and run into Harold again, I'd appreciate it if you could call me. You're very perceptive for your age and I'd appreciate anything you might have to share."

The young man held up the card, said thanks, indicated that he had a bus to catch, and left. He threw his weight against the heavy green door and walked out into the dry, smoggy heat of the evening. The city was like a giant million-car garage shut up tight with all the motors running. The last smoldering hint of the sun in the West was gone, rubbed out in the foothills and pocketed like a half-finished cigarette. The increasingly inky darkness and the lonely 2nd-rate trek of the moon, were all that were left to mark the progression of the night. Smog and city lights obscured the brilliant legions of stars, the cold diamonds of the sky. Only the moon was bright enough to compete with the neon, halogen, sodium vapor and mercury. What kind of place is it when you can't even see the stars? We throw up arcs and filaments and ballasts like Babels of illumination, swaggering about as if lighting up ballfields, airports and city streets makes any real difference in the world, let alone the universe. All of it amounting to less than a pin prick in the black, heavy, backlit Big Top of reality. We erase the night sky and forget that there's infinity all around us.

The young man inhaled the night and felt for the waitress' phone number in the back pocket of his Levi's. Goddamn she was cute. The crosswalk light flashed a white stick figure, and he ambled across the street, looking both ways for red-running psychos, his Vans rolling on and off the warm asphalt like the sticky hot slicks of a dragster. The Italian restaurant was full and spilling out onto the patio and sidewalk. Hungry people stood about outside the front door with oversized, brightly colored pagers and oversized guts to match, waiting for their turn to enter. The patio's black wrought iron torches burned seductively, syrupy tar-black smoke materializing as the orange flames licked the night air.

The young man "Excuse Me'd" his way through the crowd at the door and the crowd in the lobby and maneuvered his way to the bar. He boosted himself up onto one of only two available black vinyl swiveling bar stools. A pretty bartender with Merlot lips that parted slightly when relaxed, revealing an even top row of teeth, dropped a cardboard coaster onto the bar in front of him and asked to see some I.D. The young man obliged, she looked down and then up, and asked him, "What'll it be, hon?" He ordered beer and smiled and looked around at all the people in the bar. The bartender turned and stepped over to the taps, grabbing a clean pint glass and flipping it right-side up beneath the amber flow. She had dark, straight, shoulder-length hair, gently curled at the bottom; brown eyes, nice tits and a Celtic tattoo encircling her left arm. She wore the restaurant's t-shirt, black jeans and beat-up Docs.

Everyone in the bar was having a good time. He sat at the bar and drank his beer, occasionally pretending to be interested in the baseball game on the muted TV, but really just sitting and listening; listening to the voices rise and fall, intersecting and colliding, weaving together and coming apart like the pedestrians on the sidewalk hours before. Some people laughed and yelled and slapped each other on the back like people in beer commercials. The jocularity was contagious, but he couldn't help thinking that it really doesn't take much to amuse us humans, and maybe that's a good thing. Outside in the real world, many of these same people were irritable, moody, depressed and tired; but as soon as they sat down at a table in a bar with a few drinks and a loud crowd, they became as giddy as game-show contestants. Perfectly Pav-fucking-lovian.

"God Almighty she's got a rack," he thought, as a bleached-blonde, middle-aged waitress walked by with a roasted Italian hoagie that looked almost as good as she did. He wasn't truly hungry, but the food smelled so good and she looked so good, that he ordered a sandwich and another beer from the dark-haired, parted-lips bartender, completely forgetting about saving money for the Express. Between the blonde and the brunette, he was in heaven. The blonde's breasts were almost perfectly round and extended outward in gravity-defying perpendicularity, like grapefruits affixed to a wall.

Lost in thought, he was startled when the bartender swept by, depositing another beer and his food without missing a step. The sandwich was good: spicy pepperoni and salami with onions, peppers, melted cheese, shredded lettuce, fresh tomato and Italian dressing. It was almost as good as the one his father ordered for him on a trip to Philly when he was just a boy. His dad was born in Philly, and although he got out of the city as fast as he could, courtesy of the U.S. Army, he still felt an odd nostalgia for the place: neighborhoods of aging row-houses, grimy city streets full of trash and cars and kids playing stickball. His Dad missed the pretzels most of all. At least he talked about them most of all: the big soft, salty ones some guy standing on the curb would sell to you out of a big cardboard box. You'd pull up and buy four or five before the light turned green. When his Dad got out of the army and settled on the West Coast, there weren't any guys on the curb selling hot, soft, salty pretzels, so he settled for the store-bought, miniature, crispy versions sold in plastic bags next to the potato chips. It was weird knowing what he wanted and what he settled for; what we thought pretzels were on the West Coast and what they really were on the East Coast.

251

When his Dad took him to Philly, back to his old neighborhood, they went to this nondescript storefront sandwich place with three tables and a counter, cheap metal and vinyl chairs, a gruff man with hairy arms, and a dirty linoleum floor. He ordered two hoagies with the works. It was the best sandwich he'd ever had, unlike anything they called a sandwich out West. The old sandwich shop and the dirty old city itself had a blue collar "fuck you" pride about it, like it knew what it was, but dared you to say something about it.

The young man watched his father as they walked down dirty sidewalks, crossed busy streets, and stepped into rundown shops. He was confused, unable to discern whether his father was happy or sad. He wondered if maybe his Dad was just confirming in his mind that it had all happened the way he remembered, that the memories coursing through his mind, sharing space with dreams and illusions, had some connection to reality. Maybe when you get to be that age, you're so removed from your childhood, that it's hard to tell what, if anything, that you remember is real.

The bar and the restaurant were so full it was funny. God, we'd all be dead if there was a fire, he thought. And it was loud. Loud like a club, not a restaurant. There wasn't a single polite dinner conversation in the joint. People were getting close, talking into each other's ears, leaning in, reading lips, laughing loudly, yelling across the crowd for the waiters and waitresses, the servers themselves yelling "corner" and "behind" as they frantically rushed heavy, steaming plates of pasta and sauce from the kitchen out to the multitudes like modern-day disciples of Jesus miraculously feeding the five-thousand. He thought he heard a jukebox playing but couldn't really be sure. The beer was doing the job and he watched the waitresses and surveyed the crowd, but the bar was mostly full of guys. He had a couple of three-hundred-pound, shaved-head, Pro Wrestler types on his right wearing little paper bibs and eating crab legs over beer; and a guy about the same age as his father on his left. The guy on

252

his left was losing his hair, and what he had left was turning grey. He was looking down at an old-fashioned full of bourbon. He had a quarter of a fifth in there if he had a drop. He looked down into the copper liquid, smiling and slowly stroking the glass with his calloused right thumb. Maybe he was already drunk. Periodically, he'd look up and watch the people around him; slowly sucking in the life of the place like it was pure oxygen.

The bartender came by and replaced his empty with a full pint. In the split second before she left, he held the afternoon waitress' phone number up, figuring she'd recognize the paper, the number, the handwriting, or the M.O. She looked at the girly handwriting, smiled, and kneeled down to look at a clock hidden beneath the bar. The young man looked down her tee-shirt at the tops of her breasts. They were pure white, untouched by the blue glare of tanning booth lights, smooth and resting slightly lower than the blonde's; teardrops rather than grapefruit. She stood, realized what he was doing and smiled again, thinking he'd planned the whole thing, and slowly shook her head and yelled "She's off now, sorry!" The young man smiled and thanked her above the din. She nodded and glanced back at him over her shoulder as he admired her retreating ass. She gets hit on 8,000 times a night: how come she likes it when I do it, he wondered jubilantly, his dick and gut awash in longing. Then again, maybe it was just part of being a good bartender; making every patron feel like this bar is the only bar in the world. He motioned to her for a telephone, raising his thumb and pinky up to the right side of his face. She smiled again and nodded behind him as she dumped a bunch of empty crab legs into the trash.

The young man hesitated for a moment, nervous about his seat, but all things being equal, the almost-full pint of beer would save his place as surely as a best buddy would in elementary school. He had to take a mighty whiz anyway, might as well give the girl a call. Take a leak, call a girl. The bathroom had to be by the payphones. A restaurant, bar or the airport was about

the only place you could find a payphone these days. Back
when his Dad was a kid, payphones were a dime a dozen. Ha,
Superman wouldn't have any place to change these days.

He was feeling good already and began to suspect that he was
either a lightweight, he drank his beer too fast, or he hadn't
completely sobered up from the afternoon's drinking. The bathroom was as crowded as the rest of the place and he had to wait
in line to pee into the trough. It was cool because they threw all
their old ice into the urinal, so you were peeing into this big pile
of ice. He remembered writing his name in the snow one winter
up in Washington State when he was little, proud of the fact that
he had done it in cursive.

He washed his hands, ratcheted down a foot-and-a-half of paper
towel, dried his hands and stepped back into the hallway. The
payphones were right there. He fished two quarters out of his
pocket, wiped the phone off on his shirt, and dropped the quarters into the slot. The girl answered. It was her cell phone. He
could hear a TV in the background. The girl said she had just
stepped out of the shower. He smiled. She already had plans for
dinner, but was heading to a party a few blocks from the restaurant later that night, and he was welcome to stop by. When they
ask who you are, just tell them Carlos invited you. Carlos was
her boyfriend. The young man said "cool," hung up and smiled
to himself, running the address through his head several times so
he wouldn't forget.

"What the hell? Maybe I'll go. The worse thing they can do is
throw me out," he thought. But he better double-check what
time he was working tomorrow. He pulled two more quarters
out of his front right pocket, called the store and confirmed that
he was closing. He could party late into the night or even into
the early morning, and still have time to sleep for a few hours
and sober up before work. Wilson often warned him, with more
than a little bitterness wrapped around his words, that when
you're young, you can do things you can't do when you're old,

and that smart folks take advantage of this, within reason, before it's too late.

He slowly shuffled his way through the crowd back to his barstool. Sure enough, his seat was saved by the golden pint of beer. It stood there on the polished wood bar like a beacon, warning unsuspecting patrons away from the reserved seat like a lighthouse perched over a treacherously rocky shore. The professional wrestlers were still sucking crab meat from the dead red legs like giants sucking marrow from peasants' bones. The middle-aged guy was still drinking bourbon.

He slid his rear up onto the barstool and drank heartily from his beer. He liked the way the beer felt in his mouth and rolled over his teeth down his throat. Water and hops and malt and yeast: that's what beer is. The married buddy whose calf he'd burned had taught him about beer: he brewed his own and considered himself a connoisseur. You never knew what to expect when you walked through his front door. Sometimes, an almost overwhelming bittersweet wave of malt syrup and pungent hops would wash over you, and you knew the wort was madly boiling on the kitchen stove. Other times, it was like walking through the door of an indoor swimming pool: moist warmth and chlorine. He'd be back in the bathroom, sanitizing bottles with hot water and bleach, usually with some obscene statement fingered on the steamed-up mirror. If it was quiet and you couldn't smell anything out of the ordinary, then thick-glassed, five-gallon carboys full of maturing brew were stashed in the cool, dark closet of the back office, the yeast joyfully transforming the malt's sugars into alcohol, plastic bubble valves bubbling away the carbon dioxide produced in the process.

His friend always talked about interacting with the world on an elemental level. He made his own beer, killed and ate wild game, fished, grew vegetables in his garden, added a bush or two every year to his miniature backyard blueberry field, flew kites, showed his nephew how to make toy parachutes out of Hefty Bags, dug for clams, dropped shrimp traps into the harbor, picked wild blackberries, and raised chickens. He often pined that aside from the fact that you could die from seemingly inno-cuous injuries like an infected scratch or common ailments like the flu, he would have preferred to live in the 19th century. In so many ways, he was a walking anachronism. He even went to a psychic once to see if maybe he'd been a pioneer or farmer in his previous life, but the psychic told him he had been a cohort of Merlin the Magician who spent most of his time lounging about the drafty halls of King Arthur's castle, which was "obviously bogus" according to his friend. The young man had to agree.

The sharp sound of glass breaking back in the kitchen cut through the noise of the bar and restaurant. The bartender smiled and rang a brass bell mounted to the wall at the end of the bar. People laughed and she smiled, wiping her hands on her apron. She grabbed a plate and two glasses left behind by a hip, young, white-toothed, Hollywood-type couple. The young man saw her swear silently, noticing that they didn't leave a tip. He smiled. They were probably assholes in their previous lives, too.

A cheer erupted around him. The huge bald guys thrust hands full of crab in the air, roaring with mouths full of food. The guy on his left was looking upward at the silent TV with a big smile on his face. The waitress walked over and leaned back against the bar between them to see the TV mounted above, clapping her feminine hands and smiling a beautiful natural smile. God she smelled good, even working her ass off in a bar full of garlicky food, booze, and beer-sweating men. She lingered for a moment between them, and the young man noticed that even the old guy snuck a look at her profile before she noticed an empty pint glass at the other end of the bar and was off.

After she left, the old guy on his left leaned over and nodded up at the TV: "You know who that is?" The camera was focused on a stocky Hispanic player taking off his batting gloves on second base. The graphics indicated that he had just hit his 500th double. The young man recognized him from the papers but didn't know his name. He smiled and shook his head. The guy told him the player's name, which now appeared at the bottom of the screen, and explained as loudly as he could that this was the DH's last year, and that he'd passed up a multi-million-dollar contract with a different team so he could play his last season with the team that originally brought him up from the minors. "You don't see that much anymore," he said. "That guy's a decent one."

The young man nodded appreciatively, and the bourbon guy smiled and turned his attention back to the TV and the condensation-clad old-fashioned. It sounded like someone had turned up the volume of the jukebox, maybe in response to the increased noise in the bar. Previously, the songs were all but indistinguishable, but now the unmistakable growl of a young Mick Jagger complained about a decided lack of satisfaction. The young man remembered a movie he'd seen at Wilson's one night about the Rolling Stones and this free concert they tried to put on in California that ended up being a big brawl between all these hippies and Hell's Angels. They sang that song then. The bartender stopped what she was doing and turned to smile over her shoulder at the guy to his left. They made eye contact for just a moment while she wiggled her hips a bit and laughed. He killed the rest of the drink, smiled, left a wad of cash on the bar, and walked out into the night. The young man watched him leave and then turned to smile at the bartender and effect a "what the fuck was that about" pose when she stopped by to pick up the cash and glass and wipe down the bar. She noticed his look and leaned in with a quizzical smile on her pretty face.

"You looked at each other when this song came on," he said carefully, loudly in her ear. She pulled away and smiled, nodding and brushing her hair back over her shoulder."

"He's a regular," she leaned back in, "so he and I talk sometimes. He told me one night that this song was the meaning of life. It's kind of an inside joke." She smiled sweetly and walked away.

The song ended and some Southern Rock anthem took its place. Southern Rock, like most things Southern, was at best a guilty pleasure for the young man. His mindset was coastal, more West than East, and the Mississippi was just a big river on a map. He'd never been to The South, and he thought of it exactly as it was written, as a capitalized mythical Land; a world unto itself (as if they'd won the war); a place that elicited dictionary-definition ambivalence in everyone with whom he associated in spite of the tentative rapprochement American society seemed to be embracing. He heard things were still very "different" down South, that white people still said "nigger," and that the races still didn't mix, the paragraph about Brown vs. the Board of Education in his senior high history book notwithstanding. He heard about lynchings occurring way too close to the 21st century, turpentine-soaked castrations, and perpetual pedestrian humiliations up to the present day. And yet, there was that thing called gentility. Or was there? There was Faulkner and his sultry, lazy, sun-infused dusty roads (and murders); catfish, Huckleberry Finn, and those sweet cherry belles. Were there really still Southern Belles? How about farm girls in Daisy Maes? About the time he was born, "The Dukes of Hazzard" was a popular television show, in spite of the prominent display of the Confederate Flag and the orange American muscle car whose horn played the stirring notes of Dixie. Catherine Bach's sweet Daisy Duke ass helped quite a bit too, obviously, but at some point, between then and now, people took a moment to think about what that cross-barred flag really stood for, and they started removing it from buildings, stadiums, schools and capitols, touching off firestorms of Bible Belt indignation and Daughters of the Confederacy drama. And yet he knew that while the South held the record for racism, the East and the West were hardly immune. Bad cops in New York and L.A. made sure the country never forgot that racism is a franchise enterprise with "a location near you" popping up as unexpectedly and inevitably as the next Starbucks.

As if in eerie response to his thoughts, the distant mournful, lonely wail of a police siren pierced the bar's bubble of sound, rousting him from his reverie with its haunting nocturnal crescendo. Haltingly, spasmodically, it rose higher and grew louder; the cop manipulating the sound through intersections and setting it on automatic on the straight-aways; one moment falling off to nothing, the next crying out louder than before, like an overeager, first-year band student wrestling with his scales. It was coming closer. The young man naively looked around the bar for signs of trouble, and even turned to peer back toward the heavy, Neanderthal, steel payphones bolted to the wall by the bathrooms, but everyone was having a good time and didn't even seem to hear the sirens. He began to wonder if he was hearing things when a second siren, also close by but coming from the opposite side of town, seemed to answer the first in excited, high-pitched tones. The young man looked around: Jesus, didn't anyone else hear them? God. How crazy is this, he thought. His blood was already spiked with beer and testosterone, and the night and the day he'd had thus far had made him heady. He had that "real life" feeling people get when coming upon a car accident, mixed with the willful hedonistic bent a guy feels choosing the freeway exit leading to a strip club.

A third faint siren; barely discernable above the jukebox, the people in the bar, the restaurant, and the first two sirens, tentatively raised its voice to the night, alone in the darkness, wondering where its compatriots were racing. This one came from the part of town where he'd dropped off the beautiful lesbian chick and watched her kiss her girlfriend. Goddamn she was hot, he remembered, listening to the distant whine striving desperately to catch up to the first two. They sounded like a scattered pack of Eastern Washington coyotes calling out to each other in the ghostly, luminescent, starlit night. The scent of blood in the air raised their hackles and infused their own blood with adrenalin as they busted through cockleburs and pungent sagebrush, their sorrowful howls intersecting and yet separated, annoyingly unsynchronized, the first one closer than the second, and both closer than the third. The cries were plaintive and surprisingly devoid of authority, more desperate than commanding. The city streets were still filled with cars, and he knew the cops were weaving in and out, slowing and accelerating; tenaciously, hungrily tracking their prey; tasting the bitter tenuousness of their own existence, for they knew there was no real satisfaction even if they "won," because victories were no more than stop-gaps; the perps would be back on the streets before you knew it; the only true winner, of course, being death, which takes us all.

He wanted to go there. He wanted to go where the coyotes don't live in freeway median greenbelts and the deserted blocks of burnt-out slums. Eastern Washington was one of the lands where there were colors like the poster he'd seen in the travel agency window: an infinite, forever-blue sky echoing with vast-ness; sticky, tar-black, oil-and-gravel highways curving through millions of acres of young, verdant wheat fields stretching to-ward the sun's golden disc; distant, brown, limitless, rolling sagebrush hills. That's where his father'd done his first "real" duck hunting: the ancient, sparsely-populated, wild land of cou-lees, potholes, wasteways, dunes, seeps, canals, aqueducts, siphons and petrified wood; a land where constant, day-long, dry, buffeting, chapping winds that make you yell to be heard and fill your ears like cotton, threaten to wear the skin from your face; the land of exploding cock pheasants and sagebrush that dies and detaches itself from the earth to roll across the hard dry ground, dropping seeds as it goes like a spawning desert salmon; the land of nuclear reactors and Cold War million-gallon tanks of radioactive sludge, the poisonous cost of freedom; the dusty, arid land ironically defined by the occasional appearances of wa-ter; the land of cattail-rimmed, creek-fed ponds, and supersonic, whistling teal that rocket overhead in green and blue streaks, dodging shotgun blasts like Catch-22 pilots avoiding flak; Woo-dy Guthrie's land of massive concrete dams and reservoirs and manmade lakes and hydroelectric power that illuminates the steel and glass skyscrapers way out West across the mountains where the cities are; the land of skinny, sun-crazed coyotes that circle and howl and yip in the night's silver sunlight; circling around the poor greenhorn who must clean the hunting party's ducks on the muddy banks of the pond while the other guys, back at the pickup trucks 300 yards away, pull out their predator calls and laughingly call the hungry dogs in closer.

That's where he wanted to go, and at least for a moment he felt the urge deep in his gut, just as strong and deep as the urge to fuck, but the sirens had finally stopped, and the flashing lights lit up the picture windows of the bar, and the patrons finally noticed, standing and peering out into the darkness with morbid, drunken curiosity.

The young man hoped the middle-aged bourbon-drinking guy hadn't been hit by a car or something. As he replayed events in his mind, he realized that the first, tentative siren had pierced the night shortly after his exit. He looked up a bit too quickly at the bartender and had to wait for his vision to catch up with the upward snap of his head. Yeah, he was drunk, and that more than anything else convinced him to pay his tab and see what was going on outside. The bartender smiled at him and the substantial tip he left and he carefully "Excuse Me'd" his way through the people pressed up against the windows and stepped out into the smoggy, stagnant night and the flashing lights.

Immediately outside the restaurant, two police officers were performing CPR on a tall man in his sixties who would have looked like he was simply asleep if it hadn't been for the small pool of blood forming beneath his head and the strange pallor of his skin. Another cop was unpacking a portable defibrillator she had retrieved from the trunk of the cruiser, reading the instructions as she went. The other two kept up with the chest compressions and breaths while some more cops kept the crowd back and manned the radios. A medic was almost there, they said.

The man was at least six feet tall, white, with wispy, combed-over white hair. He wore the kind of untucked, button-down shirts old men wore in the tropics; khaki shorts, white athletic socks pulled up as high as they'd go, and brown leather loafers. His arms were at his sides, his shirt ripped open, exposing a grey, hairy chest and a substantial hairy belly. A cop the young man hadn't noticed before was interviewing witnesses. Someone said, "he just dropped and hit the ground hard." Just dropped. Jesus. What's that called when you just drop? An aneurysm. Standing there minding your own business in your old-guy clothes and WHAM. You're dead and your body falls lifelessly to the sidewalk like a sack of concrete mix. And since you're pretty much dead, or at least unconscious, you don't protect yourself when you fall. You just drop. Two professional-looking women were telling the interviewing cop that the old guy's skull hit the sidewalk with a loud, solid thunk, loud enough to be heard above the traffic and pedestrians.

It was like a newspaper article he'd read about a guy getting hit by lightning at a driving range. The weather was overcast but not indicative of thunderstorm activity, and the guy and his son were hitting their buckets of golf balls when a bolt of lightning flashed and killed the man. Everyone around him, including his son, was injured, but he was the only one who died. Once second he was fine, the next second he was dead. In a way, it was almost like being the victim of a sniper. Snipers, the young man had read, could kill a person with a single shot from more than a mile away. You were dead before the sound even reached your ears. Fifteen people standing on the sidewalk and one of them drops with a bullet in his head. That's the way it was in Sarajevo in the 1980s. The place where World War I began didn't calm down much in subsequent decades. One of Wilson's buddies, an ex-cop, made over a hundred grand tax free as a cop in one year in Eastern Europe after the U.S. stepped in to stop the ethnic cleansing. Wilson was happy for his friend, but he couldn't help feeling a little bitter too. He didn't seem to have the kind of luck his friends did.

The cops working on the old man yelled "Clear!" just like in the movies and leaned back away from the body while the cop with the defibrillator pushed a button and the man's body convulsed, just like in the movies. The guy didn't come back to life. The cop operating the defibrillator looked at a little LCD screen and shook her head, indicating that the guy's heart still wasn't beating correctly. One of the CPR cops frowned and put his ear to the man's chest as if not believing the high-tech gadget (or the cop since she was a woman), but quickly began administering CPR once again.

The young man looked around at the crowd watching the man die on the sidewalk. Some people had sad faces, others showed no emotion. A couple kids were pinching each other and laughing. Almost everyone was on their cell phone, telling whoever they were speaking with that they were watching this old guy die on the sidewalk. Cars slowly rolled by, their occupants craning their necks to see what was going on. The cop cars were blocking the lane nearest the curb, and the traffic was piling up behind them, so one of the cops went out to direct the cars past the scene with angry circular waves of his arm. "Let's go, c'mon move it there!" he yelled at the civilians in the cars. The young man doubted there'd be any impromptu memorials for the guy once everyone left; the pile of flowers and cards and stuffed animals that appeared after tragic deaths, especially after the tragic death of a child. Old guys who just drop dead don't get piles of flowers and stuffed animals; they just get a ride down to the morgue and a tag on their big toe. "At least he didn't suffer," someone in the crowed said approvingly.

The CPR cops were sweating heavily and they scanned the city streets around them with what looked like the beginning of anger on their faces. Neither one of them seemed to be in the best of health. Both looked to be in their fifties and suffering from the stereotypical propensity for donuts and aversion to the gym. CPR is hard work, and they were feeling both the physical strain and the mental burden of being the ones who were either going to be the heroes or the goats. The female cop watching them didn't try the defibrillator a second time. Instead, she relieved the cop giving breaths. He looked tired, out-of-breath and mad. Sweat poured down his face and darkened his uniform. The cop interviewing witnesses put away his pen and pad of paper and relieved the cop doing chest compressions. A paramedic truck finally rolled up and parked, effectively blocking the only open lane of traffic. Everyone look surprised, like the big red truck with dual wheels in the back had materialized out of thin air. The young man hadn't even heard a siren. The sweaty, tired cops stood slowly, rubbing their backs, and started moving the crowd farther back from the old man while the paramedics grabbed equipment from their truck and the two new CPR cops counted the chest compressions out loud. They didn't stop until the medics had both knelt down beside the body.

The young man was glad it wasn't the bourbon man, but he felt guilty since it had to be someone else. He wondered whether the old guy was a "good man," however that's defined, whether it was indeed sad that he was dying or whether he was some piece-of-shit asshole whose life had spread nothing but misery and heartache. And even then, is it good that he would soon be gone, or is every loss of life deplorable and sad, even if the life is despicable?

The medics were going through the motions of trying to save the guy, but their less-than-gung-ho attitudes seem to piss off the first CPR cops who looked at the dead guy they'd tried to save, and realizing that they'd failed, began to take their frustration out on the crowd, moving them even farther away, farther than they really needed to. It was a good time to get going. The young man felt funny being drunk around all the cops in the first place, even if he wasn't driving, so he spun around and dug his hands into the front pockets of his Levi's and sauntered down the sidewalk away from the crowd and the flashing lights, his Vans rolling onto and off of the warm concrete, pointing in the general direction in which he thought the waitress' party would be found.

After he put a couple city blocks between himself and the dead guy, he stopped in his tracks at the thought that the man might have been waiting to meet someone when he dropped. Maybe his daughter and her family were going to show him the town and take him out to dinner. Maybe he had a date with some old lady he'd met while visiting the city. No one in the crowd appeared to know him, and he didn't look like a local. He wondered if the cops would hang around for a while, kinda looking out for someone who looked like they were supposed to meet somebody, but he doubted it. Would the old guy's family show up after everyone had left and simply figure they had the wrong corner and go back home? That was one of the fucked-up parts of tragedy, he thought, people showing up on the corner and finding no one to meet.

Even if he hadn't been drunk, he wouldn't have found the party, and before any time at all had passed, he stopped walking and took stock of his situation. Number one, he needed to stop trying to remember phone numbers, names and addresses without writing them down. Number two, for some unknown reason, he was almost entirely broke. Number three, although he was working the closing shift the next day, he didn't want to spend the rest of the night walking home. For the second time that night, he found himself needing a payphone in a wireless city. If it weren't for his freakish anachronistic streak, he'd have bought a cell phone long ago like all his friends, but he hadn't, and there was no payphone in sight, so he began walking, looking for a restaurant, bar or hotel. He was so preoccupied with his search that he nearly stumbled over a wooden sandwich board set up on the sidewalk beside a red, steel pipe bike stand. Three high-tech mountain bikes and one fat-tired, beautifully restored, three-speed, vintage, purple Schwinn were chained to the rack. The brightly painted red arrow on the sandwich board pointed to a foyer on his right beyond a faded wooden door with a large window and an antique, weathered brass mail slot. A handsome, elderly man in a silk skullcap and Budweiser tee-shirt was slowly walking around in the 60-watt light of the foyer with what appeared to be a fringed, vanilla-colored, angora muffler wrapped once about his neck like some kind of vestment or prayer shawl. He was walking in slow circles with his hands clasped behind his back looking very much like a shorter, younger, healthier John Paul the Second, repeating some unrecognizable phrase over and over again like someone saying their

Hail Marys. The sandwich board described the self-consciously funky space as the neighborhood's own "living room." In addition to the old man, he saw a bunch of urban, literary, alternative types drinking bad coffee out of Styrofoam cups and milling about nervously in a loft-styled room that was actually six steps below street level. On the far wall, between two garish, orange, thickly-painted, surreal cityscapes; and almost obscured from view by a spindly, plasma-green-polyester-clothed, wild-haired, upturned-collar, starving-poet-type guy was what appeared to be a payphone.

He looked at the sandwich board again: "Open Mic 7pm – 10pm; Poetry, Prose, Performance, Comedy, Free Coffee; Sign up with Henrietta!" People on the sidewalk walked by and paid no attention to him or the sign. The old man paced the foyer's perimeter. Self-styled intelligentsia mingled uncomfortably below. Evening was slowly slipping into night. He decided to call a couple friends who owed him a favor and see if they'd come get him. He'd even be willing to buy them a couple drinks after he got some more money from his apartment. He made a mental note to finally go out and get himself a debit card and then timed his entrance into the foyer so that the old man was at the most distant point of his elliptical orbit, and slipped down the six steps and through the jittery polite smiles to the far wall between the two orange cityscapes. He fished another couple of quarters from his pocket and made the call. No one was home and he hung up a second too late to beat the machine: two more quarters down the drain.

"Help yourself to some coffee!" said an African-American woman in her fifties with graying, super-short curls, glasses and an intelligent smile. "Will you be reading tonight?" she asked, slowly stirring the contents of a white Styrofoam cup with a red plastic stir stick. She made the cheap accoutrements look elegant in her long-fingered, manicured hands. Rings of every kind adorned her fingers and a couple dozen metal bangles encircled each wrist. She was wearing a white, long-sleeved blouse and a flower-print skirt, the kind he saw women wearing at street fairs and outdoor art festivals. Sandals adorned her feet and a delicious perfume subtly imbued the air around her with an element of mystery. He caught himself wondering what it reminded him of, entirely and unconsciously preoccupied until she repeated herself with a bigger smile. He "came to" as it were, and blushed deeply, smiling an embarrassed, self-deprecating smile that women seemed to like. He shook his head "no," and looked around at the crowd nervously. "Well, then, help yourself to some coffee and make yourself at home," she said quietly. "Honestly, it's horrible coffee, but it's free and it will keep you awake during the less than vibrant pieces," she whispered, before moving on to an androgynous elderly couple in matching blue sweatshirts: "Good evening, will you be reading tonight? Well, help yourself to some coffee!"

He watched her talking with the two bright-white-haired people and couldn't help but linger on the delicious way the small of her back led enticingly into the first curve of her buttocks. One without the other would have been distracting enough, but the symbiosis of the two was utterly captivating. Then again, the young man reminded himself, he sometimes saw things in women that other guys his age didn't. His friends, in fact, made fun of his ability to find some element of beauty in almost every woman he saw. The tastes of his straight male friends, on the other hand, seemed consistently homogenous and unimaginative. The lowest common denominators were, of course, skinniness, blonde hair and big boobs. Variations from the theme were treated with more than a little skepticism, and outright contradictions of the "Hotness Orthodoxy" were openly ridiculed as heretical. As a result, the young man had long ago stopped commenting on women around his friends because he inevitably sang the praises of someone whom the other guys had summarily disqualified before the race had even begun. He wasn't perfect of course, and like anyone else he sometimes found himself flirting or making out with a girl he wouldn't have considered pursuing when sober; and at least once he'd awakened "the morning after" in utter shock and incredulity at his apparent lack of taste; but he liked to think that there was always something about each girl that caught his fancy and turned him on; whether it was the way she flipped her hair back over her shoulder, the way she glanced down shyly and then peered up at him with sultry eyes, or the way she aggressively flirted with him and boosted his ego. It was simultaneously a gift and a curse; an almost genetically-stubborn predisposition to see something good or beautiful in nearly everything around him. In one sense, it was an artist's vision: seeing the statue entombed within the roughly hewn pillar of marble. In another, it was little more than a foolish lack of discernment suspiciously akin to desperation, a weak decision to look at the world through a cliché.

"Thank you for joining us for the second half of Open Mic Night," the woman in the white blouse and flowered dress intoned warmly into the solitary microphone on the narrow, carpeted stage.

Shit.

"My name is Henrietta and if you're planning on performing tonight, you still need to talk to me first! I'll be over in my usual spot, so come on over and say hello in between sets."

Damn it. Once again, his day-dreaming left him in a lurch. There he was, still standing a few feet from the payphone, in the exact spot Henrietta had greeted him, while everyone else had long ago taken their seats in a varied assortment of Lazy-Boys, old school desks, bean bag chairs, salvaged church pews, and battered metal folding chairs. Although no one seemed to notice him, let alone care that he was the only audience member standing, he felt very much like he was in one of those dreams in which everything seems normal except you're walking around naked. Grocery shopping, dropping the car off at the shop, sitting at your desk in the office, it doesn't matter. There you are, inexplicably buck naked in a world full of fully clothed people.

"Our first performer of the second half of our evening together is a long-time supporter of, and participant in, this five-year-old tradition of Open Mic Night in the City's own Living Room, or OMNICOLoR; a long-time resident of the city; and a long-time patron of the arts, in general…"

The young man slowly backed away from the stage and slipped red-faced into an unoccupied, battered, brown upholstered easy chair about fifteen feet from the payphone. No one in the room seemed aware of his presence, let alone his embarrassment.

Henrietta finished her introduction and a short, bald, stocky man in a black turtleneck sweater, black jeans, eyeglasses with thick black frames, and black shoes took the stage and self-consciously adjusted the microphone downward about a foot. He took a deep breath and looked around at the entire crowd like they tell you to in public speaking classes, and began. He recited a poem of his own by memory in a voice reminiscent of Elmer Fudd with a Southern accent so thick you could pour it over grits. The young man'd been expecting something much, much different; a nasally German accent perhaps. Not a redneck Elmer Fudd. He stifled a gasp of surprise and covered the goofy grin that erupted on his face with his hands, pretending to stifle a sneeze. His mother had always taught him not to laugh at people and to stick up for those society picked on, but a guffaw had been his gut response. Desperate to regain control, he closed his eyes as if in concentration and did his best to focus on the words themselves, not the voice conveying them.

My Apocryphal Great Aunt Gertrude

Great Aunt Gertrude slurps hot dog water from a spoon like soup ("with a little freshly ground pepper it's real nice") and NO she ain't never watched no MTV, nor listened to rap or modern R&B; though she's a lover of the original blues, the old gut-wrenching, hardpan blues best heard through an old-fashioned full of Jim Beam Black Label Sour Mash Kentucky Bourbon Whiskey (on the rocks) which don't have nothing to do with the Delta except that it eases the pain.

Some young doctor in town said lay off the booze ("edema from cirrhosis of the liver") but Great Aunt Gertrude treats the "drop-sy" in her calves and ankles with warm cloths soaked in Parsley Root Tea and three fingers of Hollands Gin just before bed and she stops and looks at you and me and asks what's going on inside our heads 'cause Jesus cured a man with dropsy on the Sabbath as much to rock the boat as anything else; for He said the exalted ones shall be abased, and the humbled ones exalted, and if He were here today, "he'd touch my legs and make them whole."

"Four steps forward and three steps back." That's the meaning of life, says Gertrude my Great Aunt a couple dozen times a day to the point you'd wish she'd stop. Rocking in a 100-year-old chair her grandfather made before she was born, grasping its sides as if grasping life itself. Rough, arthritic, blue-veined fingers tremulously toying with the nicks and notches and scratches of six generations, connecting with something like finding a station on her old transistor radio, turning the dial back and forth: but "it's all one life" she says, "it's all one life."

"Did you know that Buddha DIED almost six hundred years before the angels visited those shepherds in the fields, watching their flocks by night?" she interrogates, wagging a gnarled finger at us, before affirming in a huff that "it would've been nice if they'd met, compared notes for a spell, for the benefit of man-

270

kind" (arms spread grandly out and wide) "but that didn't happen. Hell! They never spoke, and we're left guessing, rolling the dice before we die and hoping we get that lucky seven, that three and four that will open the door to eternal life, with a Brand New Body" she says, thinking of all the men she's had.

Speaking of which, that old slut Fannie Mae; who on a daily basis removes her false teeth in a geriatric strip-tease at precisely 2:30 in the afternoon and goes down on "Viagra Vick" in the blue-striped double-wide, only seven spaces down from Great Aunt Gertrude's artificial turf-covered porch; never walks home without offering drunk Gertie a kind word of caution regarding the dangers of DRINK, the SHAME of addiction, and the "BLESS-ED" happiness found in a personal relationship with Jesus Christ with whom she has been INTIMATELY acquainted since the tender young age of four, when she stood, stinging tears falling to the red-carpeted floor, and answered a revivalist's altar call.

Fannie Mae submitted to the Lord in much the same way she did to all the other men in her life: wholeheartedly, wide-eyed, never questioning; ready and willing to follow all directions to a "T;" enduring suffering, abuse and shame both at HIS hands and at the hands of others; like those who ridiculed her when she knelt in the middle of the junior high cafeteria and thanked God for the "bounty" he had bestowed upon her in the form of a brown bag lunch lovingly packed by her tightly-wound, weeping, loving, manic-depressive mother; who cleaned house until her fingers bled and then fled to her room for days on end, never leaving the quilted confines of her feather bed, shades drawn down tightly.

"Thanks for caring, Fannie Mae!" Aunt Gertie always says, smiling and rocking, and devilishly motioning Fannie to wipe something from her chin as she walks by, and then ol' Gert looks up at the echoing sky, craning her tortoise neck and straining her ancient, knowing eyes as if to see what hangs above the cumuli, before returning her gaze to earth to meet mine; pausing, removing her glasses and closing her wrinkled lids to say, "I see you banging your head against a wall today, young man, out of fear that you're already running out of time to accomplish the things you feel you must, but you've got to remember you've only got two decisions every waking moment: 'Do you take that next step? And if so, which way?'"

He never would have predicted it, but halfway through, the young man didn't even hear the voice anymore. His hands fell away from his face and with his eyes still closed, all he saw was Great Aunt Gertie in her rocking chair looking up through the "echoing sky." He felt like he knew her nephew and felt like maybe he was becoming her nephew and he wanted to talk to her and have her reassure him and have it make sense once and for all, but this was just a glimpse and she wasn't real and he was, after all, drunk and sitting in a room full of strangers listening to people recite poetry.

He stayed for the rest, as much because he hoped to hear something else with which he connected as the fact that there was no inconspicuous way to leave and he still hadn't reached a friend for a ride. When the reading concluded and people began to filter out, he stepped over to the payphone and used up the rest of his change without securing transportation home.

Nearly broke and without a cell phone, debit card or credit card, the young man decided to start walking home. It would take a couple hours to get there. He made his way up the six steps, through the now pontiff-free foyer, and out onto the sidewalk. He immediately noticed that the old man was twenty feet up the sidewalk peeing into a coffee can filled with sand and cigarette butts, his hands still clasped carefully behind his back. He smiled and turned away to start out on the last leg of his day's journey when an impact to his right cheek swung his head the rest of the way around at a high enough velocity to flip saliva from his mouth like those slow-motion scenes in boxing movies. If he'd been sober, he might have had the wherewithal to jump back a few steps and raise his fists to ward off additional blows. Instead, he just stood there for a second, looking back down into the city's living room and analyzing the pain on the right side of his face. He slowly reached up and checked for blood and then slowly turned to face his attacker.

"Brainiac?!?"

She slapped him again, harder. That one hurt quite a bit and a wave of anger flashed over him for a moment until he realized he had it coming.

"God-damn...." he said, rubbing the side of his face. "Would you stop hitting me please?"

"You deserve more than that you big jerk!" screeched the fluorescent green guy from the open mic night. Seeing a target about whom he could recollect no regrets, guilt or even recognition, the young man's anger reignited and he took a step toward him: "And who the bloody fuck are you motherfucker?"

"He's my friend," Brainiac responded. "He was there for me when you pulled up lame."

The young man looked at the cringing starving poet type and then looked over at Brainiac. His right eye was tearing up a bit, so it was kind of hard to see, but the look on her face doused his anger and he unclenched his fists and took a step back. "I'm sorry."

"You sure are you worthless, cowardly, selfish, short-sighted, half-witted, inconsiderate motherfucker! Do you have any fucking idea what you did to me?"

He started to answer, but he quickly realized that the question had been rhetorical.

"You think you're some hotshit lady's man? You think you can do whatever the fuck you want and not give a shit about anyone else? Think again motherfucker. You sliced off a big fucking chunk of bad karma that day motherfucker. You are SUCH an asshole. You are BEYOND asshole. And let me tell you motherfucker, you missed out on a whole shitload of really, really, REALLY nasty sex. I was on the verge of embarking on an epic journey of sexual exploration unseen since the 1960s and YOU were going to be front-row center you clueless, dickless, worth-less motherfucker."

A crowd had formed around them. Some people thought it was street theater associated with the open mic night advertised on the sandwich board sign. Others just liked watching real-life drama. If Brainiac felt uncomfortable talking about sex and rela-tionships in front of complete strangers in the middle of a busy city block, she didn't show it.

"I heard that blonde whore dumped you the day after you dumped me you fucking loser!" It had actually been three-and-a-half days but the young man decided against arguing the point. "So did you get lucky before she dumped you for a real man?" He was hoping this too was a rhetorical question, especially con-sidering the audience before which they were now performing, but to his chagrin she stopped and jutted her chin out towards him with her hands on her hips, waiting for an answer.

"No."

"What's that? What'd you say there Sport? You didn't get any fine bimbo pussy when you dumped me?"

"No."

"Oh, that's too bad Mr. Lady's Man, cause I was going to do things to you that haven't even been invented yet. I was going to suck you and fuck you like you'd never been sucked or fucked before. You see these motherfucker?" She lifted her tank top and a lacy bra to reveal two unbelievably perfect breasts. "These were going to be YOURS, you dumbfuck!" The crowd, now numbering a dozen, cheered and hooted and groaned as the young man looked at her breasts with sincere longing and regret, at least until she violently replaced her top and flung her hands outward for emphasis. In fact, his very being was caught up in an epic battle between lust and regret. The slaps, the fact that Brainiac looked really, really good, her passion and anger,

275

the color in her cheeks and lips all made him want to fuck her brains out, but the torture of reliving one of his young life's most painful mistakes in the presence of the person he'd hurt so badly had his gut twisted up in knots that hurt far worse than the residual stinging on the right side of his face where her fingers had left perfect calling cards in the form of red finger-shaped welts. He knew that he deserved everything he was getting and more, and as much as he wanted to get the hell out of there, he stood and took everything she had to give until exhausted, she strode up to him, spat in his face and thrust her middle finger up between his eyes. Then she and the fluorescent green guy stomped away across the street and into the darkness, leaving the young man to the small crowd's insults, jeers and glares. He backed slowly away and continued down the sidewalk, listening for footsteps behind him, until he came to a bar and went inside. He quickly found the bathroom and washed his face with handfuls of water, hoping the marks on his right cheek would subside enough to be somewhat inconspicuous in the dark. He took a leak, washed his hands, and then almost ordered a beer on his way out before remembering that he was broke.

He scanned the sidewalk up and down before entering the night-life flow. The crowd up the street had dispersed and he didn't recognize anyone in either direction. He was a bit turned around, so he stopped at the first bus stop he saw to orient himself with the moon and a Plexiglas-covered route map, and set out for home.

He plodded along in a haze of alcohol and guilt. On the one hand, he felt that the almost epic episode of public humiliation he'd just experienced was at least a decent down-payment on his debt to Brainiac. Add in the "big fucking chunk of bad karma" he'd apparently sliced off and he figured he was maybe a third of the way through. He was reassured that she seemed well, aside from the anger and trauma. Physically, she looked amazing, and the authority with which she delivered the slaps and spittle seemed to suggest that her confidence and will were recovering nicely. She didn't carry herself like a victim, that's for

276

damn sure. She was dishing out judgment, more avenging war goddess than dumped bookstore clerk. He'd failed her on at least two separate counts: dumping her so stupidly and then avoiding the day of reckoning; and in the space of fifteen minutes or so, had made progress atoning for both, something that might never have happened if she hadn't run into him. There would have to be more. He wasn't going to compound his error with additional errors, but he felt that he still owed her, still owed her big time. He was a shithead and a dumbfuck and beyond what he hoped he could do in the future, there was absolutely nothing he could do at the moment to make things better. He couldn't even throw his fists up toward the heavens and complain the he was "more sinned against than sinning" like Lear. It wasn't like Oedipus waking up one morning to realize that the sex and violence he'd taken part in the previous day had been with his parents. The young man's actions were petty, selfish, stupid and damaging. There was no excuse. He thought about evil and how the longer you live the more opportunity you have to commit it. He thought about men in positions of power whose sins cost lives and livelihoods and was glad that at least his evil had been overcome. Totally fucking overcome. She was a spitfire. Goddamn he'd been stupid to leave her.

He walked quietly for half an hour or so, keeping the moon above and ahead of him as he zig-zagged the city blocks. He was glad that at least the moon was still visible even if the stars weren't. Every so often a street would strike him as familiar, but for the most part he didn't recognize any of the stores, apartments, hotels, condos, bars, restaurants or offices. At least not until he reached Brainiac's used bookstore. He hadn't been there since dumping her and hadn't paid a hell of a lot of attention the times that he had been there previously, but he knew this was it. The name, the thousand-year-old wooden door with wrought iron trim, and the fake parrot in an antique birdcage in the front window. This was it. He stopped and peered in the window for a few moments, shook his head and shuffled on. He had known he'd eventually end up running into it or her, but he hadn't figured on both in one night. The fluorescent green guy must have called her or something. That wasn't a coincidence, Bountiful Living Family notwithstanding.

He walked another ten minutes or so, glad that it wasn't cold and rainy. Up ahead at the next corner, he could see cop car lights coming from the cross-street. He didn't remember hearing any sirens, but he'd also been zoning again, so he supposed they might have nearly run him over and he wouldn't have been left with the faintest recollection. When he reached the corner, he could see that there were three cop cars and two medic trucks. Three teenagers were on their bellies in the street. Two were cuffed and a third was hog-tied. All three looked like they'd had the shit beaten out of them. The medics were loading a man in his fifties or sixties strapped to a stretcher into one of the aid cars. It looked like they'd cut away most of his clothing and were administering oxygen and an IV. It smelled like someone was having a barbecue and had used way the hell too much ligh-ter fluid. The young man looked around but there were no condos or apartments nearby. What the fuck? He stopped walk-ing for a moment and listened to the various emergency personnel talking into their radios. From what he could gather, the old man was homeless and the three teenagers had set him on fire. He was being transported to the burn center. What he couldn't figure out was how the cops had managed to catch the suspects. There were few people on the street in this section of town, where skid row and the financial district crossed paths. Lots of high-rise office buildings with miniature city parks de-signed for office worker lunch breaks, but very few clubs or bars. And had the cops beaten the three? The homeless guy couldn't have wreaked that kind of havoc. The young man no-ticed a TV News van with a satellite dish on the roof pulling up and decided he'd better move along before he got involved. Up ahead, he could see someone else walking. Someone about his size walking fast just like him. It was dark, but he was walking like a guy and carrying something in his left hand. He wondered if the guy had anything to do with the fucked up shit he'd just missed.

The two of them walked together, in a sense, for about five minutes, the guy in front never turning to look behind him, never slowing or stopping to look into any of the storefronts. The object in his left hand looked to be about a foot long and three inches in diameter, almost like one of those batons the relay race runners pass to each other in the Olympics. An ancient Honda Civic drove by with a tailpipe the size of a small cannon. Other than that, the night was relatively quiet. Not quiet like back home or in Eastern Washington, but quiet for the city: ubiquitous white noise of humans packed together like the noise of a hundred beetles in an empty 2lb Folgers can.

He looked up at the moon and looked back down to the street and the guy up ahead was gone. The young man stopped and stood quietly, an uneasy feeling creeping over him as he squinted up ahead and slowly surveyed the sidewalk, the street and the sidewalk on the other side. There was no one. No one behind him. And not a sound. Both he and the unidentified relay racer were mid-block when he disappeared. No alleys. No cross-streets. "This ain't good," he thought to himself. "This ain't good at all." He waited for a few moments thinking maybe the guy had stepped into an unseen doorway to light a cigarette or something. He contemplated turning back and cutting across a couple blocks to circumnavigate the area entirely, but finally just said "fuck it" and began walking again. He walked ahead slowly, "head on a swivel" as they say, listening for footsteps on the pavement. As he approached the point at which he'd last seen the dark figure, he slowed to a stop. No alley. No doorway. The high-rise office building monopolized the entire block, standing silently, all three zillion tons, the day's heat still slowly emanating from its concrete skin into the cool night air.

He stood close to the building and looked up its face into the hazy night sky. It was wider than his peripheral vision and seemed to almost bend over to look back down at him, like a human being, hands on hips, leaning over to look at an ant on the sidewalk. The sensation messed with his already impaired equilibrium, and he took a quick step back and brought his gaze back down to street level to avoid tipping over backwards. As he did, a slight aberration in the view caught his eye like a flaw in a photograph or a hairline crack in a vase. Having regained his balance, he peered upwards once more to locate whatever it was that had caught his eye, shifting his focus from infinity to a few feet away like you would with a telephoto lens. He saw it again, just a thin line extending horizontally from the face of the building, undulating slowly, catching a bit of light now and then and becoming visible. It reminded him of those long, wavy fan-powered nylon tubes you see at used car lots. The young man backed up a few steps and noticed for the first time what appeared to be a metal vent cover set into the concrete face of the building about ten feet above the sidewalk. It was about two feet tall and three feet wide. He walked back underneath and peered up. The filament appeared to be attached to the building about where the bottom of the vent cover would be, and it extended outward by about a foot, just enough to catch his eye when he stood below and looked up. And directly below the vent, right at eye level, was another oddity: a dusty scuff mark on the building's street-level façade of polished black stone. It looked a lot like the partial footprint of someone wearing work boots or maybe Doc Martens. The print wasn't complete, just the portion from the toe to the arch, and it was distorted a bit, but it was a boot print no doubt about it. The young man wore a size nine, and this appeared to be comparable. He looked at the mark and at what he now assumed to be a human hair still waving in the air directly above, and immediately thought of one of his buddies who spends his weekends "free running" all over the city. That guy can run up and across walls like Spiderman, vault over concrete barriers and leap from roof to roof like a freakin' gazelle. He's even posted a bunch of videos on YouTube of himself doing crazy-ass shit all over town. The young man looked at the footprint and then at the vent and figured someone would have to get their head up as high as a regulation basketball hoop to leave the forensic evidence he saw before him. One hell of a move for someone wearing only size nine shoes. The young man decided to test his theory and backed up several steps into the street. Headlights appeared in the distance from where he'd come. If he was going to fall like an idiot, he wanted to do it with enough time to get to his feet before the car got there. He took a deep breath and ran at the wall with the long, exaggerated strides of someone preparing to do a lay-up after a fast break. He started his attempted ascent with his left foot on the wall, pushing off and upwards in order to get his right foot as high as the boot print. He figured if he could get his foot that far up, he'd have a decent chance of pushing the rest of his body high enough to reach the vent.

In the overly optimistic imagination of a beer-fueled, youthful mind, he could see himself soaring upwards like his free running friend, the wall no longer a barrier, but a bridge to the sky. Reality, of course, differed markedly from the visualization. His right foot hit a foot-and-a-half below the boot print and as he stretched upwards, he realized that he'd be lucky to even touch the vent, let alone get his head anywhere in its general vicinity. His right hand slapped the concrete directly below the vent and he began his descent back to the earth with a heart-felt "damnit." Fortunately, the landing was more graceful than the launch was effective, and when the car finally passed the young man, he was standing nonchalantly, pretending to look at an imaginary watch on his wrist. Making a few mental adjustments to his approach, he checked the street for more cars and finding the coast clear, made his second attempt. This time his right foot came within 10 inches of the dusty boot toe and when he reached skyward, his hands found metal, barely. His fingers curled over the lowermost horizontal cross-piece of the vent cover and he began to pull himself upward, intending to bring both feet up higher, plant them against the wall, and continue his quest for altitude. That's when he heard a very loud metallic "click" like a fence gate latch engaging, and the vent cover began to open like a mini garage door. The familiar whoosh of a hydraulic door return followed, as did the young man. By the time the vent cover stopped moving, it was almost perfectly horizontal and the young man's quickly weakening hands were twelve feet above the concrete sidewalk. He looked down, looked up at his hands and then attempted to peer into the newly uncovered recess. It was dark inside and his eyes were just shy of the height needed to see what lay beyond the entrance. He figured he had ten seconds of grip left, at the most. His curled fingers would begin to slip backwards and before he knew it, he'd be hanging by his finger tips for one painful second more before plummeting ignobly back to earth like a tired school kid washing out of the Presidential Fitness Flexed Arm Hang.

Or, he could buy some time. Swinging his legs to and fro twice cost him seven seconds up front but paid off. His heels rested comfortably on the lip of the opening, offering just enough leverage to renew his grip on the vent cover as often as he needed and pull himself up high enough to peer into the darkness of the ventilation shaft and see what appeared to be faint light emanating from within. The light was faint enough that he questioned his eyes and yet persistent enough that he recognized the undulating yellow warmth of a natural flame. He had less than a second in which to be intrigued, however, before he was yanked into the darkness with such authority that he remained horizontal even after his fingertips were ripped from the vent cover. He landed on a thin mattress on a concrete floor and immediately looked up into the muzzle of a 9mm Glock.

The 6'5", 250-pound man holding the Glock quietly said "You're dead." The semi-automatic handgun monopolized 100% of the young man's attention. People accustomed to firearms have a visceral reaction to the sight of a muzzle. Muzzle control is one of the first lessons you learn because that's what keeps everyone alive. The muzzle of a weapon is like the business end of a rattlesnake, the searing tip of a blowtorch flame, the crackling copper of a downed power line. You can feel its presence. You know where it is at all times. It doesn't belong in your face. As a result, the young man didn't notice the almost mirror-like quality of the four polished cement walls, the six candles arranged around the room's perimeter, the two other individuals sitting quietly in the lotus position or the darkness that hung over them all like a heavy black shroud.

The opening through which the young man had been unceremo-niously jerked was located in one of the longer walls of the dark rectangular space. The other long wall, lit by four equidistantly spaced candles, stood ten feet behind the man holding the gun. Cushions and thin mattresses, like the one upon which the young man lay, were scattered throughout the room. Blood-flecked nunchucks, a bottle of Stoli, a compact hiking stove, a teapot, mugs, bottled water, a baggy of pot, packages of top ramen, paint brushes and tubes of oil paint covered a low wooden table. The muted sounds of the city flowed from the opening and mixed with the sound of echoing air in the enormous cement vault. The long candlelit wall was strangely darker than the oth-ers, as if the concrete had been mixed with onyx instead of gravel. It appeared three-dimensional in the flickering light like the tormented surface of a vast vertical gray ocean.

At what appeared to be the precise midpoint of the wall's ex-panse sat a man in the lotus position, knees pressed against the wall, eyes forward as if looking through it. Two candles flick-ered on his left and two candles flickered on his right. Shadows and light engaged in a million pitched battles before him, attack-ing and retreating without victor or vanquished and he sat quietly, unmoving.

No one out in the real world would hear the gunshot. No one would find the entombed body. His parents would fly down to search. Crackpots would call in false clues. Reality television programs produced mere blocks away would reap millions in advertising dollars.

Some people live 99.99% of their lives without facing Death, while others meet Him at birth and spend the rest of their short existence dodging Him at every turn. There is an enormous dif-ference, of course, between the recognized and acceptable risk that most people in affluent, developed nations all over the world intentionally accept on a daily basis; the kind of risk incurred when driving, flying, walking down city streets, swimming in water over one's head or living in a tornado-prone area; and the imminent danger of dying to which these relatively mundane activities can on rare occasions degenerate. Until your car's brakes fail as you're exiting the freeway, the plane in which you're flying loses an engine, you're mugged, you sink exhausted below the water's surface for the second time or climb out of your storm cellar to find your home demolished, everyday activities remain just that. There is a similarly obvious difference between the lives these folks live and the lives led by people in the world's less hospitable regions, so many of which seem to congregate below the Sahara, where it's not unusual to be born without medical care in a dirt-floored hut to AIDs-infected parents in a malarial village on the verge of starvation perpetually being overrun by soldiers and rebels who regularly rob, rape, kill and kidnap. Death is in the air, it's in the dirty water carried two miles in an old petrol can, it's in the bullets, it's in the machetes, it's in the fire and explosions, it's in the mosquitoes, it's in the neighbor next door, it's in the blood, it's in the mind, it's in the gut, it's in the flies, it's in the filth.

And it's in his hand. The man's forefinger slid down toward the trigger.

"You're the young man from the bus stop," said the motionless man sitting in the lotus position whose lips remained three inches from the polished cement wall. In what would later be described by all who survived the episode as a remarkably "girly" voice, the young man squeaked an affirmative response.

"He's OK."

The simple statement was simultaneously met with pure elation and disgusted disbelief. Still hesitant to move more than his eyes, the young man peered over at his would-be executioner now standing over Harold, gesticulating wildly with a fist and a Glock, exhorting the man whose knees still pressed against the wall in a kind of guttural, shouting whisper that proved unintelligible to the young man. He contemplated diving back into the shaft through which he'd been pulled, but he had no idea if the

284

metal grate would even open from the inside. Before he had time to come up with an alternate plan, however, Harold said something the young man couldn't hear and the guy with the gun muttered "fuck" under his breath and replaced the handgun in his waistband. He turned and walked deliberately over to the young man who still had not budged.

"Were you fucking followed?"

"No. Absolutely not. I swear." The young man didn't ordinarily say things like "I swear" but he figured that if there were ever a time in his life to suck dick, this was it. And then, as if on cue, Brainiac emerged from the opening head-first.

"You fucking asshole, why didn't you answer me?" she said before wriggling out of the shaft and standing over him with her hands on her hips, nodding to the others as if it were normal for folks to be hanging out in the concrete bowels of a skyscraper in the middle of the night.

"UnFUCKINGbelievable" roared the exasperated enforcer, tattooed telephone-pole arms spread wide, sledgehammer fists clenched. He immediately stomped back over to Harold and exhorted him in his strange whispered shout once more. Once again, the young man considered running for it and once again he decided against it. "She's OK," the young man assured instead: "I didn't know she followed me, but she's totally OK." If "OK" was the key word among these people, he was going to pound that goddamn message home. Brainiac got her snotty face going and appeared ready to speak, so the young man shot her his most fervent "shut the bloody fuck up" look which she fortunately received loud and clear. At this point, however, Harold let loose a sigh that sounded more like death to the young man than the explicit threat that had greeted his dubious arrival.

The young man suddenly felt like he was going to vomit as visions of a 9mm round blowing through his brain played out before his eyes. Just like that Vietcong guy in that old picture.

A blurp of blood out the other side and then just a corpse with eyeballs you could touch. Fuck. Stupid Fuck. And now Brainiac would die too.

"We'll move again. No big deal," said Harold nonchalantly. It was like a last-second time-out quieting a packed football stadium on 4th and inches. Like Jesus silencing the storm in one of Wilson's Bible stories. In fact, the big guy deflated just like the ship's sail out in the middle of the Sea of Galilee. From hurricane to hush in 2.5 seconds. The battle of wills, if truly a battle it had been, was absolutely over. The armed man slunk off to a dark corner, turned his back to the wall and slid down its polished surface glaring dejectedly at the two assholes who had just ruined his day. The young man and Brainiac remained motionless until Harold gave up on his meditation, slowly rose to his feet and turned to face his guests for the first time.

"Please forgive the drama, but this has been a good home for us and we will be sorry to give it up." The young man began to explain that he and Brainiac wouldn't say a word to anyone but stopped when Harold raised his right hand. "We've moved many times before, we will move again. But tonight, at least, you will be our guests. In the morning, we will all leave together." He didn't allow for any other possibilities and without knowing exactly how to leave, the young man couldn't really imagine any. As if on cue, the third person emerged from the flickering shadows and offered them the bottle of Stoli from the low table. The young man recognized the green-eyed girl with strawberry-blonde dreads from the bus stop.
"Drink...listen...watch..." she said almost perkily before returning to her seat, pink satin thong still riding high above her camo cargo pants. Harold smiled and returned to his spot on the floor. Brainiac watched the girl melt back into the shadows, looked about her carefully as if reassessing the situation, gave a half shrug, cracked open the bottle and not seeing any glasses, took a swig and offered it to the young man. The young man looked over at the armed man. His eyes were closed, head tilted back against the concrete, a small glass pipe with a pungent curl of

286

smoke cradled carefully in his large right hand. He looked at the bloody nunchucks on the low table and turned his attention to Brainiac offering him the bottle. The young man took a deep breath and looked into Brainiac's eyes, his brow furrowed in concentration. He wasn't making eye contact, he was looking past all that into the darkness of her pupils as if he expected an answer to bounce about and settle into a state of purple visibility like the old Magic Eight Balls that fundamentalist preachers warned their congregations about back in the 1970's and 80's. With no such answer forthcoming, however, he was left with no other choice than to mutter "fuck it" and take a long swig. The Stoli was good. Clean. He held it in his mouth for several moments and enjoyed the coolness. Brainiac didn't know what the hell was going through the young man's mind but she wanted another drink. She reached to her left and pulled a pillow in close and then slipped it under her butt. She nestled her right shoulder and back against the young man's left side and set the bottle carefully between them when she was done. She'd remain vigilant, but having not seen the gun, she was as convinced that most of this scene was bluster and bravado as the young man was that it was deadly serious business. The five figures settled in for what was left of the night, hidden within the city like mice in a wall.

The armed man appeared to be asleep, his pipe apparently snuffed and secured at some point when the young man wasn't looking. The young man made a mental note to pay better attention for the next several hours. While it would be unwise to stare, it doesn't take much longer to pull a gun from a waistband then it does to put away a pipe. He thought he could hear Harold saying something quietly so he turned an ear in his direction and listened carefully. He wasn't talking, he was chanting; his voice low like the drone of a didgeridoo, its tones emanating outward in waves that caromed off the polished concrete walls and washed back upon themselves. The candlelight flickered tremulously as if strummed by the chant's resonance before dissipating in the farthest reaches of the dark vault like a phosphorescent mist. The young man stared forward over Harold's shoulder and saw an image of his open-eyed, open-mouthed face reflected in the mirror-like surface of the wall. The young man wondered what Harold saw, if anything, staring unblinkingly, his eyes mere inches from the burnished black surface. The chant continued and seemed to escape from Harold without movement of his jaw or lips like a ghost slipping from the maw of a grave-robbed crypt. The echoes overlapped and built upon themselves, an uninterrupted progression of sound like a room full of voices singing a song in the round. The young man felt for the flask that wasn't there before remembering the bottle beside him. He drank heavily, glancing over at the armed man, whose eyes were now half open and staring at Harold, his enormous hands resting relaxed, palms up on his knees as if in an attitude of supplication.

He felt Brainiac's body nestled into his side and the immovable concrete pressing against his back and his mind turned to the tons of concrete and girders and glass stretching upward from that point between his shoulders; 500, 600 or 700 feet into the sky; one skyscraper among a multitude, inhabited by hundreds of thousands during the day and tens of thousands even now in the middle of the night. And here he was inside the base of one mighty tower, invisible to the rest of the world, the sleeping world, the night owls, the graveyard shift workers, the partiers, the students, the insomniacs. This enormous universe of structures and creatures in itself amounting to no more than a dot on the globe. And he just a dot, within a dot, within a dot, connected to the whole through the point at which his back met the wall and through whatever unseen shit Harold was pulling into himself or broadcasting out, perhaps using the skyscraper as an antenna of sorts or a lightning rod or an enormous psychic cattle prod. Wilson told the young man that there were times in history in which a single cell within the body politic altered its health or purpose or course, and perhaps the same thing was possible in the spiritual realm if such a realm really existed. But for all he knew, the things he'd seen that day notwithstanding, that was all bullshit and the only things that mattered were the gun and the vodka and Brainiac who apparently followed him after publicly

busting his balls and was now leaning up against him for whatever reason as Harold chanted and the candles flickered and the
darkness echoed beneath thousands of tons of concrete and steel
and glass.

At some point, the young man realized he'd been zoning. He
silently swore, checked the armed guy, and looked around the
urban cave in which they all sat like modern-day Neanderthals.
The candles were half the height they'd been when he arrived
and the bottle of vodka was half gone. Across town, Wilson
flung a newspaper with his left hand and jammed the gear selector into reverse with his right. Something was going on over
Harold's head.

It looked like the kind of liquefied air illusion you get with a mi-
rage. A rarity back home, it was a common sight in this city, a
place where the sun perpetually beats down on ubiquitous concrete highways, but the young man immediately began to
wonder if the vodka, late hour, stress and monotony were beginning to play tricks on his eyes. He rubbed his eyes with the
heels of his hands and looked again. The air above Harold's
head did indeed seem to undulate like a vertical, semi-
transparent river or a collection of translucent king cobras rising
from snake charmers' baskets. As if on cue, the green-eyed girl
rose solemnly and brought what appeared to be a small, folded,
white sheet over to the low table. She opened a plastic liter bottle of water and poured it over the sheet, completely saturating it
without spilling or wasting a drop. She walked over to Harold,
carefully removed his t-shirt up over his head like a nurse assisting a patient, and draped the cold wet sheet over his back and
shoulders like you see the Red Cross people do with blankets
when they're taking care of disaster victims in commercials on
TV. She returned to her spot and the young man turned his attention back to Harold, expecting him to begin shivering within
minutes. The air in the space had grown cool, almost cold, and
there was no heat source other than their own bodies and the
candles. He knew from hunting experiences that the human
body will only tolerate inactivity for so long in a cold environ-

ment before it takes matters into its own hands and begins shivering. Harold wasn't shivering. The "heat waves" over his head had apparently subsided or been doused by the wet sheet, but Harold did not appear to be in any discomfort. He continued to stare forward; face only inches from the dark, polished, shadowed surface; chanting in that strange, low drone.

As the candles burned lower and the Stoli slowly disappeared from its bottle, the young man noticed what appeared to be occasional wisps of steam above Harold's head. This observation, however, elicited little more than a nonchalant recognition in the young man's mind as the cement vault and everything within it began to fade in his consciousness like the elements of a dream upon wakening. The point at which his back met the wall, the soft curve of Brainiac beside him, the pillow below him, the images before him; the smells of burning wax, perfume, pot, sweat and cement; the flickering light reflecting off the polished walls. These all faded away, slowly but surely, until all he was conscious of was the resounding drone of a billion bees buzzing underwater, the grinding of tectonic plates, the searing crackle of high tension power lines, the exhalation of gases from a punctured carcass, the roar of a granite-channeled mountain river, the challenge of a bull elephant, the pounding of surf on a rocky beach; the didgeridoo chant. Soon, even elements of consciousness itself seemed to disappear: language, identity, organized thought, memory, knowledge, everything but the omnipresent, eternal, echoing drone.

And then the sound began to change. Slowly. Almost imperceptibly. Like a bean sprout or bamboo shoot that grows before our very eyes without ever seeming to move. The drone rose in pitch, narrowed in definition, lost its echo. The darkness too began to retreat like an alpine lake's night grudgingly giving way to dawn; bats retreating, stars fading, moon setting. The drone moved from the gut to the lungs to the throat; transforming into a sorrowful wail and then a scream. A thought struck the young man that he was who he was and that there existed a world outside of himself and that world was beginning to erupt in a cacophony of sound and light out of a darkness about which he could remember little; and he could feel Brainiac laying on top of him, snuggled into his chest, and then Wilson's voice calling out through it all: "Hey boy!! Wake up you little shit! The damn building burned, boy. Wake up!"

Wilson grew concerned and began to wrap his jacket around his left arm to bust out the driver-side window when he noticed the empty vodka bottle and saw both the young man and Brainiac twitch and resettle themselves. He smiled, unwound the jacket and thought for a moment as he looked behind him at the smoke and steam still billowing from the apartment building; the fire trucks, fire hoses strewn everywhere like 100-foot pythons, fire-fighters with oxygen tanks and helmets rushing about, neighbors, bystanders, TV reporters and cops. He'd already checked all four doors and the keys were plainly visible in the ignition. He considered hip-checking the car to set off the alarm if it had one, but he wasn't sure what kind of reaction he'd elicit from the cops on the scene or how they'd react to the passed out young people with the open container. The overpowering smell of smoldering wood, plastic, carpet, electrical wires, linoleum, insulation and paint permeated his clothes and filled his lungs. Heavy clouds of wind-blown mist from the fire hoses trained on the roof and backside of the building wafted over him. It'd be best if the two slept it off someplace else, away from the commotion and fumes. Someone said the Red Cross had been notified because it was beginning to look like the whole building might be off limits due to structural damage and fumes for quite some time. Wilson suspected the owners would take advantage of the fire and cash out. The property was probably worth ten times what the building had been worth before the fire. He was always suspicious of coincidences and this was a huge one considering the manic pace of gentrification all around the old apartment building. At that moment, one of the fire department's huge ladder trucks rumbled by shaking the ground beneath Wilson's feet. He looked inside the car and saw the young man's eyes open.

291

Wilson yelled at him again. The young man looked confused but managed to crack a smile when he realized he had a girl asleep on top of him. Wilson laughed.

"C'mon boy, you two should get out of there! This ain't the place right now to be sleeping off last night."

The young man began to comply with Wilson's instructions but held up when a twinge of pain shot across the right side of his face and he remembered that the last time he'd seen Brainiac she was stomping away after spitting in his face. He eased himself back down and raised his finger to Wilson to let him know he'd be a sec. How the hell did they end up together in the backseat of her car? He looked down and saw the empty bottle of Stoli. He closed his eyes and tried to remember. He remembered her ripping him a new one in front of all those strangers on the street. He remembered washing his face in the bathroom of a bar and heading for home on foot. He remembered walking past Brainiac's bookstore, but that was it. Nothing else. It was like he'd walked past her bookstore and stepped right into a black hole. Nothing until waking up just now with the strangest hangover he'd ever had. He'd experienced blackouts before, but never this bad. Never involving so many lost hours. It was like being abducted by aliens and then waking up back on earth with one of them snuggling against your chest. And why the hell did it smell like they were parked in the middle of a giant campfire? What was all the noise and yelling outside? Why wasn't Wilson at work? Shit! What time was it? Was he late for work? Was Brainiac going to freak out and start slapping him again or worse when she woke up? He knew she used to carry pepper spray. He looked through the front seats and saw her keys in the ignition with the mini pepper spray canister still attached. Maybe she'd felt bad for him and followed him with a bottle of vodka and they'd driven here (where's "here?") and drank and got busy in the back seat. He sure as hell hoped they hadn't been driving through the city drunk as hell. They were both ordinarily responsible drunks and he hoped that their being in the backseat was an indication that they'd parked before hitting the bottle.

But shit, that was a lot of vodka after all the beer he'd drunk. And if Wilson was there did that mean he was home? And if he were home, why didn't they just go upstairs instead of staying in the car? And a whole bottle of vodka? He didn't see, smell or taste vomit. Then again, the only thing he could smell was smoke and Brainiac's shampoo or perfume. He couldn't tell which but he liked it. He hoped Wilson wouldn't be standing there calmly smiling if the car were on fire but he couldn't imagine why else it would smell like the inside of a fireplace. He carefully felt their hips and confirmed that they were both clothed from the waist down. Her top was intact and he was still wearing his shirt. So now there was nothing left to do but to try to gently slide her off of him as he extracted himself from the car. If he could pull off the whole maneuver and get outside before waking her, he'd avoid being pummeled or accused of taking advantage of her. He had no idea how she'd react but he felt compelled to prepare for the worse.

He carefully put the sole of his right shoe flat on the floor of the car beside the Stoli bottle and pushed himself backwards and upwards, gingerly sliding out from beneath Brainiac's inert form. God she felt good and he couldn't help but feel a little hopeful about his chances with her this second time around as long as everything was indeed as it appeared. God that would suck if it wasn't. As if in response to his thoughts, Brainiac mumbled something and he immediately froze in a particularly awkward position. She was slipping, however, so he quickly attempted to pull his left leg to safety while supporting her upper torso with his left hand. It was at that moment that she awoke suddenly to the sensation of falling and flailed wildly, striking the young man square in the nads and dropping him like the proverbial sack of potatoes. He had heard Wilson use the expression before but had never fully understood its import until his abdominal and leg muscles completely failed and his body hit the floor of the car. A wave of nausea moved over and through the young man who was now wedged between the passenger seat and the backseat, his back on the floor, his head jammed against the passenger door and his left leg still lodged below Brainiac. Wilson saw the whole thing unfold and busted out laughing in spite of the chaos and destruction around him. Brainiac righted herself and sat up straight, resting her feet on the young man still wincing below her. While obviously baffled by the situation in which she found herself, she recognized the apartment building and Wilson from previous visits and gave the man outside her car a pleasant "nice to see you again" kind of smile. Like many young women the young man had met, Brainiac allowed very little dissonance in her life, and habitually related events in a way that made sense in terms of her audience and whatever effect she hoped to achieve in a particular situation. He had learned, in fact, that in order to get what he considered "the whole truth," he often had to listen to one of her stories five or six times, preferably in the company of entirely disparate audiences and at different levels of narrator intoxication. Only then would he understand what exactly had happened and how she felt about it. Most of his male friends, on the other hand, tended to put little thought into what they said or to whom they said it. They usually came up with a version of events in a matter of seconds that portrayed them in the best possible light and used that version regardless of the audience or circumstances. Easier to follow, but just as difficult to authenticate; and certainly more prone to disastrous social errors inevitably ending with his friend standing alone, arms held out wide in oblivious incredulity, asking "What?"

By the time Brainiac looked down and asked the young man if he was alright and then suggested, as if to a child, that they get out of the car as Wilson suggested, she'd already pieced together all that she remembered from the night before and filled in the rest based on her decision to take the young man back and give the relationship another shot. As far as she was concerned, the young man deserved, and would be allowed, little say in the matter.

She got out of the car first, accepting Wilson's proffered hand and muttering "Holy Shit" as she took in her first unobstructed view of the burning apartment building. "I'm sorry," she told

Wilson as the young man emerged slowly, painfully, from the back seat, stretching stiff muscles and alternately looking to Brainiac for clues to her disposition and taking in the unbelievable scene that had unfolded around them while they slept. Unfuckingbelievable. He located his apartment's two picture windows and counted eight apartments between his own and the focal point of the firefighters' efforts. At that very moment, the section of the roof receiving most of the water collapsed in a thunderous, crashing whoosh of water, steam, asphalt, smoke, 2x4s, plywood, tarpaper and archaic skeletal television aerials. The crowd, already at a safe distance behind police barriers and fire trucks, erupted in a collective "Ohhhhhhhhhhhhh" worthy of a 4th of July grand finale and took a collective three steps back like kids on a playground playing "red-light green-light." A massive cloud of delicate white ashes, thrown a hundred feet above the original elevation of the roof, now began to drift down on all those assembled like the first, tentative snow of winter. Wilson asked Brainiac if she wanted to move her car farther down the street before the ash settled, but she just smiled at his thoughtfulness and shook her head no. The three stood and watched the ashes float softly down as the massive streams of water continued to rocket upwards and fall down upon what used to be the roof. The young man looked at all the other people watching the spectacle and for the first time realized that he was watching a disaster unfold: a commonplace disaster, a pedestrian disaster, a neatly contained disaster, but a disaster nonetheless. While he really had nothing in his apartment without which he couldn't live, he knew that some folks had a lifetime's accumulation of photos and mementos stored in boxes, hanging on walls and carefully displayed on shelves. When the section of roof caved in, dozens of people lost everything they owned, and even units some distance from the collapse, like the young man's, were still impacted by the smoke, flames and thousands of gallons of water that destroyed clothing, scrapbooks, kitchen supplies, homerun baseballs, cash, and family photos. The young man thought about the framed picture Brainiac had given him and some photos he had of his family in a shoebox under his bed. He hoped they were alright but recognized that it could have been much, much worse. He hoped no one was hurt. There were still a half dozen aid cars on the scene on this side of the building and potentially many more around the corner. The ash drifted down and the white sun rose higher in the smoggy sky. Smoke blew this way and that and clouds of mist descended on the ashes, turning them to paste. The young man finally spotted someone he knew: Mr. and Mrs. Carillo. Phillipe had managed to find a folding chair for his wife so she wouldn't have to sit on the curb with her bad leg. He stood behind her with his hand on her shoulder, watching everything happen around them. The young man spotted dreadlocked Jeff talking with a beautiful auburn-haired reporter in a bright yellow jacket with the logo of a local television station on the right breast pocket. Jeff seemed almost exuberant to be in front of the camera, leveraging this potential Big Break for everything it was worth. A few moments later, the young man recognized Mandy flirting with a young paramedic. He was obviously attempting to check her vitals, but she was about as interested in the state of her pupils as Jeff had been with the newscaster's questions about the well-being of his neighbors. The young man didn't see Jeffrey and Sid or Mrs. Lavinksy. Jeffrey and Sid were usually up pretty early in the morning and were in good shape physically: they probably got out just fine if they were home when the fire broke out. Mrs. Lavinsky, however, sometimes had trouble breathing and always stayed inside during smog alerts. She also had arthritis and couldn't move very fast when it was acting up. The young man wondered whether the smoke and fumes that were so strong there at street level would have been powerful enough upstairs to overcome someone with respiratory problems. As he scanned the crowd for Mrs. Lavinsky, someone nearby shouted that the Red Cross had arrived and as if on cue a huge Emergency Response Vehicle emblazoned with 4-foot red crosses lumbered by the three still standing next to Brainiac's car.

"Well boy, I'm guessing we won't be sleeping in our own beds tonight. I'll go see what the story is." Wilson left the two and set off for the Red Cross ERV which had parked a couple hundred yards down the street. They watched him disappear into the crowd and then turned to face each other.

"So, I'm confused," the young man offered dubiously, kicking the street with the toe of his Vans before looking Brainiac in the eye, both his hands jammed into his Levis pockets. "The last thing I remember is walking past your bookstore after you ripped me to shreds in front of all those people." Brainiac furrowed her brow and began to raise an accusing forefinger, but the young man cut her off. "Whoa, whoa, whoa: I deserved it. Obviously. I just figured that was the last time you'd ever speak to me, so I can't figure out how we ended up together. I mean, in your car. I uh….." He exhaled and looked around. "I liked seeing you when I opened my eyes. I uh….just can't fucking remember how we got to that point. And I'm hoping…I'm hoping it wasn't a goddamned total fluke or something."

Brainiac fought back a smile and looked at the young man for a moment before responding. "After I left, I watched from a distance and saw you leave. I realized you were on foot and figured you were heading home. And I knew that if you still lived here," she said, motioning to the soon-to-be condemned building, "…there was a damn good chance you'd be walking right by my store. And….I figured you were beyond pissed and probably feeling the hate so I was a little worried that you might be tempted to put a foot through a window or something. So I drove to the store and parked down the block a little ways and waited." It was at this point that her actual memory became fuzzy and then faded to black, but the young man's comment about walking past her store had filled in some details upon which she now built like a master architect. "Before too long, you showed up and I watched you walk up to the store and just look at it for a while, and then you walked on by without so much as smudging the window. That made me remember one of the reasons I used to dig you."

Even now, after everything that had happened, her use of the past tense stung a bit. The young man winced, looked up and realized the ashes had stopped falling. He looked her in the eye again and thought he saw some present tense interest, but couldn't be sure. Wilson once told him that it's easier to read a book printed with invisible ink than it is to read the heart of a woman, and the young man knew from experience that Brainiac was harder to read than most.

"So I pulled up along side of you and offered you a ride. You were surprised as hell, but I don't think you were looking forward to walking halfway across town, so you got in. It was 5 minutes before 2:00 so we stopped and you hopped out and bought a bottle of vodka from a grocery store and we drove here and parked." The young man was puzzled, because one of the few things he did remember was that he'd been basically broke. But Brainiac seemed so sure of herself that he figured it was possible he'd missed some money in a back pocket or something or that she'd handed him a twenty on his way into the store. Regardless, he liked the direction the story was headed and would have played along even if he'd been 100% sure she was making it all up.

"You invited me upstairs, but I could tell that you were turned on and I wasn't about to give you the satisfaction of nailing me so soon after giving you hell, so I crawled into the back seat with the vodka and invited you to join me with the understanding that you were still in the doghouse and we'd only be talking." She was smiling. He smiled too. It wasn't a fluke. "I realized when I picked you up that you totally accepted responsibility for what you did. And you were so sweet while we talked and drank. And you made me laugh. You fucked up beyond comprehension, but I decided last night that the fuck-up wasn't who you were. It was an aberration. It was atypical. Some guys are truly evil. You were just dumb."

"Fucking copper thieves!" Wilson exclaimed, as soon as he was within earshot of the two.

"What the fuck are you talking about old man?" the young man said, smiling. "We ain't stole no copper. We've been standing here the whole time you were gone. The only copper I got are these pennies in my pocket," he said, pulling out a handful of change and offering it as proof.

"No, no you little shit. The fire," he said pointing incredulously behind him, "..the fire was started by copper thieves. I ran into the maintenance guy on my way to the Red Cross truck and he told me the cops caught a couple of meth-heads dressed in overalls with a panel truck full of copper pipe and wire just a few blocks away. Apparently they found out that when the owners rewired and replumbed the building about fifteen years ago, they basically left the old mechanical room intact. I don't know if you ever saw it, but it was a tangled mess of wires and breakers and fuse boxes and pipes. In fact, when I first moved into the building, the maintenance guy warned me not to overload the circuits because I'd either start a fire or be out of power for days because it took that long just to track down the blown fuse. He said that whoever wired the building when it was built had to have been drunk or stupid and probably both. No rhyme or reason to the circuits, crossed wires everywhere, a veritable rat's nest. So when it came time to bring everything up to code, they basically cut off the input and output and bypassed the mess entirely. Copper wasn't worth much back then, so they just locked it up and left it. Built a brand new mechanical room with modern components so it was up to code and earthquake proof. Well these two meth-heads found out, dressed up like repairmen and walked in here in broad daylight and cleaned out the whole motherfucking mess. What they didn't realize, though, was that there was one line that was still live in that room. A capped-off gas line, buried behind wires and water pipes. They broke it when they were ripping out the last of the copper, smelled gas and took off. Didn't bother calling 911 or anything. Just left. Basically lit the fuse of a bomb and ran away. Well the gardeners came a few minutes later and were edging the grass with those gas-powered edgers, just throwing up sparks like crazy whenever they hit the cement right, and the whole room blew.

Fortunately, the walls and door were built like a bank vault and the ceiling was paper-thin, so the force of the explosion went up into the two units above. No one was home but it basically vaporized both apartments and then started burning outward from there. But the maintenance guy said he talked to one of the firefighters and there were no serious injuries. Some folks got taken to the hospital for smoke inhalation and that old guy who always yells at the kids for being too loud went because of chest pains, but no one else was hurt."

"Did you hear anything about Mrs. Lavinsky?" the young man asked.

"Yeah, she's one of the ones they took to the hospital as a precaution because of the smoke. Mrs. Stafford, too. Sounds like they're both going to be fine, though." Wilson smiled.

"So here's the scoop, kid. You need to go get in line and show your ID and they'll check you off the list and give you a hotel voucher." Wilson held his up so the young man could see. "They'll also give you this bag of emergency food and water. It looks like MREs, basically," he said, looking down into the plastic bag. "But I'll tell you boy, I don't think they'll ever let us go back. Maybe to get belongings, but this building is coming down. Red Cross lady said she's seen enough of these to be pretty sure and I'm guessing the owners are already making phone calls to potential buyers. They're going to make millions and millions off this."

Wilson looked up at the smoldering building and shook his head. "I can't say I'm going to miss this building, but I am going to miss you, you little shit."

"What are you talking about old man? I ain't going anywhere. We'll just find another building, that's all. No big deal. And maybe this is a good thing. Maybe we head farther south and find apartments closer to a beach. Get away from the traffic and noise and smog. We could split the rent on a unit and you could quit throwing papers and get a life. You could actually do shit and you might even get laid again before you die."

Wilson smiled, but couldn't bring himself to laugh.

"This ain't the Shawshank Redemption boy." He said it half-jokingly, but it came out sounding stern and almost angry. "Goddamn it. It ain't even close."

An aid car activated its siren and lights and pulled out into traffic. The three watched it leave, wondering if they'd found someone else in the building or if it was being called away to a different emergency.

"Look, boy," Wilson continued. "You were right about something, just now. This is a chance for change. It's a convenient interruption. A kick in the ass if nothing else. Like you said, there are some things I need to do before I die, getting laid among them. I ain't trying to be dramatic: that's just the way it is. There are things you need to do before you die, too. It's just that all things being equal, I'm going to beat you there by a mile. There are things I've known for a while, for as long as you've been breathing on this earth and longer, but have been too stubborn..." He breathed deeply. The acrid air filled his lungs and then coated his mouth when he exhaled. He looked up at the old building again and then back at the young man and Brainiac. He wasn't sure when it'd happened or why, really, but sometime in the few minutes between leaving them and coming back, something had changed. He'd let go. Laid down his arms and walked away from the war. It wasn't a calculated decision as much as it was a realization. A small part of him he'd given up for dead was suddenly, inexplicably alive again. "I've been too stubborn to act on. I have family spread across this country, family I should be with, but I've stubbornly held out hope that if I ignored them and focused on finding meaning in this life that transcends procreation, I could always go back. Go back after I'd figured things out. Well I'm working two jobs and ain't getting ahead and ain't figured out shit yet. I've told you before

301

that I don't understand why the majority of human beings' greatest joys are tied to their offspring when reproduction is the most basic biological act, something that the simplest of creatures engage in every second of every day. It doesn't make sense. Whether we're the most highly evolved or made in the image of God, it doesn't make sense that our entire existence is justified or realized or fulfilled by our offspring. It's not logical. It's not rational. But I can't deny the fact that they mean something to me, they mean a hell of a lot to me, and I can't continue ignoring that reality simply because I don't understand it or agree with it. I've got grandkids, boy. I see them once a year or so, but my kids miss me and they haven't completely given up on me yet. Now's the time, boy. I gave this a shot for a number of years and I can't ignore the rest of life any more. I'm going home. My oldest boy has a house on 10 acres with a barn he's converted into a shop and an apartment. He's got two boys, teenagers now. He wants me to take them fishing. He wants them to get to know me before they're grown and on their own." Wilson stopped and looked at the young man and half smiled. "Don't give me that hangdog look. You're young. You ought to be hanging out with people your own age. Like your pretty young companion here. I'll be out of your way and you can spend your time trying to impress her."

"Actually, I'm leaving too," said Brainiac matter-of-factly.

"What the fuck?" the young man protested to the sky, arms held out incredulously. "Unfuckingbelievable. I lose my house, my best friend and my ex-girlfriend...again. All in one morning. You gotta be fucking kidding me." He stomped several feet away from the two deserters, his hands holding his head as if to prevent it from splitting down the middle. The three stood like that for several moments, like the points of an isosceles triangle in one of their old middle school math books. The hoses continued to rain water down on the building but half the fire trucks had left and the remaining firefighters were cleaning up and checking for hotspots. A long line from the Red Cross ERV stretched almost to where they were standing. The young man turned around and looked back at the line and at his two friends. He shook his head and looked down at his Vans. He wondered why they made the laces so long. He had to tie big fat double-knots just to keep from tripping over them. He felt the warmth of the morning sun on the top of his head and looked up and squinted in the white glare. He ran his fingers through his close-ly-cropped hair, jammed his hands into the pockets of his Levi's and walked slowly back over to the two. He searched for an an-swer in Brainiac's eyes but aside from a particularly strong déjà vu, there was nothing there.

"Why did you do all this if you're just going to leave?"

"I didn't want to leave town without letting you know what you did to me, and then when I followed you and you were so cool, I wanted to take advantage of the time we had and thought telling you would just ruin everything."

The young man sighed and kicked at a dirty spot on the sidewalk with his toe.

"So where are you going?"

"There's a place on the Washington coast, up north towards the reservation, where a river runs down out of the hills, through the dunes and into the sea. On really low tides, you can follow the retreating ocean a mile out until the shore almost disappears from sight in the mist, and pull razor clams from the sand like carrots from a vegetable garden. And when the tide's in, you can catch shiny foot-long perch right out of the surf with just a hook and a clam neck for bait. The sky is blue and civilization is kept at arm's length out there, like a necessary evil. People stand around bonfires and watch sunsets. Bald eagles nest in hundred-foot firs and otters swim on their backs in the river." Brainiac's eyes were wide and she spoke in the awkwardly reve-rent, hushed voice of a convert unaccustomed to singing anything's praise. "My great uncle and aunt have owned a little motel and mini mart on a bluff overlooking the dunes for close to thirty years. Well he passed away about six months ago and my great aunt can't run the place herself. The motel had gotten pretty run down and they were in the process of expanding the mini mart into two of the rooms and converting the motel office into a drive-thru espresso when he died. I'm going to have to work my ass off, but I get free room and board, minimum wage and tips. In the summer it's a madhouse: they sell everything you could possibly need in the mini mart: kites, fishing gear, bait, clam guns, firewood, beer, ice, some basic groceries and souvenirs. And she's hoping that the casino being built up on the reservation will bring enough folks to make the rest of the year profitable too. I committed to a year. My great aunt figures she'll know by then whether it's going to work or not." Brainiac paused suddenly, screwing up her face in concentration. The young man smiled at the faint Milky Way of freckles that stretched from one cheekbone to the other and her perfectly shaped, petite red lips pursed and twisted below. She held up a finger between his eyes, her index finger this time, retreated a few feet down the sidewalk in the direction of her car and pulled out her cell phone to make a call. Wilson and the young man watched her dial one number and wait. Nothing. Then she appeared to look through her phone's directory and try another number. Success. She spoke for three or four minutes, gesticulating with her free hand and stepping back and forth on the sidewalk as if dancing a waltz. She closed her phone and slipped it into a pocket and looked for a moment in the direction of her car and then back at the young man and Wilson. She walked deliberately back and planted her feet on the sidewalk as if preparing to accept a blow to the gut.

"You've got no place to live, right?"

"Apparently so."

"How's the coffee house treating you?"

"We can't eat the broken pastries anymore and they're going to start making us take home the dirty aprons and wash them ourselves next month."

"Wilson is moving away."

Wilson nodded.

"You used to live up in Washington state, about three or four hours from the coast."

The young man nodded.

Brainiac nodded to both of them and paused for a moment as if running through a mental checklist.

"One year. You run the espresso, I run the mini mart. We can discreetly fuck around and all but if you dump me again or if I fall for one of the loggers in town, we still have to finish out the year like mature adults. My great aunt will not be screwed in this arrangement. No exceptions. No excuses. You get room, board, minimum wage and half the tips, just like me. Give your two-week notice at the coffee house and pay for the gas and food driving up. What do you say?" She folded her arms across her chest and shifted her weight to her back foot. The young man had been taught to work hard in life so that wouldn't be a problem, and a few quick mental calculations confirmed that the compensation including room and board would actually leave him in a better position than sticking with the coffee house and finding another apartment. He'd been to the coast as a very young boy and still vaguely remembered running across what seemed like an eternal beach of mirror-smooth saltwater sand in a world of jaw-dropping natural beauty that would complement the crossed-arm beauty before him; but he hesitated in the face of what sounded a lot like an ultimatum. He usually responded to ultimatums by opting out entirely and walking away, but to what would he be walking? He looked at Wilson with what could have been interpreted as apprehension or even fear, and Wilson smiled in response.

"I know this ain't necessarily your style, son. You tend to take a while and consider things before making a decision, but sometimes life doesn't give you that luxury. Sometimes she throws you a lifeline and you just got to grab hold and hang on. Now sure, sometimes it turns out the other end is tied to a thousand-pound anvil and you sink to the bottom, but every once in a while that lifeline turns out to be an opportunity you end up being thankful for the rest of your life. You're young. You've got very few real responsibilities or limitations. Now's the time to do shit like this. Once you get older, settle down, start a family, buy a house, it changes things. Not always, but more often than not it does. It ain't bad that it does, it's just a different time of life. Now I can't tell you what to do you little shit, but I can tell you what I'd do if I were you." He smiled, winked at Brainiac and walked away.

Made in the USA
San Bernardino, CA
13 March 2014